Dear Reader,

When we first came up with the idea for a collection of historical bride stories, we never dreamed that we would get the chance to bring you stories from writers as talented as Mary Jo Putney, Kristin James and Julie Tetel.

These three authors have won numerous awards and won the hearts of readers all over the world with their unforgettable romances, and we are delighted to have this opportunity to bring them together for you in this unique collection.

We hope that you enjoy their stories as much as we have enjoyed bringing them to you.

Sincerely,

Tracy Farrell
Senior Editor
Harlequin Historicals

Mary Jo Putney
Kristin James
Julie Tetel

Promised Brides

Harlequin Books

TORONTO • NEW YORK • LONDON
AMSTERDAM • PARIS • SYDNEY • HAMBURG
STOCKHOLM • ATHENS • TOKYO • MILAN
MADRID • WARSAW • BUDAPEST • AUCKLAND

PROMISED BRIDES

Copyright © 1994 by Harlequin Enterprises B.V.

ISBN 0-373-83296-6

The publisher acknowledges the copyright holders of the individual works as follows:
THE WEDDING OF THE CENTURY
Copyright © 1994 by Mary Jo Putney
JESSE'S WIFE
Copyright © 1994 by Candace Camp
THE HANDFAST
Copyright © 1994 by Julie Tetel Andresen

This edition published by arrangement with Harlequin Enterprises B. V.

® and TM are trademarks of Harlequin Enterprises B.V. used under license. Trademarks indicated with ® are registered in the United States Patent and Trademark Office, the Canadian Trade Marks Office and in other countries.

Printed in U.S.A.

CONTENTS

THE WEDDING OF THE CENTURY

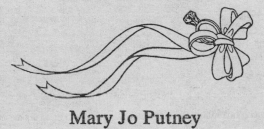

Mary Jo Putney

Chapter One

Swindon Palace
Spring 1885

After two weeks of dizzying social activity in London, a visit to the English countryside was an enchanting change of pace. Nature had cooperated by blessing the garden party with flawless weather. Puffs of white cloud drifted through a deep blue sky, the grass and trees were impossibly green, and the famous Swindon gardens were in glorious flower.

Yet the grounds were not half so splendid as the guests, who were the cream of British society. All of the men were aristocratically handsome and all of the women graceful and exquisitely dressed. At least, that was how it seemed to Miss Sarah Katherine Vangelder, of the New York Vangelders. As she surveyed her surroundings, she gave a laugh of pure delight.

The woman beside her said, "Don't look so rapturous, Sunny. It simply isn't done."

Sunny gave her godmother a teasing glance. "Is this the Katie Schmidt of San Francisco who scandalized English society by performing Comanche riding stunts in Hyde Park?''

A smile tugged at the older woman's lips. "It most certainly is *not*," she said in a voice that no longer held any trace of American accent. "I am now Katherine Schmidt Worthington, Countess of Westron, a very proper chaperon for her exceedingly well-brought-up young American goddaughter."

"I thought that we American girls were admired for our freshness and directness." A hint of dryness entered Sunny's voice. "And our fortunes, of course."

"The very best matches require impeccable manners as well as money, my dear. If you wish to become a duchess, you must be above reproach."

Sunny sighed. "And if I don't wish to become a duchess?"

"Your mother has spent twenty years grooming you to be worthy of the highest station," Lady Westron replied. "It would be a pity to waste that."

"Yes, Aunt Katie," Sunny said meekly. "If I'm very, very impeccable, may I view the rest of the gardens later?"

"Yes, but not until you've met everyone worth meeting. Business before pleasure, my dear." Katie began guiding her charge through the crowd, stopping and making occasional introductions.

Knowing that she was being judged, Sunny smiled and talked with the utmost propriety. She even managed not to look too excited, until she was introduced to the Honorable Paul Curzon.

Tall, blond and stunningly handsome, Curzon was enough to make any woman gape. After bowing over her hand, he said, "A pleasure to meet you, Miss Vangelder. Are you newly arrived in England?" His question was accompanied by a dazzling smile.

If it hadn't been for her rigorous social training, Sunny would have gaped at him like a raw country girl. Instead, she managed to say lightly, "I've been in London for the last fortnight. Before that, we were traveling on the Continent."

"If you'd like to visit the Houses of Parliament, Miss Vangelder, I'd be delighted to escort you. I'm a member." Curzon gave a deprecatory shrug. "Only a backbencher, but I can show you what goes on behind the scenes and treat you to tea on the terrace. You might find it amusing."

"Perhaps later in the season Miss Vangelder will have time," Katie said as she deftly removed her charge.

When they were out of earshot, Sunny said with awe, "Mr. Curzon is the handsomest man I've ever seen."

"Yes, but he's a younger son with three older brothers, so he's unlikely ever to inherit the title." Lady Westron gave a warning look. "Not at all the sort your mother wants for you."

"But as a Member of Parliament, he actually does something useful," Sunny pointed out. "My grandfather would have approved of that."

"Admiral Vangelder would *not* have wanted a penniless younger son for his favorite granddaughter," Katie said firmly. "Come, I want you to meet Lord Traymore. An Irish title, unfortunately, but an earl is an earl, and he's charming. You could do worse."

Dutifully Sunny followed her godmother to the next knot of guests, though she promised herself that she would slip off and view the famous water garden before she left. Until then, she would enjoy the color and laughter of the occasion.

She was also guiltily glad to be free of her mother's rather overpowering presence for a day. Augusta Vangelder was the most devoted and solicitous of parents, but she had very firm ideas about the way things ought to be. *Very* firm. Unfortunately, she was laid up in their suite at Claridge's with a mild case of the grippe, so Sunny had the benefit of the more liberal chaperonage of her godmother. Not only did Lady Westron know everyone, but she made racy comments about them. Sunny felt very worldly.

While a courtly old judge went to fetch them refreshments, she asked, "Where is the Duke of Thornborough? Since he ordered a special train to bring his guests from London for the day, I should at least know whom to be grateful to."

Katie scanned the crowd, then nodded toward the refreshment marquee. "That tall fair chap."

After a thorough examination, Sunny observed, "He's almost as handsome as Mr. Curzon, and has a most distinguished air. *Exactly* what one would expect of a duke."

"Yes, and he's delightfully witty, as well," Katie replied. "Very prominent in the Prince of Wales's Marlborough House set. I'll introduce you to him later."

Sunny glanced at the other woman suspiciously. "Am I to be paraded in front of him like a prize heifer?"

"No," Katie said with regret. "Thornborough won't do—his taste runs to ladies who are...rather excessively sophisticated. He's expected to offer for May Russell soon."

"The American Mrs. Russell?" Sunny asked, surprised.

"Mad May herself. She's a good choice—having had children by two husbands already, she shouldn't have any problems giving Thornborough an heir, and her fortune is immense." Katie gave a little sniff. "Heaven knows that Thornborough needs it."

"Who's the man standing by the duke?"

"Oh, that's just the Gargoyle."

"I beg your pardon?" Sunny glanced at her god-mother, not sure that she'd heard correctly.

"Lord Justin Aubrey, Thornborough's younger brother, better known as the Gargoyle," Katie explained. "He manages the duke's estate, which means he's scarcely more than a farmer."

A line etched between her brows, Sunny studied the dark young man. While not handsome, his face had a certain rugged distinction. "Why was he given such an unkind nickname? He's no Mr. Curzon, but neither is he ugly."

"The Aubreys are known for being tall, blond and aristocratic, and Lord Justin is none of those things. He's always scowling and has no conversation at all." Katie smiled naughtily. "One would have to question what his dear mother had been up to, except that every now and then the Aubreys produce one like him. The youngest Aubrey daughter, Lady Alexandra, resembles him, poor girl. I imagine she's around here somewhere. She's known as the Gargoylette."

Sunny's frown deepened. "I'm sorry to think that these handsome people have such cruel tongues."

"They are no more and no less cruel than New York society," Lady Westron said dryly. "Human nature is much the same everywhere."

Sunny's gaze lingered on Lord Justin. Though not tall, neither was he short; he appeared to be of average height, perhaps an inch or two taller than she. She guessed that he was in his late twenties, but his stern expression made him seem older. He also looked as if he thoroughly disapproved of the splendid gathering around him.

Her thoughts were interrupted by Katie exclaiming, "Lord Hancock is over there! I had hoped that he would be here today. Come along, dear, you must meet him."

After another wistful glance at the gardens, Sunny obediently followed her godmother.

The eighth Duke of Thornborough sampled a strawberry from one of the mounds on the refreshment table. "Splendid flavor." He reached for another. "You've been getting remarkable results from the greenhouses."

Justin Aubrey shrugged. "I only give the orders, Gavin. It's the gardeners who do the real work."

"But someone must still give the right orders, and it isn't going to be me." The duke consumed several more strawberries, then washed them down with champagne. "Relax, Justin. You've worked for weeks to make my fete a success, so you should try to enjoy the results. Everyone is having a cracking good time."

"That's fortunate, considering that this little event is costing over two thousand pounds." Money which could have been much better spent.

Gavin made an airy gesture. "The Duke of Thornborough has an obligation to maintain a certain style. After I marry May, there will be ample money for those boring repairs that you keep talking about."

Justin gave his brother a shrewd glance. "You and Mrs. Russell have reached a firm understanding?"

Gavin nodded. "We'll be making an announcement soon. A late summer wedding, I think. You can plan on fixing the roof directly after, so it will be right and tight by winter." He cast an experienced eye over the crowd. "I see that Katie Westron has a lovely creature in tow. It must be the Gilded Girl. I hear she's cutting quite a swath through

London society. The Prince has already invited her to visit Sandringham."

"Then her social reputation is made," Justin agreed with barely perceptible irony. "But who *is* the Gilded Girl?"

"Sarah Vangelder, the fairest flower of the Vangelder railroad fortune." The duke's tone turned speculative. "They say she's the greatest heiress ever to cross the Atlantic."

Justin followed his brother's gaze to where the heiress stood talking with three besotted males. As soon as he located her, his heart gave an odd lurch. Sarah Vangelder was the quintessential American beauty—tall, slender and crowned with a lustrous mass of honey-colored hair. She also had an engaging air of innocent enthusiasm that made him want to walk over and introduce himself. A beautiful woman, not his. The world was full of them, he reminded himself. Aloud, he said only, "Very fetching."

"Perhaps I should reconsider marrying May," Gavin said pensively. "They say Augusta Vangelder wants to see the girl a duchess. Should I offer her the noble name of Thornborough?"

Justin's mouth tightened. Though he loved his brother, he had no illusions about the duke's character. "You'd find a young innocent a flat bore."

"Very likely you're right," Gavin agreed. His gaze lingered. "Still, she's quite lovely."

Three peeresses and two Cabinet ministers came over to pay their respects to their host. Justin seized the opportunity to escape, for the constant chatter was driving him mad. He would have preferred to be elsewhere, but he could hardly avoid a party taking place in his own backyard.

Avoiding the formal parterre where many of the guests were strolling, he made his way to the rhododendron garden, which had been carefully designed to look like wild woods. There was a risk that he would find some of Gavin's fashionable friends fornicating beneath the silver birches, but with luck, they would all be more interested in champagne and gossip than in dalliance.

Half an hour in the wilder sections of the park relaxed him to the point where he felt ready to return to the festivities. Not that anyone was likely to miss him, but he liked to keep an eye on the arrangements to ensure that everything ran smoothly.

As he walked through a grove of Scottish pines, he heard a feminine voice utter a soft but emphatic, "Drat!"

He turned toward the voice, and a few more steps brought the speaker into his view.

It was the Gilded Girl. But that was too flippant a nickname, for the sunlight that shafted through the pine needles made her honey hair and creamy gown glow as if she were Titania, the fairy queen. He halted unnoticed at the edge of the clearing, experiencing again that strange, unsteady feeling.

A vine had snagged the back hem of Miss Vangelder's elegant bustled walking gown, and she was trying to free herself by poking with the tip of her lace parasol. Any other woman would have seemed ungraceful, but not the heiress. She looked playful, competent and altogether enchanting.

In the wooden voice he used to conceal unseemly feelings, he said, "May I be of assistance?"

The girl looked up with a startled glance, then smiled with relief. "You certainly can! Otherwise, my gown is doomed, and Mr. Worth will be terribly cross with me if he ever finds out."

Justin knelt and began trying to disentangle her hem. "Does it matter what a dressmaker thinks?"

"Mr. Worth is not a dressmaker, but an *artiste*. I'm told that I was singularly fortunate that he condescended to see me personally. After examining me like a prize turkey, he designed every ensemble right down to the last slipper and scarf." She gave a gurgle of laughter. "I was informed in no uncertain terms that any substitutions would be disastrous."

The vine was remarkably tenacious. As Justin tried to loosen it without damaging the heavy ecru silk, he asked, "Do you always do what others wish you to do?"

"Generally," she said with wry self-understanding. "Life is easier when I do."

Her skirt finally came free, and he got to his feet. "I'm Justin Aubrey, by the way."

"I'm Sarah Vangelder, but most people call me Sunny." She offered her hand, and a smile that melted his bones.

She was tall, her eyes almost level with his. He had assumed that they would be blue, but the color was nearer aqua, as deep and changeable as the sea. He drew a shaken breath, then bowed over her hand. Straightening, he said, "You should not be here alone, Miss Vangelder."

"I know," she said blithely, "but I was afraid that if I didn't take the initiative, I'd leave without having a chance to really see the gardens."

"Are you rating them for possible future occupancy?" he said dryly. "I regret to inform you that my brother is no longer in the marriage mart."

"I simply like gardens, Lord Justin," she said crisply, her aqua eyes turning cool. "Are you always so rude?"

So the exquisite Miss Vangelder had thorns. Suppressing a smile, he said, "Always. I took a first in rudeness at Oxford."

Her expression instantly transformed from reproval to delight. "You have a sense of humor!"

"Don't spread such a base rumor around. It would utterly ruin my reputation." He offered his arm. "Let me escort you back to the fete."

As she slipped her hand into the crook of his elbow, she asked, "Could we take an indirect route? I particularly want to see the famous water garden."

He knew that he should return her before her chaperon became concerned. Yet when he looked into her glorious eyes, he found himself saying, "Very well, Miss Vangelder."

As they started down the pine-needle-carpeted path, he was very aware of the light pressure of her hand on his arm and the luxuriant rustle of her petticoats. And her perfume, a delicate fragrance reminiscent of violets....

He took a deep, slow breath. "I assume you are related to Admiral Vangelder?"

"You've heard of my grandfather?"

"It would be surprising if I hadn't." He held a branch aside so that she could pass without endangering her deliciously frivolous hat. "He was one of the great American success stories."

"Yes, and something of a robber baron, as well, though he was always a darling to me. I miss him." She chuckled. "He liked people to think that he was called Admiral because of his magnificent yachts, but actually, he got the nickname because his first job was tending mules on the Erie Canal."

"Really?" Justin said, amused by her artlessness.

"Really. In fact, there are grave suspicions that his papa was not married to his mama." She bit her lip guiltily. "You're dangerously easy to talk to, Lord Justin. I shouldn't have said so much—my mother would be horrified if the Admiral's dubious parentage became common knowledge." She grinned again. "Her own family has been respectable for at least a generation longer."

"Your secret is safe, Miss Vangelder," he assured her.

She gave him another entrancing smile that struck right to the heart. For a mad instant, he felt as if he was the only person who existed in her world. She had charm, this gilded girl, a quality as unmistakable as it was hard to define. He drew a shaken breath and returned his gaze to the winding path.

Though she had said he was easy to talk to, in fact he found himself talking more than usual as they strolled through the park. He told her about the history of the estate, answered questions about the crops and tenants. Together they stood in the gazebo that was designed like a miniature Greek temple, and when they visited the picturesque ruins of an old monastery he described what the community would have been like in its heyday.

She was a wonderful audience, listening with a grave air of concentration that was occasionally punctuated by an incisive question. After she asked about the effects of the agricultural depression on the farm laborers, he remarked, "You have a wide range of interests, Miss Vangelder."

"Education is something of an American passion, so my father insisted that I have a whole regiment of tutors. Shortly before he died, he had me take the entrance exams to Oxford and Cambridge. He was quite pleased when I passed with flying colors." She sighed. "Of course there was never any question of me actually going to a university. That would have been shockingly bluestocking."

At least she had been well taught. Like most English girls, his own sisters had received the sketchiest of educations. Only Alexandra, who loved to read, had a well-informed mind. The man who married Sunny Vangelder would be lucky in more ways than one.

Justin had chosen a path that brought them out of the park's wilderness area right beside the water garden. It was an elaborate series of pools and channels that descended across three levels of terraces before flowing into the ornamental lake.

Sunny stopped in her tracks with a soft exhalation of pleasure. "Exquisite. The proportions—the way the statues are reflected in the pools—the way the eye is led gradually down to the lake. It's masterful. And the grass surrounding it! Like green velvet. How do the English grow such perfect grass?"

"It's quite simple, really. Just get a stone roller and use it on the lawn regularly for two or three hundred years."

She laughed and gave him a glance that made him feel as if he was the wittiest, handsomest man alive.

His heart twisted, and he knew that he must get away from her before he started to act like an utter idiot. "I really must take you back now."

"I suppose so." She took a last look at the water garden. "Thank you for indulging me, Lord Justin."

Their walk had taken them around three sides of the palace, and it was only a short distance to the Versailles garden where the fete was being held. As they approached the festivities, a tall man saw them and walked over swiftly. It was Paul Curzon, who had gone to Eton with Justin, though they had never been more than acquaintances. Curzon had been active in the most social set, while Justin had paid an unfashionable amount of attention to his studies.

After giving Justin a barely civil nod, Curzon said, "Lady Westron has been wondering what happened to you, Miss Vangelder."

Justin glanced at his companion and saw how her face lit up when Curzon spoke to her.

"I was in no danger, Mr. Curzon," she said, her voice proper but her eyes brimming with excitement. "I'm an avid gardener, you see, and Lord Justin very kindly consented to show me some of the lesser-known parts of the park."

In a careless tone that managed to imply that Justin was scarcely better than an under gardener, Curzon said, "You could not have chosen a better guide, for I'm sure that no one knows more about such matters than Lord Justin." He offered Sunny his arm. "Now I shall take you to Lady Westron."

Sunny turned to Justin and said with sweet sincerity, "Thank you for the tour, my lord. I enjoyed it very much."

Yet as soon as she took Curzon's arm, Justin saw that she forgot his existence. He watched them walk away together—two tall, blond, laughing people. They were like members of some superior race, set apart from the normal run of mankind.

For the first time in his life, Justin found himself resenting Gavin for having been born first. The Sunny Vangelders of the world would always go to men like Gavin or Curzon.

His aching regret was followed by deep, corroding anger. Damning himself for a fool, he turned and headed toward the house. Gavin's fete could progress to its conclusion without him.

Chapter Two

Swindon Palace
Summer 1885

Justin stared out the study window at the dreary landscape, thinking that rain was appropriate for the day he
had buried his only brother. After a gray, painful interval, a discreet cough reminded him that he was not alone.
He turned to the family solicitor, who had formally read
the will earlier in the afternoon. "Why did you ask to
speak with me, Mr. Burrell?"

"Though I'm sorry to intrude at such a time, your
grace," the solicitor said, "there are several pressing matters that must be addressed without delay."

Justin winced inwardly. Five days of being the ninth
Duke of Thornborough was not long enough to accustom
him to his new status. "I assume that you are going to tell
me that the financial situation is difficult. I'm already
aware of that."

Another little cough, this one embarrassed. "While you
are extremely well-informed about estate matters, there
are, ah, certain other items that you might not know of."

With sudden foreboding, Justin asked, "Had Gavin run up extensive personal debts?"

"I'm afraid so, your grace. To the tune of... almost a hundred thousand pounds."

A hundred thousand pounds! How the devil had Gavin managed to spend so much? Justin wanted to swear out loud.

Seeing his expression, Mr. Burrell said, "It was unfortunate that your brother's death occurred just when it did."

"You mean the fact that he died while on his way to marry May Russell? It certainly would have been more prudent to have waited until after the wedding," Justin said bitterly.

It would have been even more prudent if Gavin had stayed in the private Thornborough railway car. Instead, he had been taken by the charms of a French lady and had gone to her compartment. When the train crashed, the duke and his inamorata had both died, locked in a scandalous embrace. If Gavin had been in his own car, he would have survived the crash with scarcely a bruise.

Oh, damn, Gavin, why did you have to get yourself killed?

Justin swallowed hard. "Obviously drastic measures will be required to save the family from bankruptcy."

"You could sell some land."

"No!" More moderately, Justin said, "The land is held in trust for future generations. It should not be sold to pay frivolous debts."

Burrell nodded, as if he had expected that response. "The only other choice is for you to make an advantageous marriage."

"Become a fortune hunter, you mean?"

"It's a time-honored tradition, your grace," Burrell pointed out with dignity. "You have a great deal to offer a well-dowered bride. One of England's greatest names, and the most magnificent private palace in Great Britain."

"A palace whose roof leaks," Justin said dryly. "Even as we speak, dozens of buckets in the attic are filling with water."

"In that case, the sooner you marry, the better." The solicitor cleared his throat with a new intonation. "In fact, Mrs. Russell hinted to me this morning that if you were interested in contracting an alliance with her, she would look with favor on your suit."

"Marry my brother's fiancée?" Justin said incredulously. He thought of how May had looked earlier at Gavin's funeral, weeping copiously, her beautiful face obscured by her black mourning veil. Perhaps if he had looked more closely, he would have seen a speculative gleam in her eyes. "It's hard to believe that even she would go to such lengths to become a duchess."

"The lady implied that she has a certain fondness for you as well," Burrell said piously.

"The lady has a deficient memory," Justin retorted. It was May Russell who had first called him the Gargoyle. She had been demonstrating her wittiness. Even Gavin had laughed.

"She has a very large fortune under her own control," the solicitor said with regret. "But I suppose you're right—it would be unseemly for you to marry your brother's betrothed. Do you have another suitable female in mind?"

"No. For the last several years, I've been too busy to look for a wife." Justin returned to his position by the window and stared blindly across the grounds. Burrell was right—marriage was the only plausible answer. Justin wouldn't be the first, and certainly not the last, to marry for money.

Even as a younger son, Justin would have had no trouble finding a wife, for he was an Aubrey, had no appalling vices and he had inherited an adequate private income. Yet though Gavin's entertaining had brought a steady stream of polished, fashionable females through Swindon, there had never been one whom Justin had wanted for a wife.

Except...

He closed his eyes, and instantly the memory he had tried to suppress for months crossed his mind—a perfect spring day, a tall, graceful young woman with a smile of such bright sweetness that she was nicknamed for the sun. The image was more real than the foggy landscape outside.

Though Justin had hated himself for his weakness, he had compulsively tracked Sunny Vangelder's triumphant passage through English society. Scarcely an issue of the *Morning Post* had arrived without mentioning her presentation at court, or her glowing appearance at a ball, or the fact that she had been seen riding in Rotten Row. Rumor said that many men had asked for her hand, and daily Justin had steeled himself for an announcement of a brilliant match. Yet at the end of the season, she had left London still unbetrothed.

He drew a painful breath. It was absurd to think of such an incomparable female marrying someone as ordinary as himself. But Gavin had said that she was the greatest heiress ever to cross the Atlantic, which meant that she was exactly the sort of wife Justin needed. And it was also said that her mother wanted to see her a duchess.

Scarcely daring to hope, he asked, "Do you know if Miss Vangelder has contracted a marriage yet?"

"You want to marry the Gilded Girl?" Burrell said, unable to conceal his shock at such effrontery. "Winning her would be quite a coup, but difficult, very difficult. There's a mining heiress from San Francisco who might be a better choice. Almost as wealthy, and I am acquainted with her father. Or perhaps..."

Interrupting the solicitor, Justin said, "I would prefer Miss Vangelder. I met her once, and found her...very amiable."

After a long pause, Burrell said doubtfully, "Of course, you *are* the Duke of Thornborough now. Perhaps it could be done."

Justin smiled humorlessly at the slate-gray pools of the water garden. "How does one go about selling oneself, Burrell? My experience is sadly deficient."

Ignoring the sardonic tone, the solicitor said, "I shall visit Lady Westron. She's the girl's godmother, you know. If she thinks the idea has merit, she can write Augusta Vangelder."

"Very well—call on her ladyship before the roof collapses."

"There is one thing you should consider before proceeding, your grace," Burrell said with a warning note. "Certainly there are more American heiresses than English ones, and they tend to be much more polished, but the drawback of such an alliance is that the families usually drive hard bargains. You would probably have restrictions placed on your control of the dowry, and you might have to return the balance if the marriage ends."

Justin's mouth tightened. "I wouldn't be marrying the girl with the intention of divorcing her, Burrell."

"Of course not," the solicitor said quickly. After a shuffle of papers, he added, "If I may say so, you're very different from your brother."

"Say what you like," Justin said tersely. Yet though he told himself that a rich wife was strictly a practical matter, the possibility of marrying Sunny Vangelder filled him with raw, aching hunger.

If she came to Swindon, there would always be sunshine.

Newport, Rhode Island

Laughing and breathless from the bicycle ride, Sunny waved goodbye to her friends, then skipped up the steps of The Tides, the Vangelder summer home. Like most Newport "cottages," it would have been called a mansion anywhere else. Still, the atmosphere was more informal than in New York, and she always enjoyed the months spent in Newport.

And this summer was the best ever, because the Honorable Paul Curzon was visiting the Astors. He had arrived in Newport three weeks earlier, and the first time they had waltzed together he had confided that he had come to America to see Sunny.

She had almost expired from sheer bliss, for she had been thinking of Paul ever since their first meeting. They had carried on a delicious flirtation throughout the season, and she had sensed that there were deeper feelings on both sides; certainly there had been on her part. It had been a bitter disappointment that he had not offered for her then.

As they danced, he explained that he had not spoken earlier for he had feared that he would not be considered an acceptable suitor. But after weeks of yearning, he had finally decided to come to America and declare his love. Breathlessly she had confessed that she also had tender feelings for him.

Ever since that night, she had been living in an enchanted dream. Each morning she woke with the knowledge that she would see Paul at least once during the day, perhaps more than that. The business of Newport was society, and there was an endless succession of balls and dinner parties and polo matches.

Though the two of them had behaved impeccably in public, on two magical occasions they had had a moment's privacy, and he had kissed her with a passion that made her blood sing through her veins. At night, as she lay in her chaste bed, she remembered those kisses and yearned for more.

His courtship had culminated this morning, in the few minutes when the two of them had cycled ahead of the rest of their party. After declaring his love, he had asked her to marry him. Dizzy with delight, she had accepted instantly.

As Sunny stepped into the cool marble vestibule of The Tides, she tried to calm her expression, for she knew that she was beaming like a fool. It was going to be hard to keep her lovely secret, but she must until the next day, when Paul would ask her mother's permission. It was not to be expected that her mother would be enthralled by the match. However, Sunny was sure that she would come around, for Paul came from a fine family and he had a distinguished career in front of him.

She handed the butler her hat, saying gaily, "It's a beautiful day, Graves."

"Indeed it is, Miss Sarah." Taking the hat, he added, "Your mother has asked that you see her as soon as you return home. I believe that she is in her private salon."

Such summons were not uncommon, so Sunny went upstairs with no premonition of disaster. She knocked on her mother's door and was invited in.

When she entered, Augusta looked up from her desk with triumph in her eyes. "I have splendid news, Sarah. I'll admit I was tempted by some of the offers I received for your hand, but it was right to wait." After a portentous pause, she said, "You, my dear, are going to become the Duchess of Thornborough."

The shock was so stunning that at first Sunny could only say stupidly, "What on earth do you mean?"

"You're going to marry Thornborough, of course," her mother said briskly. "For the last several days cables have been flying back and forth between Newport and England. The essentials have been settled, and Thornborough is on his way to Newport to make you a formal offer."

"But... but I thought the Duke of Thornborough was going to marry Mrs. Russell."

"That was Gavin, the eighth duke. Unfortunately he was killed in a train wreck several weeks ago, two days before he was to marry May." Augusta smiled maliciously. "I would wager that May tried her luck with his successor, but clearly the ninth duke has better taste than his brother."

Feeling ice-cold, Sunny sank into a chair. "How can I marry a man whom I've never even met?" she said weakly.

"Katie Westron said that you did meet him. In fact, you spent a rather indecent amount of time strolling through the Swindon gardens together," her mother said tartly. "He was Lord Justin Aubrey then, younger brother to the duke who just died."

The fete at Swindon was when Sunny had met Paul. Beside that, other events of the day had paled. Dazedly she tried to remember more. The gardens had been superb, and she vaguely recalled being escorted through them by someone. Had that been Lord Justin? She supposed so, though she could remember nothing about him except that he was dark, and quiet, and . . . unmemorable.

But it didn't matter what he was like, because she wasn't going to marry him. Steeling herself for battle, Sunny said, "I can't marry Thornborough, because I'm betrothed to Paul Curzon."

There was an instant of ominous silence. Then her mother exploded. "I considered putting a stop to that earlier, but I thought it was a harmless flirtation. I couldn't *believe* that you would be so foolish as to entertain thoughts of marrying such a man." Her eyes narrowed. "I trust that at least you've had the sense not to tell anyone about this so-called engagement?"

Sunny shook her head. "Paul only asked me this morning."

"I shall send him a note saying that he is never to call on you, or speak to you, again. That will put an end to this nonsense." Augusta drummed her fingers on the elaborate desk as she thought. "Thornborough will be here in nine days. I shall give a ball in his honor a week later, and we can announce the betrothal then. The wedding should take place in October, I think. It will take that long to make suitable arrangements."

Knowing that she faced the fight of her life, Sunny wiped her damp palms on her skirt, then said evenly, "You must cable the duke and stop him from coming, Mother. Paul Curzon and I love each other, and I am going to marry him."

It was the first time she had ever defied her mother, and Augusta's jaw dropped in shock. Recovering quickly, she said in a low, furious voice, "You are a Vangelder, my girl, and I've devoted my life to training you to be worthy of the highest station. I will never permit you to throw yourself away on a worthless, fortune-hunting younger son."

"Paul is no fortune hunter! He said that if you refused permission, we could live on his income," Sunny said hotly. "And he isn't worthless! He's a British aristocrat, exactly what you wanted for me, and he has a great future in British politics. He was recently made a junior minister, and he says that with me by his side he'll soon be in the Cabinet."

"Your money would certainly help his career," Augusta said grimly, "but he'll have to find himself another heiress, because I will never give my consent."

"I don't need your consent!" Sunny said fiercely. "I'm of legal age and can marry whomever I wish. And I *will!*"

"How dare you speak to your mother this way!" Augusta grabbed Sunny's elbow, then marched her down the hall to her bedroom and shoved her inside. "If you think a humble life is so splendid, you can stay locked in here and live on bread and water until you change your mind."

As the key turned in the lock, Sunny collapsed, shaking, on the bed. She had never dreamed how painful defiance could be. Yet she could not surrender, not when her whole life's happiness was at stake.

She must see Paul; he would know what to do.

The thought steadied her churning emotions, and she began to consider what to do. Her bedroom opened onto the roof of one of the porches, and her older brother Charlie had showed her how to climb to the ground. Her mother had never dreamed that her well-bred daughter would behave in such a hoydenish fashion.

Paul was staying at Windfall, which was only a mile away. Would he be there this evening? Yes, he had mentioned that the Astors were giving a dinner party. She would wait until her mother retired, then escape and walk to Windfall. With a veil over her face, no one would recognize her even if she was seen. She'd go to the servants' entrance and ask for the butler. He knew her, and she thought that for a suitable consideration he would summon Paul and let them have a few minutes of privacy.

Once they were together, everything would be all right.

Sunny's plan went smoothly, and by ten o'clock that evening she was pacing nervously around the Windfall servants' sitting room. She hoped that Paul would be able to slip away quietly when the butler delivered her message. But what if the butler betrayed her to Mrs. Astor? Or if Mrs. Astor suspected that something was amiss and decided to investigate?

The door opened and she whirled around, ready to jump from her skin. With a wave of relief, she saw that it was Paul, devastatingly attractive in his evening dress. Coming toward her with concern on his face, he said, "Darling, you shouldn't risk your reputation like this—but it's wonderful to see you."

He opened his arms, and she went into them eagerly. She loved his height, which made her feel small and feminine. It was the first time they had real privacy, and his kiss far surpassed what they had shared before. Her resolve strengthened. She would never give up his love for the dubious pleasure of marrying a nondescript duke. *Never.*

Remembering the reason for her visit, she reluctantly ended the kiss. "Oh, Paul, something dreadful has happened!" she said miserably. "Today my mother told me that she has arranged for me to marry someone else. I told her about our betrothal, but she won't hear of it. She locked me in my room and swore I'd stay there on bread and water until I changed my mind."

"How dare she treat you in such a way!" Paul exclaimed. "I won't permit it."

"I refused to agree to her wishes, of course, but it was so difficult. I ... I think we should elope. Tonight."

"Right now?" he said, startled. "That's not what I want for you, darling. You deserve the grandest wedding of the century, not a furtive, hole-in-corner affair."

"What does that matter?" she said impatiently. "I'm trying to be strong, but my mother is ... is not easy to resist."

"Who does she want you to marry?"

"The new Duke of Thornborough, Justin Aubrey. His brother, Gavin, just died, and Justin needs a rich wife."

Before she could say more, Paul said in a stunned voice, "The Duke of Thornborough! You would be one of the most influential women in England."

"And one of the unhappiest." Tears welled in her eyes, and she blinked them back angrily. "I need to be with you, Paul."

"We must reason this out." He stroked her back soothingly. "Your mother flatly refused to consider me as a suitor?"

"She said that it was unthinkable that I should marry a nobody." Sunny relaxed again, comforted by his touch. "Such nonsense! Titles mean nothing. What matters is being a gentleman, and no one is more gentlemanly than you."

There was a long pause. Then Paul said gravely, "Sunny, I can't marry you against your mother's wishes. Though I knew that she would not be enthusiastic about my suit, I thought I would be able to persuade her. But to be Duchess of Thornborough! With that in prospect, she will never accept me."

A tendril of fear curled through Sunny. "It is not my mother's place to choose my husband," she said sharply.

"It's mine, and you are my choice. That's all that matters."

"If only it were that simple!" He sighed. "But it's not, my dear. You are not simply my own sweet love, but a national treasure—one of America's princesses. What kind of cad would I be to take advantage of your innocence to keep you from a glorious future?"

Sunny stared at him, thinking that this scene couldn't be real. Perhaps she had fallen off her bicycle and injured her head, and everything that had happened since was only a bad dream. Very carefully she said, "You're saying that you don't want to marry me?"

"Of course I do, but clearly that is impossible. If you marry me, you will become estranged from your family. I don't want to be the cause of that." He gazed lovingly into her eyes. "This won't be so bad, darling. In fact, one could see it as a piece of good fortune. With your influence to further my career, I'll be in the Cabinet in no time."

"Is that what matters most—your career?" she said brittlely.

"Of course not!" He pulled her close again. "The most important thing is our love, and your mother can't take that away from us. After you've given Thornborough an heir and a spare, we'll be free to love each other as we were meant to."

She went rigid, unable to believe what he was saying.

Feeling her withdrawal, he said tenderly, "I don't want to wait, either. If we're discreet, we can be together as soon as you're back from your honeymoon. Believe me, I would like nothing better! We'll have to be careful, of course—it wouldn't do to foist a bastard on Thornborough." He gave a wicked chuckle. "Though if the Gargoyle is unable to perform his duty, I'll be happy to help him. I look more like an Aubrey than he does."

"In other words, I make you a Cabinet minister, and my reward is adultery in the afternoon," she said numbly. "No, thank you, Mr. Curzon." Knowing that she would break down in tears if she stayed any longer, she headed for the door.

He followed her and caught her shoulders. "Don't look at it that way, darling. I promise you that this will turn out all right. We'll be able to enjoy the very cream of love, with none of the dreariness of daily living that kills romance."

He turned her around so that she was facing him. He was as heart-stoppingly handsome as ever, his golden hair glowing in the gaslight, his blue eyes limpid with sincerity.

She drew a shuddering breath. How could she have been such a fool?

His voice richly confident, he said, "Trust me, darling." Then he started to pull her toward him for another kiss.

She slapped him with all her strength. "You're right that this is a fortunate turn of events, because it's given me a chance to see what a swine you are," she said, her voice trembling. "I hope I never see you again, though I don't suppose I'll be so lucky. Goodbye, Mr. Curzon, and good riddance."

As he gaped with shock, the imprint of her hand reddening on his face, she spun on her heel and raced from the room. When she was outside the cottage, she took refuge in the shadowy lee of a huge hedge. There she fell to her knees, heart hammering and tears pouring down her face.

Ever since her childhood, she had dreamed of finding a man who would love her forever. She had wanted a marriage different from the carefully concealed hostility between her parents, or the bored civility common between many other fashionable couples. In Paul, she thought she had found the man she was seeking.

But she had been wrong, so wrong. Oh, he desired her body, and he lusted after her family's money and influence, but that wasn't love—she doubted that he knew what love was. Obviously she didn't know much about it, either. Perhaps the love she craved had never been more than a romantic girl's futile fantasy.

Blindly she stumbled to her feet and began the slow walk to The Tides. After Paul's betrayal, there was no reason to go anywhere else.

The next morning, when a maid delivered a half loaf of freshly baked bread and a crystal pitcher of water on a tray decorated with a fresh rosebud, Sunny summoned her mother and said that she would accept the Duke of Thornborough's offer.

Chapter Three

Justin found America a mixture of the sublime and the ridiculous. He liked the bustling energy of New York City and the cheerful directness of the average citizen. Yet in what was supposedly a nation of equals, he found people whose craven fawning over his title would have shamed a spaniel.

Newport society, which considered itself the *crème de la crème* of America, apparently wanted to out-Anglo the English when it came to formality and elaborate rules. Augusta Vangelder was in her element as she escorted him to an endless series of social events. She invariably referred to him as her "dear duke." He bore that stoically, along with all the other absurdities of the situation.

But the habits of the natives were of only minor interest; what mattered was Sunny Vangelder. He had hoped that she would greet him with the same sweet, unaffected good nature that she had shown at Swindon, perhaps even with eagerness.

Instead, she might have been a different person. The laughing girl had been replaced by a polished, brittle young woman who avoided speaking with him and never once met his gaze. Though he tried to revive the easy companionship they had so briefly shared, he had no success.

Perhaps her stiffness was caused by her mother's rather repressive presence, but he had the uneasy feeling that there was a deeper cause.

His fifth morning in Newport, he happened to find Sunny reading in the library during a rare hour when they were at home. She didn't hear him enter, and her head remained bent over her book. The morning light made her hair glow like sun-struck honey, and the elegant purity of her profile caught at his heart.

It was time to make his formal offer of marriage. A flurry of images danced through his mind: him kneeling at her feet and eloquently swearing eternal devotion; Sunny opening her arms and giving him that wonderful smile that had made him feel as if he were the only man in the world; a kiss that would bring them together forever.

Instead, he cleared his throat to get her attention, then said, "Miss Vangelder—Sunny—there is something I would like to ask you. I'm sure you know what it is."

Perhaps she had known that he was there, for there was no surprise on her face when she lowered her book and looked up.

"All of Newport knows," she said without inflection.

She wasn't going to make this easy for him. Wishing that he was skilled at spinning romantic words, he said haltingly, "Sunny, you have had my heart from the first moment I saw you at Swindon. There is no one else . . ."

She cut him off with an abrupt motion of her hand. "You needn't waste our time with pretty lies, Duke. We are here to strike a bargain. You need a fortune and a wife who knows what to do with a dinner setting that includes six forks. I need a husband who will lend luster to my mother's position in society, and who will confirm our fine American adage that anything can be bought. Please get on with the offer so I can accept and return to my book."

He rocked back on his heels, feeling as if he had been punched in the stomach. Wanting to pierce her contemptuous calm, he said with uncharacteristic bluntness, "We're talking about a marriage, not a business. The first duty of a nobleman's wife is to produce an heir, and knowledge of which fork to use will not help you there."

"I've heard that begetting children is a monstrously undignified business, but didn't the Queen tell her oldest daughter that a female needs only to lie there and think of England?" Sunny's lips twisted. "I should be able to manage that. Most women do."

Damning the consequences to Swindon, he said tightly, "There will be no offer, Miss Vangelder, for I will do neither of us a favor by marrying a woman who despises me."

Sunny caught her breath, and for the first time since he had arrived in Newport looked directly at him. He was shocked by the haunted misery in her aqua eyes.

After a moment she bent her neck and pressed her slim fingers to the center of her forehead. "I'm sorry, your grace. I didn't mean to imply that I despise you," she said quietly. "I recently...suffered a disappointment, and I'm afraid that my temper is badly out of sorts. Still, that does not excuse my insufferable rudeness. Please forgive me."

He guessed that only a broken heart would cause a well-mannered young lady to behave so brusquely. He had heard that Paul Curzon had been in Newport until the week before. Could Sunny have fallen in love with Curzon, who had as many mistresses as the Prince of Wales? Recalling how she had looked at the man when she was at Swindon, Justin knew it was all too likely.

The disappointment was crushing. When he had received Augusta Vangelder's invitation, he had assumed that she had obtained her daughter's agreement to the marriage. He should have known that he would never have been Sunny's choice. It was Augusta, after all, who was enthralled by the idea of a dukedom; Sunny was obviously unimpressed by the prospect.

In a voice of careful neutrality, he said, "You're forgiven, but even if you don't despise me, it's clear that this is not a match that you want." His throat closed, and it took an immense effort to add, "I don't want an unwilling bride, so if there is someone else whom you wish to marry, I shall withdraw."

She stared at her hands, which were locked tightly on her book. "There is no one I would prefer. I suppose that I must marry someone, and you'll make as good a husband as any."

He studied the delicate line of her profile, his resolve to do the right thing undermined by his yearning. Then she raised her head, her gaze searching. He had the feeling that it was the first time she had truly looked at him as an individual.

"Perhaps you would be better than most," she said after a charged silence. "At least you are honest about what you want."

It was a frail foundation for a lifetime commitment, but he could not bear to throw away this chance. "Very well," he said formally. "I would be very honored, and very pleased, if you would consent to become my wife."

"The honor is mine, your grace," she said with equal formality.

If this was a normal engagement, he would kiss his intended bride now, but Sunny's expression was unwelcoming, so he said only, "My name is Justin. It would please me if you used it."

She nodded. "Very well, Justin."

An awkward silence fell. Unhappily he wondered how achieving the fondest hope of his heart could feel so much like ashes. "Shall we go and inform your mother of our news?"

"You don't need me for that. I know that she is interested in an early wedding, perhaps October. You need only tell her what is convenient for you." Rubbing her temples, she set aside her book and got to her feet. "If you'll excuse me, I have a bit of a headache."

"I hope that you feel better soon."

"I'm sure I shall." Remembering that she had just agreed to give her life, her person and her fortune into this stranger's keeping, she attempted a smile.

It must not have been a very good attempt, because the duke's face remained grave. His thoughtful eyes were a clear, light gray, and were perhaps his best feature.

"I don't wish to seem inattentive," he said, "but my brother left his affairs in some disarray, and I must return to London the day after your mother's ball. I probably won't be able to return until a few days before the wedding."

"There is no need for romantic pretenses between us." She smiled, a little wryly, but with the first amusement she had felt since discovering Paul's true character. "It will be best if you aren't here, because there will be a truly vulgar amount of publicity. Our marriage will inevitably be deemed the Wedding of the Century, and there will be endless stories about you and me, your noble ancestors and my undistinguished ones, my trousseau, my flowers, my attendants and every other conceivable detail. And what the reporters can't find out, they will invent."

His dark brows arched. "You're right. It will be better if I am on the other side of the Atlantic."

He opened the door for her. When she walked in front of him, on impulse she laid her hand on his arm for a moment. "I shall do my best to be a duchess you will be proud of."

He inclined his head. "I'm sure you will succeed."

As she went upstairs to her room, she decided that he was rather attractive, in a subdued way. Granted, he wasn't much taller than she, but she was a tall woman. The quiet excellence of British tailoring showed his trim, muscular figure to advantage, and his craggy features had a certain distinction.

The words echoed in her mind, and as she entered her room and wearily lay on the bed, she realized that she had had similar thoughts when she first saw him at Swindon Palace.

That memory triggered others, and gradually fragments of that day came back to her. Lord Justin had been quiet but very gentlemanly, and knowledgeable about the gardens and estate. He had even showed signs of humor, of a very dry kind. It had been a pleasant interlude.

Yet he was still almost entirely a stranger, for she knew nothing of his mind or emotions. He didn't seem to be a man of deep feelings; it was his duty to marry well, so he was doing so, choosing a wife with his head rather than his heart.

Her eyes drifted shut. Perhaps this marriage would not be such a bad thing; she had heard that arranged marriages were happy about as often as love matches. She and the duke would treat each other with polite respect and not expect romance or deep passion. God willing, they would have children, and in them she might find the love she craved.

Certainly the duke had one great advantage: he could hardly have been more different from charming, articulate, false-hearted Paul Curzon.

* * *

The maid Antoinette made a last adjustment to the train of Sunny's ball gown. "You look exquisite, mademoiselle. *Monsieur le Duc* will be most pleased."

Sunny turned and regarded herself in the mirror. Her cream-colored gown was spectacular, with sumptuous embroidery and a décolletage that set off her bare shoulders and arms perfectly. After her hair had been pinned up to expose the graceful length of her neck, fragile rosebuds had been woven into the soft curls. The only thing her appearance lacked was animation. "Thank you, Antoinette. You have surpassed yourself."

The maid permitted herself a smile of satisfaction before she withdrew. Sunny glanced at the clock and saw that she had a quarter of an hour to wait before making her grand entrance at the ball. The house hummed with excitement, for tonight Augusta's triumph would be announced. All of Newport society was here to fawn over Thornborough and cast envious glances at Sunny. There would also be sharp eyes watching to see how she and the duke—Justin—behaved with each other. Antoinette, who was always well-informed, had passed on several disturbing rumors. It was said that Sunny had at first refused to marry the duke because of his licentious habits, and that Augusta had beaten and starved her daughter into accepting him.

Even though there was a grain of truth in the story about her mother, Sunny found the gossip deeply distasteful. She must make a special effort to appear at ease with her mother and her fiancé. She looked in the mirror again and practiced her smile.

The door opened and a crisp English voice said, "How is my favorite goddaughter?"

"Aunt Katie!" Sunny spun around with genuine pleasure. "I had no idea that you were coming for the ball."

"I told Augusta not to mention the possibility since I wasn't sure I would arrive in time." Laughing, Lady Westron held Sunny at arm's length when her goddaughter came to give her a hug. "Never crush a Worth evening gown, my dear! At least, not until the ball is over."

After a careful survey, she gave a nod of approval. "I'm madly envious. Even Worth can't make a short woman like me look as magnificent as you do tonight. The Newport cats will gnash their teeth with jealousy, and Thornborough will thank his stars for his good fortune."

Sunny's high spirits faded. "I believe he feels that we have made a fair bargain."

Katie cocked her head. "Are you unhappy about the match?"

Sunny shrugged and began carefully drawing an elbow-length kid glove onto her right hand. "I'm sure that we'll rub along tolerably well."

Ignoring her own advice about crushing a Worth evening gown, Katie dropped into a chair with a flurry of satin petticoats. "I made inquiries about Thornborough when his solicitor first approached me about a possible match. He'll make you a better husband than most, Sunny. He's respected by those who know him, and while he isn't a wit like his brother was, and he's certainly not fashionable, he's no fool, nor is he the sort to humiliate you by flaunting his mistress."

Sunny stiffened. "Thornborough has a mistress?"

"Very likely—most men do." Katie's lips curved ruefully. "There's much you need to learn about English husbands and English houses. Living in Britain is quite unlike being a visitor, you know."

Sunny relaxed when she found that her godmother had been talking in general rather than from particular knowledge. Though she knew that fashionable English society was very different from what she was used to, she disliked the idea of Thornborough with a mistress. Acutely.

She began the slow process of putting on her left glove. "Perhaps you had better educate me about what to expect."

"Be prepared for the fact that English great houses are *cold*." Katie shuddered. "Forget your delicate lace shawls—to survive winter in an English country house, your trousseau should include several wraps the size and weight of a horse blanket. You must have at least one decent set of furs, as well. The houses may be grand, but they're amazingly primitive—no central heating or gaslights, and no hot running water. And the bathrooms! A tin tub in front of the fire is the best you'll do in most houses."

Surprised and a little amused, Sunny said, "Surely Swindon Palace can't be that bad. It's said to be the grandest private home in Great Britain."

Katie sniffed. "A palace built almost two hundred years ago, and scarcely a pound wasted on modernization since then. But don't complain to Thornborough—English husbands, as a rule, are not solicitous in the way that American husbands are. Since the duke will not want to hear about your little grievances, you must learn to resolve matters on your own. I recommend that you take your own maid with you. That way you can count on at least one person in the household being on your side."

Sunny put a hand up. "If you say one sentence more, I will go downstairs and cancel my betrothal," she said, not knowing whether to laugh or cry. "I'm beginning to wonder why any woman would want to marry an English lord, particularly if she isn't madly in love with him."

"I didn't mean to terrify you," Katie assured her. "I just want to make sure that you won't be disillusioned. Once a woman gets past the discomforts, she may have more freedom and influence than she would in America. Here, a woman rules her home, but nothing outside. An English lady can be part of her husband's life, or develop a life of her own, in a way most unusual in America."

Since frankness was the order of the day, Sunny asked, "Are you sorry you married Lord Westron?"

Katie hesitated a moment. "There are times when I would have said yes, but we've come to understand each other very well. He says that I've been invaluable to his political career, and through him, I've been able to bring a little American democracy to some hoary bits of British law." She smiled fondly. "And between us, he and I have produced three rather splendid children, even if I shouldn't say so myself."

Sunny sighed; it was all very confusing. She was glad when a knock sounded on her door. "Your mother says that it is time to come down, Miss Sarah," the butler intoned.

"Don't forget your fan. It's going to be very warm on the dance floor," Katie said briskly. "I'll be down after I've freshened up."

Sunny accepted the fan, then lifted her train and went into the corridor. At the top of the sweeping staircase, she carefully spread the train, then slowly began descending the stairs, accompanied by the soft swish of heavy silk. She had been told that she walked with the proud grace of the Winged Victory. She ought to; as a child, she had been strapped into an iron back brace whenever she did her lessons. Perfect posture didn't come easily.

The hall below opened into the ballroom, and music and guests wafted through both. As she came into view, a hush fell and all eyes turned toward her. The cream of American society was evaluating the next Duchess of Thornborough.

When she was three-quarters of the way down, she saw that her fiancé was crossing the hall to the staircase. The stark black of formal evening wear suited him.

When she reached the bottom, he took her hand. Under his breath, he said, "You look even more beautiful than usual." Then he brushed a courtly, formal kiss on her kid-covered fingers.

She glanced at him uncertainly, not sure if he truly admired her or the compliment was mere formality. It was impossible to tell; he was the most inscrutable man she had ever met.

Then he smiled at her and looked not merely presentable, but downright handsome. It was the first time she had seen him smile. He should do so more often.

Her mother joined them, beaming with possessive pride. "You look splendid, Sarah."

A moment later they were surrounded by chattering, laughing people, particularly those who had not yet met the duke and who longed to rectify the omission. Sunny half expected her fiancé to retreat to a corner filled with men, but he bore up under the onslaught very well. Though he spoke little, his grave courtesy soon won over even the most critical society matrons. She realized that she had underestimated him. Thornborough's avoidance of the fashionable life was obviously from choice rather than social ineptitude.

When she finally had a chance to look at her dance card, she saw that her fiancé had put himself down for two waltzes as well as the supper dance. That in itself was a declaration of their engagement, for no young lady would have more than two dances with one man unless intentions were serious.

When the orchestra struck up their first waltz, Thornborough excused himself from his admirers and came to collect her.

She caught her train up so that she could dance, then took his hand and followed him onto the floor. "It will be a pleasure to waltz," she said. "I feel as if I've been talking nonstop for the last hour."

"I believe that you have been," he said as he drew her into position, a light hand on her waist. "It must be fatiguing to be so popular. In the interests of allowing you to recover, I shan't require you to talk at all."

"But you are just as popular," she said teasingly. "Everyone in Newport wants to know you."

"It isn't me they're interested in, but the Duke of Thornborough. If I were a hairy ape from the Congo, I'd be equally in demand, as long as I was also a duke." He considered, then said with good-natured cynicism, "More so, I think. Apes are said to be quite entertaining."

Though Sunny chuckled, his remark made her understand better why he wanted her to call him Justin. Being transformed overnight from the Gargoyle to the much-courted Duke of Thornborough must have been enough to make anyone cynical.

It came as no surprise to learn that he danced well. She relaxed and let the voluptuous strains of music work their usual magic. The waltz was a very intimate dance, the closest a young woman was allowed to come to a man. Usually it was also an opportunity to talk with some privacy. The fact that she and Justin were both silent had the curious effect of making her disturbingly aware of his physical closeness, even though he kept a perfectly proper twelve inches between them.

Katie had been right about the heat of the ballroom; as they whirled across the floor, Sunny realized that a remarkable amount of warmth was being generated between their gloved hands. It didn't help that their eyes were almost level, for it increased the uncomfortable sense of closeness. She wished that she knew what was going on behind those enigmatic gray eyes.

A month before, she had waltzed like this with Paul Curzon and he had told her that his heart had driven him to follow her to America. The memory was jarring and she stumbled on a turn. If Justin hadn't quickly steadied her, she would have fallen.

His dark brows drew together. "Are you feeling faint? It's very warm—perhaps we should go onto the porch for some air."

She managed a smile. "I'm fine, only a little dizzy. It's absurd that we can turn only one direction during a waltz. If we could spin the other way now and then, it would be much easier."

"Society thrives on absurdity," he observed. "Obscure rules are necessary so that outsiders can be identified and kept safely outside."

While she pondered his unexpected insight, the waltz ended and another partner came to claim her. The evening passed quickly. After the lavish supper was served, the engagement was formally announced. Augusta was in her element as even her most powerful social rivals acknowledged her triumph.

Sunny felt a pang as she accepted the good wishes of people she had known all her life. This was her last summer in Newport. Though she would visit in the future, it would not be the same; already her engagement to an Englishman was setting her apart.

The first phase of her life was ending—and she had no clear idea what the next phase would be like.

* * *

It was very late when the last of the guests left. As her official fiancé, Thornborough was allowed to escort Sunny to her room. When they reached her door, he said, "My train leaves rather early tomorrow, so I'll say goodbye now."

"I'm sorry that you'll have to travel without a proper night's sleep." Almost too tired to stand, she masked a yawn with her hand. "Have a safe and pleasant journey, Justin."

His gaze caught hers, and she couldn't look away. The air between them seemed to thicken. Gently he curved his hand around her head and drew her to him for a kiss.

Because she didn't love him she had been dreading this moment, yet again he surprised her. His lips were warm and firm. Pleasant. Undemanding.

He caressed her hair, disturbing the rosebuds, and scented petals drifted over her bare shoulder in a delicate sensual caress. She gave a little sigh, and his arms went around her.

The feel of his broad chest and his hand on the small of her back triggered a vivid memory of her last kiss, in Paul Curzon's embrace. All the anger and shame of that episode flooded back. She stiffened and took an involuntary step backward.

He released her instantly. Though his eyes had darkened, his voice was mild when he said, "Sleep well. I shall see you in October."

She opened her door, but instead of entering her room she paused and watched his compact, powerful figure stride down the hall to his own chamber. In spite of the warmth of the night, a shiver went down her spine. Her feelings about Justin were confused, but one thing was certain: it would be disastrous to continue to let the shadow of Paul Curzon come between her and her future husband.

Yet she didn't know how to get rid of it.

Chapter Four

New York City
October 1885

The Wedding of the Century.

Justin stared at the blaring headline in one of the newspapers that had just been delivered to his hotel room. It was a rude shock for a man who had disembarked in New York City only two hours earlier.

Below the headline were drawings of Sunny and himself. The likeness of him was not flattering. Were his brows really so heavy and threatening? Perhaps.

He smiled wryly as he skimmed the story; it was every bit as bad as Sunny had predicted. Apparently Americans had a maniacal interest in other people's private business. There was even a breathless description of the bride's garters, which were allegedly of gold lace with diamond-studded clasps. The item must have been invented, since he could not imagine Sunny discussing her garters with a reporter.

The thought of Sunny in her garters was so distracting that he swiftly flipped to the next newspaper. This one featured a cartoon of a couple getting married by a blindfolded minister. The tall, slim bride wore a martyred expression as she knelt beside a dissolute-looking groom who was half a head shorter.

The accompanying story implied rather strongly that the Duke of Thornborough was a corrupt specimen of European cadhood who had come to the New World to coldly steal away the finest, freshest flower of American femininity. At the same time, there was an unmistakable undercurrent of pride that one of New York's own was to become a duchess. Apparently the natives couldn't decide whether they loathed or loved the trappings of the decadent Old World.

Disgusted, he tossed the papers aside and finished dressing for the dinner that Augusta Vangelder was giving in his honor. Afterward, the marriage settlements would be signed. Yet though that would make him a far wealthier man, what made his heart quicken was the fact that after three long months, he would see Sunny again. And not only see, but touch . . .

After his Newport visit they had written each other regularly, and he had enjoyed her whimsical anecdotes about the rigors of preparing for a wedding. If she had ever expressed any affection for him, he might have had the courage to tell her his own feelings, for it would be easier to write about love than to say the words out loud.

But her letters had been so impersonal that anyone could have read them. He had replied with equal detachment, writing about Swindon and acquainting her with what she would find there. He had debated telling her about some of the improvements he had ordered, but decided to keep them as a surprise.

He checked his watch and saw that the carriage the Vangelders were sending should be waiting outside the hotel. Brimming with suppressed excitement, he went downstairs.

As he crossed the lobby, a voice barked, "There he is!"

Half a dozen slovenly persons, obviously reporters, bolted across the marble floor and surrounded him. Refusing to be deterred, he kept walking through the babble of questions that came from all sides.

The loudest speaker, a fellow with a red checked vest, yelled, "What do you think of New York, Duke?"

Deciding it was better to say something innocuous rather than to ignore them entirely, Justin said, "A splendid city."

Another reporter asked, "Any of your family coming to the wedding, Duke?"

"Unfortunately that isn't possible."

"Is it true that Sunny has the largest dowry of any American girl to marry a British lord?"

The sound of her name on the man's lips made Justin glad that he wasn't carrying a cane, for he might have broken it across the oaf's head. "You'll have to excuse me," he said, tight-lipped, "for I have an engagement."

"Are you going to visit Sunny now?" several chorused.

When Justin didn't answer, one of the men grabbed his arm. Clamping onto his temper, Justin looked the reporter in the eye and said in the freezing accents honed by ten generations of nobility, "I beg your pardon?"

The man hastily stepped back. "Sorry, sir. No offense meant."

Justin had almost reached the door when a skinny fellow jumped in front of him. "Are you in love with our Sunny, your dukeship, or are you only marrying her for the money?"

It had been a mistake to answer any questions at all, Justin realized; it only encouraged the creatures. "I realize that none of you are qualified to understand gentlemanly behavior," he said icily, "so you will have to take my word for it that a gentleman never discusses a lady, and particularly not in the public press. Kindly get out of my way."

The man said with a leer, "Just asking what the American public wants to know, Thorny."

"The American public can go hang," Justin snapped.

Before the reporters could commit any further impertinence, several members of the hotel staff belatedly came to Justin's rescue. They swept the journalists aside and escorted him outside with profuse apologies and promises that such persons would never be allowed in the hotel again.

In a voice clipped by fury, Justin told the manager, "I hope that is true, because if there is another episode like this I shall move to quieter quarters."

Temper simmering, he settled into the luxurious Vangelder carriage. The sooner this damned wedding was over and he could take his wife home, the better.

Sunny was waiting in the Vangelder drawing room. She came forward with her hands outstretched, and if her smile wasn't quite as radiant as he would have liked, at least it was genuine.

"It's good to see you, Sunny." He caught her hands and studied her face hungrily. "You were right about the publicity surrounding the wedding. I'm afraid that I was just rather abrupt with some members of the press. Has it been hard on you?"

She made a face. "Though it's been dreadful, I'm well protected here. But everyone in the household has been offered bribes to describe my trousseau."

"Gold-lace garters with diamond-studded clasps?"

"You saw that?" she said ruefully. "It's all so *vulgar!*"

She looked utterly charming. He was on the verge of kissing her when the door swung open. Justin looked up to see a tall, blond young man who had to be one of Sunny's older brothers.

"I'm Charlie Vangelder," the young man said cheerfully as he offered his hand. "Sorry not to meet you in Newport, Thornborough, but I was working on the railroad all summer. Have to learn how to run it when my uncle retires, you know."

So much for being alone with his intended bride. Suppressing a sigh, Justin shook hands with his future brother-in-law. A moment later, Augusta Vangelder swooped in, followed by a dozen more people, and it became clear that the "quiet family dinner" was an occasion for numberless Vangelders to meet their new relation by marriage.

The only break was the half hour when Justin met with the Vangelder attorneys to sign the settlement papers. His solicitor had bargained well; the minute that Justin married Sunny, he would come into possession of five million dollars worth of railway stock with a guaranteed minimum income of two hundred thousand dollars a year.

There would also be a capital sum of another million dollars that Justin would receive outright, plus a separate income for Sunny's personal use so that she would never have to be dependent on her husband's goodwill for pin money. As an incentive for Justin to try to keep his wife happy, the stock would revert to the Vangelder family trust if the marriage ended in divorce.

Gavin would have been amused to know that the value of the Thornborough title had risen so quickly. May Russell would have brought only half as much to her marriage.

Impassively Justin scrawled his name over and over, hating every minute of it. He wished that he could marry Sunny without taking a penny of her family money, but that was impossible; without her wealth and his title, there would be no marriage.

As he signed the last paper, he wondered if Sunny would ever believe that he would have wanted her for his wife even if she had been a flower seller in Covent Garden.

When her daughter entered the breakfast parlor, Augusta said, "Good morning, Sarah." She took a dainty bite of buttered eggs. "There's a letter here for you from England."

Sunny tried unsuccessfully to suppress a yawn as she selected two muffins from the sideboard. The dinner party for Thornborough had gone on very late, and she had smiled at so many cousins that her jaw ached this morning.

She wished that she had had a few minutes alone with her future husband; she would have liked to tell him how much she had enjoyed his letters. She didn't know if it had been a deliberate effort on his part, but his descriptions of life at Swindon Palace had made her future seem less alien. His dry wit had even managed to make her smile.

She slit open the envelope that lay by her plate and scanned the contents. "It's from Lady Alexandra Aubrey, Thornborough's youngest sister. A charming note welcoming me to the family."

Uncomfortably Sunny remembered that Katie had said the girl had been nicknamed the Gargoylette. Her lips compressed as she returned the note to the envelope. The girl might be small, shy and seventeen, but she was the only Aubrey to write her brother's bride, and Sunny looked forward to meeting her.

"Are you only going to have muffins for breakfast?"
Augusta said with disapproval.

"After the dinner last night, it's all I have room for."
Sunny broke and buttered one of the muffins, wondering
why her mother had requested this private breakfast.

Expression determined, Augusta opened her mouth,
then paused, as if changing her mind about what she
meant to say. "Look at the morning paper. Thornborough was intemperate."

Obediently Sunny lifted the newspaper, then blinked at
the screaming headline. *Duke Tells American Public to Go
Hang!*

"Oh, my," she said weakly. The story beneath claimed
that Thornborough had bodily threatened several journalists, then bullied the hotel manager in a blatant attempt to infringe on the American public's constitutional
right to a free press. "He mentioned yesterday that he'd
been abrupt with some reporters, but surely this story is
exaggerated."

"No doubt, but someone should explain to Thornborough that it's a mistake to pick fights with men who buy
ink by the barrel." Augusta neatly finished the last of her
meal. "A good thing that he was in England until now.
Heaven knows what trouble he would have gotten into if
he had been here longer."

Feeling oddly protective, Sunny said, "He's a very private man. He must find this vulgar publicity deeply offensive."

"Unfortunately, wealth and power always attract the
interest of the masses."

Sunny poured herself coffee without comment. Her
mother might say that public attention was unfortunate,
but she would not have liked to be ignored.

Augusta began pleating her linen napkin into narrow folds. "You must be wondering why I wanted to talk to you this morning," she said with uncharacteristic constraint. "This will be difficult for both of us, but it's a mother's duty to explain to her daughter what her...her conjugal duties will be."

The muffin turned to sawdust in Sunny's mouth. Though she didn't want to discuss such a horribly embarrassing subject, there was no denying that information would be useful. Like all well-bred young ladies, her ignorance about marital intimacy was almost total.

Briskly Augusta explained the basics of male and female anatomy. Then, rather more slowly, she went on to describe exactly what a husband did to his wife.

Sunny choked on her coffee. "That's disgusting!" she said after she stopped coughing. She had heard whispered hints and giggles about the mysterious *something* that happened between men and women in the marriage bed, but surely it couldn't be what her mother was describing.

"It *is* disgusting," Augusta agreed, "as low and animal as the mating of hogs. It's also uncomfortable and sometimes painful. Perhaps someday scientific progress will find a better, more dignified way to make babies, but until then, women must suffer for the sins of Eve."

She took a piece of toast and began crumbling it between nervous fingers. "Naturally women of refinement are repulsed by the marital act. Unfortunately, men enjoy it. If they didn't, I suppose there would be no such thing as marriage. All a woman can do is lie there very quietly, without moving, so that the man will please himself quickly and leave her alone."

Lie there and think of England, in other words. Sunny's stomach turned. Had her tall, athletic father actually done such things to her delicate mother? Was this what

Paul Curzon had wanted when he was kissing her? And dear God, must she really allow Thornborough such liberties? Her thighs squeezed together as her body rejected the thought of such an appalling violation.

Seeing her expression, Augusta said reassuringly, "A gentleman will not visit your bed more than once or twice a week. You also have the right to refuse your husband once you are with child, and for at least three months after you deliver." She glanced down at the pile of crumbs she had created. "Last night, after the settlements were signed, I took the duke aside and reminded him that you are gently bred, and that I would not permit him to misuse you."

"You spoke to Thornborough about this?" Sunny gasped, so humiliated that she wanted to crawl under the table and never come out. "How did he reply?"

"He gave me the oddest look, but said that he understood my concern for your welfare, and assured me that he would be mindful of your innocence." Augusta gave a wintry smile. "It was very properly said. He is, after all, a gentleman."

Sunny's mind was a jumble of chaotic thoughts. The marriage bed sounded revolting—yet she had enjoyed Paul Curzon's kisses, and kissing was supposed to be a prelude to doing *it*. Surely the women who carried on flagrant affairs wouldn't do so if they found the whole business distasteful. Timidly she asked, "Do all women dislike the marital act?"

"I wish that I could say that was so, but there is no denying that there are some women of our order who are a disgrace to their sex—low-bred creatures who revel in their animal nature like barmaids. I know that you are not like that, but you will meet women who are." Leaning forward, Augusta said earnestly, "I cannot emphasize enough that it is fatal to seem to take pleasure in a gentleman's embrace. If you do, he will instantly lose all respect for you. A woman who acts like a prostitute will be treated like one. Always strive to maintain your dignity, Sarah—ultimately it is all that a lady has.''

With horror, Sunny remembered that when Paul had taken liberties, she had responded eagerly. Was that why he had made his degrading suggestion that she marry Thornborough, then have an affair with him? She still thought his behavior despicable—but perhaps she had brought it on by her wantonness. Paul had seen her acting like a slut, so he had treated her like one. It was exactly what her mother was warning her about.

Apparently a woman who gave in to her animal nature also risked unleashing a man's worst traits. That had been bad enough in the case of Paul Curzon, but Thornborough was going to be her husband; if he didn't respect her, the marriage would be hellish.

Feeling ill, Sunny said, ''I shall remember all you have said and I will strive to behave in a manner that you would approve.''

''I'm sure you will not disgrace your upbringing.'' Augusta bit her lip, her usual confidence gone. ''Oh, Sarah, I'm going to miss you dreadfully. You'll be so far away.''

Sunny resisted the temptation to point out that her mother should have thought of that before accepting the proposal of a foreigner. ''I'll miss you, too. You must visit us at Swindon soon.''

Augusta shook her head. ''Eventually, but not right away. I know that I'm a strong-minded woman, and I don't want to cause trouble between you and your husband. Marriage is a difficult business, and you and he must have time together with as little interference as possible.''

At moments like this, Sunny loved her mother with painful intensity. It was true that Augusta was often domineering—yet her love for her children was very real. She was a woman of formidable energy; if she had a railroad or a bank to run, she might have been less absorbed in her daughter's life.

"I'll be fine," Sunny said with determined optimism. "Thornborough is a gentleman, and I am a lady. I'm sure that we can contrive a civilized marriage between us."

She wished that she was certain that was true.

Chapter Five

Tears flowing down her face, Sunny stood patiently while her maid laced up her white brocade bridal corset. Then Antoinette dropped the wedding gown over her head. It was magnificent, with foaming layers of Brussels lace and billows of white satin spangled with seed pearls and silver thread. Augusta had been so confident of her daughter's future triumph that she had ordered the gown from Worth when they visited Paris in March, before Sunny had ever set foot in London.

When the gown was fastened, Antoinette lifted the tulle veil and carefully draped it over the intricate coils of Sunny's hair. As the gauzy fabric floated down to her knees, the bride bleakly wondered if it was dense enough to conceal her tears.

Antoinette secured the veil with a coronet of orange blossoms, saying soothingly, "Don't fret, mademoiselle. Every girl is nervous on her wedding day. *Monsieur le Duc* is a fine gentleman, and he will make you very happy."

Sunny's shoulders began shaking with the force of her sobs. Antoinette frowned and gave her a handkerchief, muttering, "Madame Vangelder should not have gone ahead to the church. A girl needs her mother at a time like this."

As Sunny wept into the crumpled muslin square, a knock sounded at the door. Antoinette answered and returned with a large white flower box. "For you, mademoiselle."

"You can open it if you like," Sunny said drearily.

Less jaded than her mistress, Antoinette opened the package, disclosing an exquisite orchid bouquet nestled in layers of tissue paper. "There is a card for you, mademoiselle."

Sunny's puffy eyes widened when she read, *These flowers are from the Swindon greenhouse. If they are suitable, perhaps you might wish to carry them. Fondly, Justin.*

Oblivious to the fate of her five-yard-long train, Sunny dropped into a chair and wept even harder.

"Oh, mam'zelle," Antoinette said helplessly. "What about the orchids makes you weep? They are very lovely."

"Yes, they are." Sunny made a desperate effort to collect herself. "I was...touched by Thornborough's thoughtfulness in having them sent all the way from England."

Though it was not something she could say to her maid, she was even more moved by the fact that he was actually letting her choose whether or not to carry them. Every other detail of the wedding—the trousseau, the decorations, the extravagant reception—had been determined by her mother. Even the eight bridesmaids—including two Vangelder cousins, a Whitney, a Jay and an Astor—had been selected by Augusta for reasons of her own. Sunny had been swept along like a leaf in a torrent.

But Justin had given her a choice. Surely with such a considerate man, she could be happy. Unsteadily she said, "I must look like a fright. Please bring me some cold water and a facecloth." She glanced at the enormous bouquet Augusta had ordered. "You can set that aside. I will carry the orchids."

"But..." After the beginning of a protest, the maid nodded. "Yes, mademoiselle. An excellent choice."

As Antoinette went for the cold water, Sunny found herself wondering if the maid had ever endured the grotesquely undignified process of mating that Augusta had described. The thought almost sent her off in tears again.

For the last two days, at the most awkward moments, she had wondered the same thing about others: her brother Charlie, who was very fond of female company; the wife of the Anglican bishop who was going to perform the ceremony; Thornborough himself. Her morbid imaginings were turning her into a nervous wreck.

Antoinette returned with a basin of water and a cloth, then flipped the veil back over Sunny's head so that her face was bare. "You must hurry, mademoiselle, or you will be late."

As she sponged her stinging eyes with the cool, moist cloth, Sunny snapped, "They can all *wait*."

The day became increasingly unreal. Fifth Avenue was lined on both sides with policemen assigned to prevent the thousands of spectators from breaking through. The wedding was to be at St. Thomas's Anglican church. Though the Vangelders didn't usually worship there, it was the only fashionable church with enough space for the seventy-voice choir Augusta had chosen.

Inside the church, huge arches of orange blossoms spanned the aisle, and banks of palms and chrysanthemums seemed to cover every vertical surface. Twenty-five excruciating minutes behind schedule, Sunny waited for her entrance, one icy hand clenched around her orchid bouquet and the other locked on her brother Charlie's arm. Though she could not see the guests clearly in the dim light, every pew seemed to be filled.

As the bridesmaids marched smartly down the aisle to the music of the sixty-piece orchestra, Charlie whispered, "Buck up, Sunny. Show them that an American girl is every bit the equal of any European princess."

The wedding march began, and Sunny started the long walk to the altar. If it hadn't been for her brother's firm support, the "American princess" might have fallen flat on her face.

With hysterical precision, she calculated that in the months since she had met Thornborough, they had seen each other for ten days, and been alone together for less than an hour. *Why was she marrying a stranger?* If it hadn't been for the five-yard train, she might have turned and bolted.

The dark figure of her fiancé waited impassively at the altar. Next to him was his best man, a pleasant fellow called Lord Ambridge, an old school friend of Justin's who was currently serving in the British Embassy in Washington.

As Sunny drew closer to her future husband, she saw that his expression was grim. Then she looked into his eyes and realized that he was as nervous as she. Her lateness must have made him wonder if she had changed her mind.

Dear God, how humiliating those long minutes of waiting must have been for him. As Charlie handed her over, she gave Thornborough an unsteady smile of apology.

His expression eased. He took her hand, and the warmth of his clasp was the most real thing she had experienced all day.

They turned to face the bishop, and the ancient, familiar words transformed the stranger beside her into her husband.

* * *

The wedding night was a disaster. Later Justin realized that it had been foolish of him to think it could have been otherwise, yet he had had the naive hope that once he and his bride were alone together, they would be able to relax. To become friends.

Instead, the "wedding breakfast" had proved to be a huge reception that seemed as if it would never end. By the time they reached their hotel suite, Sunny's face was gray with fatigue.

He wanted to hold her but restrained himself, for she looked as if she would shatter at a touch. They had a lifetime ahead of them; it would be foolish to rush matters now.

She mutely followed his suggestion that she relax with a long bath. Much later, after Sunny's maid had finished her ministrations and left for the night, he joined his wife in the spacious bedchamber. He expected to find her in the canopied bed, perhaps already asleep. Instead, she stood by the window, gazing out on the lights of New York.

He found her a far more interesting sight than the city. The glossy, honey-gold hair that flowed over her shoulders was even lovelier than he had imagined, and he longed to bury his face among the silken strands. Her white negligee frothed with lace and delicate embroidery, and was so translucent that he could see the lithe shape of her body beneath. It must be another Worth creation; only a master could make a woman look simultaneously pure and provocative.

His wife. He was still awed by the miracle of it.

Justin had been introduced to the dark mysteries of passion when he was sixteen. Deciding it was time his young brother became a man, Gavin had taken Justin to a courtesan. With his usual careless kindness, Gavin had chosen the woman well. Lily was a warmhearted, earthily sensual Frenchwoman who had known exactly how to initiate a shy youth half her age.

Justin's shamed embarrassment had been gone by the end of his first afternoon with Lily. With her he had discovered not only passion, but kindness and mutual affection. He had visited her many times over the ensuing years. When her looks faded and she could no longer support herself as a courtesan, he had quietly bought her a cottage in the south of France so that she could retire in comfort. They still corresponded occasionally.

Because of Lily, he was now able to give his wife the gift of passion. Praying that desire would not make him clumsy, he went to join her by the window. Her delicate violet scent bewitched him, and his hands clenched with the effort of not touching her. Needing a safe, neutral topic, he said, "New York is lovely in a way quite distinct from London or Paris."

"I shall miss it," she whispered.

He glanced over and saw tears trembling in her eyes. "It must be hard to leave one's home," he said quietly, "but you can come back whenever you wish."

"Yes." She drew an unsteady breath. "Still, it hurts knowing that I am no longer an American. Though I understood that marrying a foreigner meant that I would lose my citizenship, I didn't expect to feel it so much."

"The law might say that you are now an Englishwoman, but it can't change what you are in your heart. America made you, and nothing can take that away."

After a long pause, she said in a low voice, "Thank you. I needed to be reminded of that."

Thinking the time was finally right, he put an arm around her waist. For the barest instant, she was pliantly yielding. Then she went rigid, like a small woodland creature holding still in the desperate hope that it would escape a predator's notice.

He turned her toward him and pulled her close, stroking her back in the hope that she would relax, but he was unsuccessful. Though she submitted without protest, her body remained as stiff as a marble statue.

Shyness or nerves were to be expected, but her reaction seemed extreme. He put his hands on her shoulders and held her away from him. "Sunny, are you afraid of me?"

"Not...not of you, really," she said, her eyes cast down.

It wasn't a heartening answer for an eager bridegroom. Patiently he said, "Then are you afraid of...marital intimacy?"

"It's more than that, Justin. I don't know quite how to explain." She pressed her hands to her temples for a moment, then looked into his eyes for the first time in days. "I was raised to be a wife. In the whole of my life, there was never any thought that I would ever be anything else." She swallowed hard. "Only now, when it's too late, does it occur to me that I don't really want to be married to anyone."

Though she claimed that he was not the problem, it was hard not to take her comments personally. Feeling a chill deep inside, he lowered his hands and said carefully, "What do you want me to do—set you up in a separate establishment so that you never have to see me? File for an annulment on the grounds that your mother coerced you into marriage against your will?"

She looked shocked. "Oh, no, of course not. I pledged my word today, and that can't be undone. I will do my best to be a good wife to you—but I don't know if I will succeed."

Some of the pain in his chest eased. As long as they were together, there was hope for building a loving marriage.

Though he had been counting the hours until they could be together, he said, "We needn't share a bed tonight, when you're so tired. It might be better to wait a few days until you're more at ease with me."

She hesitated, clearly tempted, before she shook her head. "I think it will be best to get it over with. Waiting will only give me more time to worry."

He wanted to make love to his wife, and she wanted to "get it over with," like a tooth extraction. Dear God, this was not what he had dreamed of. Yet perhaps she was right. Once she learned that intercourse was not as bad as she feared, she could relax and find pleasure in physical intimacy.

Yet he could not quite suppress the fear that his wife might never come to welcome his touch. He had been concerned ever since Augusta had ordered him to try to control his beastly animal nature. Obviously Augusta had loathed her own marital duties, and there was a strong possibility that she had passed her distaste on to her daughter.

His mouth tightened. Brooding would solve nothing. If his wife wanted the marriage consummated tonight, he would oblige—partly because it might be the wisest course, but more because he wanted her with an intensity that was painful.

"Come then, my dear." He untied the ribbons of her negligee and pushed it from her shoulders so that she was clad only in a sheer silk nightgown that revealed more of her tantalizing curves than it concealed. He drew a shaky breath. It was how he had dreamed of her—and at the same time, it was utterly wrong, for she looked at him with the despairing eyes of a wounded doe.

She colored under his hungry gaze and glanced away. "Could you . . . would you turn the lamps out?"

Though he yearned to see her unclothed, he said, "As you wish."

As he put out the lights, she drew the curtains so that the windows were covered and the room became suffocatingly dark. Then she climbed into the bed with a faint creak of springs.

After removing his robe, he located the bed by touch and slid in beside her. He would have liked to take his nightshirt off, as well, but a man's naked body might upset her more, even in the dark and under blankets.

He drew her into his arms and kissed her with all the tenderness he had been yearning to lavish on her. Though she did not reject him, her mouth was locked shut and her whole frame was tense and unyielding. No amount of patient skill on his part could soften her; in fact, his feather kisses and gentle stroking seemed to make her more rigid. He felt as if he was trying to ravish a vestal virgin. Despairing, he pushed himself up with one arm and said hoarsely, "This isn't right."

"Please, just *do* it," she said, an edge of hysteria in her voice.

His better nature surrendered, for despite his doubts, his body was hotly ready, burning for completion. He reached for the lotion he had provided to ease this first union.

She gasped when he raised the hem of her gown, separated her legs and touched her intimately. He hoped that she might respond positively to his sensual application of the lotion, but there was no change. She simply endured, her limbs like iron, her breath coming in short, frightened gulps.

Though his blood pounded in his temples, he forced himself to go slowly when he moved to possess her. Her body resisted and he heard the scratch of her nails digging into the sheets, but she made no protest.

When the frail membrane sundered and he thrust deeply into her, she gave a sharp, pain-filled cry. He held still, waves of exquisite sensation sweeping through him, until her breathing was less ragged.

Then he began to move, and his control shattered instantly. He loved her and she was his, and he groaned with delirious pleasure as he thrust into her again and again.

His mindless abandon had the advantage of swiftness, for he could not have prolonged their coupling even if he tried. After the fiery culmination, he disengaged and lay down beside her, trembling with reaction. He yearned to hold her close and soothe her distress, but hesitated to touch her. "I'm sorry I hurt you," he panted. "It won't be this painful again."

"I'm all right, Justin," she said, voice shaking. "It... wasn't as bad as I expected."

It was a lie, but a gallant one. No longer able to restrain his impulse to cradle her in his arms, he reached out. If she would let him comfort her, something good would come of this night. But she rolled away into a tight little ball, and his searching fingers found only her taut spine.

The silence that descended was broken by the anguished sound of her muffled sobs. He lay still, drenched with self-loathing at the knowledge that he had found intoxicating pleasure in an act that had distressed her so profoundly.

After a long, long time, her tears faded and her breathing took on the slow rhythm of sleep. Quietly he slid from the bed and felt his way to the door that led to the sitting room, cracking his shin on a stool as he went.

A gas lamp burned in the sitting room, and he saw his haunted reflection in a mirror on the far wall. He turned away, unable to bear the sight of his own misery.

The suite was the most luxurious in the hotel, though not as richly furnished as the Vangelder houses. A porcelain bowl filled with potpourri sat on a side table. He sifted it through his fingers, and the air filled with a tangy fragrance.

He had reached for heaven and landed in hell. Their disastrous wedding night had not been the result of anything simple, like shyness on her part or ineptness on his; it had been total rejection. The woman of his dreams couldn't bear his touch, and there seemed little chance that she would change in the future.

Vases of flowers were set all over the room. Some he had ordered, others were courtesy of the hotel, which was embarrassingly grateful to have the Duke and Duchess of Thornborough as guests. He pulled a white rose from an elegant cut-glass vase. It was just starting to open, at the perfect moment when promise met fulfillment.

Inevitably, he thought of Sunny when he had first seen her at Swindon. Exquisite, laughing, without flaw.

And now she lay weeping in the next room, her bright gaiety gone. He supposed that part of the blame for that could be laid to a false lover, and part to Augusta, who loved her daughter with utter ruthlessness. But most of the fault was his. By the simple act of wanting to marry her, he might have destroyed her blithe sweetness forever.

He began plucking out the satiny white petals, letting them drop one by one. She loved him, she loved him not, over and over, like a litany, as the scent of rose wafted around him.

The last petal drifted to the floor. She loved him not.

He lifted the vase and studied the artistry of the cut glass. Then, in one smooth, raging gesture, he hurled it across the room, where it shattered into a thousand pieces.

She loved him not.

Chapter Six

Justin glanced out the train window at the rolling English landscape. "We'll reach Swindon station in about five minutes."

Sunny lifted her hat from the opposite seat and secured it to her coiled hair with a pearl-headed hat pin. Since they were traveling in the luxurious solitude of the Thornborough private car, she had had ample space for her possessions.

As she prepared for their arrival, she surreptitiously studied her husband. His expression was as impassive as always, even though he was bringing his bride home for the first time. Didn't he ever feel anything? In three weeks of marriage, he had never been anything but unfailingly polite. Civil. Kind. As remote as if he were on the opposite side of the earth.

Not that she should complain, for his calm detachment had made it possible to reach a modus vivendi very quickly. In public, she took his arm and smiled so that they presented a companionable picture to the world.

Naturally neither of them ever referred to what happened in the silence of the night. Justin always ordered suites with two bedrooms so they could sleep separately. Every three or four days, with his gaze on the middle distance, he would ask if it was convenient for him to visit her.

She always gave her embarrassed assent, except for once when she had stammered that she was "indisposed." She would have died of mortification if he had asked what was wrong, but he had obviously understood. Five days passed before he asked again, and by then she was able to give him permission to come.

As he had promised, there had been no pain after the first occasion, and soon her fear had gone away. Dutifully she obeyed her mother's dictum and lay perfectly still while her husband did what husbands did. The marital act took only a few minutes, and he always left directly after.

Once or twice, she had felt his fingers brush through her hair before he climbed from the bed. She liked to think that it was a gesture of affection, though perhaps it was mere accident, a result of fumbling in the dark.

But her mother had been right; passive acceptance of her wifely role had won Justin's respect. Besides treating her with the utmost consideration, he also encouraged her to speak her opinions. That was certainly an unusual sign of respect, as well as a pleasure few wives had.

They discussed a wide variety of topics—British and American politics, art and music, architecture and history. Though Justin was never talkative, his observations were perceptive and he seemed to genuinely enjoy listening to her chatter. Best of all, the conversations were slowly building a rapport between them. It wasn't love—but perhaps someday it might be.

She prayed that that would happen, for living without love was a sad business.

Getting to her feet, she pulled on her sable-lined coat. Though it would warm her on the raw November day, that practical use was secondary. Before they left New York, her mother had emphasized that it was essential to wear her furs as a sign of wealth when she was first introduced to her new home and family. A good thing it wasn't August. Unable to see all of herself in the mirror, she asked, "Do I look all right?"

Her husband studied her gravely. "You look very lovely. Exactly as a duchess should, but seldom does."

The train squealed to a halt, and she glanced out to see a bunting-draped platform. "Good heavens," she said blankly. "There are hundreds of people out there."

"I did warn you." He stood and walked to the carriage door. "It's probably the entire population of Swindon Minor and everyone for five miles around. The schools will have given a holiday so that the pupils can come and wave flags at you."

"It's different actually seeing them." Observing her husband's closed expression, she said, "You don't look very enthusiastic."

"Gavin was much better at this sort of thing."

Perhaps that was true, but when Justin opened the door and stepped onto the platform, a roar of welcome went up. He gave a nod of acknowledgment, then turned to help Sunny step down. Another cheer went up, so she gave a friendly wave.

She met a blur of local dignities, all of whom gave speeches of welcome. Luckily she was good at smiling graciously, and the sables kept her from freezing in the damp air.

The only part that stood out in her mind was the little girl who was pushed forward, clutching a bouquet in her tiny hands. "Give the posies to the duchess, Ellie," her mother hissed.

Unclear on the theory, Ellie swept the bouquet around in circles. With a grin, Sunny intercepted it, then dropped a kiss on the child's soft brown curls. "Thank you, El-lie."

Another cheer arose. Sunny blushed; her gesture had not been calculated, but apparently kissing babies was good policy everywhere.

The mayor of the borough assisted her into the waiting carriage and Justin settled beside her. However, instead of starting for the palace, there was a delay while the horses were unhitched. A dozen men seized the shafts and began pulling the carriage up the village high street as the church bell began to ring clamorously. Sunny gave her husband a doubtful glance. "This seems dreadfully feudal."

He lifted his hand in response to a group of exuberant uniformed schoolchildren. "This isn't really for you, or for me, either. It's a celebration of continuity—of a life lived on this land for centuries. Swindon Palace belongs as much to the tenants as it does to the Aubreys."

She supposed he was right, and certainly the crowd seemed to be having a very jolly time. Nonetheless, her democratic American soul twitched a bit. Trying to look like a duchess, she smiled and waved for the slow two miles to Swindon Palace.

Another crowd waited in the courtyard. After the new-lyweds had climbed the front steps, Justin turned and gave a short thank-you speech in a voice that carried easily to everyone present. Gavin might have had a talent for grand gestures, but the tenants had had more daily contact with Justin, and they seemed to heartily approve of him.

After one last wave, she went inside with her husband. The greetings weren't over yet, for a phalanx of Aubrey relations waited with a sea of servants behind them.

As she steeled herself for more introductions and smiles, two huge wolfhounds galloped toward the door, nails scrabbling on the marble floor. The sight of the enormous dogs charging full speed at her made Sunny give a small squeak of alarm.

Before the beasts could overrun them, Justin made a quick hand gesture and commanded, "Sit!"

Instantly the wolfhounds dropped to their haunches, though they wriggled frantically for attention. Justin stroked the sleek aristocratic heads, careful not to neglect either. "These were Gavin's dogs. They miss him dreadfully."

To Sunny, it looked as if the wolfhounds were perfectly satisfied with the new duke. It took a moment to realize that Justin's comment was an oblique admission of his own grief. She was ashamed of the fact that she had not really considered how profoundly he must feel his brother's death. Though the two men had been very different, the first time she had seen them they had been standing side by side. They must have been close, or Justin would not have chosen to manage the family property when he could have done many other things.

While she was wondering if she should say something to him, the relatives descended. First in consequence was the dowager duchess, Justin's mother, who wore mourning black for Gavin. Her forceful expression reminded Sunny of her own mother, though Augusta was far more elegant.

After a fierce scrutiny of the colonial upstart, the dowager said, "You look healthy, girl. Are you pregnant yet?"

As Sunny flushed scarlet, Justin put a protective arm around her waist. "It's a little early to think about that since we've been married less than a month, Mother," he said calmly. "Sunny, I believe you already know my older sisters, Blanche and Charlotte, and their husbands, Lord Alton and Lord Urford."

Sunny had met all four in London during the season. The sisters were in the same mold as Gavin: tall, blond, handsome Aubreys whose self-absorption was tempered by underlying good nature. They examined Sunny's furs with frank envy, but their greetings were friendly. After all, it was her money that would keep up the family home.

Next in line was Lady Alexandra, the Gargoylette. She hung back until Justin pulled her into a hug. It was the most affectionate Sunny had ever seen him. "I don't believe you've met my little sister, Alexandra."

He accompanied his introduction with a speaking look at his wife. Sunny guessed that if she was dismissive or abrupt, he would not easily forgive her.

Alexandra stammered a greeting, too bashful to meet her new sister-in-law's eyes. Dark and inches shorter than the older girls, she looked very like Justin. There was nothing wrong with her appearance except that her mother dressed her very badly.

Following her instinct, Sunny also hugged her smallest sister-in-law. "Thank you so much for your letter," she said warmly. "It was good to know that I would have a friend here."

Alexandra looked up shyly. Her gray eyes were also like Justin's, but where he was reserved, she was vulnerable. "I'm glad you're here," she said simply. "I saw you when you came to the garden fete last spring, and thought you were the loveliest creature in the world."

A little embarrassed at such frank adoration, Sunny said lightly, "It's amazing what a good dressmaker can do."

Then it was onward to sundry Aubrey cousins and shirttail relations. After that, the butler and housekeeper—two *very* superior persons—welcomed her as their new mistress and presented her with a silver bowl as a wedding gift from the household. While Sunny wondered how much the poor servants had been forced to contribute, she was paraded past ranks of maids and footmen as if she were a general reviewing troops.

Finally it was time to go upstairs to prepare for dinner. Justin escorted her to her new rooms.

The duchess's private suite was rather appallingly magnificent. Eyeing the massive, velvet-hung four-poster bed, Sunny asked, "Did Queen Elizabeth sleep there?"

"No, but Queen Anne did." The corner of Justin's mouth quirked up. "I know it's overpowering, but I didn't order any changes because I thought you'd prefer to make them yourself."

Sunny thoughtfully regarded a tapestry of a stag being torn apart by a pack of dogs. "I don't care if it is priceless—that tapestry will have to go. But I can bear it for now. How long do I have until dinner?"

"Only half an hour, I'm afraid. There's more to be seen, but it can wait." He gestured to a door in the middle of one wall. "That goes directly to my bedchamber. Don't hesitate to ask if there's anything you need."

"I'm too confused to know what I need, but thank you." Sunny took off her hat and massaged her throbbing temples. "Should you and I go down together for dinner?"

"Definitely," he replied. "Without a guide to the dining room, you'd probably get lost for a week."

After Justin left, Antoinette emerged from the dressing room. "While everyone was welcoming you, madame, I had time to unpack your clothing. What do you wish to wear tonight? Surely something grand to impress the relations."

"The butter-cream duchesse satin, I think." Sunny considered. "I suppose I should also wear the pearl and diamond dog collar, even though it chafes my neck."

The maid nodded with approval. "No one will be your equal."

After Antoinette disappeared to prepare the gown, Sunny sank into a brocade-covered chair. It was hideously uncomfortable, which was fortunate, because otherwise she might fall asleep.

It was pleasant to have a few minutes alone. In spite of the wretched chair, she was dozing when Antoinette bustled back. "Madame, I have found something wonderful! You must come see."

Sunny doubted that anything was worth such enthusiasm, but she obediently rose and followed her maid into the dressing room. Two doors were set into the opposite wall. Antoinette dramatically threw open the right-hand one. "Voilà!"

Sunny's eyes widened. It was a bathroom that would have impressed even Augusta Vangelder. The mahogany-encased tub was enormous, and the floor and walls had been covered in bright, exquisitely glazed Spanish tiles. "You're right—it's the most gorgeous bathroom I've ever seen."

"And the next room over—" the maid pointed "—is a most splendid water closet. The chambermaid who brought in the towels said that *Monsieur le Duc* had all this done for you after the betrothal was announced."

Amused and touched, Sunny stroked a gleaming tile. It appeared that she would not have to suffer the country house horrors that Katie Westron had warned her about. "Perhaps later tonight I will take advantage of this."

Wanting to give credit where credit was due, she went to her bedchamber and opened the connecting door to the duke's suite. "Justin, I have found the bathing room and—"

In the middle of the sentence, her gaze found her husband and she stopped dead. She had caught him in the middle of changing his clothing. He had just taken off his shirt, and she blushed scarlet at the sight of his bare chest.

Though his brows rose, he did not seem at all discomposed. "Having seen the wonders of modern American plumbing, I knew that you would find Swindon rather primitive," he said. "Making some improvements seemed like a more useful wedding gift than giving you jewels."

Though she tried to look only into his eyes, her gaze drifted lower. He was broad-shouldered and powerfully muscled, which was why he didn't have a fashionable look of weedy elegance. She wondered how the dark hair on his chest would feel to her touch. Blushing again, she said hastily, "Your idea was inspired. I've always loved long baths, and I'd resigned myself to having to make do with a tin tub in front of the fire."

"Speaking of fires, I decided that it was also time to install central heating." Justin casually pulled on a fresh shirt, though he didn't bother to button it. "It will be a long time until the whole building is completed, but I had the workers take care of this wing first, so you would be comfortable. I know that Americans like their houses warm."

Only then did she notice that the rooms were much warmer than she should have expected. "Thank you, Justin. I think you must be the most considerate husband on earth." She crossed the room to her husband's side and gave him a swift kiss.

It was the first time she had ever done such a thing, and she wondered belatedly if he would think her too forward. But he didn't seem to mind. His lips moved slowly under hers, and he raised his hand and massaged the back of her neck. He had a tangy masculine scent that was distinctly his own. Succumbing to temptation, she let her fingers brush his bare chest as if by accident. The hair was softer than she had expected, but she felt unnerved when his warm flesh tensed at her touch. Hastily she lowered her hand.

But the kiss continued, and she found that she was in no hurry to end it. Very gently, his tongue stroked her lips. It was a new sensation, but pleasant. Very pleasant. . . .

The clamor of a bell reverberated brassily through the corridors. Both of them jumped as if they had been caught stealing from the church poor box.

After he had caught his breath, Justin said, "The predinner bell. We must be downstairs in ten minutes."

"I barely have time to dress." Embarrassed at how she had lost track of time, Sunny bolted to her own room. As soon as the connecting door was closed, Antoinette started unfastening her traveling dress so that the duchesse satin could be donned.

Yet as her maid swiftly transformed her, Sunny's mind kept returning to the kiss, and her fingertips tingled with the memory of the feel of her husband's bare body.

Dinner was another strain. Sunny sat at the opposite end of the table from her husband, so far away that she could barely see him. Before the first course had been removed, it was obvious that the dowager duchess was a tyrant, with all the tact of a charging bull. She made a string of remarks extolling Gavin's noble spirit and aristocratic style, interspersed with edged comments about the deficiencies of "poor dear Justin."

Charlotte tried to divert the conversation with a cheerful promise to send Sunny a copy of the table of precedence so that she would never commit the cardinal crime of seating people in the wrong order. That inspired the dowager to say, "There are about two hundred families whose history and relationships you must understand, Sarah. Has Justin properly explained all the branches of the Aubreys and of my own family, the Sturfords?"

"Not yet, Duchess," Sunny said politely.

"Very remiss of him. Since he wasn't raised to be a duke, he hasn't a proper sense of what is due his station." The dowager sniffed. "So sad to see poor dear Justin in his brother's place—such a comedown for the family. You must be quick about having a child, Sarah, and make sure it's a boy."

Sunny was tempted to sling the nearest platter of veal collops at her mother-in-law, but it seemed too soon to get into a pitched battle. A quick glance at her husband showed that he had either not heard his mother, or he chose to ignore her. Clearly Alexandra had heard, for she was staring at her plate.

Carefully Sunny said, "The eighth duke's death was a great tragedy. You all have my sympathies on your loss."

The dowager sighed. "Gavin should have betrothed himself to you, not that Russell woman. If he had, he might be alive now, in his proper place."

Sunny had heard enough gossip to know that the fatal problem had not been Gavin's fiancée, but his inability to keep his hands off other women, even when on the way to his own wedding. Hoping to end this line of discussion, she said piously, "It is not for us to question the ways of heaven."

"A very proper sentiment," the dowager said. "You have pretty manners. One would scarcely know you for an American."

Did the woman suppose that she was giving a compliment? Once more Sunny bit her tongue.

Yet in spite of her good intentions, she was not to get through the evening peacefully. The gauntlet was thrown down at the end of the lengthy meal, when it was time for the ladies to withdraw and leave the gentlemen to their port. Sunny was about to give the signal when the dowager grandly rose to her feet and beat Sunny to it.

As three women followed the dowager's lead, Sunny's blood went cold. This was a direct challenge to her authority as the new mistress of the household. If she didn't assert herself immediately, her mother-in-law would walk all over her.

The other guests hesitated, glancing between the new duchess and the old. Sunny wanted to whimper that she was too *tired* for this, but she supposed that crises never happened at convenient times. Though her hands clenched below the table, her voice was even when she asked, "Are you feeling unwell, Duchess?"

"I am in splendid health," her mother-in-law said haughtily. "Where did you get the foolish idea that I might be ailing?"

"I can think of no other reason for you leaving prematurely," Sunny said with the note of gentle implacability that she had often heard in her mother's voice.

For a moment the issue wavered in the balance. Then, one by one, the female guests who had gotten to their feet sank back into their seats with apologetic glances at Sunny. Knowing that she had lost, the dowager returned to the table, her expression stiff with mortification.

As she waited for a decent interval to pass before leading the ladies from the table, Sunny drew in a shaky breath. She had won the first battle—but there would be others.

* * *

The evening ended when the first clock struck eleven. Accompanied by the bonging of numerous other clocks, Justin escorted his wife upstairs. When they reached the door of her room, he said, "I'm sorry that it's been such a long day, but everyone was anxious to meet you."

She smiled wearily. "I'll be fine after a night's sleep."

"You were a great success with everyone." After a moment of hesitation, he added, "I'm sorry my mother was so...abrupt. Gavin was her favorite, and she took his death very badly."

"You miss him, too, but it hasn't made you rude." She bit her lip. "I'm sorry, I didn't mean to sound impertinent."

"My mother is a forceful woman, and I don't expect that you'll always agree. Blanche and Charlotte used to have terrible battles with her. Just remember that you are my wife, and the mistress of Swindon."

"I shall attempt to be tactful while establishing myself." She made a rueful face. "But I warn you, I have trouble countenancing unkind remarks about other people."

That sensitivity to others was one of the things he liked best about her. A volatile mix of tenderness and desire moved through him, and he struggled against his yearning to draw her into his arms and soothe her fatigue away.

He might have done so if he hadn't been aware that the desire to comfort would be followed by an even more overwhelming desire to remove her clothing, garment by garment, and make slow, passionate love to her. With the lamps lit, not in the dark.

Innocently she turned her back to him and said, "Could you unfasten my dog collar? It's miserably uncomfortable."

The heavy collar had at least fifteen rows of pearls. As he undid the catch and lifted the necklace away, he saw that the diamond clasp had rubbed her tender skin raw. He frowned. "I don't like seeing you wearing something that hurts you."

She sighed. "Virtually every item a fashionable woman wears is designed to hurt."

He leaned forward and very gently kissed the raw spot on her nape. "Perhaps you should be less stylish."

She tensed, as she did whenever he touched her in a sensual way. "A duchess is supposed to be fashionable. I would be much criticized if I didn't do you credit." Eyes downcast, she turned and took the jeweled collar, then slipped into her room.

He felt the familiar ache as he watched her disappear. Who was it who said that if a man wanted to be truly lonely, he should take a wife? It was true, for he didn't recall feeling lonely before he married.

But now that he had a wife, his life echoed with loneliness. The simple fact was that he wanted more of her. He wanted to hold her in his arms all night while they slept. He wanted her to sigh with pleasure when he made love to her. He wanted to be with her day and night.

He drew a deep breath, then entered his room and began undressing. He had hoped that with time she might come to enjoy intimacy more, but every time he came to her bed, she became rigid. Though she never complained, or spoke at all, for that matter—it was clear that she could scarcely endure his embraces.

Yet she didn't seem to dislike him in other ways. She talked easily and was willing to share her opinions. And she had given him that shy kiss earlier. In her innocence, she had not understood that she set the blood burning through his veins. But even going to her bed would not have quenched the fire, for he had found that quick, furtive coupling was more frustrating than if he had never touched her.

As he slid into his bed, he realized how foolish it was of him to object to a necklace that chafed her neck when his conjugal demands disturbed her far more. He despised himself for taking that which was not willingly given—yet he was not strong enough to prevent himself from going to her again and again. His twice weekly visits were his compromise between guilt and lust.

He stared blindly into the darkness, wondering if he would be able to sleep.

If you would be lonely, take a wife.

Chapter Seven

Swindon
February 1886

Sunny abandoned her letter writing and went to stand at her sitting room window, staring out at the gray landscape. In the distance was a pond where long ago a footman had drowned himself in a fit of melancholy. As the dreary winter months dragged by, she had come to feel a great deal of sympathy for the poor fellow.

The loudest sound was the ticking of the mantel clock. Swindon was full of clocks, all of them counting out the endless hours. She glanced at the dog curled in one of the velvet-covered chairs. "Daisy, how many of the women who envied my glamorous marriage would believe how tedious it is to winter on an English country estate?"

Daisy's floppy-eared head popped up and she gave a sympathetic whimper. Unlike the beautiful but brainless wolfhounds, Daisy, a small black-and-tan dog of indeterminate parentage, was smart as a whip. Sunny liked to think that the dog understood human speech. Certainly she was a good listener.

Sunny's gaze went back to the dismal afternoon. Custom decreed that a bride should live quietly for a time after her wedding, and at Swindon, that was very quietly indeed. Apart from the newlyweds, Alexandra and the dowager were the only inhabitants of the vast palace. There were servants, of course, but the line between upstairs and downstairs was never crossed.

The best part of the daily routine was a morning ride with Justin. Sunny never missed a day, no matter how vile the weather, for she enjoyed spending time with her husband, though she couldn't define the reason. He was simply...comfortable. She only wished that she understood him better. He was like an iceberg, with most of his personality hidden from view.

After their ride, she usually didn't see him again until dinner, for estate work kept him busy. Occasionally he went to London for several days to attend to business. He was gone now, which made the hours seem even longer.

The high point of country social life was making brief calls on neighbors, then receiving calls in turn. Though most of the people Sunny met were pleasant, they lived lives as narrow and caste-ridden as Hindus. Luckily even the most conventional families usually harbored one or two splendid eccentrics in the great British tradition. There was the Trask uncle who wore only purple clothing, for example, and the Howard maiden aunt who had taught her parrot all the basic social responses so that the bird could speak for her. Such characters figured prominently in Sunny's letters home, since little else in her life was amusing.

A knock sounded at the door. After Sunny called permission to enter, her sister-in-law came into the sitting room. "A telegram arrived for you, Sunny, so I said I'd bring it up." Alexandra handed it over, then bent to scratch Daisy's ears.

Sunny opened the envelope and scanned the message. "Justin finished his business early and will be home for dinner tonight."

"That's nice. It's so quiet when he's away."

"Two months from now, after you've been presented to society and are attending ten parties a day, you'll yearn for the quiet of the country."

Alexandra made a face. "I can't say that I'm looking forward to being a wallflower at ten different places a day."

"You're going to be a great success," Sunny said firmly. "It's remarkable what good clothing can do for one's confidence. After Worth has outfitted you, you won't recognize yourself."

Unconvinced, Alexandra returned to petting Daisy. Though young in many ways, the girl was surprisingly mature in others. She was also well-read and eager to learn about the world. The two young women had become good friends.

Deciding that she needed some fresh air, Sunny said, "I think I'll take a walk before I bathe and change. Would you like to join me?"

"Not today, thank you. I have a book I want to finish." Alexandra grinned, for at the word "walk," Daisy jumped to the floor and began skipping hopefully around her mistress. "But someone else wants to go. I'll see you at dinner."

After Alexandra left, Sunny donned a coat—not the sables, but a practical mackintosh—and a pair of boots, then went down and out into the damp afternoon, Daisy frisking beside her. Once they were away from the house, Sunny asked, "Would you like to play fetch?" Foolish question; Daisy was already racing forward looking for a stick.

Sunny had found Daisy on a morning ride not long after her arrival at Swindon. The half-grown mongrel had been desperately trying to stay afloat in the overflowing stream where someone had probably pitched her to drown. Driven frantic by the agonized yelps, Sunny had been on the verge of plunging into the water when Justin had snapped an order for her to stay on the bank. Before she could argue, he dismounted and went in himself.

When Sunny saw her husband fighting the force of the current, she realized that he was risking his life for her whim. There had been one ghastly moment when it seemed that the water would sweep him away. As her heart stood still, Justin managed to gain his footing, then catch hold of the struggling dog. After sloshing out of the stream, he had handed her the shivering scrap of canine with the straight-faced remark that it was quite an appealing creature as long as one didn't have any snobbish preconceptions about lineage.

The sodden pup had won Sunny's heart with one lap of a rough tongue. Sunny had almost wept with gratitude, for here was a creature who loved her and whom she could love in return.

Naturally the dowager duchess had disliked having such an ill-bred beast at Swindon, but she couldn't order the dog out of the house when Justin approved. The dowager had resorted to mumbled comments that it was natural for Sunny to want a mongrel, since Americans were a mongrel race. Sunny ignored such remarks; she had gotten very good at that.

As always, Daisy's desire to play fetch exceeded Sunny's stamina. Abandoning the game, they strolled to the little Greek temple, then wandered toward the house while

Sunny thought of changes she would make in the grounds. A pity that nothing could be done at this time of year, for gardening would cheer her up.

In an attempt to stave off self-pity, she said, "I'm really very fortunate, Daisy. Most of Katie Westron's dire warnings haven't come true. Justin is the most considerate of husbands, and he is making the house very comfortable." She glanced toward the palace, where men were laboring on the vast roof, in spite of the weather. "My ceiling hasn't leaked since before Christmas."

She made a wry face. "Of course, it might be considered a bit strange that I talk more to a dog than to my husband."

One of Katie's warnings haunted her—the possibility that Justin might have a mistress. Could that be the real reason for his business trips? She loathed the thought that her husband might be doing those intimate, dark-of-the-night things to another woman. She tried not to think of it.

The dull afternoon had darkened to twilight, so she summoned Daisy and headed toward the house. If the best part of the day was riding with Justin, the worst was dining with the dowager duchess. Familiarity had not improved her opinion of her mother-in-law. Most of the dowager's cutting remarks were directed at Justin, but she also made edged comments about Alexandra's lack of looks and dim marital prospects. She usually spared Sunny, rightly suspecting that her daughter-in-law might strike back.

Sunny wondered how long it would be before she disgraced herself by losing her temper. Every meal brought the breaking point closer. She wished that Justin would tell his mother to hold her tongue, but he was too courteous—or too detached—to take action.

When she got to the house, she found that her husband was in the entry hall taking off his wet coat. She thought his expression lightened when he saw her, but she wasn't sure; it was always hard to tell with Justin.

"Hello." She smiled as she took off her mackintosh. "Did you have a good trip to London?"

As the butler took away the coats, Justin gave Sunny a light kiss on the cheek, then rumpled Daisy's ears. He was rather more affectionate with the dog. "Yes, but I'm glad to be home."

He fell into step beside her and they started up the main stairs. The thought of a possible mistress passed through Sunny's mind again. Though she knew that it was better not to probe, she found herself saying, "What are all these trips about, or wouldn't I be able to understand the answer?"

"The Thornborough income has traditionally come from the land, but agriculture is a chancy business," he explained as they reached the top of the stairs. "I'm making more diverse investments so that future dukes won't have to marry for money."

She stopped in mid-stride, feeling as if he had slapped her. When she caught her breath, she said icily, "God forbid that another Aubrey should have to stoop to marrying a mongrel American heiress."

He spun around, his expression startled and distressed. "I'm sorry, Sunny—I didn't mean that the way it sounded."

Her brows arched. "Oh? I can't imagine any meaning other than the obvious one."

When she turned and headed toward the door of her suite, he caught her arm and said intensely, "You would have been my choice even if you weren't an heiress."

Her mouth twisted. "Prettily said, but you needn't perjure yourself, Justin. We both know this marriage wouldn't have been made without my money and your title. If you invest my money wisely, perhaps our son, if we have one, will be able to marry where he chooses. I certainly hope so."

Justin's hand fell away and Sunny escaped into her sitting room, Daisy at her heels. When she was alone, she sank wretchedly into a chair. She had been better off not knowing what Justin really felt. Before she had wondered if he had a mistress; now, sickeningly, she wondered if he had a woman who was not only his mistress, but his beloved. There had been a raw emotion in his voice that made her think, for the first time, that he was capable of loving deeply. Had he been forced to forsake the woman he loved so that he could maintain Swindon?

Sensing distress, Daisy whimpered and pushed her cool nose into Sunny's hand. Mechanically she stroked the dog's silky ears. What a wretched world they lived in. Yet even if Justin loved another woman, he was her husband and she must make the best of this marriage. Someday, if she was a very good wife, perhaps he would love her, at least a little.

She desperately hoped so, for there was a hole in the center of her life that the frivolity of the season would never fill.

Sunny's depression was not improved by the discovery that the dowager duchess was in an unusually caustic mood. Throughout an interminable dinner, she made acid remarks about the neighbors, the government and most of all her son. As fruit and cheese were served, she said, "A pity that Justin hasn't the Aubrey height and coloring.

Gavin was a much more handsome man, just as Blanche and Charlotte are far prettier than Alexandra."

Sunny retorted, "I've studied the portraits, and the first duke, John Aubrey, was dark and of medium build. Justin and Alexandra resemble him much more than your other children do."

The dowager sniffed. "The first duke was a notable general, but though it pains me to admit it, he was a very low sort of man in other ways. A pity that the peasant strain hasn't yet been bred out of the family." She gave an elaborate sigh. "Such a tragedy that Justin did not die instead of Gavin."

Sunny gasped. How *dare* that woman say she wished Justin had died in his brother's place! Justin was worth a dozen charming, worthless wastrels like Gavin. She glanced at her husband and saw that he was carefully peeling an apple, as if his mother hadn't spoken, but there was a painful bleakness in his eyes.

If he wouldn't speak, she would. Laying her fork beside her plate, she said, "You must not speak so about Justin, Duchess."

"You forget who I am, madame." The dowager's eyes gleamed with pleasure at the prospect of a battle. "As the mother who suffered agonies to bear him, I can say what I wish."

"And you forget who *I* am," Sunny said with deadly precision. "The mistress of Swindon Palace. And I will no longer tolerate such vile, ill-natured remarks."

The dowager gasped, her jaw dropping open. "How dare you!"

Not backing down an inch, Sunny retorted, "I dare because it is a hostess's duty to maintain decorum at her table, and there has been a sad lack of that at Swindon."

The dowager swept furiously to her feet. "I will not stay here to be insulted by an impertinent American."

Deliberately misinterpreting her mother-in-law's words, Sunny said, "As you wish, Duchess. I can certainly understand why you prefer to have your own establishment. If I were to be widowed, I would feel the same way. And the Dower House is a very charming residence, isn't it?"

The dowager's jaw went slack as she realized that a simple flounce from the table had been transformed into total eviction. Closing her mouth with a snap, she turned to glare at Justin. "Are you going to allow an insolent American hussy to drive me from my own home?"

Justin looked from his mother to his wife, acute discomfort on his face. Silently Sunny pleaded with him to support her. He had said that she was the mistress of Swindon. If he didn't back her now, her position would become intolerable.

"You've been complaining that the new central heating gives you headaches, Mother," Justin said expressionlessly. "I think it an excellent idea for you to move to the Dower House so that you will be more comfortable. We shall miss you, of course, but fortunately you won't be far away."

Sunny shut her eyes for an instant, almost undone by relief. When she opened them again, the dowager's venomous gaze had gone to her daughter. "The Dower House isn't large enough for me to have Alexandra underfoot," she said waspishly. "She shall have to stay in the palace."

Before her mother-in-law could reconsider, Sunny said, "Very true—until she marries, Alexandra belongs at Swindon."

"*If* she ever marries," the dowager said viciously. Knowing that she was defeated and that the only way to salvage her dignity was to pretend that moving was her own idea, she added, "You shall have to learn to run the household yourself, Sarah, for I have been longing to travel. I believe I shall spend the rest of the winter in southern France. England is so dismal at this season." Ramrod straight, she marched from the room.

Sunny, Justin and Alexandra were left sitting in brittle silence. Not daring to meet her husband's eyes, Sunny said, "I'm sorry if I was disrespectful to your mother, but...but I'm not sorry for what I said."

"That's a contradiction in terms," he said, sounding more weary than angry. After a long silence, he said, "By the way, I saw Lord Hopstead in London, and he invited us for a weekend visit and ball at Cottenham. I thought the three of us could go, then you could take Alexandra on to Paris for her fittings."

Relieved that he didn't refer to her confrontation with the dowager, Sunny said, "That sounds delightful. Are you ready for your first ball, Alexandra? I have a gown that will look marvelous on you with only minor alterations."

"That's very kind of you," a subdued Alexandra said.

For several minutes, they stiffly discussed the proposed trip, none of them making any allusion to the dowager's rout. It was like ignoring the fact that an elephant was in the room.

Finally Sunny got to her feet. "I'm very tired tonight. If you two will excuse me, I'll go to bed now."

Her temples throbbed as she went to her room, but under her shakiness, she was triumphant. Without the dowager's poisonous presence, life at Swindon would improve remarkably.

She changed to her nightgown and climbed into bed, wondering if Justin would visit her. Ordinarily he did after returning from a journey, but perhaps he would stay away if he was displeased with the way she had treated his mother.

Though it shamed her to admit it, she had come to look forward to his conjugal visits. One particular night stood out in her mind. She had been drifting in the misty zone between sleep and waking when her husband came. Though aware of his presence, she had been too drowsy to move her languid limbs.

Instead of waking her, he had given a small sigh, then stretched out beside her, his warm body against hers, his quiet breath caressing her temple. After several minutes he began stroking her, his hand gliding gently over her torso. She had lain utterly still, embarrassed by the yearning sensations that tingled in her breasts and other unmentionable places. Pleasure thickened inside her until she had had to bite her lip to keep from moaning and moving against his hand.

Fortunately, before she disgraced herself, he dozed off, his hand cupping her breast. Slowly her tension had dissipated until she also slept. Her rest was remarkably deep, considering that she had never in her life shared a bed with another person.

But when she awoke the next morning, he was gone. She might have thought she had dreamed the episode if not for the imprint of her husband's head on the pillow and a faint, lingering masculine scent. It had occurred to her that people who could not afford to have separate bedrooms might be luckier than they knew.

She had been mortified by the knowledge that she had the nature of a wanton. The next time she saw Katie Westron, she must find the boldness to ask how a woman could control her carnality, for surely Katie would know. Until then, Sunny would simply have to exercise willpower. She could almost hear her mother saying, "You are a lady. Behave like one."

Yet still she longed for her husband's company. She had almost given up hope that he would join her when the connecting door quietly opened and he padded across the deep carpet. As he slipped into the bed, she touched his arm to show that she was awake and willing. He slid his hand beneath the covers and drew up the hem of her nightgown.

Perhaps the evening's drama was affecting her, for she found it particularly difficult to keep silent while he prepared her for intercourse. Those strange feelings that were part pleasure, part pain, fluttered through her as he smoothed lotion over her sensitive female parts.

When he entered her, heat pulsed through those same parts, then expanded to other parts of her body. She caught her breath, unable to entirely suppress her reaction.

Immediately he stopped moving. "Did I hurt you?"

"N-no." She knotted her hands and pressed her limbs rigidly into the mattress. "No, you didn't hurt me."

Gently he began rocking back and forth again. The slowness of his movements caused deeply disquieting sensations. Yet curiously, instead of wanting them to stop, she wanted more. It was hard, so hard, to be still....

His breathing quickened in the way that told her that the end was near. He gave a muffled groan and made a final deep thrust. Then the tension went out of him.

She felt a corresponding easing in herself, as if her feelings were intertwined with his. She was tempted to slide her arms around him, for she had a most unladylike desire to keep his warm, hard body pressed tightly against her. Perhaps he might fall asleep with her again.

But that was not what men and women of good breeding did. Her parents had not shared a room. After Sunny's birth, they had probably not even had conjugal relations, for she was the youngest in the family. Once her father had two sons to work in the business and her mother had a daughter for companionship, there had been no need for more babies.

Justin lifted his weight from her. After pulling her gown down again, he lightly touched her hair. She wanted to catch his hand and beg him to stay, but of course she didn't.

Then he left her.

When the connecting door between their chambers closed, Sunny released her breath in a shuddering sigh, then rolled over and hugged a pillow to her chest. She felt restless impatience and a kind of itchy discomfort in her female parts. Her hand slid down her torso. Perhaps if she rubbed herself there . . .

Horrified, she flopped onto her back and clenched her hands into fists. Her nurse and her mother had made it clear that a woman never touched herself "down there" unless she had to.

She closed her eyes against the sting of tears. She was trying her very best to be a good wife. But from what she could see, a good wife was a lonely woman.

In a flurry of trunks and contradictory orders, the Dowager Duchess of Thornborough moved herself and a substantial number of Swindon's finest antiques to the elegant Dower House on the far side of the estate. Then she promptly decamped to the French Riviera, there to flaunt her rank and make slanderous hints about her son's inadequacies and her daughter-in-law's insolence. The one thing Justin was sure she would not say was the truth—that a slip of a girl had maneuvered the dowager out of Swindon Palace.

Life was much easier with his mother gone. He and Sunny and Alexandra dined *en famille*, with much less formality and far more enjoyment. His sister was blossoming under Sunny's kind guidance, and no longer dreaded her social debut.

What wasn't prospering was his marriage. Ever since his incredibly clumsy remark about sparing future dukes the necessity of marrying for money, there had been strain between him and Sunny. What he had meant was that he wanted financial considerations to be irrelevant.

Unfortunately, she had believed the unintended insult rather than his heartfelt declaration that he would have wanted to marry her anyhow. Because he had accidentally hurt her, she had struck back, hurting him in return when she had underlined the fact that their marriage had nothing to do with love.

Fearing that more explanations would only make matters worse, he hadn't raised the subject again. Eventually memory of the incident would fade, but in the meantime Sunny had pulled further away from him. She was courteous, compliant—and as distant as if an ocean still divided them. Sometimes she trembled during their wordless conjugal couplings, and he feared that she was recoiling from his touch. If she had verbally objected, perhaps he could have controlled his desires and stopped inflicting himself on her. But she said nothing, and he did not have the strength to stay away.

As they prepared to go to the ball at Cottenham Manor, he hoped that Sunny's return to society would cheer her. She deserved laughter and frivolity and admiration.

Yet though he wanted her to be happy, the knowledge that she would be surrounded by adoring, predatory men terrified him. If she was miserable in her marriage, how long would it be before she looked elsewhere?

If you would be troubled, take a wife.

Chapter Eight

Cottenham Manor
March

Cottenham Manor, seat of the Earl of Hopstead, was almost as grand and large as Swindon Palace. Lord and Lady Hopstead were famous for their entertainments, and Sunny had spent a long and happy weekend at Cottenham the previous summer. It was a pleasure to return, and as her maid fastened a sapphire and diamond necklace around her neck, she hummed softly to herself.

"Madame is happy tonight," Antoinette observed as she handed Sunny the matching eardrops.

Sunny put on the eardrops, then turned her head so she could see the play of light in the sapphire pendants. "I've been looking forward to this ball for weeks. What a silly custom it is for a bride to rusticate for months after the wedding."

"But think how much more you will appreciate society after wintering in the depths of the English countryside."

"That's true." Sunny rose with a rich whisper of taffeta petticoats. She was wearing a sumptuous blue brocade gown, one of Worth's finest, and she was ready to be admired.

"You must sit until I have put on your tiara," Antoinette said reprovingly.

Obediently Sunny sat again and braced herself for the weight of the Thornborough tiara. The massive, diamond-studded coronet would give her a headache, but it wouldn't be proper for a duchess to attend a ball without one, particularly since the Prince of Wales would be present.

Just as the maid was finishing, a hesitant knock sounded at the door. Antoinette crossed the room and admitted Alexandra. Dressed in a white silk gown that shimmered with every movement, the younger girl had a fairylike grace. Her dark hair had been swept up to show the delicate line of her throat, and her complexion glowed with youth and good health.

"You look marvelous," Sunny said warmly. "Turn around so I can see all of you."

Her sister-in-law colored prettily as she obeyed. "You were right about the gown. Even though this one wasn't made for me, it's so lovely that one can't help but feel beautiful."

"It looks better on you than it ever did on me. You'll be the belle of the ball."

"No, you will." Alexandra chuckled. "But at least I don't think that I'll be a wallflower."

Another knock sounded on the door. This time it was Justin, come to take his wife and sister down to the dinner that would precede the ball. Sunny had hoped that there would be so many people at Cottenham that they would be put in the same room, but such intimacy was unthinkable in the fashionable set. The previous night, she had slept alone. Perhaps tonight . . .

Hastily she suppressed the improper thought.

After he examined them both, Justin said gravely, "You will be the two most beautiful women at the ball. Alex, I shall have a dozen men clamoring for your hand before the evening is over."

As Alexandra beamed, he offered one arm to his wife and one to his sister, then led them into the hall. As they descended the broad stairs, Sunny asked, "Will you dance with me tonight?"

He gave her a quizzical glance. "You would dance with a mere husband?"

"Please." Afraid that she might sound pathetic, she added lightly, "I know that it's not fashionable to dance with one's spouse, but it isn't actually scandalous."

He gave her one of the rare smiles that took her breath away. "Then it will be my very great pleasure."

As they entered the salon where the other guests had gathered, Sunny's heart was already dancing.

The Hopsteads' ball was an excellent place to rejoin society, and Sunny enjoyed greeting people she had met the year before. During a break after the fourth dance, she came across her godmother, who was resplendent in coral-and-silver silk. "Aunt Katie!" Sunny gave her a hug. "I hoped you would be here. You're not staying at Cottenham, are you?"

"No, I'm at the Howards'. Every great house in the district is full of guests who have come for this ball." Katie affectionately tucked a tendril of Sunny's flyaway hair in place. "You're in fine looks. By any chance are you . . . ?"

"Please, don't ask me if I'm expecting a blessed event! I swear, every female at the ball has inquired. I'm beginning to feel like a dreadful failure."

"Nonsense—you've only been married a few months."
Katie chuckled. "It's just that we're all such gossips, and
like it or not, you're a subject of great interest."

Sunny made a face. "Luckily there will soon be other
heiresses to capture society's attention." The two women
chatted for a few minutes and made an engagement for the
next morning.

Then Sunny glanced beyond Katie, and her heart froze
in her breast. On the far side of the room was Paul Curzon, tall and distinguished and heart-stoppingly handsome.

As if feeling her gaze, he looked up, and for a paralyz-
ing instant their eyes met. Shocked by the way her knees
weakened, Sunny turned to Katie and stammered, "I must
go now. I'll see you tomorrow."

Then she caught her train up with one hand and headed
for the nearest door, scarcely noticing when she bumped
into other guests. Sometimes escape was more important
than manners.

One of the drawbacks of socializing was the number of
people who hoped to enlist ducal support for some cause
or other. This time, it was a junior government minister
talking about an upcoming bill. Justin listened patiently,
half of his attention on the minister, the other half antici-
pating the next dance, which would be with Sunny. Then,
from the corner of his eye, he saw his wife leave the ballroom, her face pale. He frowned, wondering if she was
feeling ill.

He was about to excuse himself when he saw Paul Curzon go out the same side door that Sunny had used. Justin's face stiffened as a horrible suspicion seized him.

Seeing his expression, the minister said earnestly, "I swear, your grace, the scheme is perfectly sound. If you wish, I'll show you the figures."

Justin realized that he couldn't even remember what the damned bill was about. Brusquely he said, "Send me the information and I'll give you my decision in a week."

Hoping desperately that he was wrong, he brushed aside the minister's thanks and made his way after his wife and the man whom she might still love.

Without conscious thought, Sunny chose the conservatory for her refuge. It was at the opposite end of the house from the ball, and as she had hoped, she had it to herself.

Cottenham was noted for its magnificent indoor garden, and scattered gaslights illuminated banks of flowers and lush tropical shrubbery. Though rain drummed on the glass panels far above her head, inside the air was balmy and richly scented.

She took a deep breath, then set out along one of the winding brick paths. It had been foolish to become upset at the sight of Paul Curzon, for she had known that inevitably they would meet. But she had not expected it to be tonight. If she had been mentally prepared, she would have been able to accept his presence with equanimity.

Yet honesty compelled her to admit that in the first instant, she had felt some of the excitement she had known in the days when she had loved him. In the days when she *thought* she loved him, before she had discovered his baseness.

As always, nature helped her regain her composure. If she hadn't been dressed in a ball gown, she would have looked for some plants to repot. Instead, she picked a gardenia blossom and inhaled the delicate perfume.

As she did, a familiar voice said huskily, "The conservatory was a perfect choice, darling. No one will see us here."

"Paul!" The shock was as great as when she had first seen him, and spasmodically she crushed the gardenia blossom in her palm. After a fierce struggle for control, she turned and said evenly, "I didn't come here to meet you, Paul, but to get away from you. We have nothing to say to each other."

Unfortunately the way out lay past him. As she tried to slip by without her broad skirts touching him, he caught her hand. "Sunny, don't go yet," he begged. "I'm sorry if I misunderstood why you came here, but I wanted so much to see you that hope warped my judgment. I made the worst mistake of my life with you. At least give me a chance to apologize."

Reluctantly she stopped, as much because of the narrow aisle as because of his words. "I'm not interested in your apologies." As she spoke, she looked into his face, which was a mistake. He didn't look base; he looked sincere, and sinfully handsome.

"If you won't let me apologize, then let me say how much I love you." A tremor sounded in his voice. "I truly didn't know how much until I lost you."

Reminding herself that he had looked equally honest before he had broken her heart, she tried to free her hand, saying tartly, "Perhaps you think that you love me *because* you lost me. Isn't that how people like you play at love?"

His grip tightened. "This is different! The fact that you were willing to marry me is the greatest honor I've ever known. But I let myself be blinded by worldly considerations, and now I'm paying for my folly. Both of us are."

"There's no point in talking like this! The past can't be changed, and I'm a married woman now."

"Perhaps the past can't be changed, but the future can be." He put his hand under her chin and turned her face to his. "Love is too precious to throw away."

His gaze holding hers, he pressed his heated lips to her gloved fingers. "You are so beautiful, Sunny. I have never loved a woman as much as I love you."

She knew that she should break away, for she didn't love him, didn't really trust his protestations of devotion. Yet her parched heart yearned for warmth, for words of love, even ones that might be false.

Her inner struggle held her paralyzed as he put his arms around her and bent his head for a kiss. In a moment, she would push him away and leave. Yet even though it was wrong, for just an instant she would let him hold her....

The conservatory seemed like the most likely spot for dalliance, but Justin had only been there once, and he lost precious time with a wrong turn. His heart was pounding with fear when he finally reached his destination and threw open the door. He paused on the threshold and scanned the shadowy garden, praying that he was wrong.

But through the dense vegetation, he saw a shimmering patch of blue the shade of Sunny's gown. Down a brick path, around a bend...and he found his wife in Paul Curzon's arms.

The pain was worse than anything Justin had ever known. For a moment he stood stock-still as nausea pulsed through him.

Then came rage. Stalking forward, he snarled, "If you expect me to be a complaisant husband, you're both fools."

The two broke apart instantly, and Sunny whirled to him, her face white. Justin grabbed her wrist and pulled her away from Curzon. Then he looked his rival in the eye and said with lethal precision, "If you ever come near my wife again, I will destroy you."

"No need to carry on so, old man," Curzon said hastily. "It was merely a friendly kiss between acquaintances."

Justin's free hand knotted into a fist. *"I will destroy you."*

As Curzon paled, Justin turned and swept his wife away, heedless of the difficulty that she had keeping up in her high-heeled kid slippers. When she stumbled, his grip tightened to keep her from falling, but he did not slow down.

Wanting to ease the rage in his face, she said desperately, "Justin, that wasn't what you think."

He gave her a piercing glance. "It looked very much like a kiss to me. Am I wrong?"

"Yes, but... but it didn't really mean anything."

"If kisses mean nothing to you, does that mean you'll give them to any man?" he asked bitterly. "Or only those with whom you have assignations?"

"You're deliberately misunderstanding me! I went to the conservatory to avoid Paul, not to meet him. I know that I shouldn't have let him kiss me, but it was just a...a temporary aberration that happened only because there were once...warmer feelings between us."

"And if I hadn't come, they would have become warmer yet. If I had been ten minutes later..." His voice broke.

Guilt rose in a choking wave. Though she had not sought the encounter with Paul, she had not left when she should, and she had allowed him to kiss her. Might the warmth of Paul's embrace have dissolved her knowledge of right and wrong? She wanted to believe that morality would have triumphed—but treacherous doubt gnawed at her. Since she had discovered her wanton nature, she could no longer trust herself.

They reached the hallway below the main staircase. Several couples were enjoying the cooler air there, and they all turned to stare at the duke and duchess. Dropping her voice, Sunny hissed, "Let go of me! What will people think?"

"I don't give a tinker's dam what anyone thinks." He began climbing the staircase, still holding tightly to her wrist to keep her at his side. "Your behavior is what concerns me."

He followed the upstairs corridor to her bedchamber, pulled her inside, then slammed the door behind them and turned the key in the lock. The room was empty, lit only by the soft glow of a gas lamp. She edged uneasily away, for this furious man was a stranger, and he was starting to frighten her.

They stared at each other across the width of the room. With the same lethal intensity he had directed at Paul, Justin growled, "In the Middle Ages, I could have locked you in a tower or a chastity belt. A century ago, I could have challenged any man who came near you to a duel. But what can a man do about a faithless wife in these modern times?"

His words triggered her secret fear. "What about faithless husbands?" she retorted. "I've been told that men like you always have mistresses. Is the real reason for your trips to London another woman—one that you couldn't have because you had to marry for money?"

Renewed fury blazed in his gray eyes, and a dark hunger. "I have not looked at—or touched—anyone else since I met you. I wish to God that you could say the same. But since you choose to act like a whore, I will treat you as one."

Then he swept across the room and shattered her with a kiss.

Sunny had thought that her months of marriage had educated her about what happened between husband and wife, but nothing had prepared her for Justin's embrace. The quiet consideration to which she was accustomed had been replaced by blazing rage.

Trapped in the prison of his arms, she was acutely aware of his strength. Even if she wanted to resist, any effort on her part would be futile. Yet as they stood locked together, his mouth devouring hers, she sensed that his fury was changing into something that was similar, but was not anger at all. And it called to her.

Her head tilted and the heavy tiara pulled loose and fell to the carpet, jerking sharply at her hair. When she winced, his crushing grip eased and he began stroking her head with one hand. His deft fingers found and soothed the hurt. She didn't realize that he was also removing the pins until coils of hair cascaded over her shoulders.

He buried his face in the silken mass, and she felt the beating of his heart and the soft exhalation of his breath against her cheek. "Oh, God, Sunny," he said with anguish. "You are so beautiful—so painfully beautiful."

Yet his expression was harsh when he straightened and turned her so that her back was to him. First he unhooked her sapphire necklace, throwing it aside as if it was a piece of cut-glass trumpery. Then he started to unfasten her gown.

She opened her mouth to object, but before she could, he pressed his mouth to the side of her throat. With lips and tongue, he found sensitivities she hadn't known she possessed. As he trailed tiny, nibbling kisses down her neck and along her shoulder, she released her breath in a shuddering sigh, all thoughts of protest chased from her mind. Potent awareness curled through her, pooling hotly in unmentionable places.

When the gown was undone, he pushed it off her shoulders and down her arms. The rough warmth of his fingers made an erotic contrast to the cool silk that skimmed her flesh in a feather-light caress, then slithered in a rush to the floor, leaving her in her underthings. Instinctively she raised her hands to cover her breasts, stammering, "Th-this is highly improper."

"You have forfeited the right to talk about propriety." He untied her layered crinolette petticoat and dragged it down around her ankles. Then he began unlacing her blue satin corset. Stays were a lady's armor against impropriety, and she stood rigidly still, horribly aware that every inch of her newly liberated flesh burned with life and longing.

Then, shockingly, he slid his hands under the loose corset and cupped her breasts, using his thumbs to tease her nipples through the thin fabric of her chemise. It was like the time he had caressed her when he thought she slept, but a thousand times more intense. Unable to suppress her reaction, she shuddered and rolled her hips against him.

"You like that, my lady trollop?" he murmured in her ear.

She wanted to deny it, but couldn't. Her limbs weakened and she wilted against him, mindlessly reveling in the waves of sensation that flooded through her. The firm support of his broad chest, the silken tease of his tongue on the edge of her ear, the exquisite pleasure that expanded from her breasts to encompass her entire being, coiling tighter and tighter deep inside her....

She did not come to her senses until he tossed aside her corset and turned her to face him. Horrified by her lewd response and her near-nakedness, she stumbled away from the pile of crumpled clothing and retreated until her back was to the wall. "I have never shirked my wifely duty," she said feebly, "but this . . . this isn't right."

"Tonight, right is what I say it is." His implacable gaze holding hers, he stripped off his own clothing with brusque, impatient movements. "And this time, I will have you naked and in the light."

She could not take her eyes away as he removed his formal garments to reveal the hard, masculine body beneath. The well-defined muscles that rippled beneath his skin . . . the dark hair that patterned his chest and arrowed down his belly . . . and the arrogant male organ, which she had felt but never seen.

She stared for an instant, both mortified and fascinated, then blushed violently and closed her eyes. No wonder decent couples had marital relations in the dark, for the sight of a man's body was profoundly disturbing.

A Vienna waltz was playing in the distance. She had trouble believing that under this same roof hundreds of people were laughing and flirting and playing society's games. Compared to the devastating reality of Justin, the outside world had no more substance than shadows.

Even with her eyes closed, she was acutely aware of his nakedness when he drew her into his arms again, surrounding her with heat and maleness. Her breath came rapid and irregular as he peeled away the last frail protection of chemise, drawers and stockings. His fingers left trails of fire as they brushed her limbs and torso.

She inhaled sharply when he swept her into his arms and laid her across the bed, his taut frame pinning her to the mattress. Though she tried to control her shameful reactions, she moaned with pleasure when his mouth claimed her breast with arrant carnality.

No matter how hard she tried, she could not lie still as he caressed and kissed and tasted her, the velvet stroke of his tongue driving her to madness. His masterful touch abraded away every layer of decorum until she no longer remembered, or cared, how a lady should act. In the shameless turmoil of intimacy, she was tinder to his flame.

She was lovely beyond his dreams, and everything about her intoxicated him—the haunting lure of wild violets, her tangled sun-struck hair, the lush eroticism of removing layer after layer of clothing until finally her flawless body was revealed. Her lithe, feminine grace wrenched his heart.

Yet side by side with tenderness, he found savage satisfaction in her choked whimpers of pleasure. His wife might be a duchess and a lady, but for tonight, at least, she was a woman, and she was *his*.

This time there would be no need of lotion to ease their joining. She was hotly ready, and she writhed against his hand as he caressed the moist, delicate folds of female flesh. Her moan gave him a deep sense of masculine pride, dissolving the aching emptiness he had known in their inhibited marriage bed.

When he could no longer bear his separateness, he entered her. The voluptuous welcome of her body was exquisite, both torment and homecoming. Trembling with strain, he forced himself to move with slow deliberation. This time he would not let their union end too quickly.

Vivid emotions rippled across her sweat-sheened face. But he wanted more; he wanted communion of the mind as well as the body. He wanted acknowledgment of the power he had over her. Hoarsely he asked, "Do you desire me?"

"You . . . you are my husband." She turned her head to the side, as if trying to evade his question. "It is my duty to comply with your wishes."

Mere obedience was not what he wanted from his wife. He repeated, *"Do you desire me?"* Slowly, by infinitesimal degrees, he began to withdraw. "If not, perhaps I should stop now."

"No!" she gasped, her eyes flying open for an instant and her body arching sharply upward. "Don't leave me, please. I couldn't bear it. . . ."

It was what he had longed to hear. He responded to her admission by surrendering to the fiery need that bound them. No longer passive, she was his partner in passion, her nails slashing his back as they thrust against each other. She cried out with ecstasy as long, shuddering convulsions rocked them both, and in the culmination of desire he felt their soaring spirits blend.

In the tremulous aftermath, he gathered her pliant body into his arms and tucked the covers around them. As they dozed off together, he knew they had truly become husband and wife.

Justin was not sure how long he had slept. The ball must have ended, for he could no longer hear music and laughter, but the sky outside was still dark. He lay on his side with Sunny nestled along him, her face against his shoulder.

Not wanting to wake her, he touched the luscious tangle of her hair with a gossamer caress. He had never known such happiness, or such peace. Not only was she the loveliest and sweetest of women, but she was blessed with an ardent nature. If he hadn't been so blasted deferential, he would have discovered that much sooner. But now that they had found each other, their lives would be different.

Her eyes opened and gazed into his. For a long moment, they simply stared at each other. He stroked the elegant curve of her back and prepared to make the declaration of love that he had never made to any other woman.

But she spoke first, saying in a thin, exhausted voice, "Who are you?"

A chill touched his heart as he wondered if she was out of her senses, but she seemed lucid. Carefully he replied, "Your husband, of course."

She gave a tiny shake of her head. "You are more a stranger to me now than on the day we married."

He looked away, unable to face the dazed bleakness in her aqua eyes. He had known that she had not yet been unfaithful; not only was she not the sort of woman to engage lightly in an affair, but buried at Swindon she hadn't even had an opportunity. Yet seeing her in Curzon's arms had devastated Justin because it was a horrific preview of the possibility that he would lose her.

Despair had made him furiously determined to show her what fulfillment was. He had wanted to possess her, body and soul, to make her his own so profoundly that she would never look at another man. He realized that he had also hoped to win her love by demonstrating the depth of his passion.

But the fact that he had been able to arouse her latent ardor did not mean that she suddenly, miraculously loved him. With sickening clarity, he saw that in his anger he had ruthlessly stripped away her dignity and modesty. Instead of liberating her passion, he had ravished her spirit, turning her into a broken shadow of the happy girl who had first captured his heart.

His unspoken words of love withered and died. Instead he said painfully, "I am no different now from what I was then."

He wanted to say more, to apologize and beg her forgiveness, but she turned away and buried her face in the pillows.

Feeling that he would shatter if he moved too suddenly, he slid from the bed and numbly dragged on enough clothing to make his way the short distance to his room.

As he left, he wondered despairingly if he would ever be able to face his wife again.

Chapter Nine

Sunny awoke the next morning churning with tangled emotions. The only thing she knew for certain was that she could not bear to face a house full of avid-eyed, curious people. With a groan, she rolled over, buried her head under a pillow and did her best not to think.

But her mind refused to cooperate. She could not stop herself from wondering where Justin was and what he thought of the events of the previous night. She was mortified by memories of her wantonness, and angry with her husband for making her behave so badly. But though she tried to cling to anger over his disrespect, other things kept seeping into her mind—memories of heartwarming closeness, and shattering excitement....

At that point in her thoughts, her throat always tightened. Justin had said he would treat her as a whore, and her response had confirmed his furious accusation.

For the first time in her life, Sunny understand why a woman might choose to go into a nunnery. A world with no men would be infinitely simpler.

Eventually Antoinette tiptoed into the dim, heavily curtained room. "Madame is not feeling well this morning?"

"Madame has a ghastly headache. I wish to be left alone." Remembering her obligations, Sunny added, "Tell

Lady Alexandra not to be concerned about me. I'm sure I'll be fine by dinner.''

There was a long silence. Even with her eyes closed, Sunny knew that her maid was surveying the disordered bedchamber and probably drawing accurate conclusions. But tactful Antoinette said only, ''After I straighten the room, I shall leave. Perhaps later you would like tea and toast?''

''Perhaps.''

As the maid quietly tidied up the evidence of debauchery, someone knocked on the door and handed in a message. After the footman left, Antoinette said, ''*Monsieur le Duc* has sent a note.''

Sunny came tensely awake. ''Leave it on the table.''

After the maid left, Sunny sat up in bed and stared at the letter as if it were a poisonous serpent. Then she swung her feet to the floor. Only then did she realize that she was stark naked. Worse, her body showed unaccustomed marks where sensitive skin had been nipped, or rasped by a whiskered masculine face. And her body would not be the only one marked this morning....

Face flushed, she darted to the armoire and grabbed the first nightgown and wrapper she saw. After she was decently covered, she brushed her wild hair into submission and pulled it into a severe knot. When she could delay no longer, she opened the waiting envelope.

She was not sure what she expected, but the scrawled words, *I'm sorry. Thornborough* were a painful letdown. What was her husband sorry about—their marriage? His wife's appallingly wanton nature? His own disproportionate rage, which had led him to humiliate her? The use of his title rather than his Christian name was blunt proof that the moments of intimacy she had imagined the night before were an illusion.

Crumpling the note in one hand, she buried her face in her hands and struggled against tears. The wretched circle of her thoughts was interrupted by another knock. Though she called out, "I do not wish for company," the door swung open anyhow.

In walked Katie Westron, immaculately dressed in a morning gown and with a tray in her hands. "It's past noon, and you and I were engaged to take a drive an hour ago." She set the tray down, then surveyed her goddaughter. "You look quite dreadful, my dear, and they say that Thornborough left Cottenham this morning at dawn, looking like death."

So he was gone. Apparently he couldn't bear being under the same roof with her any longer. Trying to mask the pain of that thought, Sunny asked, "Are people talking?"

"Some, though not as much as they were before I said that Thornborough had always intended to leave today because he had business at Swindon." Briskly Katie opened the draperies so that light flooded the room. "And as I pointed out, who wouldn't look exhausted after a late night at such a delightful ball?"

"He *was* planning to leave early, but not until tomorrow." Sunny managed a wry half smile. "You lie beautifully."

"It's a prime social skill." Katie prepared two cups of coffee and handed one to Sunny, then took the other and perched on the window seat. "There's nothing like coffee to put one's troubles in perspective. Have a ginger cake, too, they're very good." After daintily biting one, Katie continued, "Would you like to tell me why you and Thornborough both look so miserable?"

The scalding coffee did clear Sunny's mind. She was in dire need of the advice of an older and wiser woman, and she would find no kinder or more tolerant listener than her godmother.

Haltingly she described her marriage—the distance between her and her husband, her loneliness, her encounter with Paul Curzon and the shocking result. Of the last she said very little, and that with her face burning, but she suspected that her godmother could make a shrewd guess about what went unsaid.

At the end, she asked, "What do you think?"

"Exactly why are you so upset?"

After long thought, Sunny said slowly, "I don't understand my marriage, my husband or myself. In particular, I find Justin incomprehensible. Before, I thought he was polite but basically indifferent to me. Now I think he must despise me, or he would never have treated me with such disrespect."

Katie took another cake. "Do you wish to end the marriage?"

"Of course I don't want a divorce!"

"Why 'of course'? There would be a ghastly scandal, and some social circles exclude all divorced women, but as a Vangelder, you would be able to weather that."

"It...it would be humiliating for Thornborough. If I left him, people would think that he mistreated me horribly."

Katie's brows arched. "Aren't you saying that he did exactly that?"

"In most ways, he's been very considerate." She thought of the bathroom that he had had installed for her, and almost smiled. Not the most romantic gift, perhaps, but one that gave her daily pleasure.

"You'd be a fool to live in misery simply to save Thornborough embarrassment," Katie said tartly. "A little singed pride will be good for him, and as a duke he will certainly not be ruined socially. He can find another wife with a snap of his fingers. The next one might not be able to match your dowry, but that's all right—the Swindon roof has already been replaced, and you can hardly take it back. What matters is that you'll be free to find a more congenial husband."

The thought of Justin with another wife made Sunny's hackles rise. "I don't want another husband." She bit her lip. "In fact, I can't imagine being married to anyone else. It would seem wrong. Immoral."

"Oh?" Katie said with interest. "What is so special about Thornborough? From what you say, he's a dull sort of fellow, and he's not particularly good-looking."

"He's *not* dull! He's kind, intelligent and very witty, even though he's quiet. He has a sense of responsibility, which many men in his position don't. And he's really quite attractive. Not in a sleek, fashionable way, but very . . . manly."

Her godmother smiled gently. "You sound like a woman who is in love with her husband."

"I do?" Sunny tried the idea on, and was shocked to realize that it was true. She was happy in Justin's presence; on some deep level that had nothing to do with their current problems, she trusted him. "But he doesn't love me—he doesn't even respect me. Last night he said that since I had behaved like a . . . a woman of no virtue, he would treat me like one." A vivid memory of his mouth on her breast caused her to blush again.

"Did he hurt you?"

"No, but he . . . offended my modesty." Sunny stared at her hands, unable to meet her godmother's gaze. "In fairness, I must admit that I did not behave as properly as I should. In fact . . . I was shocked to discover how wantonly I could behave."

"In other words, your husband made passionate love to you, you found it entrancing as well as alarming, and are now ashamed of yourself."

The color drained from Sunny's face, leaving her white. "How did you know?"

Setting aside her coffee cup, Katie said, "The time has come to speak frankly. I suppose that your mother told you that no decent woman ever enjoyed her marriage bed, and that discreet suffering was the mark of a lady."

After seeing her goddaughter nod, she continued, "There are many who agree with her, but another school of opinion says that there is nothing wrong with taking pleasure in the bodies that the good Lord gave us. What is the Song of Solomon but a hymn to the joy of physical and spiritual love?"

Weakly Sunny said, "Mother would say you're talking blasphemy."

"Augusta is one of my oldest and dearest friends, but she and your father were ill-suited, and naturally that has affected her views on marital relations." Katie leaned forward earnestly. "Satisfaction in the marriage bed binds a couple together, and the better a woman pleases her husband, the less likely he is to stray. And vice versa, I might add." She cocked her head. "If you hadn't been raised to believe that conjugal pleasure was immodest, would you have enjoyed the passion and intimacy that you experienced last night?"

The idea of reveling in carnality was so shocking that it took Sunny's breath away—yet it was also powerfully compelling. She had come to look forward to Justin's visits and to long for more of his company. The idea that her response was natural, not wanton, was heady indeed.

More memories of the previous night's explosive passion burned across her brain. Though the episode had been upsetting, there had also been moments of stunning emotional intimacy, when she and her husband had seemed to be one flesh and one spirit. If such intensity could be woven into the fabric of a marriage, it would bind a man and woman together for as long as they lived. And if passion made a marriage stronger, surely fulfillment could not be truly wicked.

There was only one problem. "I'd like to think that you're right, but what does it matter if I love my husband and he holds me in contempt? Justin has never said a single word of love."

Katie smiled wryly. "Englishmen are taught to conceal their emotions in the nursery, and the more deeply they care, the harder it is for them to speak. In my experience, the men who talk most easily of love are those who have had entirely too much practice. The more sparingly a man gives his heart, the more precious the gift, and the less adept he is at declarations of love. But deeds matter more than words, and an ounce of genuine caring is worth a pound of smooth, insincere compliments."

Abruptly Sunny remembered that Justin had said that he hadn't looked at another woman since meeting her. She had thought that was merely a riposte in their argument, but if true, it might be an oblique declaration of love. Hesitantly she said, "Do you think it's possible that Justin loves me?"

"You would know that better than I. But he seems the sort who would be more of a doer than a talker." Katie's brows drew together. "Men are simple creatures, and for them, love and passion often get knotted up together. If he does love you in a passionate way, the kind of restrained marriage you have described must be difficult for him."

And if he was finding the marriage difficult, he would withdraw; that much Sunny knew about her husband. She had regretted the fact that he had never reached out to her with affection—yet neither had she ever reached out to him. Perhaps she was as much responsible for the distance between them as he was. Attempting lightness, she said, "I suppose that the way to find out how he feels is to hand him my heart on a platter, then see whether he accepts it or chops it into little pieces."

"I'm afraid so." Katie shook her head ruefully. "All marriages have ups and downs, particularly in the early years. I was once in a situation a bit like yours, where I had to risk what could have been a humiliating rejection. It wasn't easy to humble myself, but the results were worth it." She smiled. "A witty vicar once said that a good marriage is like a pair of scissors with the couple inseparably joined, often moving in opposite directions, yet always destroying anyone who comes between them. The trick is for the blades to learn to work smoothly together, so as not to cut each other."

That's what she and Justin had been doing: cutting each other. Feeling a century older than she had the day before, Sunny gave a shaky smile. "Apparently I must learn to speak with American bluntness."

"That's the spirit. But first, you might want to ask yourself what you want out of your marriage."

"Love, companionship, children. I certainly don't want to withdraw entirely from society, but the fashionable world will never be the center of my life, the way it is for my mother." Her brow wrinkled. "Perhaps if my parents had been happier together, my father would not have worked so hard, and my mother would not have cared as much about society."

"I've often suspected that many of the world's most dazzling achievements are a result of a miserable domestic situation." Katie considered. "You might want to wait until both you and Thornborough have had time to recover from what was obviously a distressing episode. You were about to take Alexandra to Paris, weren't you? In your place, I would carry on with my original plans. That will give you time to think and decide exactly how to proceed."

"I'm going to need it." Sunny rose and hugged her godmother. "Thank you, Aunt Katie. What can I do to repay you?"

"When you're old and wise like me, you can give worldly advice to other confused young ladies." Katie smiled reminiscently. "Which is exactly what I was told by an eccentric, sharp-tongued Westron aunt who sent me back to my husband when I was a bewildered bride."

Sunny nodded gravely. "I promise to pass on whatever womanly wisdom I acquire."

But before she was in a position to give good advice, she must fix her own frayed marriage. And that, she knew, would be easier said than done.

Chapter Ten

Alexandra looked eagerly from the carriage window. "Almost home! It's hard to believe that it's been only a month since we left Swindon. I feel *years* older."

Sunny smiled, trying to conceal her frayed nerves. "Paris has that effect on people. You really have changed, too. You left as a girl and are returning as a young woman."

"I hope so." Alexandra grinned. "But I'm going to go right up to my room and take off my wonderful Worth travel ensemble. Then I'll curl up in my window seat and read that new Rider Haggard novel I bought in London. Though Paris was wonderful, there's nothing quite like a good book."

"You've earned the right to a little self-indulgence." Sunny gave her sister-in-law a fond smile. Petite and pretty, Alexandra would never be called the Gargoylette again, and the difference was more than mere clothing. Now that Alexandra was free of her mother's crushing influence, she was developing poise, confidence and a quiet charm that would surely win her whatever man she eventually honored with her heart.

The carriage pulled up in front of the palace and a footman stepped forward to open the door and let down the steps. Even though Sunny had lived at Swindon for only a few months, and that interval had been far from happy, she felt a surprising sense of homecoming. It helped that the full glory of an English spring had arrived. All nature was in bloom, and the sun was almost as warm as high summer.

As they entered the main hall, Sunny asked the butler, "Is my husband in the house or out on the estate?"

She assumed the latter, for Justin was not expecting them to return until the next day. But the butler replied, "I believe that the duke is taking advantage of the fine weather by working in the Greek gazebo. Shall I inform him of your arrival?"

Sunny's heart lurched. She had thought she would have several hours more before confronting her husband about the state of their marriage, but perhaps it would be better this way. "No, I shall freshen up and then surprise him."

As she walked toward the stairs, a black-and-tan whirlwind darted across the hall and leapt against her, barking joyfully. "Daisy! Oh, darling, I missed you, too." Sunny knelt and hugged the slender little dog, feeling that such a warm welcome was a good omen.

A moment later, the wolfhounds thundered up and greeted Alexandra eagerly, then escorted her upstairs. Canine snobs of the highest order, they could tell aristocratic British blood from that of an upstart American, and they reserved their raptures for Justin and his sisters.

Sunny didn't mind. Her charming mongrel at her heels, she went to her room and changed from her traveling suit to her most flattering tea gown, a loose, flowing confection of figured green silk that brought out the green in her eyes.

She chose the costume with care, and not just because it was comfortable. The free and easy design of a tea gown was considered rather daring because it hinted at free and easy morals. She hoped that Justin would see her garb as the subtle advance that it was.

Because he always seemed to like her hair, she let it down and tied it back with a scarf. She needed all the help she could get, for she was terrified by the prospect of baring her heart to the man who could so easily break it. Apart from a brief note that she had written to inform Justin of their safe arrival in Paris, there had been no communication between them. For all she knew, he was still furious over Paul Curzon's kiss.

Fortunately, she had news that should mollify any lingering anger. God willing, it would also bring them together.

Chin high, she sailed out of the house and down the path toward the gardens.

A breeze wafted through the miniature Greek temple, carrying exuberant scents of trees and spring flowers. Justin scarcely noticed. He was hardly more aware of the pile of correspondence that lay on the cushioned bench beside him, for thoughts of his wife dominated his mind. All of his grief, guilt and anguished love had been intensified by that night of heartbreaking passion, when he had briefly thought that their spirits and bodies were in total harmony.

Sunny had sent him a single impersonal note from Paris. Though it gave no hint of her feelings, its civility implied that she was willing to go on as if nothing had happened.

Yet he feared her return almost as much as he longed to see her. Having once found passion in her arms, it was going to be almost impossible for him not to try to invoke it again, whether she was willing or not.

Absently he slit an envelope with the Italian dagger that he used as a letter opener. Before he could pull out the folded sheet inside, a soft voice said, "Good day, Justin."

He looked up to see Sunny poised on the edge of the folly, her right hand resting on one of the Ionic columns that framed the entrance. She wore a flowing green tea gown that made her look like an exquisite tree nymph. The garment was distractingly similar to a nightgown, and the breeze molded the fluttering, translucent layers of fabric to her slim figure.

For an instant all his tormented desire must have showed in his face. He wanted to cross the marble floor and draw her into his arms and never let her go. But he didn't. She looked ready to run if he made a move toward her, and it was unbearable to think that she might fear him.

He set the pile of letters on the bench beside him and courteously got to his feet. "I hope you had a good journey. I wasn't expecting you and Alex until tomorrow."

"Rather than spend another night in London, we decided to come home early."

"I'm glad. The house has seemed empty without the two of you." Afraid to look at her because of what his expression would reveal, he turned the dagger over and over in his hands. The impact of her presence had driven away all of the eloquent, romantic speeches he had been rehearsing in his mind.

After a strained silence, she said, "I have good news. I'm almost certain that... that I am with child."

His first reaction was delight, but that was instantly shadowed by the implications. Augusta Vangelder had told him that once her daughter conceived, she was not to be troubled by husbandly lust. The fact that Sunny was brandishing the possibility of her pregnancy like a shield was clear proof that she welcomed the excuse to ban him from her bed.

His fingers whitened around the handle of the dagger. If she bore a son, her obligation to the Aubrey name would be fulfilled, and their marriage would effectively be over. Driving the dagger into his belly would have hurt less than that thought.

During the last lonely month, he had resolved to take advantage of the quiet intimacy of the marital bed to speak more openly to his wife. If she was willing, perhaps they could build a closer, warmer relationship. Now that hope was gone; any discussions between them must endure the harsh light of day.

Knowing that the silence had been too long, he said, "Excellent. I hope you are feeling well?"

She nodded.

After another awkward pause, he said, "Good. We shall have to get a London physician here to make sure that your health is all it should be." He laid the dagger precisely on top of his correspondence so that the letters would not blow away in the wind. "You need not worry that I will continue to... force my attentions on you."

"Very well." She bent her head, and a slight shiver passed through her. Relief, perhaps. "I'm a bit tired. I think that I'll skip dinner and have a tray in my room."

Thinking that she looked pale, he said, "Of course. You must take good care of yourself."

Back straight and head high, she turned and started down the grassy path. Every inch a lady, and as unapproachable as Queen Victoria herself.

He watched her leave, very aware of what an effort it was to breathe. Inhale, exhale. Inhale, exhale. He had been breathing all his life, yet never noticed before how difficult it was.

There was a tearing sensation deep inside, as if his heart was literally breaking, and he knew that he could not let the deadly silence continue. He called out, "Sunny!"

She halted, then turned slowly to face him. In the shadows cast by the tall boxwoods that lined the path, he could not see her face clearly.

He stepped from the folly and moved toward her, then stopped when she tensed. "Sunny, I want to apologize for what I did at Cottenham. I am profoundly sorry for distressing you."

"You were within your rights, and your anger was justified," she said expressionlessly.

"Perhaps, but that doesn't make it right to mistreat you. It won't happen again."

"Should I be grateful for that?" she said with sudden, chilling bitterness. "That night was upsetting, but it was also the one time in our marriage that you have shown any feelings about me. I have begun to think that even anger is better than indifference."

The gay ribbons on her gown shivered as she bowed her head and pressed her fingertips to her brow. When she looked up, her eyes were bleak. "We can't continue to live together as strangers, Justin. I can't endure it any longer."

Her words struck with the force of a blow, nearly destroying his fragile control. It seemed impossible that their marriage could be ending like this, on a day full of sunlight and promise. Yet he could not hold her against her will; somehow he must find the strength to let her go. "If you wish to be free of me," he said tightly, "I will set no barriers in your way."

Her mouth twisted. "Is that what you want—to end our marriage now that you have your damned roof?"

"I want you to be happy, Sunny." Hearing the anguish in his voice, he stopped until he could continue more steadily. "And I will do anything in my power that might make you so."

The air between them seemed to thicken, charged with indefinable emotions. Then she said passionately, "What I want is to be a real wife! To be part of your life, not just another expensive bauble in Swindon Palace." Her hands clenched at her sides. "Or perhaps I should wish to be your mistress, since English lords seem to save their hearts for women who are not their wives."

Stunned, he stammered, "I don't understand."

"It's a simple matter, Justin. I want you to love me," she said softly. "Do you think that you ever could? Because I'm horribly afraid that I love you."

He felt as if his heart had stopped. Her declaration was so unexpected that it seemed she must be mocking him. Yet it was impossible to doubt the transparent honesty in her eyes.

Before he could find the words to answer, her face crumpled and she spun away from him. "Dear God, I'm making a fool of myself, aren't I? Like the brash, vulgar American that I am. Please—forget that I ever spoke."

Justin's paralysis dissolved and he caught her arm and swung her around before she could dart down the path. To his horror, tears were coursing down her face. The sight delivered a final, shattering blow to his reserve. Crushing her in his arms, he said urgently, "Don't cry, Sunny. If you want my love, you already have it. You always have."

Though her tears intensified, she did not pull away. Instead, she wrapped her arms around him and hid her face in the angle between his throat and shoulder. She was all pliant warmth, honeyed hair and the promise of wild violets.

He groped for the best way to tell her how much he loved her until he realized that words had always failed and divided them. Action would better demonstrate the depth of his caring. He raised her head and brushed back her silky hair, then kissed her with all of the hunger of his yearning spirit.

Salty with tears, her lips clung to his, open and seeking.

Subtle currents flowed between them—despair and comfort, wonder and promise, trust and surrender. In the stark honesty of desperation, there was no place for shame or doubt or misunderstanding. One by one, the barriers that had divided them crumbled away to reveal the shy grandeur of love.

At first the sweetness of discovery was enough, but as the kiss deepened and lengthened, sweetness slowly blossomed into fire. Murmuring her name like a prayer, he kneaded the soft curves that lay unconstrained beneath her flowing gown. She pressed against him, breathless and eager, and he drew her down to the sun-warmed grass.

They had had dutiful conjugal relations, and once they had come together with chaotic, disquieting passion. This time, they made love. She yielded herself utterly, for the awesome needs of her body no longer frightened her now that she knew she was loved.

Rippling layers of green silk were easily brushed aside, buttons undone, ribbons untied. Then, too impatient to wait until they were fully disrobed, they joined in the dance of desire. Swift and fierce, their union was a potent act of mutual possession that bound them into one spirit and one flesh.

Only afterward, as she lay languidly in the haven of his arms, did she realize the scandalousness of her behavior. The Duchess of Thornborough was lying half-naked in the garden, as bold as any dairymaid in a haystack. How strange. How shocking. How right.

His head lay pillowed on her shoulder, and she slid her fingers into his tousled dark hair. "How is it possible for us to say so much to each other in ten minutes when we didn't speak a single word?" she asked dreamily.

"Words are limiting. They can only hint at an emotion as powerful as love. Passion comes closer because it is itself all feeling." Justin rolled to his side and propped himself up on one elbow, his other arm draped over her waist to hold her close. Smiling into her eyes, he said, "For someone who seemed to hate being touched, you have developed a remarkable talent for physical intimacy."

She blushed. "At first I was afraid of the unknown. It wasn't long until I began to look forward to your visits, but I was ashamed of my desire. And... and my mother said that a man would never respect an immodest woman who reveled in her lower nature."

"In this area, your mother's understanding is sadly limited. There may be men like that, but for me, the knowledge that we can share our bodies with mutual pleasure is the greatest of all gifts." He leaned over and dropped a light kiss on the end of her nose. "Let us make a pact, my love—to pay no attention to what the world might say, and care only about what the two of us feel."

With one hand, she unbuttoned the top of his shirt and slipped her fingers inside so she could caress his warm, bare skin. "I think that is a wonderful idea. I only wish that we had started sooner. I was so sure that you married me only because you needed my fortune."

Expression serious, he said, "Don't ever doubt that I love you, Sunny. I have since the first time we met, when you were the Gilded Girl and I was an insignificant younger son who could never dare aspire to your hand."

Her eyes widened. "We hardly even spoke that day."

"On the contrary—we walked through the gardens for the better part of an hour. I could take you along the exact route, and repeat everything you said. It was the most enchanting experience of my life." His mouth quirked up wryly. "And you don't remember it at all, do you?"

"I do remember that I enjoyed your company, but I was meeting so many people then. You were simply a quiet, attractive man who didn't seem interested in me." She looked searchingly into his eyes. "If you loved me, why didn't you say so sooner?"

"I tried, but you never wanted to hear." He began lazily stroking her bare arm. "Since it never occurred to me that you could love me, there was no reason to burden you with my foolish emotions, even if I had known how to do it."

A vivid memory of his proposal flashed through her mind. He had said then that she had had his heart from the moment they met. There had been other occasions when he had haltingly tried to declare himself, plus a thousand small signs of caring, from his wedding orchids to the way he had risked his life to rescue a puppy for her. Yet because of her pain over Paul's betrayal and her conviction that Justin had married her only for money, she had spurned his hesitant words and gestures, convinced that they were polite lies. Dear heaven, no wonder he had preferred to conceal his feelings.

"I'm the one who must apologize. Because I was hurting, I ended up hurting you as well." She laid her hand along his firm jaw, thinking how handsome he looked with that tender light in his eyes. "Yet you were always kind to me."

He turned his head and pressed a kiss into her palm. "We gargoyles are known for kindness."

"I *hate* that nickname," she said vehemently. "How can people be so cruel? You are intelligent, amusing, considerate, and a gentleman in the best sense of the word."

"I'm very glad you think so, but society loves cleverness, and a good quip counts for more than a good heart," he said with dry amusement. "The fact that you love me is clear proof that much of love comes from simple proximity."

"Nonsense," she said tartly. "Proximity can just as easily breed dislike. But it's true that I would never have learned to love you if we hadn't married. You are not an easy man to know."

"I'm sorry, my dear." He sighed. "As you know, my mother can be...difficult. I learned early that to show emotions was to risk having them used against me, so I became first-rate at concealing what I felt. Unfortunately, that made me at a flat loss at saying what matters most. I promise that from now on, I will say that I love you at least once a day."

"I'd rather have that than the Thornborough tiara." Shyly she touched her abdomen, which as yet showed no sign of the new life within. "Are you happy about the baby? You didn't seem very interested."

"I'm awed and delighted." A shadow crossed his face. "If my reaction seemed unenthusiastic, it was because I feared that if it was a boy, you would go off to Paris or New York and never want to see me again."

"What a dreadful thought." She shivered. "May I ask a favor?"

"Anything, Sunny. Always." He laced his fingers through hers, then drew their joined hands to his heart.

"I would very much like it if we slept together every night, like people who can't afford two bedrooms do." Her mouth curved playfully. "Even with central heating, it's often chilly here."

He laughed. "I would like nothing better. I've always hated leaving you to go back to my own cold and lonely bed."

"We can start a new fashion for togetherness." She lifted their clasped hands and lovingly kissed his finger-tips.

He leaned over and claimed her mouth, and the embers of passion began glowing with renewed life. As he slid his hand into the loose neckline of her gown, he murmured, "We're both wearing entirely too many clothes, especially for such a fine day."

Remembering their surroundings, she said breathlessly, "Justin, don't you dare! We have already behaved disgracefully enough for one day."

"Mmm?" He pulled her gown from her shoulder so that he could kiss her breasts, a process that rendered her quite unable to talk. She had not known that there was such pleasure in the whole world.

She made one last plea for sanity as he began stripping off his coat. "If someone comes along this path and sees us, what will they say?"

"They'll say that the Duke of Thornborough loves his wife very much." He smiled into her eyes with delicious wickedness. "And they'll be right."

* * * * *

Dear Reader,

I adore weddings, and I always, *always* cry, even if I don't know the happy couple myself. The first wedding I can remember was that of my cousin Delores when I was about six. She was beautiful, I was madly envious of the flower girl, and at the reception, little white boxes of cake were given out as souvenirs. I loved the little boxes and looked for them at receptions for years to come, but, alas, without success.

Weddings are almost always great fun, but so are birthday parties, and I never cry at those. (Well, almost never.) The difference is that marriage is the cornerstone of all human societies, so a wedding is one of life's great rites of passage, along with birth and death. The emotions invoked are profound: the hope that springs from new beginnings, tempered by the knowledge that the couple's future will hold trials as well as laughter, loss as well as joy.

No matter how "suitable" a match is in worldly terms, ultimately a marriage boils down to one man and one woman who must come to terms with each other, preferably in an emotionally satisfying way. Great wealth and power can make the challenges of marriage even more difficult.

I got the idea for "The Wedding of the Century" years ago when I first read about the real-life marriage of Consuelo Vanderbilt and the ninth Duke of Marlborough at the height of the Gilded Age. Their wedding was one of the great media events of the late nineteenth century, but the marriage ended in divorce after producing two sons.

My own story is about two very human, vulnerable people who are almost overwhelmed by the trappings of wealth and the expectations of others. I hope you enjoy reading about how Justin and Sunny find each other.

Mary Jo Putney

JESSE'S WIFE

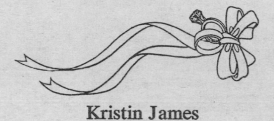

Kristin James

Chapter One

Amy McAlister had never done anything so daring.

She glanced up at her companion as she tucked her hand in his arm and strolled out through the hall and kitchen onto the back porch. The color was high in Amy's cheeks, partially from the exercise of dancing in which they had been engaged, but just as much from her heightened excitement. It would not be terribly improper to walk with Mr. Whitaker out onto the front porch, for there was such a crush of people inside the house that more than one gentleman and lady had stepped outside this balmy October evening for a breath of air.

However, it was quite another matter for them to have slipped out onto the small back porch, where there was no one but them. Still worse, Mr. Whitaker was taking her hand and leading her down the steps onto the packed earth of the backyard and across toward the corral. To be alone with a man in the darkened night was not at all proper, especially when he had asked her to slip away with him for a moonlight stroll. In any other woman, such behavior would have been termed loose. In herself, Amy knew, such carelessness would be classified as mere naiveté, for the quiet, plain Amy was "such a *good* girl," and, moreover, not the sort to drive a man to an act of unbridled passion.

The idea rankled. It wasn't that Amy wished to be thought of as a "bad" girl, or to have some harridan like old Mrs. Gooden call her an "incorrigible flirt"—as she had Amy's sister, Corinne. She simply found it singularly depressing to know that everyone thought her so indifferent in looks and boring in personality that she would never even be afforded the opportunity to break society's rules.

Amy had unhappily admitted the truth—that she was, indeed, just plain and uninteresting. All the looks in their family had fallen to her younger sister, Corinne, whose blond curls, sparkling blue eyes and creamy complexion had entranced most of the men of the area ever since she grew old enough to put her skirts down and her hair up.

Amy, on the other hand, had rather mousy light brown hair, which she usually wore carelessly screwed up into a knot, a style that did nothing for her features. Her eyes, though large and expressive, were an ordinary brown. Her skin was nice enough, her figure was neat and becomingly curved, and her features were not unpleasing. But Amy had none of her sister's vivacity. Rather than sparkling and flirting, she was apt to be tongue-tied in a man's presence. She tended to look down when she talked, and she avoided talking to people if she possibly could. Moreover, she was well-known around the county as a scholar, and few people were interested in the sort of things she liked to talk about.

As a result, Amy was something of a wallflower. It was a good thing, her mother maintained, that Amy was a calm, sensible girl, obviously happy being immersed in her books, and with no interest in a husband or family.

In that, Mrs. McAlister was wrong. Although Amy was generally calm and sensible, inside her beat the heart of a romantic. She read everything she could get her hands on, from dull histories to the thoughts of philosophers, but what she loved most of all were novels, especially romantic ones, and those she read over and over. Therefore, when Charles Whitaker had leaned down and whispered in her ear at the end of the dance, suggesting that they slip away from this tiresome crowd and go for a stroll in the moonlight, she had readily agreed.

Her pulse was skittering madly now as she walked with him across the yard. One of his hands covered hers as it lay in the crook of her elbow, warm and full of meaning. He glanced down at her and smiled, his eyes caressing her face. Amy drew in a little breath and gazed up into his face, which was washed romantically by moonlight. Looking at him made her knees a trifle weak.

Charles Whitaker was a handsome man, one who could, indeed, have stepped from the pages of one of her novels. His hair was jet black and thick, springing back from a high, fair brow, and his eyes were dark and intense. From the moment he had ridden into Portersville a few weeks before, he had been the center of intense female interest.

There was a faint air of melancholy about him, and though he was mysteriously silent regarding his past, one or two things he had let drop indicated that his family, once the proud possessors of a plantation in Virginia, had lost it all in the war some twenty-four years before. Amy didn't hold his loss against him. After all, Amy's own father had come to Texas after the war from his native Louisiana with his friend Cal Boudreaux. He had worked hard and built up one of the biggest ranches in the state.

To Amy's surprise, however, her father seemed to have little sympathy for Charles Whitaker. He had accepted Whitaker in the friendly way people had here, without questions as to his past, but after a few weeks he had taken a dislike to Charles. He had said Charles was lazy and frivolous, and wondered why he hadn't taken a job, as any other man would have. He had told his daughters grimly that he suspected the man was a fortune hunter, and warned them to stay away from them.

Corinne, of course, had merely laughed and continued to do as she pleased, flirting with Mr. Whitaker as she did with her other many beaux. Even Amy, usually obedient to her father's wishes, thought he was being unkind and unfair, and when Charles had begun paying decided attention to her, she had disregarded her father's warnings. She was thrilled that a man like Charles Whitaker had stopped hanging about her beautiful sister and had chosen her company instead.

They reached the corral, and Whitaker drew Amy into the shadow of the barn. In the distance, Amy heard a trill of laughter from the porch, but it merely blended into the soothing night noises—the shuffle of horses' hooves within the corral, the croak of frogs down by the stock tank, the call of a night bird. She felt wrapped in the darkness, and giddy to be standing so close to Charles and in such a situation.

He smiled down at her, taking her hands in his. "You must think me very presumptuous."

Amy mutely shook her head. She was more afraid that he would think her overly bold than the other way around.

"I had to speak with you . . . to be alone with you."

"Why?" she asked honestly.

Whitaker looked a trifle taken aback by her bluntness. "But surely you have guessed . . ."

Amy continued to look at him uncertainly. She had noticed that the past few times she had seen Mr. Whitaker, he had paid particular attention to her, no longer dangling after Corinne. But she had refused to let herself believe it, certain that she simply had been reading too much into a look or into the number of times he asked her to dance.

"Mr. Whitaker, I'm not sure—"

She broke off, whirling as the barn door scraped across the earth with a loud noise. A man stepped out of the barn and into the moonlight. He stopped abruptly when he saw them, and his eyes narrowed.

"Oh! Jesse!" Amy breathed a sigh of relief. "You startled me."

The man walked toward them, his eyes flickering over Charles Whitaker, then coming to rest on Amy. His gaze was expressionless, but still Whitaker shifted a little beneath it. Jesse Tyler was young, no more than twenty, and he was not a big man, but he was leanly muscled and strong. There was about him an air of toughness. Whitaker wasn't sure what it was—perhaps the hard expression in his cool green eyes, or the carefully blank, hard set of his face or even the rough clothes he wore and his slightly shaggy, too-long hair—but it was clear that Jesse Tyler was not a man to tangle with.

"What are you doing out here, ma'am, so far from the party?" Tyler asked Amy mildly, but the suspicious look he shot at Whitaker was anything but mild.

"Just taking a stroll," Amy answered. "It was awfully hot in there, dancing. You know."

Jesse nodded, biting off the end of his cheroot, then putting it in his mouth and lighting it. Amy eyed him uncertainly. She liked Jesse; he was one of her dearest friends. Though others often said he was tough, even mean, Amy had never seen anything like that in him. She reached out and placed a hand affectionately on Jesse's arm. He paused in the act of lighting his cheroot and looked up at her. His gaze was long and considering.

"You won't say anything about my being out here, will you, Jesse?"

"I don't think your pa would like it," he responded.

"Perhaps not, but there's nothing wrong with it. You know I wouldn't do anything wicked or reckless, don't you?"

"*You* wouldn't," he said with careful emphasis, and his eyes flickered to Whitaker.

"I'm in good hands with Mr. Whitaker," Amy replied blithely, and smiled. "You mustn't worry about that."

Tyler continued to stare at Whitaker, his gaze hard. "Yes. I'm sure Mr. Whitaker will be very careful to take good care of you."

Charles raised his brows in lazy disdain at the hint of a threat in the other man's words, but he sketched a little bow, inclining his head to show that he understood Tyler's implication.

"Good night, Miss Amy."

"Good night, Jesse."

Tyler strolled away in the direction of the house. Charles and Amy did not watch him go, so neither of them saw him stop when he reached the shadows of the house and turn back to look at them. He ground out his cheroot in order to rid himself of its red glow, and he crossed his arms over his chest and leaned back against the side of the house, studying the couple by the corral.

Charles took Amy's hands in his. "Please, Miss McAlister, come for a stroll with me—away from the yard. If we stay here, we'll only be interrupted again."

Amy paused uncertainly. She was dazzled by the attention Mr. Whitaker was paying her; no man had ever flirted with her so assiduously, or paid her such pretty, extravagant compliments. It made her feel almost beautiful, as if she were a belle of the county like her sister, instead of a washed-out nonentity, relegated to line the wall with the matrons and the other spinsters while the sought-after girls danced.

She knew that it would be improper to walk out of the yard alone with a man late at night. Why, it wasn't really proper to have come this far away from the others with him! Yet she could not bear to give up this chance to be with him and hear the wonderful things he had to say. He seemed to actually be smitten with her, and it would have taken a stronger woman than she—or one far more sure of herself—to give up this opportunity.

"All right," she murmured, her pulse racing as he took her hand and led her away from the corral and barn. "But only for a little while."

"Of course."

They took the path that led toward Rock Creek. The moonlight made it easy for them to pick their way along. Some distance behind them, Jesse Tyler left the shadow of the house and followed.

Amy was grateful that Charles kept up a constant flow of conversation as they walked along, for she usually found herself without anything to say around gentlemen.

They reached the creek, whose banks were lined with trees, and Amy started to turn back, assuming that this was as far as they would go. But to her surprise, Charles led her along the bank of the creek. The moonlight filtered down through the branches, and now and then, in an open place, it sparkled on the water, a beautiful and romantic sight. They reached a grove, and Amy came to an abrupt stop. There, at the edge of the grove, was a horse and buggy, unattended. Amy stared at it in surprise.

"What in the world? Who—" Her heart began to thump, and she glanced around nervously. There must be someone else here.

"Charles, let's go," she whispered urgently.

"No. Wait. Don't be scared. This is my buggy. There's no one here."

"Yours?" Amy looked at him in blank surprise. "But what is it doing here?"

"It's a surprise." Again that beautiful white smile flashed on his face, asking her to share in his pleasure. "I put it here because I wanted to surprise you."

"Surprise me? But I don't understand." Amy was puzzled, yet she let him pull her along to the buggy.

"You'll see." He put his hand at her elbow to help her into the buggy. When she hesitated, he murmured, "Please, don't spoil the moment, darling."

Darling! Heat rose in her face at his use of the endearment, and her stomach knotted. She knew that her mother would not approve of her doing this, but... Was it really so improper? After all, it was merely a ride in the moonlight with a gentleman. No doubt Corinne and other girls like her had done it many a time; it was just an indication of her own inexperience that she had never been asked to do it. She felt silly, yet at the same time thrilled by the loving word that had slipped from his lips, and both sensations served to drown her unease at being alone in a buggy at night with a man.

She climbed into the buggy, and they started off across the land, coming out at last on a narrow, rutted road that marked the end of her father's land on the south side. The land was lovely, bathed in moonlight, and it was breathlessly exciting to be alone with Charles, but gradually her uneasiness won out. She was sure she should not be doing this.

"Perhaps we'd better start back now," she murmured.

"In just a moment," Charles replied. "There's a place I want to show you."

The buggy rattled across the old wooden bridge spanning the creek and stopped on the small rise just beyond. It was a pretty view. Even the old sheepherder's hut below them, abandoned years before, took on a romantically ruined aspect in the pale wash of the moonlight.

Charles got down and came around to help Amy out of the buggy, taking her arm and drawing her over to look at the view.

He turned and looked down at her seriously. "Miss McAlister, I don't know whether you are aware of the high esteem in which I hold you."

Pleased, Amy smiled, but could think of no way to answer his remark.

"I have tried to contain my feelings. I know I am unworthy of you."

Amy's heart began to beat faster. She had never received a proposal, but she had heard about several of them secondhand from Corinne and some of her friends, and this sounded suspiciously like one. However, she could hardly believe that Charles Whitaker would actually be making an offer of marriage to *her!*

"Amy—my love makes me bold to call you that—"

"It's all right," Amy reassured him softly.

Annoyance flickered in his eyes for an instant at her interruption, but was quickly gone, replaced by a look of melting love.

"Amy, my dearest, I cannot hold back my feelings any longer. I have fallen deeply, desperately, in love with you. I want you for my wife. Say you'll marry me, and you'll make me a happy man." He smiled down into her face.

Amy gazed at him in amazement and uncertainty. *She had finally had a proposal of marriage!* No one could ever again say that she had been utterly unwanted. Her heart swelled with feeling. Charles Whitaker was everything a woman could want in a man—handsome, courteous, sophisticated. It would be very easy to fall in love with him; in fact, already she thought she was halfway to that point—aflutter with nerves whenever he was around, dreamily imagining him as the hero of her stories. The only problem was...

"But I don't know you!" she blurted out.

His expectant face fell, and Amy realized how graceless her response had been.

"I'm sorry. It's not that I don't have a—a great deal of regard for you, Mr. Whitaker. But, well, I haven't known you long. And marriage is such a major step. A lifetime, in fact." It occurred to her that she sounded deadly dull and sensible. Corinne, she knew, would have groaned at such a practical response.

Charles took her hands in his, squeezing them and saying passionately, "Love can happen in an instant! I cannot stop thinking about you, dreaming about you."

He raised her hands to his mouth and began to press his lips feverishly against them. Amy stared at him, feeling ridiculous and embarrassed. She had imagined many times a man saying words such as this to her, and now, when it was actually happening, it sounded rather absurd.

"Mr. Whitaker, please..." Amy tugged her hands out of his grasp. "I think it's time we returned to the house."

Charles grabbed her shoulders. "Please!" he exclaimed passionately. "Tell me that you return my feelings! I burn for you!"

He jerked her to him and kissed her hard. Amy, shocked, froze for a moment, unable to move or even think. Then his tongue thrust against her lips, wet and disgusting, and she began to struggle, twisting her face away.

"No! Stop!" She wriggled and squirmed, trying to break the bond of his arms around her, but he was stronger than she. Strangely, he seemed to enjoy her struggles.

"Ah!" he said, the loverlike tone gone from his voice, replaced by a coarse quality. "Maybe this won't be such a chore after all. You might be a little interesting."

"What!" Amy went still, all the color leaving her face. "What do you mean?"

He grinned, one hand coming up to crudely encircle her breast. "Just that there's some fire in you, after all. I think I may enjoy 'compromising' you."

Hurt and rage surged through her, and Amy brought her foot down with all her might on his instep, wishing that her dancing slippers had higher heels.

What they did have proved quite enough. Whitaker let out a howl of pain, and his arms slackened around her.

Amy tore out of his grasp and darted off.

Chapter Two

Whitaker stood between Amy and the buggy, so when she ran away from him, she ran away from it, too. Instinctively she headed toward the only shelter within reach: the decaying sheepherder's hut. She knew that even though she had gotten a head start on Whitaker, he would soon catch up with her, hampered as she was by her dress and petticoats, her flimsy dancing slippers and the stays that fashionably bound her waist. Her only hope was to reach the hut before he did and somehow bar it against him.

But before she could reach the shack, Whitaker caught her. He grasped the back of her dress, pulling her to a stop. Her dress ripped, tearing down to her waist in back. Amy twisted, trying to pull loose, but she succeeded only in tearing her bodice further, so that it slid down her arms, exposing her chest, which was clad in only her chemise and stays.

Whitaker threw her to the ground, knocking the breath out of her. He dropped down to his knees, straddling her prone body, and began to rip at the laces of her stays. Amy struggled, but her arms were hampered by her fallen bodice. He grabbed the bodice, twisting it around her wrists and jerking them up above her head, immobilizing her arms.

Amy bucked and struggled impotently, sobbing, but Whitaker only leered down at her, his grin widening. She realized with horror that her movements were arousing him. She let out a scream of rage, and he slapped her, almost casually, then chuckled.

"Who do you think's going to hear you out here?"

"My father will kill you!" she spat.

"I doubt it," he retorted cheerfully. "More likely he'll insist that I marry you."

Fury surged through Amy. She hated him, and she hated herself for letting him trick her so. She redoubled her efforts to escape, twisting and kicking. Her pulse hammered in her ears, so hard that for a moment she thought the drumming she heard was merely that. Then it registered that it was hoofbeats, bearing down on them fast.

She turned her head, hope dawning on her face. A horse was thundering toward them, and a man leaned low over its neck. Amy recognized both horse and man in the bright moonlight.

"Jesse!"

A look of such dismay crossed Whitaker's face that Amy would have laughed in any other circumstances. He scrambled to his feet and started to run, but the horse was upon them now, and Jesse leaped off the horse onto him. The men tumbled onto the ground and rolled. Quickly Jesse was on top, his fists pummeling Whitaker. Amy scrambled to her feet, impatiently disentangling her torn bodice from her wrists. She stumbled toward the men.

"Jesse! No! Please! Stop! You'll kill him!" The rage drained from her at the sickening sounds of his fists thudding into flesh. She ran to Jesse and tugged at his arm.

He turned and looked up at her. His pale eyes were bright, close to madness, and Amy drew in a quick breath, almost afraid of him. Then reason returned to his face, and he was once again the Jesse she knew well. He rose to his feet, brushing back his hair with his hand. His eyes ran down her body, and then he averted his head.

Amy realized then that she was embarrassingly close to nakedness. Her bodice was completely gone, and her stays, with their laces halfway undone, sagged open, exposing her chest almost to her waist in only the thin covering of her chemise. She looked down at herself. The dark circles of her nipples showed through the thin cloth, plainly visible to Jesse, and as the breeze brushed over her naked shoulders and arms, she shivered and her nipples tightened, turning into hard little buds.

Thoroughly humiliated, Amy crossed her arms over her chest, huddling into herself, as a burning blush spread over her throat and face. Tears sprang into her eyes, and she struggled not to cry in front of Jesse, feeling that somehow that would be the final humiliation. *Whatever must he think of her?* Somehow it seemed the worst of the whole mess that she should be humiliated in front of a man who had for many years been her friend.

"I'm sorry," she mumbled miserably, tears leaking out of her eyes.

"Sorry!" Jesse exclaimed, impulsively going to her and curling his arm protectively around her shoulders. "What in the blue blazes do you have to be sorry for? That scoundrel over there's the one who ought to feel sorry, and, by God, he will by the time I get through with him."

"No!" Amy leaned against Jesse, grateful for his strength and reassurance, her hand clenching in the front of his shirt. "Please, don't do anything else. It'll only make it worse! I've created such a scandal. Oh, what will Mama and Papa say?"

She burst into sobs at the thought, and Jesse held her, murmuring soft words of sympathy and stroking her hair awkwardly. He couldn't help but be aware of Amy's nearly naked chest against his. Her breasts pressed into him, the nipples pointing, and he could feel the warmth of her skin beneath his arms. Her hair, tumbling down from its elegant roll, was sweet-smelling, and soft as satin. He could feel his own body hardening. He was a scoundrel himself to respond to her that way, he thought, when she was in such distress from the lustful pawings of another man.

But he could not help it. Holding Amy in his arms was something he had wanted to do for years, though under normal circumstances he would never have allowed himself to. He knew it was hopeless, but he had loved Amy for years—from the first moment he'd seen her, when he was fifteen and she was thirteen, and she'd come charging in like a wildcat to save him.

Jesse had been an orphan, and had made his way in the world since he was ten years old, when he went to work for a brutal man named Olen Sprague. Amy and her father had come to Sprague to purchase a horse from him, and they had arrived just as Sprague was whipping Jesse for yet another infraction. Amy, horrified, had run in between Sprague's belt and Jesse, and had commanded him to stop, her usual shyness and reserve melted by her anger. Mr. McAlister had wound up offering Jesse a job at his ranch, and they had left, without the horse for Amy, but with Jesse.

He had remained with them ever since, and had become one of Mr. McAlister's most trusted employees, breaking and training cow ponies. He held McAlister responsible for changing his life, and there was nothing he would not do for the man—or for Amy. Amy, he thought, was pure gold, clever and sweet, worth ten of her prettier sister. She was far out of the reach of most men, though, including himself. She was an innocent, a child, and it made him burn with rage to think what Charles Whitaker had tried to do to her—and made him feel ashamed of himself that he could have such a basic masculine response to the feel of her in his arms.

"Come, I'll take you back to the house," he said quickly to cover his discomfort. He looked down at her state of undress. He couldn't take her back this way. Quickly he stripped off his jacket and handed it to her. "Here, put this on."

Gratefully Amy slipped into his jacket. It looked ludicrous, of course, and its buttons started so far down that one could easily see that she had no dress on beneath it, but at least she was decently covered. She clung to Jesse, still sniffling, as he led her to his horse and helped her up onto it. Then he swung up behind her and, cradling Amy in his arms, turned the animal toward home.

Amy snuggled into Jesse's chest, grateful for his strength—and his silence. She was unbearably humiliated, and knew she could not answer any questions or face a lecture right now. Jesse, however, was comforting and uncensorious. He had long been one of the few people to whom she could talk easily; he was quiet and undemanding, the only man she knew besides her father who seemed to pay any attention to her. She often sat out on the corral fence and watched him break a horse, and it was easy to smile at him and chat with him when he took a break for a drink of water. He had even sat, his fingers busy cleaning and polishing the tack and saddles, and listened to her talk about the exciting things she discovered in books, something that even her father usually didn't have time for.

Thank God it was Jesse who had found her in that awful situation, and not someone else.

Tears started to leak from her eyes again as she thought about what had happened, but after a while they subsided. It was so comfortable leaning against Jesse. She began to feel calmer. She had been a fool, she thought wearily. She should have known that no man would truly be interested in her, as Charles Whitaker had pretended to be. She had doubtlessly mired her family in an awful scandal. Just thinking of that man's hands and mouth on her made her shudder. Jesse had rescued her from the horror of what Charles had tried to do, and she was enormously grateful to him, but that would not prevent a scandal. All she could do was pray that somehow she could keep all the people at the party from finding out what had happened.

Jesse was thinking the same thing. He hoped that if he rode quietly into the yard and left his horse by the corral, perhaps he could get Amy in the back door without anyone seeing her. Then he could find Mr. McAlister and explain to him what had happened and trust in him to hush the matter up.

Unfortunately, there was no possibility of entering the ranch house secretly. When they were still some distance from the house, Jesse caught sight of the bobbing lights of lanterns and torches all around the yard and outbuildings and even beyond.

He slowed down, wondering how he could manage to evade the well-meaning searchers, but just then a man's voice cried, "There! Miss Amy! Is that you?"

A rider moved out of the shadow of the trees and trotted toward them. It was Hank Westruther, a neighboring rancher, and the husband of one of the biggest gossips in the county. Grimly Jesse pulled up.

"Mr. Westruther, please, could you—"

He interrupted gleefully. "Miss Amy! It is you!" The man turned, waving his lantern wildly, and shouted in the direction of the house, "I've found her! Here! McAlister!"

He turned his attention back to Jesse and Amy. "You're one of Lawrence's men, aren't you? What happened?"

"Yes, sir, I'm Jesse Tyler."

"Of course. The wizard with horses." Westruther peered at Amy, who kept her face turned into Jesse's chest. "Is she all right? What happened to the girl? Don't seem like that little Amy to go wandering off like this."

"She's fine," Jesse replied, ignoring Westruther's other questions. He touched his heels to his horse's side, urging him into a trot. The best thing he could do now was get Amy into McAlister's hands as quickly as possible.

But as they rode into the yard, people on foot and horseback seemed to converge on them from all directions. The yard was soon full of lights and people, babbling questions. McAlister and his wife came out onto the porch, their faces white and worried, followed by their daughter Corinne, who looked sulky. They stopped when they saw Jesse and Amy and stared at them. Corinne's mouth fell open.

Amy, in an agony of embarrassment, hid her face against Jesse's chest. He had to dismount and help her down, however, and when he did so, she was fully exposed to everyone in her state of deshabille—hair tumbling down to her shoulders and a man's coat over her almost bare chest.

Amy wrapped Jesse's jacket tightly around her and ducked her head. The crowd pressed in on her from all sides, and she whirled back to Jesse. "Jesse..."

"Stand back," he ordered the people around them, then swept Amy up into his arms to carry her up the steps to her parents.

"Oh, Amy!" Mrs. McAlister reached out her hand to her daughter's head. "Are you all right, honey?"

"Take her into the back parlor, Jesse," her father ordered gruffly. Mrs. McAlister followed Jesse, leaving her husband to reassure all the guests, and Corinne trotted behind her, her face alight with curiosity.

"What happened?" Corinne asked breathlessly. "Amy, what did you do?"

"Is she hurt?" Mrs. McAlister's forehead was knotted with worry. "Corinne, honey, stop asking questions and go get a wet cloth for your sister."

Corinne grimaced, but turned and went off to the kitchen. Mrs. McAlister gripped Jesse's arm, pulling him to a stop. "What happened, Jesse? Where's that Whitaker fellow? Pat Spielman said they left the house together. Did he—"

"*Nothing* happened," Jesse stated firmly. "I found them and I took care of the son—of Whitaker. I don't think he really hurt her, only scared her."

"Oh, thank God."

"I'm all right," Amy said, turning her head and looking at her mother for the first time. "I'm so sorry, Mama."

Unlike Jesse, Mrs. McAlister was not at all surprised at her daughter's apology, and she understood very well why she offered it. Tears began to pour afresh from Mrs. McAlister's eyes. "Oh, Amy! What are we going to do?"

Jesse carried Amy into the parlor and carefully set her on the sofa. Amy took his hand, reluctant to let him go. His quiet strength had been so reassuring.

"Thank you," she whispered.

"No need to thank me." He squeezed her hand.

Corinne hurried into the room, carrying a wet cloth, and handed it to her mother, who began to bathe Amy's face. She stepped back, looking down at her sister. "Everybody's been running around like chickens with their heads cut off," she announced, looking rather put out.

"I'm sorry," Amy murmured again.

Mr. McAlister came into the room and shut the door firmly behind him, turning the key in the lock. "Damned busybodies," he growled. "I wouldn't put it past that Mrs. Bowen to come bustling in here on some excuse or other." He strode over to the sofa and shook Jesse's hand firmly. "Thank you, Jesse. I could never repay you for what you've done."

Jesse looked embarrassed and shook his head. "There's no need to thank me, sir. Anyone would have done the same. When I saw Whitaker take her off like that, I figured he was up to no good. I'm just sorry I didn't get after them any quicker. I had to go back and saddle my horse. I hadn't figured on him having a horse and buggy hidden."

"You were wonderful, Jesse," Amy told him, her eyes glowing. She turned to her father. "Papa, you should have seen him! He knocked that—that *man* right to the ground, and—"

"Yes, dear," Lawrence McAlister said, interrupting her. "I'm sure Jesse did what was necessary and proper. But now I want you to tell me what happened. *Exactly* what happened."

Amy blushed and swallowed, seeming to search for the right words to say. Finally she began to talk, in a hurried, trembling voice. Jesse edged toward the door. He didn't want to be a party to such an intimate family scene. But he couldn't escape unnoticed; Mr. McAlister had locked the door and pocketed the key. He retreated to a corner of the room and leaned against the wall, crossing his arms and doing his best to appear invisible.

Amy's voice faltered as she told of agreeing to go for a ride with Charles Whitaker, and then dropped almost to a whisper as she described how he had proposed to her, then attacked her. Corinne gasped, and her eyes grew huge as she stared at her sister. Mrs. McAlister moaned and leaned back in her chair, as if the last ounce of strength had been drained from her.

"What are we to do now?" Sylvia McAlister wailed. "Amy's reputation is ruined! Utterly ruined!"

"But, truly, he didn't do anything to me," Amy protested weakly. "Except for a few bruises. He didn't...well, violate me."

"Hush!" Mrs. McAlister cried. "Don't even say such a thing!" She began to cry, her hands going up to her face. "You're ruined anyway. It's almost two o'clock in the morning! To have been out at that hour with a man—and to come home looking like that, with Jesse carrying you on his horse! Well, anyone could guess what happened. Except that they'll all presume it was even worse. I don't know what we're going to do."

"Amy, how could you!" Corinne added. "What if people stop inviting us to parties? What if—"

"Well, there's nothing for it. Amy has to marry the fellow," Mr. McAlister announced heavily. "Whitaker's seen her in an indecent state of dress, he's ruined her name, he's...he's touched her in a lewd way."

Jesse stirred uneasily. *His sweet little Amy couldn't be made to marry that villain!* The whole idea was repulsive. His fists clenched as he remembered seeing the man holding Amy down on the ground, his hands moving over her.

Amy colored to the roots of her hair at the disgust on her father's face, but her agitation was greater than her embarrassment, and she leaped to her feet, her fists clenching. "No! I could not marry that man! I won't!"

"You have to," her father said wearily. "I don't like it, either. He's a blackguard. But the only thing that can save your reputation is for you to marry, and at once. Why, half the county was in the yard and saw you ride in. Hell's bells, Amy, it's you I'm thinking of. You'll be snubbed. People will gossip about you. You won't have a chance of marrying."

"I didn't, anyway," Amy replied, fighting back her panic.

"*None* of us will be able to hold up our heads," her mother went on tearfully. "What happened was bad enough, but if you don't get married, then everyone will say you're outright brazen."

"But I don't want to marry him!"

"You should have thought of that before you went out riding with Charles Whitaker at eleven o'clock at night!" Mrs. McAlister retorted. Now that she knew her daughter was safe, her former worry was rapidly turning into anger.

"I can't! I can't marry him!" Amy wailed. "Papa, you don't understand. He did it so this very thing would happen. He as good as told me so. He was trying to...to force you to make me marry him."

"Well, he was right," Mr. McAlister said grimly. "He knew that the only thing that could bring you out of this disgrace would be an immediate marriage. I know he's a cad. That's obvious. But if I pay him something, no doubt he'll be willing to give you his name and then disappear. Hopefully you won't have to be bothered by his presence."

Amy stared at her father. "But then I'll be married and have no husband!" It seemed a worse fate than being a spinster or a widow or even an outcast: to be tied legally to a man she despised, with no hope of ever finding love. It would be a kind of living death. "I can't. Please, Papa, don't ask me to do that! I'll do anything else. I'll go away somewhere, so that you all won't have to bear the stigma of what I've done. Or... or..."

Her voice trailed off miserably. She could think of nothing else she could do. No other man would want to marry her, now or ever. She would be regarded as Charles Whitaker's leavings. Her family would bear the burden of the awful scandal that had been caused by her own thoughtlessness. It was only right that she should be punished, not they. But Amy quailed at the thought of the price she would have to pay to make up for her folly. Whatever infatuation she had felt for Charles Whitaker had fled as soon as he began to kiss her. She hated and feared him, and the thought of marrying him made her feel ill.

But how else could she get out of this mess she had created? She glanced up at her father's stern countenance. He was a good man, but he abhorred the idea of any sort of blot on his family's name. He was a man who lived by a strict code of honor, and he expected everyone else to follow that code, no matter what sacrifices were involved. For once, Amy knew that she could expect no leniency from him.

She let out a long, shuddering sigh. She would have to marry Whitaker. She drew a breath to speak.

Suddenly Jesse shoved away from the wall, blurting out, "Then marry me."

Chapter Three

There was a moment of stunned silence in the room. Everyone turned to stare at Jesse. Amy went white, then pink, and dropped her face into her hands.

"Are you serious?" Lawrence McAlister studied Jesse, frowning.

"Yes, sir." Jesse came toward him. "You know I wouldn't normally have asked. I'm not nearly good enough for Amy."

"Don't say that!" Amy stuck in fiercely, raising her face from her hands, eyes blazing. "You're the best man in the world!"

Jesse cast her a faint smile. "I'm glad you think so, ma'am. But your father knows as well as I do that I'm not the sort of man you should be marrying." He turned and fixed Mr. McAlister with a serious gaze. "But you can't deny that I'm a hell of a lot better than that blackguard Whitaker. Sir, you can't be easy at the thought of giving Amy to him."

"No, of course I'm not. But, Jesse, there's no reason why you should sacrifice—"

Jesse's face tightened, and he said shortly, "It's no sacrifice!"

"Well, of course, I didn't mean that marrying Amy would—" McAlister bumbled to a stop, reddening. "What I meant was, you're young, and you have your whole life in front of you. You'd be giving up the chance to find and marry a woman you love someday. There's no reason for you to do that. Why, you saved Amy!"

"I know. But the same applies to me as to Whitaker. I saw her with her dress torn off. I—I touched her." His color heightened a little as he remembered the wayward reaction of his body to touching her, and he hoped her father wouldn't guess how lascivious his own response had been. "I held her in my arms all the way back to the house. The only difference is that I didn't try to harm her."

"No. Of course not." McAlister was still somewhat stunned by Jesse's offer, but he couldn't help but feel relief. He loved his daughter, and he hated to think of her marrying a man like Whitaker. She would be safe with Jesse. He would respect her and care for her, even if he did not love her. Jesse knew Amy well, and would not be impatient with her or scornful of her odd, dreamy, bookish ways.

He glanced toward his wife, who was still staring at Jesse, openmouthed, then toward his daughter. Amy was gazing at Jesse, her face troubled. "Well, Amy, what do you say?"

She turned to him, frowning. "But, Papa...it wouldn't be fair. Jesse, it wouldn't be right!"

Jesse flushed at her words. "I know it's not. I told you that. But I don't see what else to do."

"I don't mean that nonsense about you not being good enough to marry me," Amy retorted scornfully. "I mean, it wouldn't be fair to you. *You* haven't done anything wrong. I was the one who...who was so stupid and wicked.

And there's no reason why you should be punished because of what I did!''

Jesse gazed back at Amy levelly. "Sometimes you *are* foolish. Why do you insist on saying that marrying you would be punishment? Any man would be honored to be your husband.''

She averted her face. "No. That's not true. I'm in disgrace. And that's not all—I'm difficult to live with. Ask anyone in my family." She gestured vaguely toward the others. "They can tell you. Half the time I don't pay attention, I've always got my nose stuck in a book, I'm not much of a housekeeper, and I don't care about cooking or clothes or...oh, all kinds of things.''

Jesse grinned. "Well, now, that is too bad, 'cause I don't care much for those things, either. We just might starve.''

Amy couldn't keep from smiling at his words, and she cast him a glance of amusement. "You think you're joking." She stood up and faced him, setting her face into stern lines. "The truth is, I'm not...I'm not like other people.''

"Now, Amy..." protested her father with a groan.

"No, it's true, Papa, and you know it, however much you love me." She looked Jesse straight in the eye. "I'm a bookworm. I read all the time. I read poetry and novels and...and everything I can. And that's not all. I write things, too...poems and stories..." she said with the melancholy of one confessing to murder. "I can put my hair up in only one style, and my favorite dress is three years old, and I wear it because it's comfortable, not because it's pretty.''

Jesse's lips twitched. "You may not believe me this, ma'am, but I count that an advantage. I don't know what I'd do with a wife who wanted new clothes all the time.''

"Jesse! Stop being obtuse. You know that's not the worst of it. That's just what makes daily life with me so uncomfortable. After tonight, my reputation is in shreds. You can't want a wife whom everyone in the county has branded a slut!"

Jesse's face hardened. "No one would call you such a thing," he retorted. "I'd like to see anyone try!"

"Well, they might not in your presence," Amy admitted candidly. "But they'd say so behind your back. People would—would ridicule you. They'd say that you had to marry me, that Papa made you. That he bought me a husband because I was such a disgrace. I would ruin your name just as surely as I've ruined mine."

"That's not true, dear," Mrs. McAlister answered, feeling on firm ground when it came to social problems. "Not if you married Mr. Tyler. Now, if you remained unmarried, it's true that it would cast a shadow over you all your life, but if you marry, why, it'll all blow over in a few months. Before you know it, everyone will have completely forgotten about it. Or at least they'll stop talking about it."

"Mama, you don't understand." Amy shot her mother a dark glance. "I can't bear for Jesse to be forced into marrying me to save my name. And for Jesse's name to be tarred with the same brush because he married me!"

"I'm not being forced," Jesse put in quietly. He looked over at Amy's father. "Sir, could I talk to Amy alone just for a moment?"

McAlister hesitated. It wouldn't be proper, of course, but, after what had happened already tonight, it seemed a minor breach of society's rules. "Well, all right, I suppose so, but only for a few minutes."

He took his wife's arm and led her out of the room, Corinne trailing reluctantly after them, and pulled the door almost completely shut. Jesse walked over to Amy and took her hand.

"Let's sit down."

Amy nodded, and they sat down side by side on the sofa. Jesse was still holding her hand. It felt odd, she thought, to have a man's hand around hers. Jesse's hand was strong and roughened by calluses, and it completely covered hers. She thought about Jesse and the way he handled the horses, his hands patient and gentle yet strong. It made her feel warm and safe to have his hand on hers, and she remembered how pleasant it had been to lean her head against his chest.

"It could never be a burden to marry you," Jesse told her. "It would be a privilege. An honor. You must believe that. You and your father have done so much for me. You took me away from Sprague and showed me how good and kind people can be. Before that I had given up hoping, given up believing that things could be any better. Before I knew you I was nothing.... I had nothing."

"That's not true. You're very talented. Papa has said so often. Why, remember how that man from San Antonio tried to hire you away from Papa?"

Jesse shrugged. "I'm good with horses. But that's not what I'm talking about. Nobody ever considered me as a person before. But you and your pa took me in and...and were good to me. Ah, hell, ma'am, I'm no good at saying things!"

"I understand what you're saying," Amy said reflectively. "You want to marry me so you can repay your debt to Papa and me."

Jesse's mouth tightened. "You persist in looking at everything the worst possible way. I want to marry you," he said obstinately. "Why can't you just accept that?"

Amy cast a sideways glance at him, a smile touching the corners of her mouth. "Don't you agree that this desire came upon you rather suddenly?"

He couldn't tell Amy that he wanted to marry her because he loved her, that he had loved her for years. It would only make her feel bad and guilty. To Amy he was merely one of the workers, someone to whom she was kind, as she was to everyone. It was impossible that she would have any interest in him. She was too smart and educated for an ignorant cowpoke like himself. She had spent her life among fine things and people of good manners. And he was a man who had grown up hardscrabble, fighting for everything he got.

Besides, she was in love with another man. She was so infatuated with Charles Whitaker, in fact, that she had thrown caution to the winds and gone out driving with him late at night. Jesse was sure that it had hurt Amy terribly to discover that Whitaker was using her for his own ends, that he had not loved her as she had loved him and was not the sterling man she thought he was, but a fortune hunter who was willing to do anything to gain a rich wife. For that reason, she had been repelled by the idea of having to marry Whitaker, but Jesse didn't fool himself that her refusal meant she didn't still love Whitaker.

Jesse was an astute young man, however, and he'd been around Amy long enough to have some idea how to get around her. So he sighed now and stood up, moving away from her.

"All right. I won't press you. I know I'm not a proper husband for you. I was presumptuous to even ask you. It'd be absurd for a lady like you to be married to me."

"Jesse! That's not the reason at all!" Amy protested, as he had known she would, her face filled with dismay. "It's not because I'm a 'lady,' or whatever strange notion you've gotten into your head.''

"It's the truth. Everyone would say we wouldn't suit. They'd talk about how you had 'married beneath you,' and you shouldn't have to put up with that. I wouldn't even have suggested it if it hadn't been for the circumstances. I thought maybe marriage to me would be preferable to the scandal and all. But likely you'll live that down after a while. No one could seriously believe you've done anything wicked. Whereas if you married me, you'd have to put up with that inequity all your life.''

"How can you talk such nonsense?'' Amy said fuming, her cheeks pink with indignation. "Do you really believe I'm that shallow, that snobbish?''

"You know I don't think anything bad of you. I just told you I don't blame you for not wanting to marry me.''

"Jesse!'' Amy frowned in frustration. "You're turning my words all around. It's not that I don't want to marry you. I don't want to marry anyone!''

"I know that, ma'am. The only thing is, you really sort of have to, don't you, or else you and your family are going to be dragged through the dirt? I know you don't want that.''

Amy looked anguished. "No, I don't. It would be so awful for Corinne and Mama. Papa, too, though he'd try hard to bear up under it. But, Jesse, I can't ask you to make that sacrifice for my family!''

"I keep telling you, it's not a sacrifice. It's what I want to do. It's the only chance I've ever been given to help you and your father. Besides, it'd be my chance to have a family. I've never had that.''

Amy hesitated, looking at him uncertainly. Everything Jesse said made sense. The thought of marriage was rather frightening, but it would be less so with Jesse than with anyone else she could think of. But she could not help feeling guilty at the thought of Jesse marrying her in order to save her reputation. It seemed so unfair to him!

Seeing her hesitation, Jesse went on, "I wouldn't push you, if that's what you're worrying about. I mean, I wouldn't presume to, well, exercise my—my marital rights."

He looked highly uncomfortable, and Amy blushed scarlet at his words. She wasn't sure exactly what marital rights were, but it was something women talked about in hushed tones, which meant it was secret and rather scandalous.

"I know I shouldn't say anything like this to a lady, but, well, I don't know how else to reassure you, if that's what you're worried about. I would never try to force you like Whitaker did, just because we're married. I'd, well . . . I mean, I know you don't love me, and you'd feel awkward." He stumbled to a halt, unnerved by Amy's beet red face and the anguish of embarrassment in her eyes.

"Thank you," Amy said softly. She might not know exactly what he was talking about, but she would certainly be grateful not to be subjected to the kind of pawing and kissing that Charles Whitaker had done to her—not that she could really imagine Jesse acting that way, anyway. "I— Well, all right, I will marry you. I mean, if you're still sure that that's what you want."

"Yes, ma'am." He smiled at her, suddenly looking shy. "I'm positive."

"Well. Then, I—I guess we better tell Mama and Papa."

She went to the door and looked out into the hall. Her parents and sister were huddled together at the foot of the stairs, and they turned at the sound of the parlor door opening and hurried back into the parlor. Mr. and Mrs. McAlister were obviously relieved to hear that Amy had accepted Jesse's offer, and they fell immediately to making plans.

"It will have to be soon, I'm afraid," Sylvia McAlister mused. "I'd like to wait, just to prove to everyone that she doesn't have to...but that would keep the gossip alive that much longer. Better to get it over with, and then everyone will begin to forget."

"You're right," her husband agreed. "Can you manage it in a week or two?"

"Yes. We'll keep it small. Just the family."

Amy retreated from the group, feeling lonely and cold—not at all the way a bride should feel. And her wedding wouldn't resemble the romantic occasion she had dreamed of. She could feel tears welling up inside her, and she had to struggle to hold them back. Amy turned away. She wished she could run away, wished she did not have to face all this.

But she could not do that, of course. She had already brought too much disgrace upon the family. She would simply have to endure it.

Amy glanced back over her shoulder at Jesse. He was standing, listening to her father talk. As she looked at him, he suddenly seemed a stranger to her. She did not really know him, and yet before long she would be living with him, married to him for life! It was a disturbing thought, and she turned quickly and left the room.

She started toward the stairs and the peace and safety of her own room, but before she reached the bottom stair, Corinne came after her and grabbed her by the arm and pulled her back around.

"What did you think you were doing?" she asked furiously. "Now you've ruined everything!"

"I know." Tears welled up in Amy's eyes. "I'm sorry." She and Corinne were not the good friends that some sisters were, but she hated to have her angry at her.

"People will talk about me," Corinne went on, fueled by her favorite topic—herself. "They'll wonder if I'm loose like my sister."

"Corinne!" Amy cried, stung. "I'm not! You know I'm not!"

Corinne made a dismissive gesture. "Of course not," she said disgustedly. "You would never do anything wrong. But that's what people will say. How could you have been so stupid? Did you actually believe that Charles was interested in you?"

"I—I couldn't quite believe it," Amy admitted. "But he *seemed* to be."

"Oh, for heaven's sake! I knew right away what he was. That's why I turned him down. It was me he wanted, you know. He was always hanging around. He asked me twice to marry him, but I turned him down. That's the only reason he started dangling after you."

Amy looked down at the floor, struggling not to burst into tears. Corinne was right, of course; she should have known that a man could not possibly be interested in her, especially not with a beauty like her sister around. She had been foolish to let Charles turn her head, and now her whole family would pay for her misdeed. Even though she could contain the scandal by marrying Jesse, there would still be whispers.

And Jesse would pay most of all. It seemed awful that he, innocent of any wrongdoing, should have to suffer for her foolishness. But how else could she save her family? She told herself that she would not have agreed to his proposal just to save herself the shame and scandal. She would have endured it, knowing that she deserved it. She was marrying Jesse for Mama's and Papa's sake. And Corinne's, too. Corinne had been blameless and, for once, far wiser than Amy had.

"I know," Amy admitted, her voice barely a whisper. "I was so silly and wrong. I'm sorry. Oh, I wish I could go back and do it all over. Poor Jesse!"

"Poor Jesse?" Corinne repeated scornfully. "I wouldn't waste my time feeling sorry for him. He gets to marry the rancher's daughter! He's gaining wealth and position. Why, I bet Papa even gives him some land for you all to live on. He'll make quite a profit off the deal."

Amy's head snapped up, and she glared at Corinne. "Jesse would never do it for that!" she protested fiercely.

Corinne's eyes widened with surprise at her meek sister's transformation, and she took a step backward.

"He did it to be kind, not for any thought of profit," Amy went on. "He is giving up his whole life, his chance at ever loving someone, just to save me! Just to help our family! Now, you take back what you said about him!"

"All right, all right." Corinne turned her hands out, palm up, in an exculpatory gesture, though her voice was still laced with sarcasm. "I'm sure Jesse has done no wrong."

"Well, he hasn't!" Amy thrust her chin out defiantly, and she gave her sister a look of warning. "And I don't want to hear anyone around here saying another bad word about him."

With that, Amy turned and stalked up the stairs, leaving Corinne staring after her in amazement.

Chapter Four

The next two weeks went by in a whirlwind of activity. Amy did not realize it, but much of the work was orchestrated by her mother with the primary purpose of keeping Amy's mind off the scandal and the approaching nuptials. Mrs. McAlister took her youngest sister's wedding dress, only seven years old, down from the attic and tailored it to fit Amy's smaller frame. She also bought two lovely bolts of material from the mercantile store in town and made Amy new dresses, declaring that she could not send her off to her husband looking like a ragamuffin.

She set the girls to washing the linens in Amy's hope chest, making sure that all of them were as fresh and neat as the day they had sewn them. When they weren't busy sewing, they were cooking or cleaning the house, for even though it was to be a small wedding, attended only by family, there would be plenty of guests, since Sylvia McAlister had been born here and had dozens of aunts, uncles and cousins. Also, a few very close friends, like the Boudreaux family, would be invited, and, of course, all the ranch hands. It added up to quite a few people, and there would be a celebration afterward. Sylvia McAlister was not about to send her elder daughter off without any ceremony, no matter what the haste. Therefore, the house must be spotless and the larder well stocked.

As Corinne had predicted, Amy's father had decided to give the young couple a piece of land as a wedding present. It was not large, but it was plenty for Jesse to break and train wild horses and sell them, which was what he wanted to do. The land had an old line shack on it at present, and Jesse and a couple of the other hands were staying there until the wedding, getting the house in suitable shape. So Amy did not see her future husband until the wedding.

She thought many times about what her marriage would be like, and was nervous, scared and excited by turns. She wondered about the wedding night, and what it was exactly that Jesse had promised not to demand of her. *Was it the same thing that happened when animals mated?* Amy couldn't quite imagine how it would work, and it made her blush to think of it.

Sylvia tried to talk to her about her marital obligations once, but she stumbled and blushed and tiptoed around the subject so much that Amy could make little sense out of it—although she assured her quickly that she understood, just to put her mother out of her misery.

Amy knew that Jesse would keep his promise, and that she did not need to be nervous or shy, but she thought that surely he would *someday* expect her to be a real wife to him. He was probably giving her time to get adjusted to the idea, to him...unless, of course, he found her so unattractive that the thought of coupling with her repelled him. Perhaps that was why he had been so quick to promise not to push her sexually. Saddened by that thought, Amy found herself hoping that he didn't really intend to keep his promise forever.

Amy might not know anything about her "marital duties," but she knew well enough that she did not want to spend the rest of her life being a sham of a bride—a wife in name only—with a husband who tolerated her just because he had to pay back a debt to her father.

Such thoughts kept her worried and on edge until the day of the wedding. She had seen Jesse only once since their wedding was announced, and that had been the day before the wedding, when he had returned from the line shack he was rebuilding for them. He had come up to see her that evening, but both of them had been awkward and had little to say to one another. Jesse had seemed like a stranger to Amy, and her stomach had knotted more tightly than ever.

The wedding ceremony was late morning the next day. Amy's mother and sister helped her into her aunt's wedding dress, and Sylvia arranged her hair into a thick roll, with little tendrils of hair escaping and curling around her face. Then she stepped back and smiled into the mirror at her daughter's image.

"You look beautiful," Sylvia assured her. "Just as a bride should. Doesn't she, Corinne?"

"Yes," Corinne responded grudgingly.

Amy looked at herself in the mirror. She thought that she did, in fact, look rather good today. So often the fussy frills and bows of fashionable dresses overwhelmed her petite figure, but the elegant simplicity of this dress, a few years out of fashion, suited her, and its creamy yellow color warmed her pale skin. Her mother's pearls, lent for the occasion, glimmered at her ears and throat, as smoothly beautiful as the satin of the dress. Her cheeks were faintly flushed, and her big brown eyes were bright with excitement. She smiled back at her image. *Would*

Jesse look at her and find her beautiful? Suddenly she wanted that more than anything in the world.

Corinne and Mrs. McAlister left Amy's bedroom and swept down the staircase. Amy followed them, alone, a moment later. As she neared the bottom, Amy drew in her breath sharply. The parlor was filled with people, and at the sound of her footsteps they all turned to look at her. Amy was not used to being the center of attention, and her stomach turned to ice. She faltered on the stairs and reached out to grasp the banister to steady herself. She went down the last few steps, feeling more and more nervous with each movement.

How could there be this many people here? Her nerves multiplied the number until the waiting crowd seemed like a vast blur of unfamiliar faces. Then her eyes fell on Jesse, standing at the front of the parlor with the minister from their church. He was smiling at her, and her nerves settled a trifle. She started walking toward him. As long as she concentrated on Jesse and ignored the staring faces around her, she was all right. She didn't even look over to where her mother and father sat, suddenly afraid that looking at them would make her start to shake or, worse, to cry.

She reached the front, and Jesse took her hand. Her hands were freezing, and she knew he must feel that through her lace mitts. He squeezed her hand reassuringly, and she was grateful for the warmth and strength that seemed to course through his hand into hers. She looked up at him, and he smiled down at her, giving her a wink that somehow relaxed her.

The minister began the ceremony. Jesse's replies were strong and sure. Amy had been afraid that she would stumble over her words or forget what she was saying, but she managed to get everything out, even if it was in a rather soft voice.

Then, suddenly, it was over. The minister was smiling at her, and Jesse turned and bent to give her a brief kiss. His lips barely brushed hers, but she could feel his breath against her skin, the warmth of his flesh, and it was a strange sensation—but not unpleasant. It reminded her of the way it felt when she ran her horse—a little scary, but exciting, too.

They turned away, and Amy's parents came up to them immediately, shaking Jesse's hand and hugging her. Tears sparkled in Mrs. McAlister's eyes, and she squeezed Amy to her tightly before she stepped back to let her husband and Corinne have their turns. After that, there were all the relatives to greet, as well as the ranch hands, but for once Amy felt too relieved to dislike the crush of people.

Afterward, they ate at trestle tables set up in the side yard, for the day was sunny and mild, despite the fact that it was almost November. Of course, the men got into games of skill, as they usually did, while the women cleaned up after the meal. The men laughingly excluded Jesse from the riding competitions, such as racing or leaning down out of the saddle to swoop up an object from the ground, saying that as groom he wasn't allowed to enter. Jesse protested, saying that they were cutting him out only because they knew he would win. But his protests were faint, and he seemed quite happy to sit beside Amy on the porch with the older relatives and watch the sport.

Later in the afternoon, when the games finally wound down and the children had been put down for naps upstairs, Uncle Tyrah got out his fiddle and struck up a tune, accompanied by another man, who pulled an harmonica from his back pocket.

"First the bridal couple has to dance!" Amy's Great-aunt Hope called out as people began to gather around.

"Well, I reckon we'd better oblige," Jesse said, holding out his hand to Amy and leading her into the center of the yard, where a circle had formed to watch the bridal couple.

Amy followed him, picking up the train of her skirt and looping it over her arm. Her stomach was dancing with nerves, and she hoped she wouldn't stumble or do anything to disgrace herself. "I—I don't dance very well," she said in a stifled voice, keeping her eyes down.

Jesse reached out and put his hand on her waist, taking her other hand in his. "You'll do fine."

Amy looked up into Jesse's face, warmed by his reassuring words. *How handsome he was!* She wondered why she had never noticed before. But, no, she realized, he wasn't handsome, exactly. His hair was a little too long and shaggy, and his features were a trifle too rough. He looked like a man who had seen more of life than anyone should have had to at his age, and yet... there was a certain sensitivity to his wide mouth, a kind of wary vulnerability in his eyes that refuted the wildness. He looked, not handsome, but... intriguing. Desirable.

At that thought, Amy glanced quickly away. The music started, and they began to dance. Jesse danced competently, and he kept a firm grasp on Amy's waist, guiding her without hesitation. Amy found that it was easy to follow his lead, and she looked up at him again and smiled.

He grinned back at her triumphantly, and his face lit up, his eyes taking on a twinkle and suddenly very green. He looked different—younger and even a little mischievous, a lurking charm overwhelming his usual tight, tough control.

A funny fluttering started inside Amy. She was very aware of her hand in his, his callused palm rough against her skin. His other hand felt very large upon her side, the fingers curling around onto her back. She could feel their heat even through the cloth of her dress. It was curiously exciting.

This man seemed like a different Jesse from the one she had known for five years. He was no longer just one of her father's employees whom she liked, but one of those vaguely frightening creatures known as eligible males, the sort of person with whom she was expected to talk and dance and around whom she was tongue-tied and stumbling. She could feel the smooth power of his muscles as he guided her around the outdoor dance floor, the leashed force of the male being, and the thought made her shiver. She wondered if Jesse had any idea of the effect he was having on her. Amy hoped not; she imagined that he would be disappointed in her if he learned that only two weeks after he'd found her in a compromising situation with one man, she was feeling these strange stirrings about another man.

Amy wondered if she was abnormal. She had heard other girls talk of love, of feeling faint or dazzled or breathless when this man or that talked to them or took their hand for a dance, but she had never heard any of them mention the odd, faintly sizzling sensations that she was experiencing right now. No one spoke of being supremely aware of a man's body close to her own, of the sinew and muscle that lay beneath the firm flesh, or of the heat of the skin. She had never heard anyone describe the hot, melting feeling growing in the pit of her stomach. And it seemed to her decidedly unladylike to be imagining Jesse's hand gliding down her back, where it now rested, and over her hips and legs.

Amy blushed at her own thoughts. *Did the things she was thinking about have anything to do with the "marital duties" Jesse had spoken of?* She suspected that they did, and she suspected, further, that Jesse would be shocked to know what she was thinking. He believed her to be pure and innocent, the sort of woman who would recoil from bedding a man she did not love. Yet here she was thinking about doing that very thing, and feeling not repulsed but excited. She knew that she must not let him know what she was thinking. When the dance ended, Jesse's arms relaxed and fell away from her slowly. Amy murmured, "Thank you," and looked up into Jesse's face. He was not smiling, and there was an odd glint in his eyes. Amy wasn't sure what it meant, but her heart began to beat a little faster.

"Thank *you*." Jesse's voice came out a trifle hoarse, and he had to clear his throat. His eyes moved over her face, and Amy wondered what he was thinking.

As the next song started, other couples broke from the circle around them and began to dance. Jesse raised his eyebrows questioningly, and Amy nodded. He took her in his arms again, and they began to waltz. Amy felt as if her feet were floating across the ground.

They danced several more dances, but then her mother pulled her away, reminding her that they'd better be on their way before it grew dark. Her father's buggy was brought up from the barn. Amy's trunk and a carpetbag were strapped to the back. The rest of their things, including furniture, had been taken over to their new home in a wagon the day before, as had their riding horses.

There was no getting away without a shivaree, a wedding custom in which the bridal couple were sent off with a maximum of noise. A couple of boys set off firecrackers, and everyone shouted out good wishes and jests, many of them bordering on the bawdy. Amy suspected that they got off lightly because she was the daughter of most of the men's boss, although sometimes the jests were enough to make women cover their ears. Cal Boudreaux's son, Joe, and two of her cousins mounted their horses and rode madly around the buggy and across the yard, firing their guns in the air and letting out rebel yells. Jesse grinned and slapped the reins across the horses' backs, letting them have their heads. Amy twisted around in her seat and looked back. Her parents and Corinne stood on the steps in front of the porch, waving.

Tears filled Amy's eyes, and an ache bloomed in her chest. She was leaving her family forever; after this, she would return only as a visitor. She waved and blew them a kiss, continuing to wave until the figures had receded into the distance and she could no longer make out anything but the shape of the house. At that point their last two pursuers pulled up and swept their hats from their heads, waving goodbye. Amy and Jesse tossed them a last salute, and Amy turned back around to face the fast-approaching sunset. Her throat felt tight with unshed tears, and a confusion of emotions tumbled inside her. She glanced over at Jesse, and he smiled at her.

Amy smiled back tremulously. *She was a married woman now, and this man was her husband.*

Chapter Five

It was almost twilight when Jesse and Amy reached their new home. The sun was slipping below the horizon, and the area was bathed in a golden glow. As they approached the house, Amy, who had seen the place several times in the past, looked at it with new interest. She leaned forward, and as they drew closer, she sucked in her breath sharply.

"Why, Jesse! It looks so...so different!"

He smiled, casting her an uncertain glance. "Do you like it?"

"Oh, yes! It's wonderful." Jesse had obviously replaced the bad boards and painted the whole thing a crisp, clean white. He had even added dark green shutters to the windows.

"I want to put on a porch in front, too," he told her, "but I didn't have time. I'll get it done before next spring, though. That way we can sit out and look at the wildflowers over there. There's a pastureful of them every spring."

"And watch the fireflies in the evening," Amy added, her lips curving upward into a smile.

"Sure."

"I can plant flowers in front of the porch. Mama'll give me cuttings from her rosebushes."

They smiled at each other in perfect agreement, the sweet pride of ownership swelling in their breasts. Though Amy had grown up in comfort, she had never really had anything of her own except for her books, and Jesse had had less than that, not even a true home. This small house with the new corral beside it was a treasure to them.

They pulled up in front of the house, and Jesse leaped down to help Amy out of the buggy. She looked at the house, then back at him. Jesse smiled at her, relieved that she liked the place. He'd worked like a demon on it the past two weeks, and he'd driven the other two men with him until they regretted agreeing to help him. He was proud of the results and already filled with love for his first home, but he had been afraid that Amy, used to the large main house of the ranch, would not like it. He had known that she would be too kind to say anything bad, yet had worried that her face would fall in disappointment. But even a sweet disposition such as Amy's would not account for the clear joy that he had read in her unguarded face as she looked at their home.

"Come on, I want to see what it's like inside," Amy said, starting forward.

"No, wait. It's bad luck." Jesse stopped her and bent to sweep her up in his arms. "I have to carry you across, or we'll have bad luck."

Amy giggled. It was strange to be held like this by a man, to have his arms around her at the knee and chest, to feel his hand there, just below her breast, and his own chest so firm and warm against her other side. She could see straight into Jesse's face. His eyes looked so green this close, and she was fascinated by the texture of his tanned skin, and the blending of blond and brown strands in his hair.

He felt her gaze and turned his head to look into her eyes. He went still, and for a moment they remained motionless, gazing at each other, aware of nothing except how close they were and every place that their bodies touched. Amy felt suddenly hot and breathless, and she wanted to move her hand from its place on Jesse's shoulder and weave her fingers into his hair. Her eyes went to his mouth, and she wondered what it would feel like if he kissed her— really kissed her, not like the respectable peck that he had placed on her lips at the end of the wedding ceremony.

Then Jesse moved, breaking their trance, and carried her through the front door. He set her down, and Amy looked around delightedly. No one would have recognized this for the line shack it had once been. It was still only one big room, of course, kitchen, bedroom and parlor all in one, but it had been transformed with loving care. The walls had been sanded and painted, and the floor, which had been merely packed earth, was now laid with pine planks, carefully varnished. There were only a few pieces of furniture, and though it was not new, it had been hand-picked by Amy from the things in the McAlister attic. The big brass bed and the lyre-backed oaken washstand had been her grandmother's. The hutch and table in the kitchen area were the ones they had used when she was a child, replaced years ago by more expensive ones her mother had ordered from San Antonio. The braided rug in front of the couch came from Amy's own bedroom at home; her grandmother had given it to her when she turned sixteen. She loved everything in the room, and it made the house seem immediately her home.

"Oh, Jesse!" she breathed, her eyes shining as she turned slowly, taking it all in. "It's beautiful. It's perfect."

Jesse grinned. "You really think so?"

"Oh, yes!"

"I didn't have time to get everything done, of course, but I can get to the rest of it this winter. I thought that I could build shelves for your books along that wall behind the couch."

"Really?" Amy turned big eyes brimming with gratitude and happiness toward him. "Jesse, you are so sweet. How could I ever thank you?"

"You don't need to thank me, ma'am." He looked embarrassed. "You're my wife now. Why wouldn't I try to make you comfortable here?"

"Since I'm your wife now," Amy told him teasingly, "you might stop calling me ma'am."

"I know. I'm sorry. It slipped out. It seems so odd.... It'll take me a little while to get used to it."

"Me, too," Amy admitted. She turned back to survey the room once more, and was filled with housewifely pride and a sudden nesting instinct. "I'll need to make curtains for the windows. That's all it's lacking. And maybe braid a rug for beside the bed."

She colored faintly and turned away. Abruptly the free-and-easy camaraderie between them, the shared happiness, was gone. Amy could have kicked herself for mentioning the word *bed*.

"I, uh...I better unharness the horses and turn them out in the pasture," Jesse said stiffly, and left the house.

While he was gone, Amy spent the time exploring the house more thoroughly, opening the doors and drawers in the kitchen and bedroom areas. When Jesse returned, carrying her trunk, Amy turned, her brow knit in puzzlement.

"Jesse, where's the stove?"

He checked for an instant, then continued to carry the trunk over to the wardrobe. "Well, there isn't one, for the moment."

"There isn't one," Amy repeated blankly.

Jesse nodded. "I'm sorry. I know it's not convenient, but the line shack didn't have one, and Hansom's Store didn't, either. He had to put one on order for me. It should be in in a week or two."

"But, Jesse, what are we going to do until then? How will I cook?"

He jerked a thumb toward the fireplace at the kitchen end of the room. Amy turned and looked at it, and her eyes widened.

"The fireplace!" She turned back to Jesse, panic on her face. "But, Jesse, I don't know how to cook over an open fire!"

"Well," Jesse said reasonably, "it can't be all that hard. People did it for years before they had stoves. Mrs. Sprague still cooked that way."

"But you don't understand." Amy's voice rose in a wail.

Jesse's face tightened. "I'm sorry, Amy. I know it's not what you're used to."

Heedless of what he was saying, Amy plunged on. "You don't know what an awful cook I am! Even Ines said so, and you know how sweet she is. I was already afraid that you'd hate what I cooked for you, so I was going to start out with the two or three things that I know I can do all right, like scrambled eggs and stew and bean soup. But I don't even know how to cook *them* in a fireplace." Tears started in her eyes. "It'll be awful, and you'll be sorry you ever married me, and— Oh!" She broke off, the tears rolling out of her eyes and down her cheeks, and she looked at Jesse with such exaggerated distress that it was almost comic.

Jesse couldn't help but chuckle, relieved to find that Amy wasn't upset because cooking in the fireplace was "beneath her." "Ah, Amy..." he said, starting toward her.

"Don't you laugh at me!" She took a step backward. "It's not funny."

"Well, maybe not, but it's not a tragedy, either." He took her arms in his and gave them a gentle shake. "I don't care whether you can cook. I'm sure I've eaten worse than anything you could dish out. There've been times when I've had nothing but hardtack or jerky for days."

Amy looked at him doubtfully. "But at least it wasn't burned—or, worse, half burned and half raw."

He laughed at her expression. "Then we'll eat jerky and hardtack instead. We have a supply, you know. Or I can manage a pot of beans over the fire, I think. Besides, it's only for a little while. The stove'll come in soon enough."

"I guess you're right." Amy heaved a sigh. "But I'd hoped I could conceal my ineptitude from you for a time, at least. Now you know."

"So you aren't a good cook. It's not the end of the world. There are lots of people who can't do things that you're good at. It all evens out."

"No." Amy shook her head. "I'm not good at anything practical." She moved away and plopped down in one of the chairs by the table. "All I'm good at is reading and daydreaming."

"It's hard to get by if you can't read," Jesse said tersely. "Believe me."

Amy looked at him oddly. "Why do you say it that way?"

Jesse shrugged and turned away. "No reason. I'm just saying that you don't think enough of yourself. You're always trying to make less of yourself than you are. Imagination's a grand thing, and there are plenty of people who could use a little of it. Why, how else would all those people who write those books you like to read do it? You know a lot about all sorts of things—history and such. You've got what somebody like me will never have. I've heard you. You know dates and places, and the why and wherefore of things. That's more important than knowing how to cook, isn't it?''

''Not if you're hungry,'' Amy replied dryly.

Jesse chuckled, shaking his head. ''I forgot to mention, you know how to argue, too. I never met such a one for always having to have the last word.''

''That's not true!''

Jesse cast her a speaking look, and Amy burst out laughing. ''All right, point taken.'' She paused, looking at him, and said finally, ''You really don't mind?''

''Well, I doubt I'll enjoy it. But it won't last forever. Anyway, I know you, and you're too clever to let something buffalo you. Pretty soon, you'll be cooking up a storm.''

''I've never done it before.''

''Ah, but this is the first time there won't be somebody there to cook something good when you ruin it.'' He cocked an eyebrow at her.

''Jesse Tyler! Are you saying I ruined my dishes on purpose just to get out of doing it?''

''Nope. Just saying that you never had much reason to learn before. I wouldn't think there's anything you can't learn if you put your mind to it.''

Amy smiled. ''Thank you. I hope you'll say the same after you've eaten a few of my meals.''

''Well, at least that won't start tonight,'' Jesse said jovially, crossing to the front door and picking up a box there. ''Before we left, Ines gave me this. Said she reckoned we wouldn't have any interest in trying to fix a meal tonight."

Amy grinned. "She was trying to save me embarrassment on my first night in our new home."

"Well, whatever, she sent us quite a spread." He set the box down on the table and began taking things out of it. "What do you think of this, Mrs. Tyler?"

Amy glanced up, startled, then smiled shyly at Jesse. It sent a funny fizzy sensation through her to hear herself called by her new married name. There was something even more tingling about hearing Jesse say the words.

"I think it looks scrumptious," she retorted. "And," she continued, leaning across the table and putting her hand on his, "I think you are the best and dearest of men, and I'm terribly, terribly lucky to have you for a husband."

He was still for a moment, his eyes gazing deeply into hers, almost as if he were searching for something there. Then he grinned in his usual way and said lightly, "Now, there is one of the few times when you aren't right. *I'm* the one who's lucky. Let's sit down and sample Ines's present."

They sat down to eat the delicious meal. Amy found it easy to be with Jesse. He made some light conversation, but he seemed just as content to be silent. Normally, when Amy sat in silence with someone, she was very aware of her inability to make conversation and felt guilty for the awkwardness, and then she became even more tongue-tied. But Jesse's easy acceptance of the quiet, perversely enough, freed Amy to talk, and she soon was chatting away about her plans for their home.

After the meal, when Jesse went out to check on the animals and Amy cleared the table and washed up, she began to think about the night ahead of her and wonder what was going to happen. Jesse had told her that he wouldn't expect anything like that from her, so tonight would not be a real "wedding night."

She cast a glance at the large brass bed in one corner of the house. Did Jesse expect them to sleep together in the same bed? There really was nowhere else *to* sleep, but, on the other hand, Amy could not imagine climbing into bed with a man and going to sleep, cocooned with him there under the blankets, with nothing between them except a few inches of air and the cotton of her nightgown. Amy drew in a shaky breath just thinking about it.

The dishes were few, and she finished them quickly. Then Amy turned to unpacking the things from her trunk. Keeping busy helped hold off the thought of what this evening would bring.

After a while Jesse came in, carrying a hammer and nails, and went over to the bedroom area, where Amy was working. Amy glanced over her shoulder at him. She felt awkward, being with him here, so she turned away quickly and resumed her task, keeping an eye on him as she worked. Jesse pounded a stout nail into the wall at a level with the top of his head, and left it protruding an inch or so, then tied a piece of thick twine to it. Stretching the twine out, he curved it around the back of the large wardrobe, making a ninety-degree angle, and up to the side wall, where he pounded another nail into the wall and tied the other end of the twine to it.

Amy glanced at the twine, puzzled. It formed a sort of imaginary wall, enclosing the bedroom on the two open sides. "What's that?" she asked. "Are you going to build walls there?"

"Nah. I thought about it, but I figured it'd make the bedroom too small and dark." He finished tying the twine and stepped back to look at it. "I'm probably going to have to tack it into the back of the wardrobe, if you don't mind. I'll use a little nail so it won't leave much of a hole."

"That's all right. But what's it for?"

"Cloth walls," Jesse replied with a flash of a grin. "We can hang some of those sheets and things in that trunk your ma sent out here." He nodded his head toward the cedar hope chest.

"Oh! I see. We can pin them up like on a clothesline."

"Right. Then you can have some privacy. I'll bunk down out there." He gestured toward the living area.

"But where? On the sofa? It's too short, surely."

"You're right about that. Then I'll just spread out my bedroll on the floor."

"Oh, no! Jesse, you can't mean to sleep on the floor!"

He shrugged. "Why not? I've slept on the floor before, believe me."

"That may be, but not here—not in your own house."

"But where else am I going to sleep?" he asked reasonably. "There isn't another bed, and I prefer the floor to that couch—I hate running up against the back of it every time I turn over." He paused and looked at her. "What did you think, Amy? That I was going to break my promise to you?"

"No! No, of course not." Amy hastened to reassure him, worried that she had hurt him, that he would think she didn't trust or believe him.

"Because I won't," he went on flatly. "Ever."

"I know you wouldn't. I just didn't think about . . . the practicalities of the situation before. It seems so awful that you should have to sleep on the floor in your own house."

He smiled at her, and Amy thought what a warm green his eyes turned when he smiled like that, like leaves struck by the sun. "You're too softhearted. I don't mind, really. Later, when I have the time, I'll build me a truckle bed."

"All right. If you're sure." Amy went to the trunk and pulled out several sheets.

Together they hung them on the twine with clothespins. They met in the middle, and their hands happened to reach up to the line at the same time, and they brushed against each other. A little thrill ran through Amy at the contact, and she pulled her hand back self-consciously, unable to look at Jesse. She felt more than saw him turn away.

He gathered up his hammer and nails, saying stiffly, "Well, I'll take these back out to the toolshed."

Amy nodded. She suspected that he was giving her this time to undress and put on her nightgown. She was grateful to him for that. Even with the sheets up, she thought, she would have felt embarrassed at undressing in the same room with him. As soon as he closed the front door behind him, she skinned out of her clothes as fast as she could.

Jesse was gone long enough that she was able to not only undress, but wash up and go through her other nightly routines, as well. She blew out the oil lamp beside the bed and crept in under the covers. She curled up and closed her eyes. The bed was deliciously soft, and the sheets smelled faintly of lavender, but these things made little impression upon Amy. She was more aware of the tight, cold little ball of loneliness that was centered in her chest.

Sometime later she heard the door open and Jesse come in. She did not open her eyes, just lay still, listening to the soft noises he made as he laid out his blankets on the floor and rolled up in them. Somehow the sound of his presence only made Amy lonelier. She thought how pleasant and comforting it would be to have Jesse's arms around her, as he had held her that night when he rescued her from Charles. Amy could not recall ever having felt quite that safe and warm.

Did Jesse mean to keep his promise not to touch her forever? If that was his intention, then she knew that he would stick to it. Jesse was a strong person. *Or perhaps,* she thought, *it wouldn't require any strength of will on his part. Perhaps it was just that he found her too unappealing to even desire to sleep with her.*

With that thought, tears seeped out from between her lids, and she turned her face into the pillow and cried, softly, so that Jesse would not hear her.

Chapter Six

Jesse paused, wiping the sweat from his brow, and looked over his shoulder at the western horizon. The sun was sinking fast, and soon the light would fade too much for him to see. It was time to quit.

Amy would have supper ready soon, anyway, and he couldn't deny his eagerness to get back inside and see her. His stomach rumbled, and he grinned to himself. It wasn't desire for food that was calling him home. If he was lucky, enough of the meal would be salvageable to fill his stomach, but with Amy's cooking, even that wasn't always a possibility.

They had been married for a little over a week now, and in that time decent meals had been few and far between. The first meal Amy had cooked, breakfast the day after their wedding, had been an unmitigated disaster, with blackened bacon, fried eggs that were raw on top and scorched on the bottom, and toast that was the color and consistency of charcoal. Even Jesse, despite a valiant effort, had been unable to eat it. They had wound up eating the leftovers from their packed supper of the night before.

Amy had finally gotten the knack of cooking eggs and bacon over the fire, and her toast now was only a little burned around the edges, making breakfast the best meal of the day. A rump roast the other evening had been charred on the outside and still raw in the center, and her vegetables usually wound up a big, gluey blob that was almost unrecognizable. Jesse still wasn't sure what the thick green mass the other night had been, though he suspected beans or peas. Her corn bread was passable, as long as he left the bottom crust stuck to the pan and ate only the top portion.

Jesse drove in a final nail, hung the hammer through his belt and climbed lithely down from his perch on the crosstimber of the barn. He strode toward the house, stretching out his tired muscles. He was working harder than he ever had, but he didn't mind it. Everything he did was for him and Amy, and that made it a joy. Once he finished getting this barn built for the protection of their horses and the hay, he would be able to start doing the work he really loved: hunting, capturing and training the wild mustangs that still roamed the range. His life, he thought, was almost perfect. He was married to the woman he loved, they had their own cozy little home, and he was doing the work he loved, the work he excelled at. It couldn't have been better—except for the fact that he couldn't sleep with his wife.

The frustration was eating him alive. He had sworn not to make love to his wife, thinking that he could live like that. After all, he had loved Amy for years, had seen her often at the ranch, and he had managed to keep his desire and love for her in check, hiding it from everyone.

But he was finding out how different a situation it was, actually living in the house with Amy, sitting across from her at every meal, seeing her when he awoke and at night before he went to sleep, talking and laughing with her, sharing thoughts with her. His love for her seemed to grow with each passing day, and his promise became harder and harder to keep.

He was coming to know all her different expressions—the bemused, vague look she turned on him when his voice pulled her away from the book she was reading, the flashing anger that made her eyes huge and glowing when she talked about some wrong, the way her eyes brimmed with merriment and her mouth twitched upward when she was amused. He was learning her thoughts and dreams, discovering the fascinating breadth of her imagination. He had heard that familiarity bred contempt, but in him it was drawing forth a deeper, stronger love—and an equally strong desire. The more he knew Amy, the more he wanted her.

Yet he could not have her. He was sworn to keep his hands off her, and if he broke that promise, if he tried to seduce her, to kiss and caress her into giving in to him, then she would lose faith in him. Once her trust in him was gone, he would have no chance of winning her love. The only hope he had with Amy was to give her time to get over her love for Charles Whitaker, and then maybe, just maybe, she would come to return *his* love. He knew how to be patient; he used that skill every time he broke and trained a horse. He knew how to coax and wait, how to take his gains in small increments.

He also knew how badly a mistake could ruin the whole careful plan and make a horse skittish again, setting him back. That was why he had to move so carefully with Amy, why he had to stick to his promise until *she* urged him to break it. Unfortunately, maintaining that promise was the hardest thing he'd ever had to do. Sometimes he thought that he would rather put up with ten Olen Spragues than have to live like a eunuch with the woman he loved.

Jesse reached the house and went inside. It was warm and scented with the smell of a wood fire. There was also a charred odor, one with which he had grown quite familiar the past few days. Jesse stopped, and his eyes went warily to the fireplace. Well, at least there was no food actually in flames, as the sausages had been last Thursday.

He strode over to the fireplace, picked up the hot pad lying there and pulled out the spider skillet. Lifting the lid, he found several pork chops. They were barely brown on the top, but Jesse had learned not to be fooled by that. He grabbed a fork from the table and lifted one of them from the skillet. It came up slowly, sticking to the hot metal, and when he got it turned over he saw that the bottom was almost black. Shaking his head, he turned the other two, covered the pan again and set it back at the edge of the fireplace. The other pot was causing the smell. In it were four small, blackened, roundish objects; he wasn't sure what they were, but they had obviously gone long past the point of being cooked.

Jesse set the pan down on the counter and turned, looking for Amy. As he had expected, she was curled up in the comfortable chair in the corner of the room beside the window. In one hand she held a meat fork, in the other, a book, tilted to catch the last dying rays of the sun. Her lower lip was caught between her teeth, and her eyes were darting back and forth, devouring the lines. She whipped the page over and started avidly down the next one.

Jesse had to grin. It was impossible for him to get angry with Amy. She looked so sweet and intent, so amusingly lost to the world. Sometimes he felt as if he had married a sprite or a fairy, blissfully disconnected from the concerns of other human beings because she was attached to another world, one in which mere men like him could never enter.

"Amy..." he began. Then, he cleared his throat and said, in a much louder voice, "Amy!"

She jumped, her eyes flying up from the book to where he stood. "Jesse!"

A delighted smile broke across her face, and whatever fragments of irritation he felt with her quickly flew away. "Good afternoon, Mrs. Tyler." The term of address was the closest he allowed himself to come to an endearment. It carried for him the warm, even titillating knowledge that she belonged to him now.

Amy uncurled her legs and stood up. "I didn't hear you come in. I was reading my favorite book, and I was at the very best part." She paused and sniffed the air. "What's that smell?"

He said nothing, only raised his brows, and Amy wailed, "Have I burned dinner again?"

She dropped her book and raced toward the fireplace, but Jesse caught her by the shoulders. "It's all right. I already turned the pork chops, and I took the, uh, the other things off the fire."

"The other things?" Amy looked at him blankly, and then her eyes widened in horror. "You mean the potatoes?"

"Is that what they were?" An amused grin tilted up the corners of Jesse's mouth.

"Yes! Where are they?" He gestured toward the counter, and she went over to them. When she saw them, her hands flew to her cheeks, and she cried, "Jesse! They're ruined!"

She turned to him, her eyes filling with tears. "I've done it again! I am so sorry."

"It could happen to anyone," he replied soothingly.

Amy's lips twitched with disgust. "No, it couldn't, and you know it. Honestly, Jesse, I'm such a mess! I'm the most awful wife, and you are always so sweet and kind about it. I feel terrible!''

"Would you rather I growled at you or banged on the table?" he inquired politely, his eyes lighting with amusement. "I suppose I could manage to work up a tantrum or two."

Amy managed a small, watery smile. "Sometimes I almost wish that you would. I feel so guilty—you're so good to me, and I'm managing wretchedly. Oh, Jesse! You must regret marrying me!" Tears began to spill over out of her eyes.

"Never!" Jesse retorted fiercely, reaching out to grasp her shoulders. At his touch, she gave way to her tears and threw herself against his chest, crying.

"You don't even know the worst," she told him, sobbing, "I—I finished the curtains this afternoon, and they're horrid! I ruined them!"

"Sweetheart . . ." Jesse uttered the endearment without thinking as he curled his arms around her. She felt so good in his arms that he almost let out a sigh of pure pleasure. Amy was warm and pliant against him. He could feel the soft pressure of her body all the way up and down his, and it sent an enticing, sensual thrill through him. Jesse ached to help her, to comfort and reassure her. Yet he ached just as much to squeeze her closer to him and let his hands run free over her body.

But he knew that she trusted him, and so he could not do what he wanted. It would be taking advantage of her weakness and her unhappiness, it would be going back on his word to her. And no matter how painful it might be at times to keep his promise, he was determined to do so.

So Jesse contented himself with laying his cheek against her soft hair and breathing in the delicious scent of it as he cuddled her body against his. He hoped that Amy was too naive to notice or that the clothing between them was thick enough to hide the instinctive reaction of his body from holding her this close.

Amy's tears stopped, and she let out a little sigh, snuggling closer. That little movement almost undid Jesse's resolve, expressing as it did Amy's enjoyment of being held by him. Jesse wondered if she might feel some bit of desire for him, too. Could she sometimes feel lonely in that bed by herself at night and wish that their marriage was of a different kind?

He could not let himself believe it. It was just his wishful thinking, his own willful longings, that made him impute his desires to Amy. Amy was too sweet and naive, too innocent, to think of such things. He remembered how disgusted and angry she had been when Charles Whitaker started mauling her that night—and she had been in love with him. How much less would she welcome the advances of a man she didn't even love!

Jesse forced himself to loosen his arms around her and move back a little. Amy, too, stepped back and raised her face to look up at him. Tears glistened on her pale cheeks and swam in her eyes, making them huge and luminous. Her mouth was soft and almost trembling, deliciously pink and moist; it seemed to call out to be kissed. Instinctively he began to lower his face toward hers, but then he caught himself. Drawing in a harsh breath, he released her completely and moved away.

"Uh...well, why don't you show the curtains to me? They couldn't be that bad."

Amy hesitated, then said in a muted voice, "All right."

She went listlessly to her bedroom, which was still roped off by sheets, and returned a moment later, two pieces of material in her hands. Mutely she held them out to Jesse, and he took them.

"Why, they look fine to me," he told her heartily, and carried them over to the window. The material was attractive, and the two sides looked to be the same length; his fear had been that one was longer than the other. "Look," he said cheerfully as he held them up on either side of the window. "Oh."

Now he could see the problem. Both sides might be the same, but they were too short. The curtains ended, ludicrously, a good two inches higher than the windowsill. He looked back at Amy, who was standing watching him, her arms folded across her chest. He hoped she wouldn't start crying again. He could think of nothing to say to make her feel any better about the curtains.

To his surprise, a smile twitched across Amy's face, and she had to bring up her hands to cover a laugh. Her eyes twinkled merrily above her hands, and suddenly she couldn't hold it in anymore. She began to laugh. "Oh, Jesse! I—I'm sorry." She tried to swallow her laughter and regain a sober expression, but it was a losing battle from the start, and she once again burst into giggles. "But that look on your face!"

She gave way to her laughter, and Jesse couldn't keep from joining in. The curtains were, after all, absurd. So, for that matter, were the potatoes she'd cooked. He laughed harder, thinking of all the silly mistakes she'd made over the past week and how hard-pressed he'd been not to laugh at most of them. Now he released the amusement he had so valiantly held in—and, with it, much of the tension that had strung his nerves taut. The more he laughed, the more Amy laughed, too, until finally their sides were aching from their merriment.

His laughter slowed, then stopped as Jesse released a sigh and leaned against the wall, recovering his breath.

Amy flopped down onto a chair, holding her sides. She wiped her eyes and looked at him.

"I didn't know being married would be this much fun," Amy confessed naively.

Suddenly, as hard and fast as a fist to the gut, desire slammed through Jesse. He wanted to charge across the room and pull Amy to her feet and kiss her again and again, so deep and hard that they melted into one another. He clenched his teeth together hard to keep back the words that threatened to tumble from his mouth, words of love and yearning and hot, youthful passion.

"Do you really not mind the things I do?" Amy went on.

Jesse levered himself away from the wall. "No, I don't mind." His voice came out hoarsely. He jammed his hands in his pockets and turned aside, clearing his throat. "Amy, I didn't marry you to get a cook or a seamstress. I've told you before."

"But why? What do you get out of it? I mean, I got my reputation saved. I can sit around and read and let the dinner burn, and you don't mind. But what do you get?"

"I get you," he answered honestly.

Amy blinked. "But that's not much."

"It's all I want."

Realizing how much he had revealed, Jesse swung around. "Come on," he said brusquely. "Enough of this. Let's see if there's anything we can save out of those potatoes."

Amy watched him, frowning, as he crossed the room to the ruined potatoes. She looked as if she would like to question him further, but in the end she said nothing, just followed him to the table.

They scooped out the centers of the burned potatoes and ate the half-burned pork chops. Jesse said little. He was aware of Amy studying him curiously from time to time, but he couldn't bring himself to meet her eyes. He wondered what she was thinking, and whether she had guessed his feelings from what he had said. He cursed his wayward tongue.

Later, after they had eaten, Amy cleared off the table and washed the dishes. Jesse watched her, thinking it must be a sign of how badly he was smitten that he enjoyed so much watching Amy do even a simple thing like washing dishes. It was knowing that she did it for him, that she was his wife, in his home, that made his loins turn hot. He thought about going up to Amy and slipping his arms around her waist, bending down to nuzzle the bare back of her neck. He thought about sliding his hands up her torso to her breasts and cupping them possessively. He could imagine their soft, warm weight through the cotton of her dress, the hard prickling of her nipples as he touched them.

Jesse knew he was insane to do this to himself. He should leave and let his senses calm down. He should force his mind onto something else. But he could not. Instead, his imagination rolled onward, picturing how he would take her in his arms and kiss her, how he would lift her up and carry her to this very table and lay her down upon it, shoving up her skirts and letting his hands roam her legs...

"Jesse? Are you all right?"

"What?" He came back to reality with a crash. Amy was standing at the counter, staring. "I—I'm sorry. I didn't hear you. I was daydreaming."

"It must have been an odd daydream," Amy commented. "You looked as if you were in pain."

"No, I— Really, it was nothing. Just foolishness. Now, what were you saying?"

"I was asking you if you'd mind reading to me while I worked. Corinne and I used to do that sometimes. It made the work go faster."

Jesse went cold inside; her words were as effective in cooling him down as a bucket of ice water in his face. "Read?" he repeated blankly. "Read what?"

"I don't know. Whatever you want to. Why don't you pick out a book from one of the boxes?"

"Uh..." Jesse stood up, glancing from Amy to the boxes of books stacked in the corner. "If you don't mind, I have some chores I need to finish outside. I really should do them first."

"In the dark?"

"I'll take a lantern."

"Oh. All right, if that's what you want." Amy looked disappointed, but she went back to her work without any complaint.

Jesse hurriedly left the room. He went to the corral and looked at the horses, resting his arms on the upper rail. He tried to think of some chore to do out here. At least it would make his words a little less of a lie. He hated lying to Amy, who was so trusting and sweet.

But he hadn't known what else to say. And he couldn't tell her the truth. It would be too humiliating. Not that Amy would say anything unkind. But he could imagine the dismay that would leap into her eyes, quickly followed by pity. And he could not bear to see her look at him like that.

The following Saturday, Amy and Jesse rode into town to get their stove, stopping at the McAlisters' ranch house to borrow their wagon. The McAlisters greeted Amy with hugs and cries of glee. It was less than two weeks since they had seen her, but somehow the fact of her marriage made it seem as if it had been longer.

They picked up their supplies in town, and Jesse and the store clerk loaded the small but heavy stove into the back of the wagon while Amy watched them, fairly bubbling with excitement over their new purchase.

Afterward, as Jesse started to help her into the wagon, Amy said, "No, wait. We have to go to the post office and pick up Papa's mail. I promised him that we would."

"All right." They walked across the street, and Jesse got Mr. McAlister's mail.

As he returned, Amy asked eagerly, "Is the *Hancock's Quarterly* there? It has a continuing story I've been reading."

"I don't know. Here, you look for it." Jesse handed her the stack of mail.

"Why, silly," Amy said with a smile, "it's right here on top. See?" She pointed to the cover of the magazine on the top of the stack.

"Oh," Jesse said shortly, glancing at the periodical. "I—I guess I didn't look at the name."

Amy gave him an odd look, but she said nothing, just walked with him out to the wagon and climbed in. But inside, her brain was busily whirring. It was hard to see how Jesse could have missed seeing the name on that magazine. It was written in huge letters across the top of the cover. She thought back to the way he had left the house so abruptly the other night after she asked him to read aloud while she finished the dishes. It had seemed odd that he had such urgent chores to do, when up until then he had been sitting around, obviously enjoying the opportunity to relax after a hard day's work. She remembered, too, the time when he had been reminding her of her abilities and accomplishments, and reading had been the first thing he mentioned. Could it possibly be that Jesse could not read?

But he had signed his name on their wedding certificate. She had seen him do it. How could he write if he couldn't read? That didn't make any sense. Amy told herself that she must be wrong, and yet she could not quite get rid of her suspicions. She thought about it on the way home, and she soon concocted a plan.

That night after supper, she asked casually, "Jesse, would you help me take some of these books out of the boxes? I'm looking for something."

"Sure." He rose with alacrity and walked over to the boxes. Squatting down beside one, he opened it and began to pull out books.

"Why don't you look in that box?" Amy suggested, kneeling in front of another box. "I'll look in this one. I'm looking for *Gulliver's Travels*."

Jesse's hands stilled. He pulled another two handfuls of books out and said slowly, "Why don't I take them out, and you look for the book? That'll be quicker."

He set the books down beside Amy and delved into the box again, avoiding her eyes. Thoughtful, Amy shuffled through the books he had given her. Then she suddenly held one out in front of Jesse, saying, "Why, look what I found!"

He gazed at the book blankly. "Yes. I see. The book you wanted."

"No," Amy said, watching him carefully. "It's not *Gulliver's Travels*. It's a book of poetry."

"Oh." A dull flush mounted in Jesse's cheeks. He turned away. "Do you want me to keep on looking, then?"

"No, I don't. I never wanted the book."

He glanced at her in surprise. "Then why the hell—"

"I just wanted to see something. You can't read, can you?"

Jesse's eyes flashed, and he rose quickly to his feet. "That's why you asked me to help you? It was a trick?"

"Yes, I guess it was," Amy admitted, rising. "I suspected you couldn't, but you didn't tell me, so I thought I could find out if I—"

"Congratulations!" Jesse snapped. He looked so furious that Amy stepped back involuntarily. "You proved it. I can't read. I can't write. Now you know. You married a fool who doesn't know anything but horses!"

Jesse whirled around and strode out of the house, slamming the door behind him.

Chapter Seven

"Jesse! Jesse, wait!" Amy cried, running after him. She caught up to him near the corral and grabbed his arm. "Jesse, I'm sorry. Please, wait, listen to me."

He stopped and swung around. His face was dark with anger, and he snapped, "What?"

"I'm sorry," Amy went on breathlessly. "Please believe me, I didn't mean to upset you. I—I shouldn't have done that. Mama always said I was far too inquisitive for a lady. I'm sorry."

"Stop apologizing. It's not your fault," he responded tightly. "You didn't do anything wrong. Anyone would be shocked to find that a grown man can't read or write."

"I wasn't shocked," Amy protested. "There are lots of grown men who can't read or write. Why, old Herman, for one, and Sam Dougherty, and I bet lots of other hands that I never even knew about."

"Yeah, but you didn't make the mistake of marrying one of them."

"Mistake? Why do you say that? Just because you can't read?"

"Just?" he repeated sarcastically. "Maybe not, if you were some poor nester's daughter, or a washerwoman. But you— My God, Amy! You're the smartest person I've ever met, man or woman. Why, your dad swears that you've read all the books in his library twice over, and some of them a lot more than that. How are you going to feel sometime when we're around other people, people like your family, and somebody realizes that I can't read?''

Amy shrugged. "I don't know. I haven't thought about it."

"Well, I'll tell you. You'll be humiliated. It's not right. I—I used to watch you sometimes, sitting out on your front porch, reading...."

"You did?" Amy looked at him, surprised.

"Yes. I saw how you devoured those books. I've seen you writing in your pad, too."

Amy colored. "Well, yes, sometimes I do. I— Mama says it's foolish."

"It's not foolish. It's wonderful. But don't you see? How can you bear to have a dumb lump of a husband like me? I don't even know what you're talking about half the time."

"Well, how could you, if you've never read the books?"

"That's what I mean! I don't know anything."

"Don't talk that way!" Amy retorted fiercely, reaching out to grab his hand and squeeze it tightly between her own. "You know lots and lots! There's nobody around here who knows horses like you do."

Jesse snorted derisively, but Amy pressed on. "Well, that's a lot more useful knowledge than some of the things I know, like...like when the Battle of Hastings was, or Marco Polo's trade route to the Orient. There are lots and lots of things that I can't do, but you don't hold me in contempt for them. You saw how my curtains turned out, and you know how terrible my cooking is. I could never build a barn, the way you're doing. Why, I hardly know how to hammer a nail. I wish I could do it, but nobody ever thought it was a fit thing to teach a girl. But that doesn't make me a dummy or a fool, any more than it makes you one not to be able to read. I would never, *never* feel humiliated because you are my husband.

Jesse gazed at her, his brows drawn together in puzzlement. He lifted his forefinger and trailed it softly down her cheek. "You're something special. It truly doesn't bother you that I can't read?"

"No. Why should it?" Amy smiled up at him. "Am I forgiven now? Will you come back inside with me?"

"Of course. I wasn't angry with you. It was with me. With life."

Amy linked her arm through Jesse's, and they started back to the house. "Tell me something—why can't you read?"

Jesse shrugged. "'Cause I never learned. I didn't go to school. My ma couldn't read, either, and she didn't see the sense in it. Besides, she always needed me at home to help her, so she didn't send me. And after she died, I had to make my way in the world. I didn't have time to go to school, and anyway, I was getting too old."

"How were you able to sign your name on our marriage certificate? That made me think I must be wrong about you not being able to read."

Jesse grinned shamefacedly. "Oh, that. I knew I was going to have to sign it, and I didn't want you to see that I couldn't write. So I had one of the other hands teach me how to write my name. He wrote it down for me, and I practiced it over and over until I could do it. That's all."

Amy remembered the slow, careful way Jesse had made his signature. She had thought he was taking his time because it was an important thing. "Oh. I see."

They reached the house and went inside. Amy went over to the boxes and piled the books back in. Jesse began to help her. Amy turned to him impulsively and laid her hand on his arm.

"I truly am sorry about what I did. I didn't mean to hurt you. I didn't realize why you wouldn't tell me, or how much it meant to you. So many people think reading and history and things like that are pretty useless knowledge."

"It's all right." He smiled at her. "You didn't do anything wrong."

"Jesse... would you like to learn to read? I was thinking that I could teach you."

He glanced at her sharply. "No, that's too much trouble for you."

"How can that be trouble? I love books—you just told me that yourself. It would be fun for me."

"Teaching me my ABCs?" He looked skeptical.

"Yes. That's something that I *am* good at, something I can help you with. And it would make me happy. You've been so good and patient with me, it's the least I could do for you. And with you, I don't think it'd be boring at all."

Something flashed in Jesse's eyes, and a thrill ran through Amy. She thought about sitting beside Jesse every night and working with him. It didn't sound dull to her.

"But I'm too old to learn it now."

"Why? You're not senile yet, are you?"

He shrugged. "I don't know. It just seems foolish. It would take so long, and there are so many things I need to do. It'd waste a lot of time."

"Reading is *not* a waste of time," Amy told him severely. "Besides, I was thinking I could help you more with the outside chores. I mean, all I do now is feed the chickens and cook and keep the house clean. Keeping this place clean is hardly anything, it's so small. Now, with the stove, cooking's going to be a lot easier, too. Anyway, it doesn't take up all my time, either. The fact is, I don't have enough to do. I'm being lazy.''

"That's all right."

"Not while you're working yourself into the ground, it's not. I bet there are lots of things I could do to help you, and that way you'd have time to spare for learning. I could even help you build the barn. You could show me how to do some things—I'd really like to learn!—and I could help you. Hold things in place while you nail them down, maybe, or fetch and carry for you, at least. Please?"

Amy folded her hands in an exaggeratedly prayerful attitude, and Jesse had to chuckle. "Sure, you can help me if you want."

"And you'll let me help you with reading?"

Confusion flitted across his face. Finally he said, "Amy, what if I can't? What if I really am stupid, like Sprague said?"

"Jesse Tyler." Amy put her hands on her hips and gave him an exasperated look. "You are *not* stupid. Tell me something—who do you think knows more, me or Olen Sprague?"

Jesse chuckled. "What a question! You, of course."

"Then why do you persist in believing him over me? I'll tell you why." She shook her forefinger sternly at him. "Because you're flat scared of something you don't know. You know the way to get over something you're scared of is to just do it. So you *have* to let me teach you."

"I never knew what a bossy woman I was marrying," Jesse marveled, grinning.

"Well, you did marry me, and now you're stuck with me."

His grin broadened. "I don't mind."

Amy felt suddenly breathless. Jesse's eyes were so warm when he looked at her, and the way his mouth curved upward did strange things to her stomach. She wished he would lean over and kiss her. She wanted to feel his mouth against hers, to taste his lips.

She looked away, confused and embarrassed, and Jesse stood up. The moment was over. "All right," he said, reaching down a hand to pull her to her feet. "We might as well get started . . . teacher."

Over the course of the next few weeks, Amy and Jesse were always together. During the day she helped him build the barn, and in the evenings they worked on Jesse's reading. Amy felt that neither of those occupations could really be called work. Though the carpentry was sometimes tiring, she found it fun and intriguing, as well. She caught on quickly for she did not find it boring, unlike most of her house chores. Jesse's praise of her ability made her smile and flush with pleasure.

To her amazement, she found that her other skills even began to improve. The new stove was a vast help with her cooking, and now that she had chores outside to help with, she had less time to spend on the cooking, and consequently she cooked the meal all at once, remaining at the stove the whole time, instead of getting distracted by a book and forgetting what she was doing. She began to realize that Jesse was right; she wasn't incompetent in all practical matters.

Another thing Amy discovered she could do well was teach. Jesse was learning how to read by leaps and bounds. She taught him the alphabet quickly, and after that she rode over to her parents' house one day to retrieve a small trunk full of her old schoolbooks. They started on the primer, chuckling a little over the childishness of the book. Amy found herself looking forward all day to teaching Jesse his lessons in the evening. She enjoyed helping him.

She enjoyed watching his earnest concentration. Quite frankly, she liked simply sitting beside him or watching his hand move across the paper.

She loved his hands. They were strong and slender, callused yet capable of gentleness. She found herself looking at his hands often as they worked together, and she could not keep from thinking wild, crazy things about his touching her. It was embarrassing, even though, of course, Jesse had no idea what she was thinking.

At first Jesse was embarrassed to be seen struggling over the simple words, but after a time, when Amy was neither impatient nor scornful of his efforts, he shed most of his embarrassment and concentrated on his studies. He worked his way steadily through the primer, and as he conquered each new word or sentence, Amy was as proud of his success as he was.

When Jesse read the last sentence of the last page of the primer, he closed the book with a snap and turned to smile triumphantly at Amy, who was seated beside him at the kitchen table.

Amy let out a squeal. "You did it! I knew you could!"

Without thinking, she leaned across the few inches that separated them and hugged him enthusiastically. Jesse froze for an instant, and then his arms clamped around her like steel bands and his mouth came down, seeking hers.

His kiss startled Amy, and she let out a little squeak of surprise. But then the feel of Jesse's mouth against hers drove out all other thoughts and feelings. His lips were pliant, but insistent and determined, pressing deeper and deeper into hers. Their velvet pressure threw Amy's insides into turmoil, opening her up to wild, chaotic yet delightful sensations.

Jesse's tongue slid delicately along the joining line of her lips, and Amy drew in a startled breath. He seized the opportunity, thrusting his tongue between her lips and into her mouth, his own lips pressing hers open for him. Amy remembered that Charles Whitaker had tried to do the same thing, but it felt incredibly different when Jesse did it. It wasn't scary, it was exciting. Amy shivered and leaned into him, giving herself up to the delightful exploration of his tongue.

With a groan, Jesse pulled Amy out of her chair and into his lap, cradling her tightly against his chest. One of his arms was around her shoulders, pressing her to him, and the other drifted lower, his hand sliding down her back and over the curve of her buttock. Heat blossomed between Amy's legs, growing as Jesse kissed her again and again. His skin was feverishly warm and his breath came out in a hot shudder against her cheek. The evidence of his response to her excited her almost as much as his mouth on hers. Amy had never experienced this sort of heat within herself before, this odd feeling of ripeness, as though she were loosening and opening to him. Her breasts seemed swollen and heavy, aching, and she wanted Jesse to touch them. It was a scandalous thought, she supposed, but at the moment she didn't care. She wanted to stretch and purr on his lap like a cat and have him stroke her all over.

She shifted on his lap, bracing her hands on his shoulders, and Jesse went still. He lifted his head, and his hands fell away from her. Amy looked up at him, her eyes wide with surprise and confusion. *Why was he stopping?*

"Jesse?" she began uneasily.

"Oh, God." He looked appalled. "No. No. I'm sorry. Oh, Amy, I didn't mean to—"

He jumped to his feet, setting her away from him hastily. "Please, Amy, I—I don't know what happened. But I swear, I'll be more careful next time. I won't let it happen again."

She gazed at him blankly, seeing disgust, even horror, in his eyes. *What had she done wrong?* Panic-stricken, she couldn't think what to say or do.

"I'm sorry," he said again, stiffly. "I—I'll leave you alone now."

He turned on his heel and strode quickly out the door. Amy stood for a long moment, gazing at the blank door. Everything had happened so fast that it left her stunned. She turned and walked blindly into the bedroom area, seeking the illusive protection of the cloth walls. She sat down on the bed and thought about what had happened. *Why had Jesse stopped kissing her so abruptly? Why had he left?*

Obviously he didn't want any passion between them. When he had made her that promise, she had thought that he was doing it for her sake, so that she would feel at ease until she got to know him better. Now she began to wonder if he had not meant it for his sake, as well. Perhaps Jesse had no interest in making love to her, now or ever. Maybe he found her uninteresting. Unattractive.

But if that was true, Amy couldn't understand why he had kissed her. She had leaned over to hug him in her enthusiasm, but Jesse had kissed her. He had pulled her right out of her chair and onto his lap. She remembered the sound of his labored breathing, the searing touch of his skin. *Surely those things betokened desire, not indifference.* He had wanted her. She didn't think she could be that wrong about what had transpired.

She tried to remember exactly when he had broken off their kiss. It had been when she squirmed in his lap, restlessly seeking satisfaction for the fiery ache within her, and her hands clamped onto his shoulders.

Amy frowned, thinking. Jesse had stopped when she responded to him, not just letting him take her lips, but actively urging him on with her body. She remembered her mother talking once about Mabel Holloway and how she was always chasing the boys. "Men don't like an aggressive female," Mrs. McAlister had declared, casting an admonishing eye toward Corinne. "You mark my words. She'll have trouble ever getting a husband. I heard she went out in the garden alone with Henry Smithson at the Patterson dance last month—and was gone for ten minutes. Well, she'll get a reputation acting that way, I can tell you."

And even Corinne, who had grimaced at her mother's remark, had once said something similar to her. "Men like a chase," Corinne had told her, explaining why she had turned down Geoffrey Ames for a dance, even though she had one open on her dance card. "You can't let a fellow know that you like him, or he loses interest."

It had sounded rather strange to Amy at the time, for it seemed to her that a man ought to be pleased and reassured to know that a woman he was interested in was interested in him, too. But now, thinking about the way Jesse had just acted, she wondered if Corinne and her mother were right. Maybe men didn't want a woman to be too eager.

It was obviously terribly important to a man that a woman be pure; that was why her driving out with Charles that night had ruined her. Perhaps a man even wanted his wife to be so pure-minded that she did not want to touch him or to rub herself against him as Amy had just done.

Jesse must have been appalled at her wantonness. That was why there had been disgust in his eyes. He had thought her too bold, too forward. Maybe he even thought she would respond like that to any man. After all, only a few weeks ago, she had driven out with Charles Whitaker at night, which no lady should have done. Jesse might think that she had acted the same way with Charles as she had with him. He wouldn't know that she had never felt for Charles Whitaker the kind of passion she felt for him. Jesse couldn't know how much she loved him.

Amy sat bolt upright. *Where had that thought come from? She loved Jesse Tyler?*

But of course, she realized, a tiny smile playing at her lips. It was obvious: She loved him. She had probably loved him for a long time and not realized it. Love was not the silly infatuation she had had for Charles Whitaker for a time. That had simply been her overactive imagination. Love was the emotion inside her now, this sweet, aching yearning. Love was wanting to be around Jesse all the time. It was enjoying talking to him and laughing with him. It was the quiet, certain knowledge of Jesse and what he would do, the faith and trust she had in him.

She wasn't sure when it had happened, if love for Jesse had grown from being married to him or if it had been inside her earlier, hidden and waiting to reveal itself. The important thing was that she did love him.

Amy slid off the bed, about to run out and find Jesse and tell him. She would explain that she loved him, that she wanted to be a real wife to him, that she had never really loved Charles Whitaker.

But she stopped herself before she reached the front door. There was that boldness again, that impulsiveness that always got her into trouble. She seemed to have difficulty acting in a proper, maidenly way. However, this time she had to make herself do what she should. Jesse and her marriage were too important for her to make a mistake.

Amy turned and walked back into the bedroom and sat down once again on her bed to think. She realized that she should not boldly announce her love and her intention to have a real marriage. For one thing, Jesse would no doubt be appalled at this further demonstration of her forwardness. Secondly, he did not return her love. He had married her merely to pay back the debt of gratitude that he owed her and her father. Therefore, Amy realized, she must conceal her own feelings, while at the same time getting Jesse to fall in love with her. For him to feel right about it, he must pursue her.

She almost started crying at that thought. It seemed hopeless. She had never been the kind of girl men fell in love with. Jesse probably thought of her as a sort of sister.

Well, perhaps not exactly as a sister. A wicked grin touched her lips. He hadn't kissed her as if she were his sister tonight. He did feel desire for her. She could not be mistaken about that. What she needed to do was to entice and attract him, to encourage that passion, so that he would start to kiss her again and want to share her bed. Then, surely, when they were truly husband and wife, he would grow to love her.

The trick, she knew, would be in enticing him without appearing bold or sluttish. Her actions must appear entirely innocent. It seemed impossible. But Amy was a smart girl with a fertile imagination, and as she got undressed and crawled into bed to go to sleep, her brain was buzzing with schemes.

She embarked on her plan first thing the next morning. First, she knew, she must follow her sister's advice and look as alluring as she could. She spent much more time than usual over her hair, finally getting it pinned into a full, soft style that flattered her face. Next she pulled out one of the new dresses that Corinne had insisted enhanced her coloring. The final touch was a spot of rose water behind her ears and on her wrists. Then she walked out of the little bedroom to face Jesse, her color high with excitement.

Jesse was putting wood in the new stove, and he swiveled around at the sound of her approach. His expression was uncertain, and he wiped his hands down his trouser legs nervously. "Amy."

Amy smiled brilliantly at him. "Hello, Jesse."

Jesse blinked in surprise, but he smiled back and returned to laying the fire. Amy walked over to the stove and bent down beside him to peer into the firebox. He glanced at her, his eyes traveling over her body, then hastily turned back to finish his job.

Over the next few days, Amy did her best to subtly entice her husband. Every evening as they worked together on Jesse's reading, she leaned close to him on the pretext of looking at his book. When she refilled his glass at dinner, she made sure her hand or arm brushed his. Once, in the evening, she came out of the bedroom pretending to remember that she had to tell Jesse something. She was careful to forget her dressing gown, so that she was clad only in her lace-trimmed white nightgown. Of course, it was hardly revealing, being high-necked and long-sleeved and made of cotton, but at least it flowed down along the lines of her body, without all the petticoats and undergarments that a lady wore under her dresses.

Seeing the way Jesse's eyes flickered down her body and the way he rose from his bed on the floor, almost as if drawn up by force, Amy was certain that her attire had had the effect she desired. She deliberately walked up to him, gazing into his face. He reached out to touch her hair, which was flowing loosely over her shoulders, then snatched his hand back and clasped his hands behind his back. Amy could almost feel the heat from his body, and she could see the tension in his face, the involuntary slackening of his lips, and a triumphant satisfaction rose up in her. Her doubts were resolved. She had been right; he *did* want her, no matter how much he tried to hide or deny it.

After that night, she had the courage to take her sensual teasing to a new level. In the past she had waited modestly each evening for Jesse to make his nightly trip around the yard before she went into her bedroom area and undressed. But the next night, instead of waiting for him to leave, she bid him a pleasant good-night, picked up her kerosene lamp and sailed into the bedroom, leaving Jesse gazing after her.

She set the lamp down on the night table and began to unpin her hair. Though the sheets hung around the room ostensibly gave her privacy, Amy was aware that with the light of her lamp behind them, the sheets were almost transparent. Though the image would not be clear, Jesse would be able to see her every move. She brushed out her hair and began to undress, her ears cocked for the sound of the front door opening and closing. It didn't come, and Amy smiled to herself, knowing that Jesse must be watching her.

It was embarrassing to know that he could see her pull off her skirt and blouse, then her undergarments, until finally she was completely nude, and she blushed as she did it. But it was exciting at the same time, and she felt a delicious thrill at the thought of Jesse watching her.

However, much to her disappointment, it seemed as though all her efforts were doomed to failure. Jesse did not try to kiss her, did not even make a move toward her. If anything, he began to avoid her company. Amy suspected that if not for their lessons, she would hardly have seen him at all. Sadly she began to wonder if, instead of luring him into loving her, she was actually driving him away!

She would give it a few more days, she thought, and then, if Jesse still had made no move toward her, she would give up and let things return to the way they had been.

Chapter Eight

Jesse dunked his head and chest under the pump spout outside. The water was bitterly cold, and he shivered, but he grimly continued to wash off. It helped to cool him down, which, heaven knew, he needed before he went into the house and saw Amy. The pain seemed an apt punishment for the sins he usually contemplated when he was with her.

Jesse wasn't sure how much longer he could last. It seemed as if nowadays all he could think about was making love to Amy. He knew it would be disastrous if he did, that he would be breaking every vow he had made to her, that he would be letting his lust destroy their marriage. But it was reaching the point where the need was so strong in him that he almost didn't care about the consequences, as long as he could finally satisfy the craving that was rampant in him.

Ever since that night when he had kissed her, his life had been a living hell of desire. He had managed to pull himself together then and get out, to quell the hunger that was raging in him, and he had sworn that after that he would keep a firmer hold over his passions. But no matter how hard he tried, the yearning in him only grew worse. Amy seemed prettier and more desirable every day. He knew it must be only his hunger that made it appear so, but everything Amy did now seemed full of sexual allure. Now it seemed as if she accidentally brushed against him frequently, as if she leaned in closer to look at his schoolwork, tantalizingly warm and smelling of roses, as if when she smiled at him her eyes were warm with sensual promise.

Worst of all had been the one night she had gone into her bedroom to undress before he left the house. He had been surprised, but he supposed he must have been late in going, and she had gotten tired of waiting. He knew that she did not realize how her lamp turned the barrier of the white sheets translucent, making all her movements visible to him. She had undressed and put on her nightgown, and he had stood and watched. He had known guiltily that he should go, that he was invading her privacy, that he was only making his own situation more untenable. But he had been unable to tear himself away. Every night now he waited for her to go into the bedroom and innocently undress before his gaze. He hated himself for doing it, yet he could not make himself leave. Every night he vowed that this night would be different, but it never was. No matter how much he reviled himself for it inwardly, he could not walk out the door.

Shivering, Jesse blotted his chest and arms dry with a towel and pulled back on his shirt. He buttoned it quickly and grabbed his jacket from the hitching post, where he had hung it while he washed up. He cast a last look toward the barn. They had finished it days ago, and now the horses were safe inside its shelter. Every time Jesse looked at it, he was filled with pride.

He strode across the yard and into the house, bracing himself mentally against the desire that always flooded him when he saw his wife. Amy turned and smiled at him as he stepped inside. She was prettily flushed from the heat of the stove, and little tendrils of hair had escaped her bun and were curling softly around her face. Even knowing how he always reacted to her, Jesse was amazed by the desire that slammed into his gut.

They ate supper. Though Amy's meals were much improved since the arrival of the stove, Jesse hardly tasted his food. He was too aware of Amy's presence, desire already tightening his loins just from looking at her and listening to her voice.

Afterward they got out the books and worked at the table. Jesse tried to lose himself in the work, but he found it almost impossible to concentrate with the scent of Amy's perfume tickling his nostrils. She laid her hand on his arm while she explained a word to him, and his skin burned where she had touched it.

Finally they finished their lesson and Jesse put away the books. Amy picked up the kerosene lamp and turned to go into the bedroom area. Jesse watched her, knowing that he should leave. He stood up, but he did not move toward the door. His breathing accelerated, and his flesh tingled in anticipation. He gripped the back of his chair, his eyes remaining on Amy's form, visible through the sheets.

She set the lamp down on the nightstand and began to unpin her hair. Jesse's loins tightened. He knew what was coming, and that made it somehow even more exciting. Her hair tumbled down slowly. Then she picked up her brush and began to brush through it in long, even strokes. Watching her dark form, he could almost feel her hair sliding through the brush, could almost hear the crackle of electricity.

When she finally set down the brush, her fingers went to the buttons of her bodice, and she undid them slowly, then peeled the bodice off. She folded it neatly, put it away, and began on her skirt. Soon it drifted down over her hips and along her petticoats, pooling at last at her feet. Jesse watched as she bent to pick it up. He wished he could see her in detail, not just this dark figure against the sheets. He wanted to see the tones of her skin, each individual feature of her face and body.

Slowly, one by one, she took off her petticoats. With each movement, Jesse's skin flamed hotter, until he felt as if he were on fire. His hands clenched tightly around the posts of the chair, his knuckles white with tension. Amy reached down and removed her shoes, then rolled down each stocking, her hands gliding along her legs. Jesse swallowed hard as her fingers went next to the ribbons of her chemise. She untied them and pulled the chemise off, and he could see the globes of her breasts swing free, high and firm, swaying with her movements. Heat flooded his loins, and his manhood swelled, pressing against his trousers.

Jesse wanted her so much he thought it might kill him. He could think of nothing but her, the beauty of her body and the sweet wonder of taking her. She untied her pantaloons and pulled them down, revealing her soft feminine shape entirely. Jesse was on fire, hard and throbbing. She reached for her nightgown. He began to walk to the bedroom.

He knew he should stop, should go back, but tonight he could not bring himself to listen to reason. He was drawn to her in a way that surpassed all reason, all thought. There was nothing in him right now but need. Jesse reached out his hand and took the edge of one sheet, pulling it aside.

Amy jumped, gasping, and instinctively jerked the nightgown in her hand up to her torso, partially concealing her nakedness. "Jesse!"

She stared at him, her eyes wide and startled, yet luminous. His eyes went down to her mouth, soft and pink, then farther down, to her bare shoulders and arms, above the nightgown crumpled to her chest. Her skin was just as satiny as he had known it would be, a lovely creamy white. His eyes moved down the line of her hips and legs. She was perfectly formed.

Hunger pulsed in him. He wanted to snatch away the gown and reveal all her body to him. He wanted to lay her down on the bed and crawl on top of her, to sink into her delicious softness.

"Oh, God, Amy..." He closed his eyes. He thought he might explode. "Please...I want you."

Amy stared at Jesse's tortured face. Her heart twisted within her. As much as she wanted him, as much as she had tried to get him to desire her, she had never intended that he feel the kind of pain that was in his eyes now.

"Jesse." Tears clogged her voice. She didn't know what to say. It occurred to her that she had done nothing but bring misery to this man whom she loved so much.

"I'm sorry," he went on hoarsely. "I know I promised you, and I meant it. I— But, Lord, when I see you, I—I don't think I can keep from making love to you."

Amy forgot about concealing her boldness, about pretending that she did not feel the wanton desire that blossomed inside her. She could not think about the consequences, or about how Jesse's feelings for her might change if he knew how she really felt. All she could see was Jesse and his anguish. All she could think of was easing it.

"Then don't try to," she said, dropping her nightgown to the floor.

Jesse blinked, unable to believe his ears or eyes. He stared at Amy's naked body—slender and feminine, inviting. Blood roared in his head and coursed through his body. *Amy was giving herself to him.*

He started toward her. He half expected her to back away from him or blurt out that she didn't mean it or even suddenly run away. But she did not. She simply stood, watching him with wide eyes.

There was something a little frightening about Jesse, Amy thought. Power and heat radiated from him intimidatingly, and there was something more—a wildness barely held in check. But that very wildness was exciting, too. It was a heady feeling to know that she had the ability to arouse him to such overwhelming desire.

Jesse stopped only inches from her. Carefully he put his hands on her shoulders. His fingers seared her skin. He gazed down into her eyes, his face taut, his eyes blazing bright green. Slowly he bent and sealed her mouth with his. Heat flamed up instantly in Amy, and she moved into him, her arms going around his waist. It was strange and rather titillating to feel his clothes against her naked flesh. Amy moved against him, provoking a deep groan from Jesse, and her nipples hardened as they rubbed against the cloth of his shirt.

His kiss was hungry and deep, and his hands slid over Amy's body, as though he wanted to touch her everywhere at once. His tongue plunged deep into her mouth, and his fingers dug into her buttocks, lifting her up into him. The denim cloth of his trousers was rough upon her skin, and under it she could feel the hard insistence of his desire. She shivered, trembling with need for him.

"I'm sorry," he murmured, releasing her. "You're cold." He pulled down the bedspread and picked her up and settled her in the deep feather mattress. He reached down and jerked off his boots, then began to unbutton his shirt.

Amy was a trifle chilled, but she didn't pull the cover up over her. She liked the way Jesse gazed at her all the time he was undressing, as if he could not get his fill of looking at her body. He peeled his shirt back off his shoulders and down his arms; when it stuck at the still-buttoned cuffs, he swore and yanked at it. Amy heard the buttons pop off and bounce across the floor. He unfastened his belt buckle and started on the metal buttons of his trousers, but then he broke off, as if he could not hold back a moment longer, and bent to kiss her thoroughly, his hands plunging into her hair. He pulled away and continued to undress, his eyes eating her up all the while.

Finally he finished and stood naked in front of her. Amy gazed at him in love and wonder. He was lean and ridged with muscle, his skin smooth and tanned. Amy longed to reach out and run her hand along the washboardlike expanse of ribs and muscles. It was like satin laid over rock. Her eyes drifted lower, to his flat abdomen and the naked, thrusting maleness riding between his legs. She drew in a shuddering breath.

"Oh, Jesse, how can—? Do you think it'll work?"

Her naive remark drew a chuckle from him, despite the passion now tearing at his vitals. He climbed into the bed and lay down beside her, saying, "I'm not sure, sweetheart. I've never actually tried it. But I presume it must, given all the children that are produced."

"Do you mean—?" Amy sat up, amazement stamped on her face, and she gazed down intently into his face. "Are you saying that you've never—?"

He shook his head, smiling faintly. "No. Disappointed?"

"No! I—" She began to smile. "It's rather nice, actually, to know that you haven't—that no other woman has ... well, you know."

"Yes, I know." He stroked his knuckles down her cheek. "I feel the same about you."

"It's just, well, I suppose it would be better if one of us knew what he was doing."

His grin grew broader, and he curved his hand around her neck, pulling her down toward him. "I think we'll muddle through well enough."

Amy melted into him, delighting in the feel of his naked chest against hers. Their mouths met and clung, and the heat that had abated slightly while Jesse undressed flared up with renewed force. Jesse rolled over, taking Amy under him. They kissed deeply, tongues entwining.

Jesse pulled his mouth free and rained kisses over her face and down her neck, murmuring, "Sweet, so sweet. I'm glad I have never lain with another woman. I want to learn every pleasure with you. I want every flicker of your desire to be for me."

"It is," she assured him, her hands sweeping down his back and buttocks onto his hair-roughened thighs.

His mouth moved lower, onto the soft curve of her breast, and Amy drew in her breath sharply.

His head came up, and he frowned in concern. "Did I hurt you?"

"No! Oh, no. Please . . . keep on."

She moved a little beneath him, urging him on, and he quickly returned to what he had been doing. His mouth trailed across her breast, and his hand came up to cup it. Her nipple hardened at the soft, moist touch of his mouth, and Jesse stroked his thumb across the little bud, watching in fascination as it tightened even more. He teased the nipple with his thumb and forefinger, gently squeezing and caressing it until Amy's breath was ragged and she was rolling her head restlessly from side to side, eyes closed against the sweet, almost painful pleasure. Jesse looked at her face, drinking in the passion there, and then, at last, he lowered his head and took her nipple into his mouth. Amy let out a shuddering moan as he began to suck, enveloping her sensitive nipple with moist heat as his mouth pulled gently at it.

Amy had never experienced anything like the hot tremors of sensation that ran through her now. Passion blossomed in her abdomen, turning it waxen and heavy. Heat throbbed between her legs, where she suddenly, embarrassingly, flooded with moisture. She clamped her legs together to ease the sensation, but it wasn't enough; it wasn't what she wanted.

But Jesse seemed to know exactly what she wanted. His hand slid down her smooth stomach and abdomen and into the tangle of curls there. His movement startled her, but she reacted instinctively, opening her legs. His finger slipped down between her legs, delving into the slick, satiny folds of flesh. Amy groaned and moved her legs restlessly.

Jesse lifted his head and looked down into her face as his fingers explored her; the desire on her face excited him almost past bearing. He leaned down and teased her other nipple into hot, pulsing life with his tongue, while his fingers searched her soft secret flesh, delving into her heat, until she was panting and writhing with passion.

"Please, Jesse, please," Amy murmured.

Jesse moved quickly between her legs, lifting her buttocks and probing gently, his shaft instinctively seeking its home. He pushed into her, feeling her tighten at the pain. He wanted to stop, to not hurt her, but he was past that point now. He thrust into her, quick and hard, and she gasped, but now he was deep inside her, gloved by her sweet, tight femininity. Jesse groaned and took a long, slow breath, fighting the desire that threatened to swamp him. He had never felt anything so pleasurable, so good. It was as if he had found his home. His life.

He pulled back and plunged more deeply, sending waves of pleasure through them both. He tried to move slowly, but the pleasure was too intense, the passion too strong. It swept him along, making him move faster and faster. Amy was moving beneath him, panting, her fingers digging into his back. Her desire multiplied his, driving him higher and higher, until finally Amy convulsed around him, letting out a noise of surprised pleasure. Feeling her passionate release ignited his own, and Jesse cried out, releasing his seed into her and sweeping them both into a dark, mindless whirl of pleasure.

Finally Jesse rolled off her, curling his arm around her and cradling her head on his shoulder. They lay together silently, dazed by the storm of pleasure they had just experienced. Jesse turned his head to look into Amy's eyes. She smiled shyly at him, suddenly a little embarrassed by what she had just done. *Would he think her loose now? Overly bold?* But he had enjoyed it; innocent as she was, Amy could not believe that she was mistaken about his response. Jesse had been in the grip of passion, and surely he would not blame her for feeling the same way. She remembered the words of desire he had spoken, the endearments he had murmured as he kissed and caressed her. Why, he had called her "sweetheart" and "love"! Hope fluttered in her chest.

Jesse smoothed a finger down Amy's cheek. "You are so beautiful," he murmured. "Even more beautiful than I imagined."

Amy blushed and had to look away, thrilled by his words. "Thank you." Her voice was barely audible.

"Thank *you*." He kissed the top of her head. "You gave me a glimpse into heaven tonight."

"Jesse! That's blasphemous!" But she had to giggle, warmed by his words. She hesitated, then went on, "Did you really...enjoy it? Was it what you wanted?"

"Couldn't you tell? Of course it was what I wanted. It was everything I have ever dreamed of."

"I'm glad." She looked at him with glowing eyes. "I was afraid you might be disappointed with me."

"Don't be absurd." He brought her hand up and placed a kiss on the back and then on the palm. "You're everything any man could want." He spoke slowly, punctuating every word with a kiss on one of her fingertips.

He was quiet for a moment, and then he went on in a constrained voice. "What about you? Were you...content? I hope I didn't hurt you."

She shook her head, her hair brushing across his skin. "No. Only a little. And after the hurt, it was so wonderful." Amy blushed furiously. "I didn't know what to expect, what I would feel, but I never dreamed it would be like that."

Jesse smiled and twisted down to kiss her lips. Then he lay back with a sigh of contentment. He gazed up at the ceiling, idly twisting a strand of Amy's hair around his finger. Finally he asked softly, "Why did you— do that this evening? Why did you drop your nightgown and invite me in?"

"Oh. Were you upset with me?"

"For that? Good God, no, why would I be upset with you for giving me what I wanted?"

"I mean, because I so bold. I didn't act much like a lady. But you looked so unhappy—I never meant to make you unhappy."

"You made love with me because I looked unhappy? Because you felt sorry for me?"

"No. I didn't say I made love with you because you were unhappy. I already wanted to do that. I said I *dropped the gown* tonight because I couldn't bear to go on hurting you. Before then, I really hadn't thought about whether I was causing you pain—you know, with the things I was doing."

"Things you were doing?" he repeated, realization dawning in his voice. "You mean you did that on purpose?" Jesse sat straight up and gazed down at her in shock. "Undressing in here with the lamp on? You meant for me to see that every night?"

Amy glanced at him uncertainly. "Yes. And the other things, like sitting too close to you while you studied and wearing rose water all the time."

"My God." Jesse rubbed his hands over his face. "I can't believe this. All that time you were *trying* to get me to break down? You *wanted* to seduce me?"

"I'm sorry." Amy's voice trembled, and she bit her underlip. "Oh, please, Jesse, don't be mad. I didn't realize that it would upset you so. I just wanted you to love me, and I didn't want you to think I was too bold. Mama and Corinne told me how men like to pursue a woman. I saw how you looked that time after we kissed, and you were so disgusted with me. When you said that it would never happen again. I didn't want you to think I was loose and terrible. So I figured if I made all those things seem innocent, then maybe you wouldn't be repulsed."

"Repulsed!" He shoved his hands back into his hair. "I must be going mad. I was not repulsed by you. I never have been—I don't think I could be. I didn't sleep with you because I had promised you I wouldn't! I couldn't break my vow! And how could I try to seduce you, knowing that you loved another man?"

Amy frowned, looking puzzled. "Ano— Oh! You mean Charles Whitaker?"

"Yes. Charles Whitaker," he agreed grimly. "Unless there's someone else that you love lurking around."

"Only you," Amy replied simply. "I never loved Charles. I was infatuated with him for a time, but I never really loved him."

But Jesse seemed to have heard only the first part of her statement. "Only me?" he repeated in a dazed voice. "Are you saying that you love me?"

"Of course! That's what I've been talking about. That's why I was trying to trick you into desiring me. The night we kissed, I realized that I loved you. I thought if I could make you want me, then maybe that desire would grow into love. I wanted you to love me. I wanted to be truly your wife. I wanted to have you kiss me again and touch me and—make love to me."

Jesse groaned comically and flopped back onto the bed. He began to laugh, and Amy stared at him. "Oh, Amy, Amy... what a pair of fools we are! You didn't have to seduce me into loving you. I already loved you! Why do you think I offered to marry you? Why do you think I never slept with any of the whores in town? I went there with the other hands, but when I got into a room with the girl, I looked at her and knew I couldn't—because she wasn't you. You were the only one I wanted. I've loved you for years, almost from the first moment I saw you."

"Me?" Amy asked in disbelief. "You love me?"

"Yes!" He rolled onto his side, bracing his head on his bent arm. "Yes, I love you." He leaned over and began to kiss her lightly all over her face and neck, saying, "I love you, I love you, I love you."

Amy laughed out loud and threw her arms around his neck. "Oh, Jesse, how can we have been so foolish?" She smiled brilliantly up at him.

Jesse bent to kiss her again, but he stopped abruptly. Amy frowned up at him, puzzled. "What is it? What's the matter?"

"I don't know. I thought—I thought I heard something." He turned his head, listening. Suddenly his body went taut. "The horses! I did hear something."

He got up and went over to the window, pulling aside the curtain and peering out into the night. "I don't see anything...."

With an uneasy expression he turned back to her. "I better check."

"What is it?" Amy sat up, clutching the sheet to her naked bosom, his sudden odd mood infecting her, too.

"I'm not sure." Jesse quickly pulled on his trousers and shoved his feet into his boots. He grabbed his shirt from the floor, where he had dropped it earlier, and headed for the door.

Alarmed, Amy got out of bed and began to put on her clothes, too. She heard Jesse open the door, and then she heard a loud, abrupt oath from him, and he exclaimed, "The barn's on fire."

"On fire!" Amy ran to the window, and now she could see what Jesse had not been able to earlier: Flames were licking up from the back of the barn, eerie and orange against the night sky.

She saw Jesse run across the yard toward the barn. She knew he would first run to save his horses. But then he would return to fight the fire, she knew, and her mind busily spun ahead to what she should do to help him.

Quickly she thrust her feet into her shoes, not bothering to tie them, and ran from the room. She finished buttoning her dress as best she could as she hurried into the kitchen and began pulling out her largest tubs and pots, as well as the pails in which she carried water and feed for the chickens. She carried them out to the pump outside.

The horses thundered out of the barn past her, terrified by the fire. She knew Jesse had released the horses from their stalls and he would be here in a moment to grab the pots of water. She pumped as hard as she could, filling up the two pails and then starting on the largest tub.

She realized that Jesse should have gotten one of the pails by now, and fear clutched at her heart. She straightened and looked toward the barn. There was no sign of Jesse. Her fear deepened. She picked up the pails and began to walk to the barn, expecting at any moment to see him come running toward her to take the pails.

He did not.

Amy's heart began to thunder in her chest, and she set down the pails and ran to the barn. Just as she reached the barn door, a figure came out of the darkened corral, stretching out an arm toward her. Amy shrieked and jumped, startled.

"Shh . . . Don't be afraid. It's me."

Amy stared through the darkness at the man, only a few feet away from her. "Charles?" she asked in astonishment. "What in the world are you doing here?" Then she shook her head; there was no time for explanations. "Come on and help me. Jesse's still in the barn."

She started forward again, and he grabbed her arm, pulling her to a halt and turning her around. "No, don't!"

"What? Let go of me." She twisted, but he clung to her tightly.

"Don't go in there! You'll ruin everything. Besides, you can't save him. He's out cold."

"Out cold! Why? What do you mean?" Amy went icy inside, too scared to move.

"I hit him. I had to. He discovered me."

Amy glanced toward the barn, now blazing brightly. She could feel the heat from its flames. "You mean you set this? And then you hit Jesse and left him to die in there?"

He nodded. "I had to. I told him I'd get back at him. No one can get away with treating Charles Whitaker like that."

"Let go of me!" Amy began to struggle wildly, released from her momentary paralysis.

"No, wait!" He grabbed her with both hands, holding on tightly even though she kicked and swung and twisted, fighting to get away from him. "Don't! Think— Once he's gone, you won't have a cowhand for a husband. You and I can be married. You wouldn't have turned me down if you'd known that you'd have to marry your father's horse trainer instead. You deserve better than that. Leave him alone, and we—"

"Are you insane!" Amy brought her heel down hard on his instep and twisted away with all the strength she possessed, driven by fear. At last she was able to tear free from him. She ran straight into the burning barn, screaming, "Jesse! Jesse!"

"Amy, no!" Whitaker came after her, trying to pull her back.

Amy grabbed the closest thing she could find, a shovel that was leaning against the barn wall, and she whirled around, slamming it into Whitaker. She connected solidly with his head and shoulders, and he crumpled to the floor. Amy dropped the shovel and ran deeper into the barn, calling Jesse's name.

Smoke roiled through the barn, blinding her and making her cough. The heat was intense. High above her head, flames licked at the rafters of the barn. But Amy thought of none of it, only of Jesse and the fact that she could not let him die. She screamed his name over and over as she made her way toward the back of the barn, peering through the smoke.

Her foot hit something soft, and there was a groan. "Jesse!"

She sank down on her knees beside him, coughing from the smoke, and shook his arm. "Jesse! Jesse, wake up! We have to get out of here."

He stirred and mumbled, coughing, but he didn't open his eyes. Grimly Amy shoved her arms under his shoulders and locked them across his chest. She pulled and tugged frantically, but she could budge him only inches. Tears streamed down her face, and she repeated his name over and over, begging him to wake up, to help her. She pulled, straining every muscle, digging in her heels, and slowly she moved his body. Inch by precious inch they moved across the floor, and all the while the flames licked over the rafters, sending down sparks and waves of heat.

Finally Jesse groaned, and his eyes fluttered open.

"Jesse!" Amy exclaimed in relief and collapsed beside him. "Get up! Help me! Come on."

His eyes rolled, and for an awful instant she thought he had lost consciousness again, but then he groaned and rolled over, coughing, and began to try to rise. Jesse made it up to his hands and knees, and Amy put her shoulder under his arm, lifting with all her strength.

He staggered to his feet and, with him leaning woozily against her, they stumbled and weaved toward the barn door. It was an agonizingly slow journey, and Amy's heart was in her mouth with each step as the rafters groaned above them. Then, at last, they were free of the barn and sucking in the fresh air of the outdoors. They collapsed against the corral fence, coughing.

"What—what happened?" Jesse gasped.

"Charles Whitaker tried to kill you." Quickly Amy related what had happened.

"You mean—" Jesse looked back at the barn. Flames licked across the roof and up the walls. A rafter crashed, engulfing the rear of the barn in flames. "You mean Whitaker's in there?"

"Yes." Amy, too, looked at the barn, frowning with worry. Charles was a low human being, but she hated to think of him burning to death in the inferno he had created.

Jesse sighed and started back to the barn.

"No! Jesse! You might get killed, too! He's not worth it."

He smiled at her, but shook off her restraining hand. "I can't just let a man burn to death."

Jesse loped into the barn, and Amy waited in breathless suspense. Moments later, Jesse reemerged, dragging Charles Whitaker. A great groan sounded from the barn, and the central beam broke and crashed in flames to the ground. The barn roof collapsed, sending flames leaping and sparks shooting out.

Jesse stood looking at the barn for a long moment, then sighed and turned away. "We better tie this fellow up. I'll take him in to the sheriff tomorrow. This time I'm not letting him get away."

As soon as they had tied Whitaker up, Jesse and Amy raced to water down the area around the barn. Although the barn itself was beyond help, they had to keep the fire from spreading to the corral and the grass beyond. They soaked the corral fences nearest the barn, as well as the ground around it for several feet.

By the time they finished, they were tired and sore, but they saw with satisfaction that the fire was not spreading.

Amy turned from the grim sight of the barn burning to the ground and looked down at Jesse. He reached up and wiped a smudge of soot from her cheek, and then he smiled tenderly into her eyes.

"You saved my life." His voice was soft, almost wondering.

"Of course. I love you. I couldn't let you die."

Any lingering doubts he had had about her love melted away. She had risked her own life to save his.

Amy looked back at the barn, and her eyes flooded with tears. "Oh, Jesse. I'm so sorry. All your hard work..."

Jesse glanced at the rubble of the barn, then turned back to Amy. "I can rebuild a barn. What's important is that I have you. You're my wife, in every way, and that's all that matters to me. We can do anything together."

Amy threw her arms around his neck and went up on tiptoe to brush her lips against his. "Oh, Jesse, I love you so."

"And I love you, Mrs. Tyler." His arms tightened around her, and he kissed her deeply. "I love you."

* * * * *

Dear Reader,

I hope all of you enjoy reading "Jesse's Wife." It is set in one of my favorite times and locales, central Texas in the second half of the nineteenth century. I have lived in central Texas for the last fourteen years, and there's something special about writing a book when I can look out my study window and see in the distance the same landscape of live oaks, scrub juniper and tumbling, rocky creeks in which my characters lived.

"Jesse's Wife" is an idea that I've had in my head for years, but I could never seem to find the right format for it. When Harlequin Historicals asked me to write a story for their upcoming *Promised Brides,* I knew that I had found the place for Jesse and Amy. I hope that you will agree.

Best Wishes,

Kristin James

THE HANDFAST

Julie Tetel

Chapter One

Castle Tomain nam Mòd
The Scottish Highlands, 1703

Anne Chisholm felt herself being tossed in the air, then released. It was pleasant at first, that feeling of weightlessness. With the part of her mind that was no longer fully asleep, she anticipated that she would soon awaken with a start to realize that she had been dreaming of the bumpy carriage ride that had brought her so far north. In that same dreamily wakeful half second, she decided that when she floated to ground again, she would roll over, snuggle farther into the warm feather bed, and recapture sleep.

She was jolted awake with a very real and bone-jarring thud. Instead of being surrounded by lavender-scented linen and goose down, she found herself wrapped in wool that smelled sharply of wood smoke and peat; and instead of lying comfortably in a safe bed, she was coming to the rapid and terrifying conclusion that she had been slung over a man's broad shoulder, rump up. Disoriented, she caught only snatches of sounds that formed a fractured whole: scuffling boots in various corners of her bedroom, whispered commands, the creak of a door opening, the muffle of two bodies colliding, low curses, the rumble of a male laugh, a harsh "Shh!"

Suddenly she was whirled about as her captor turned, and she felt her body graze the doorjamb as she was shouldered out of the bedroom. She guessed that she must be in the hallway, but when she lifted her head to get her bearings, she could see nothing of her upside-down world beyond the black of night. At her minimal movement, and before she could cry out for help, her head was pushed down and her face was flattened against her captor's back.

Because she was muffled in a blanket, her arms were nearly useless, so she began to thrash in earnest with her legs. Although those movements brought her the indignity of her captor's hands on her ankles and thighs and backside, her head was momentarily released, and she lifted it again to cry out. No sound left her panic-stricken throat. She tried again, only to have her captor push her head down again against his back, stifling her.

"Dugald!" her captor whispered to a man ahead of him in the hallway. "She's awake!"

"Way you took her, no won—no wonder," came the reply, unsteadily and with indifferent reproach.

"She's heavier than I thought," her captor complained. "Had t' try twice."

"Shh!" This from farther down the hallway.

She squirmed again in an attempt to free herself, or at least to throw her captor off-balance. He had not yet released her head, but she was beginning to think she might have success escaping his grasp until he whispered again, "Dugald! The wench is—is—tryin' t' cry out. Bind her mouth, there's a good lad."

"So ye need help now, Duncan?" Dugald replied with exaggerated condescension. He performed the favor nevertheless, for the next thing Anne knew, her head was jerked upward and a cloth was hastily but securely tied around her mouth.

"Shhhhhhh!" Insistently, this time.

In that moment of contact with the man called Dugald, she was engulfed by the smell of whiskey, strong and sweet on sour breath, and was confirmed in her suspicions that her abductors were uncommonly drunk. Her mouth bound, terrified now, she tried again to effect her release with her legs—to no avail. None of her efforts had slowed her captor down, and she was aware that they had already traveled the length of the hallway. She worried now whether her captor, in his drunken state, was capable of descending the spiral stairs that led to the main hall without dropping her. She halted her thrashing long enough to be carried with alarming carelessness down the black funnel of the stone steps, which were tricky enough when taken sober and in the bright light of day.

At their improbably safe landing, Anne began to squirm again, and prayed that the castle guard was alert and on duty. Then the horrible idea assailed her that these men were of the Clan Ross, for she did not think they could have entered the fortress castle otherwise. For all she knew of Scottish ways, particularly those of the Highlands, this late-night abduction was standard practice, and the men had permission to carry her off. The obvious goal of such a practice did not fail to occur to her. She began to struggle harder.

"Oof!" Her captor grunted and tried to tame her as he crossed the hall in long strides. He opined, none too quietly, "She's a feisty one. Wouldna ha' thought it."

Dugald's voice could be heard in reply, "Gavin said she was a quiet one."

"Gavin's not had t' carry her weight. Heavier than I thought."

"Gavin said she was a frail thing, too."

"What does Gavin know, I'm wonderin'?"

"Shhhhhhh!"

"Shh yerself, Gavin lad!" returned the two in unison.

So her captors were Duncan, Dugald and Gavin. She did not recall having met any Ross men with those names at Castle Tomain nam Mòd, but that meant nothing in a manor with fifty or more inhabitants, when she had been here only a day and a half.

Soon they had crossed the hall, without being stopped. After a few more twists and turns down short, dark hallways, they left the stealthy gloom of the castle and entered the swirling night mists of the courtyard. She lifted her head, but could see little more than clammy white. Against one side of her face, she felt the restless night winds, which were fresh even in July. The blanket that wrapped her kept the winds off the rest of her body. Blood beat at her temples, causing them to throb with fear and the effects of her prolonged inverted position.

A new voice whispered impatiently from across the courtyard. "Hurry now! Come!"

"Hey, now, Alex!" one called back in a stentorian whisper.

She closed her eyes against the horror of it. Four men, now? As her captor carried her across the courtyard, she thought that her quick disgrace was to take place, appropriately, in the stables.

But no. With the bit of reason left to her, she realized that they were leaving the castle through a wicket in the main portal. Then the unsyncopated sounds of boots on stone rang in her ears, and she felt her stomach heave and sink as she was whisked down a narrow stone staircase that seemed to be built into an exterior fortification. At the thought of entering the dark, desolate hills just beyond the castle gates, her fear expanded to incorporate despair. She wished, pitifully, that custom allowed the men to have done with her in her own bed.

At the bottom of the stairs, she heard the stamp and wheeze of horses close by, along with the clink of metal bit and bridle. She caught a whiff of warm horseflesh. Her captor shifted her ungently from one hard shoulder to the other, nearly letting her fall headfirst to the ground before he righted himself and her.

After the shock of these shifts had coursed through her body, she lifted her head wearily. In that moment, dim night light penetrated a tatter of mist, and she was able to perceive the dress of the man who held her. She saw that his back was covered not by the distinctive red plaid of the Clan Ross, but by a less vivid one. Green, she guessed, gridded with fine lines of blue or black. She had no knowledge of tartans, and so could not have said to which clan these men belonged. It struck her as a further measure of the awful dimensions of her situation that she was being borne off by savages from a clan with no name.

They moved toward the horses. She closed her eyes again and let her head fall, her temples fit to explode from the throbbing pain. The blood was drumming in her ears and darkening her eyeballs.

"That's us away now, laddies," said one of the men. It was Gavin, she reckoned. He had been the most impatient of the three in the castle.

"T' the southmost bothy, as we agreed," another said, swinging into the saddle. This was Alexander, she guessed, their leader. "We've washed—wasted enough time here." Their *drunken* leader.

"Nay, then, we were quick," a third man, likely Dugald, protested. He emphasized his point by belching with supreme satisfaction.

"As quick as the bothy's old woman," Alexander replied with a drunkard's insulting dignity from high on his horse.

"Ye've not had t' carry this weight, my fine-talkin' lad." This from her captor, belligerently.

"Ye're weakened by drink, Duncan," Alexander tossed down at him. He clucked his tongue. "'Tis a sorry day for the Sutherlands, I'm thinkin'."

Through her dulled senses, she registered the information. Duncan, Dugald, Gavin, Alexander. Sutherlands, then. They were not nameless savages, after all.

"Then ye can take her, Alexander," Duncan said, rolling his *r*s with fierce challenge.

The next thing she knew, she was heaved from Duncan's shoulder and flung up and across a horse. Mercifully, Alexander's reflexes were still good enough to protect her from injury. He captured her wrapped form neatly and nestled her in the wedge between his legs and the circle of his arms. Now that she was upright, the blood rushed from her temples, making her light-headed.

Duncan's voice came from below. "Ye see, then, Alex? She's no frail thing, as we were led t' believe!"

Alexander seemed to think this comment called for immediate verification. He passed inquisitive hands over her person, rousing her deflated spirits to life and her body to squirming, angry protest. She strained against the cloth in her mouth, growling with the effort. She struggled to retain consciousness after the rapid draining of blood from her head.

Alexander lifted the folds of the blanket from her face and peered owlishly at her in the dark. She managed to snarl her opinion of him and his manners before he let the folds of the blanket fall back over her face. "Best t' keep the rag in her mouth," he decided, picking up the reins and flicking them. Then, with apparent reference to her lack of frailty, he declared solemnly, "But ye speak the truth, Duncan." He turned his horse. Apparently as an afterthought, he added, "Evan will thank us. That he will."

Evan? A *fifth* man? she thought wildly. Sutherlands, all of them, no doubt. She could not help it—she swooned. Before she lost consciousness, the thought came to her that they might not be nameless, but they were still savages.

Sometime later, she roused to half awareness, wanting to disbelieve that she was still tramping over the wilds of northern Scotland, jostled on a lathered horse. Her backside was as close to a man as it had ever been—or ever could be—and had been rubbing up against him over a period of hours by now. She cracked bleary eyes open. The dawn had not yet broken, but the sky was no longer pitch, and the thinnest thread of a crimson line held the promise of day on the horizon on her right. The night mists still grazed on the hillsides, but they were friendlier now, like the ghosts of old flocks.

She looked up. She noted that Alexander, reeling slightly though he was, seemed less in danger of falling off his horse than did the others. She looked down and saw now that her blanket was a tartan of rich hunter green, black-patterned. So this was the Sutherland plaid. It was surprisingly soft. Of the many discomforts she felt, the chill of dawn was not one of them, for she was warm down to the tips of her bare toes. The smell of woodsmoke and peat that clung to the wool was not so suffocating out in the open.

Suddenly the terror of the occasion gripped her so thoroughly that only the solid bones and flesh of the man holding her had reality. She shuddered violently.

"Hey, then!" Alexander called out. "The lass is awake! Just in time!"

This occasioned more yelping and hooting from Duncan, Dugald, and Gavin, and it coincided with the appearance of a thatched bothy, or shelter, nestled in a rocky outcropping of an adjacent hill. Swiftly the horses ate up the distance and Alexander drew his stallion to a halt and dismounted. He deftly maneuvered his charge so that she slithered down to the ground, where she was caught again in his arms.

The folds of the tartan fell away from Anne's head and face when she was set upright. It was light enough now to discern the features of her present captor, and she noted that he was returning her regard keenly. It seemed to her that Alexander looked vaguely troubled. He turned smartly on his heels and left her to walk toward the hut, some twenty feet away.

The others had drawn rein and dismounted. They were heading toward the door of the bothy, as well. As they entered, she heard them talking loudly about breaking their fast, obviously pleased with themselves and the world. One man produced a flask, and its appearance was greeted with spirited early-morning enthusiasm.

She stood stock-still for a moment or two, amazed to be so ignored. First things first, she decided, and raised her arms to untie the cloth that bound her mouth. She worked her jaw and took a deep breath, while her terror shaded insensibly into puzzlement.

Another moment passed before one of the men emerged and scanned the scene until he spotted her. As he walked toward her, she could see in the ever-lightening dawn of day that his brows rose high in question and his eyes seemed to come in and out of focus. When he was close enough to take her arm, he rubbed his face vigorously. He was a short, stocky man, black-browed and swarthy, and as ugly a Highlander as she had ever seen. When he uncovered his face again, he shook his head. She could see that he was even more troubled than Alexander had been.

"She doesn't look like Claire," he said to no one in particular, his tone suggesting that he disbelieved his own two eyes.

"That is because I am not Claire," she said, pulling the plaid around her haughtily and standing up straight, so that her eyes were a fraction above his. She eyed him with magnificent condescension. "But I have guessed that you, sir, are Duncan Sutherland."

He fairly flinched at her words, and his gasp was audible. He put his finger to his lips and hissed, "Say no more!" Then he turned toward the hut and bellowed, "Come, ye slummocky gawks! There's been a terrible mistake!"

"What, she's fled?" one said as he ran out of the bothy, the others tumbling behind him. They came to a halt a few feet from her, forming a haphazard semicircle behind Duncan. Their eyes were uniformly wide.

An expectant second passed before one man pointed an accusatory finger at her. "That's not Claire!" he announced angrily. He was of the same build and coloring as Duncan, and was as similar to him as a squat creamer to its sugar. She guessed this was Dugald.

"Where's Claire?" the tall, slim, fair one demanded. Gavin, she determined. He was holding the uncorked flask, and he took the opportunity to bolster his senses, which were obviously deranged at the sight of the woman before him. He gargled, then swallowed, and looked around him suspiciously, as if expecting to see Claire.

Anne was feeling her courage gather in the face of her abductors' disarray. Her eyes flashed fire and dignity around the group until they fell on Alexander, who had not yet said anything. His sapphire blue eyes met hers. She saw that he was making a visible effort to clear his brain of the alcohol-laced cobwebs clouding his mental functions. He had some success, for he was able to form an intelligent question: "If ye're not Claire—and I can see ye're not—then who in God's name are ye?"

"I am Anne Chisholm," she said with icy hauteur. "And you, sir, I presume, are Alexander Sutherland."

He nodded dumbly.

"She doesn't sound like Claire, neither." This from Duncan, with great perception.

"Sounds haughty," Dugald opined, nodding wisely.

"Oh, aye, haughty," Duncan agreed.

"Where's Claire?" Gavin demanded with drunken tenacity, still looking around, his eyes glaring.

"If you are referring to Claire Ross," Anne informed him, "she is presumably safe in her bed at Inverness."

"Very haughty," Duncan insisted.

Alexander shoved hands that were slightly unsteady through thick black hair, further disordering his disorderly mane. He drew a deep breath, then said, "There's been a mistake."

She smiled scornfully and said slowly, "There *has* been a mistake." She paused for effect, then continued, "A very grave mistake. One that is, no doubt, punishable by law. I have no notion of the laws governing Scotland, but I am sure that the arm of English law will reach as far as this godforsaken edge of the world." She took the strong offensive. "If I remember correctly, hanging is the punishment for the abduction of an Englishwoman."

The statement failed to produce any reaction of fear or remorse or even consternation on the part of her misguided captors. Instead, the faces of Duncan, Dugald, Gavin and Alexander froze a moment in surprise, and then all four broke into merriment. They exhaled on great gusts of laughter, exclaiming, each in turn, "Anne Chisholm is English!"

"Oh, aye, and Duncan Sutherland is Italian!"

"I'm French!"

"I'm Greek!"

"She's Chinese!"

If Anne could have seen herself through their eyes, she would have understood their merriment. She looked the perfect Highland lassie, from the wild wisps of her red hair escaping her night braid, which had long since disintegrated, to her clear white skin, to her wide green eyes and her milkmaid's figure. Even her bare feet fit the picture, for not wearing shoes or boots was a common Highland practice in the summer among men and women of all stations in life. Wrapped as she was in a Sutherland plaid, she looked like every sister and sweetheart these men had ever known.

Anne's fear evaporated. Anger seized her. She could not see herself through their eyes. "I am Anne Chisholm, daughter of Walter Chisholm, chamberlain of the court of Queen Anne," she stated grandly. "I was born and raised in London, and I am an Englishwoman. I am in Scotland for the first time—" here she faltered "—visiting relatives. *Distant* relatives."

Dugald nodded. "I knew she wasn't a Sassenach."

They all paused to absorb the truth of that.

Gavin plopped down on the ground, cross-legged, with his head in his hands and the flask cradled in his lap.

Of the four of them, Alexander seemed to be the only one whose wits were functioning. "That explains, at least," he said, "how Duncan came to mistake you. He knows Tomain nam Mòd like the back of his hand. You must have been given Claire's chamber while she's away."

She confirmed coldly, "I have been given her chamber, yes."

Duncan clapped his hand to his brow and exclaimed, "So that was it!"

Anne listened with growing indignation as Duncan and Dugald, sobered now, engaged in a brief professional discussion, opened by Duncan on the opinion that, "Well, 'twas a good plan anyhow."

"Very good," Dugald agreed, a little solemnly.

"But for the fact that we nabbed the wrong lassie."

"Oh, aye, wrong lassie." This very solemnly.

"So, then. What are we going t' do with her?"

"Take her back."

Duncan shook his head. "Can't do it."

"Why not?"

"Haven't got a plan t' get her back into the castle. Only had a plan t' get her *out*."

"And it'll soon be broad daylight."

As if on cue, the first shimmering line of the sun crested the horizon.

Duncan suggested, "We'll have to storm the castle."

Here Alexander entered the discussion. "I didn't kill the guards, only knocked their heads together. I reckon they're awake by now and have put the entire castle on high alert."

While Duncan and Dugald considered this valuable piece of information, Alexander shook his head, then his limbs, as if to loosen them. With an impatient, dismissive gesture, he left the group and wandered off into some far bushes. Anne was insulted that he would abandon so important a discussion, until she realized that he had gone off to relieve himself. She blushed and returned her attention to Duncan and Dugald, who were still busily sorting out the problem of what to do next.

After a moment of great concentration, Duncan said, "I have a plan."

"How t' get round the castle guards a second time?"

Duncan shook his head. "Not as good as that, but it'll save us from disgrace." With a nod to Anne, he added, "And her."

"What, then?"

Duncan said, "Handfastin'."

Dugald's brows rose. He looked impressed. "Handfastin', then. 'Tis a good plan."

"A very good plan."

"But which among us?" Dugald wanted to know.

Duncan frowned, looking down first at Gavin, then off to where Alexander had wandered. His frown vanished. In unison, he and Dugald cried happily, "Alexander! Oh, aye!"

"The ladies like him," Duncan said.

"And he's got naught t' lose," Dugald offered.

"It wouldn't be a sacrifice for him. Not really."

"Not really."

Together they called out over their shoulders, "Alexander!"

At the brutal noise, Gavin moaned and held his head.

Chapter Two

Anne was not quite sure she liked the sounds of what she was hearing. She had no idea what they were talking about, but at mention of their disgrace and hers, some very unpleasant visions arose in her mind's eye, principally involving her father. Although she no longer feared for her immediate bodily safety, she was beginning to perceive other, disagreeable dimensions to her present predicament, especially now that daybreak was upon them. She was not sure what Alexander Sutherland had to do with the new plan—if plan it was—or what it had to do with her, but she needed to clarify one important detail first.

"Handfasting?" she queried.

Duncan explained, "Pledgin' the hand."

"Pledging the hand?"

Dugald chimed in. "It's a betrothal."

"Almost as good as a marriage," Duncan added.

"Nay, then, it counts as marriage."

"Marriage for twelve months and a day."

She asked warily, "And what is your plan, exactly?"

At that moment, Alexander returned to the group. "Marriage for a year and a day?" he repeated, evidently having heard only the last of the discussion. "Why are ye speakin' of handfastin' at such a moment, lads?"

Duncan and Dugald looked cheerfully at him. "Why, Alex, me lad," Duncan informed him, "we've hit on a plan!"

"A very good plan!" Dugald seconded.

Alexander invited them to explain.

"We've proposed a handfastin'," Duncan was pleased to tell him.

"T' preserve our honor and hers, ye might say," Dugald added.

"Have ye the man in mind?" Alexander asked.

Duncan and Dugald did not alter their cheerful expressions. "Oh, aye, we've the man in mind, Alex!"

After a moment, Alexander blinked in comprehension, then uttered a soft, knowing "Ahh!"

Anne was surprised when Alexander did not immediately reject what she was beginning to suspect was no plan at all, but an absurdity. He glanced at the horizon and squinted against the rising sun. He looked back at her. He rubbed his chin. He said, "It's down with the applecart for us, I can't deny." He rubbed his chin again and looked at her. His remarkable blue eyes were clear now, but still shadowed. "What do ye think, lassie?"

"About what?" she asked icily, denying even to herself her increasing apprehension at the nature of this "plan."

"Duncan and Dugald here think that the only way t' preserve our honor and yours—and prevent a bloody clan war, I might add—is t' rectify the mistake with a handfastin'. Ye and me."

She took a deep breath and tried to control a wild surge of emotion. From force of long habit, she mastered herself, and drew on her strict and proper upbringing. "To put the matter in proper English—" She rounded on Duncan when he opened his mouth. "Yes, *English*, Duncan Sutherland! You are proposing that I enter into handfast with—" she gestured toward Alex, but would not look at him "—this man. A betrothal, in fact."

"That's right."

"She understands."

Anne maintained her dignity. She continued, "For a year and a day."

"That's right."

"She understands."

"This is outrageous!" Anne declared angrily. "You... you...*gentlemen,* are, I must inform you, ignorant of several highly relevant factors that make such a handfasting impossible." At their obliging expressions of inquiry, she deployed an argument she had never imagined would be to her advantage. "Please understand, sirs, I am already betrothed."

Duncan and Dugald waved this away as if it were of no consequence. "Handfastin' is more like a marriage," said one.

"It takes precedence over a mere betrothal," said the other.

Alexander ran his eye over her and said, "He'll wait."

At this embarrassing scrutiny, Anne pulled the tartan more tightly around her and stood up straighter. "You, sir," she said, "are insulting."

Alexander smiled a charming, lopsided smile. "Och, now, lass, I meant t' be flattering."

For some reason, she did not find a ready reply to that absurd gambit. Her silence permitted Duncan to ask, "And what is the other— What was it, now?" Here he scratched his head. "'Highly relevant factor'?"

Anne quickly gathered her forces again. She smiled the smile of the daughter of the chamberlain to the queen. "My father will not permit it."

"Nay, then, lass, yer father's permission is no' necessary for a handfastin'," Dugald was happy to inform her. "Oh, aye, I see that ye're surprised, but we Scots think that a man and woman can decide for themselves if they're inclined toward one another, and that they should live together t' see if they'll suit."

She felt irrationally chastened by Dugald's high-minded attitude. "Live together?" she asked, quite amazed. "Just like that? No parental approval?"

Alexander joined in the discussion at this point. "Nor the interference of a priest."

Anne was visibly startled by this.

"'Tis a reasonable enough arrangement," Alex explained, "and the custom serves us well. At the end of the year and a day, the couple can be permanently married, if they so desire. Or, if either of them objects, the union is dissolved. If there is a child as a result of the union, it has to be supported by the one who objected to going forward with the marriage."

Anne had difficulty assimilating the idea that a man and woman should arrange their own marriage, outside the family, outside the church, but she dimly perceived some advantages to it. However, based on her experiences of the past several hours, she decided that this practice of handfasting must be of a piece with the rest of the wild Scottish ways.

She said confidently, "It's barbaric."

Duncan and Dugald looked nonplussed for a moment. "'Tis right proper," said one.

"'Tis legal," said the other.

"It spares a lot of bastards," said Alexander, not mincing words, "and secures many a legitimate claim t' a chieftainship of a clan, thereby saving us a lot of disorder and confusion. At the same time, it's not so bad for a man and a woman t' take responsibility for a child they conceive out of a union of passion."

Anne sniffed at these explanations, and Duncan and Dugald seemed to have had enough of them, too. They declared themselves ravenous, and matched word to deed by turning to go off to the bothy, where they said they had left some green cheese and eggs the night before. As an afterthought, Duncan turned back and commanded Alexander to proceed with his courting so that they could get on with the handfasting. Then he stumbled across Gavin, whose head was still in his hands. With a nod to Dugald, they picked the sick lad up by his arms, and then they were gone.

Alexander turned to Anne, a slight, whimsical smile softening the hard planes of his jaw and deepening the creases that ran from his straight nose to his well-formed mouth. He lifted black brows in invitation and motioned toward his right. "Shall we?" he asked. "As ye've heard, I have orders t' court ye."

"So that we can get on with the handfasting?" Anne returned, accepting his escort. They headed in the direction of a large boulder on the side of the hill. The emerald green turf beneath her feet was thick and damp. She shook her head. "You're not serious, and I'll not fall victim again to one of your pranks."

Alexander said, "We're very serious. What ye have not yet understood is that ye have no choice in the matter."

She dared to look at him, and could not quite read his expression, which was, indeed, as matter-of-fact as his tone. She managed a pretty shrug, not wishing to appear gullible, or to panic at this new turn of events.

They arrived at the boulder, from which a chip had fallen eons before, thus making a natural seat. With Alexander's kind attention, she disposed herself there and arranged the plaid around her shoulders, maintaining her modesty, as all that she wore beneath was a thin cambric night shift. The chip had fallen in front of the boulder, and served as a footrest. Clusters of tiny bluebells bloomed in a circle at her feet.

Alexander stood beside her and placed one foot on an indentation in the boulder that had been worn by the finger of time. He flipped his plaid so that it hung off one shoulder and fell front and back. Its edges grazed the ground. He wore neither neckcloth nor doublet, but his linen shirt was fine, and had been sewn and embroidered with great skill and care. Trews covered his shapely legs, a dirk was thrust in his belt, and leather brogues were laced around his feet.

He propped an elbow on his raised knee and set his chin on his fist. "Ye see, lass," he told her, looking off to the east, "we can't take ye back t' Tomain nam Mòd. The guards are awake by now, yer kin will see that yc've gone, and they'll guess it's the work of the Sutherlands."

"But it was a mistake," Anne said, feeling surprisingly calm in the face of this great disaster. "Can you not return me this morning and explain it? Or are you afraid?"

Alexander shook his head. "Not of the Rosses—begging your pardon, Anne o' Siosal." He called her by the Celtic version of Chisholm. "It's yer honor that's been compromised, and naught will undo that but the protection of my name."

She still retained the shred of a notion that he was not serious. With the yellow sun peeping up over the horizon, warming the raw dawn, surrounded by the fresh, fragrant air of the summer Highlands, and speaking to a man whose rough parts added up to a surprisingly smooth whole, she did not feel equal to arguing the issue. She felt, in fact, lighthearted, but that might well have been due to her continuing relief that she had not been borne off by vicious rapists.

"Any other questions, lass?" he asked after a moment, not unkindly.

She bethought herself of a detail that had been rattling around in her mind with no place to settle. "Who is Evan?"

His eyes, as deep a blue as the Highland sky, suddenly sparkled. "Ye've hit the nail, as we say, with the very question that needs asking! Why, he is the cause of all yer troubles, Evan Sutherland is. A more mournful lad ye'll never meet! Deep in love with his Claire Ross, and not an ounce of gumption t' win her!"

Anne put two and two together. "So *that's* why Claire was sent to Inverness," she said, narrowing her eyes in speculation as she looked off into the shadowy distance. "Upon arriving yesterday—the day before yesterday, now—I heard that Claire had resisted her father's orders to marry a Munro, I think it was. She was sent to an aunt's so that she could reconsider her poor behavior. It was intimated that she had given her heart elsewhere." She glanced back at Alexander. "To Evan, I expect?"

"I expect so," said Alexander.

Anne felt a tiny spurt of vindication. "So a man and a woman don't always get to decide for themselves whom they wish to marry? Why do not Evan and Claire simply pledge themselves in handfast?"

"Well, now, that's what we were thinkin' last night as we sat at Dunrobin, tryin' t' humor a most morose lover boy. Och, now, there was no persuadin' him that he had t' take the bull by the horns, so to speak. So when he took t' his bed—he being worn out from so much soulful emotion— we devised a plan for defeatin' the defenses at Tomain nam

Mòd, with the brotherly thought of doin' his work for him!''

"I can certainly think of less dramatic ways of accomplishing the same end," Anne said, rather primly.

"Name but one, lass."

"You could have had Evan send Claire a note to meet him outside castle walls, for instance, and they could have pledged their hands anywhere—why, right here, in fact. That way, when Claire did not respond to the note, you would have discovered that she had been sent away, and Evan could have gone to get her in Inverness."

Alexander rubbed his chin. "Ah, but ye see, we did not want t' compromise Claire by havin' her go directly against her father's wishes. We thought it would be better for her honor within her family t' have her carried off and be forced into marryin' Evan."

Anne's mind boggled at this cockeyed notion of honor, but she thought it wiser at the moment not to try to penetrate the mysteries of a Highland man's mind. "But why is the Ross against his daughter's union with Evan Sutherland?"

Alexander looked at her as if she were extremely simpleminded. "Why, lass, the Rosses and the Sutherlands have been at a feud for generations, now. It is unthinkable that a Ross would *give* his daughter, freely, to a Sutherland!"

"How would I know that?" she returned huffily. "I've been in Scotland hardly two full days, and only one of them has been in any surroundings nearing civilization!"

Alexander assumed a knowing look. "Sent away from London were ye, t' rusticate? Disobedient, I suspect ye are, like yer distant cousin, Claire."

Anne's mouth dropped open, and she betrayed herself with a question that she immediately regretted, "How could you know that?"

Alexander smiled smugly as he eyed her vivid flush. "'Tis yer temper, lass. Pure Scots."

With effort, she recovered her composure and complexion. "I came to Scotland," she said with great dignity, "to meet the relatives I have never known. My father thought it proper."

Alexander smirked. "Ye didn't like yer betrothed, either, lass, and ye were sent away to reconsider?"

She resented his insight. "My betrothed is—" she could not choke out the words *entirely acceptable to me,* and chose instead "—none of your business."

Alexander shrugged and said, "Ye've the right of it, and I couldn't be less interested in him, when all is said."

Anne was not going to be put at a disadvantage. She plucked from thin air the first thing that came to mind. "And I suppose you are *not* going to tell me why Duncan and Dugald thought that *you* were such a likely candidate for a handfasting?" She smiled in what she hoped was a superior manner. "They seemed to think that you had nothing to lose, and that such a turn would not be a sacrifice for you."

Alexander surprised her by saying, "I'll be happy to tell ye. I've nothin' t' lose in this wee project of handfasting, since there's a price on my head."

Anne edged away from him. "You're a thief or a murderer, perhaps?"

Alexander laughed heartily at that, the sound of merriment rumbling down the hill into the dark glen and echoing back up again. "I've killed and stolen, ye might say, but only in times of war, when it's not called killin' and stealin'. Nay, then, I'm considered a political undesirable by yer friends the Sassenachs, who have perceived the nuisance value of the Scottish Parliament and wish t' annex it t' their own." He forestalled her obvious retort by waving a hand and adding, "Aye, lass, yer friends, although ye're dyin' t' claim them as yer kin."

She did not choose to engage in a discussion of her heritage, in which she could not see victory for herself. "What did you do to earn a price on your head?"

"I've objected to the Act of Union, and even helped prevent it thus far," he said, blithely exposing himself to a woman who claimed to be English, at least by upbringing. "It's a low price on my fine head, too, which mortal wounds my vanity, but that's not t' the point just now. I bring it up rather t' show ye that ye've not much t' be worried about in pledgin' your hand t' me. I'll doubtless be hangin' from the gallows in Crown Square well before the end of the year and day."

Anne was amazed, and not a little impressed, that he could speak of his own death so carelessly, even dispassionately. At the same time, it occurred to her that he might be leading her down a false trail. She said, "You may well hang before the year is out, but by that time— whenever it comes—I'll be ruined!"

Alexander frowned thoughtfully, then said, "Nay, lass, ye'll be a widow."

Anne gasped on a laugh, but would have none of it. "I'll be *ruined!*" she insisted severely.

"Ye're ruined now," he said, "if ye'd but recognize it."

At that timely moment, a diversion was created when Gavin dashed out the bothy door and, in a blur of green, shot for the far bushes, over which he bent.

Alexander stood up straight and offered Anne his arm. He said politely, "I imagine the bothy is a more fit place for yer company now, with Gavin's evacuation, and I'll be pleased to take ye in, so that ye may eat and raise yer courage for the handfastin'."

Anne rose and accepted his arm. At her movement, her plaid slipped off one shoulder, exposing an expanse of breast easily visible through her thin shift. She hastily covered herself and glanced at her companion to see if he had noticed. He was looking respectfully away. Standing next to him now, she remembered having rubbed her backside up against him for several hours. She felt her skin pinken, and hated, not for the first time, her perfect Scottish complexion.

She said coolly, "I'll eat, but there will be no handfasting. I don't suppose you've been considering my feelings about all of this?"

Alexander looked up into the clouds in bewildered supplication. "And here I was thinkin' I'd convinced her that her feelin's were precisely what I *was* considerin'!" To Anne he said, "When ye've broken your fast, ye'll feel better about the handfastin'."

"You think a little food in my stomach will change my mind about marrying you?"

Alexander nodded. "I like to think positive, ye see."

This, she thought whimsically, from a man with a price on his head. That is, if he was telling her the truth.

Within mulled a small fire, spreading blue smoke throughout the dim interior. The pleasing smell of properly cooked food assailed her nostrils, and did, in fact, raise her spirits. But not so far as to make her accept the notion of a handfasting.

Duncan and Dugald had plainly taken the matter as settled. When Anne and Alexander darkened the door, they were arguing amiably in a language Anne did not understand. At their entrance, Duncan and Dugald turned toward them, all smiles, and gestured them to their places on the bench at the rough trestle table and offered to serve them a meal "in celebration."

"But there's nothing to celebrate," Anne told him, maintaining what she hoped was a strong position.

Duncan nodded gravely, then winked broadly at Alexander. Dugald said, "Naught like a wee bit of resistance t' pique a man's desire," then served up eggs and bacon and cheese. He also put before her a bowl full of "porritch," the like of which she had seen the morning before at Tomain nam Mòd. Before arriving in Scotland, she had heard rumors of the vile character of this dish that she had previously thought grossly exaggerated. They were not, and she refused the dish this morning, as she had the morning before. Otherwise, the breakfast was delicious, and more than satisfying to an appetite sharp-set from the exertions of the morning.

Anne and Alexander ate at a leisurely pace, speaking idly of this and that. Their companionable silences were bridged by the domestic bustle of Duncan and Dugald. At length, Duncan asked, "Have ye told her how it's done, Alex?"

Alexander shook his head. "Not yet."

"How is it done, then?" she asked, curious by now about this practice of handfasting.

Alexander stood up before her. He held out his hands and pulled her to her feet. "It's very simple," he said. "Ye have t' be afore witnesses." Here he nodded to Duncan and Dugald. "Under most circumstances it's human witnesses, of course," he added, drawing rude ripostes from the pair, "but these black sheep will do. Now, ye hold hands, as we're doin', and ye say, 'I pledge ye my troth.'"

"I pledge you my troth," Anne repeated. "That's all?"

"Aye, I pledge ye my troth." He smiled warmly. He had, she noted, a very charming smile. "That's all there is t' it, lass."

Chapter Three

Alexander gave her hands a squeeze before releasing them. "Well, now, 'tis settled," he said. He sat back down on the bench, facing away from the table, stretched out his long legs, and propped his elbows on the table so that he could lounge comfortably.

Anne felt a spasm in the region of her heart. "What do you mean, 'It's settled'?" she demanded, her eyes wide.

"Why, the handfastin'," he said, looking up at her with an amicable smile.

"It is *not* settled!" she said. She looked around, turning an accusing eye on each man in turn. "Not by any measure!"

Duncan looked taken aback. "How can it not be settled, lass? I heard you pledge yer troth t' Alexander, plain as day."

"It was a trick!" Anne said.

"What trick, then?" Dugald wanted to know. "I neither saw, nor heard, no trick. Ye were holding hands. Ye made the oral pledge. Afore witnesses."

"But I didn't *mean* the words!" Anne cried, aghast.

Duncan cocked a heavy brow and put his hands on his hips. "Is it not just like a Sassenach," he said in a tone of righteous disgust, "t' take back the very words they speak?'' He shook his dark head. "Ye've lived too long among them, lass, and adopted their dishonest ways. I'm sorry for it!''

Anne knew when she was being hoodwinked. She looked angrily down at Alexander, who was looking up at her with a slightly amused expression on his face. "Say something!''

" 'Tis only for a year and a day,'' he said. "Less, if I'm t' hang.''

Anne stamped her foot in fury at having been foiled. "I won't stand for this!''

Alexander put his hand to his ears. "Och, now, lass, so soon the wife, already scolding! And we haven't even taken our pleasure yet.'' At that, he stood up. "Ah, that's it! Ye've not been properly bussed as a married woman!''

He reached out and drew Anne toward him. The plaid slipped from her shoulders to be caught in her elbows, and her lightly clad figure was pressed to his length. He put his lips to hers and kissed her, well and without reserve. She tasted on his lips whiskey and, unexpectedly, wild heather honey. The kiss dizzied her, and she experienced a feeling similar to the one she had had when Duncan threw her over his shoulder and twirled her through her bedroom door. When Alexander ended the kiss and released her, she was momentarily speechless. She put her hand to her cheek, where his early-morning stubble had burned her skin.

He sat himself down on the bench again. Looking to Duncan and Dugald, he said, " 'Tis what she needed t' keep her quiet.''

This observation was clearly not calculated to keep Anne quiet. "How dare you?'' she demanded in magnificent rage. "I did nothing, and performed no ceremony. I did not mean the words I said, and was merely repeating what you told me!'"

Here Dugald entered the discussion. By the knitting of his brows, it seemed he had been concentrating deeply on the point she had raised. "I'm not at all sure, as ye say, that yer not *meanin'* the words has any bearin' whatsoever on the *effect* of yer words." He pointed a studied finger in the air. "Now, then, where'd we all be, if a man says 'I bet ye a pound it won't rain on the morrow'? Then it rains, and the man says 'I did not mean it' and won't pay his bet? What then, lass?"

Anne did not know; nor did she care. "We are not speaking of a frivolous bet, but of something very close to marriage!"

Dugald nodded. "With even more reason, then, ye see, must yer words be taken at face value. I'm inclined t' think now, that if ye were t' go back t' London and marry yer fainthearted Sassenach, ye'd be a bigamist."

Anne's mouth fell open. "I still say there must be an inward feeling for the words to count."

At this point, Alexander entered the discussion with a string of incomprehensible words in what Anne took to be Greek. After a moment of dumbfounded silence, he cited his source, "*Hippolytus,* by Euripides."

Duncan jerked his thumb at Alexander. "He's had an education," he said by way of apology for this lapse into literature, "but we are glad t' discover that it hasn't addled his brain any worse than the same time spent drinkin' bad whiskey."

Alexander explained, "I was citing the classical expression of Dugald's point, namely line 612, when Hippolytus says, 'My tongue swore, but my heart did not.' Ye see, then, 'tis a very old problem, this one of disclaiming yer words by arguing other intentions. But we've a plain saying in the Highlands: Your word is your bond."

Anne felt a mental abduction similar to the bodily one she had earlier experienced. Something was not right in all of this, but she did not know, and so could not say, exactly what was wrong. In all the slipperiness of this argumentation, one detail was graspable. She turned to Alexander. "Exactly where was this education?"

"Paris," he answered.

Her brows shot up. "Paris?"

"Aye, 'tis a bonny city, and I hope t' see it again some day."

"Before you die, perhaps?" she asked, a little waspishly.

He nodded and said, "'Tis the best way t' see it." He added pleasantly, "Maybe I'll take ye there."

"Trying to divert me from the issue at hand, Alexander Sutherland?"

"Nay, then, I'm tryin' t' divert my morbid thoughts from dwellin' on my own premature death."

"Which, I hope, will be soon," she retorted.

He caught the point of her remark before it touched him and riposted quickly. "Then ye'll be free t' marry the man yer father has chosen for ye." He asked seriously, "What do ye not like about him, by the by?"

She thought involuntarily, *Narrow shoulders*. She did not like many things about the man her father had chosen for her, but the shorthand for her dislike was his narrow shoulders. She looked around the room and noted that she was among a broad-shouldered clan of men, the Sutherlands. Duncan and Dugald were dark and squat and seemed broader of shoulder than they were tall. Gavin, who had returned from the bushes and was leaning weakly against the doorframe, was their opposite in his height and slimness and fairness, yet he was similarly broad-shouldered. Alexander was dark like Duncan and Dugald and tall like Gavin, and he had the Sutherland shoulders. To perfection.

She realized that she could not say "narrow shoulders" to this particular roomful of men without sounding extremely provocative. Instead, she asked sweetly, "Did I say that I did not like something about him?"

From his sprawling position on the bench, Alexander was regarding her meditatively. "Considering the length of time it took ye t' answer, aye. So what is it ye mislike about him?"

"I thought you weren't interested in him," she said primly.

Alexander slapped his thighs and stood up. "Ye've the right of it. I'm not the least bit interested in a borin' Sassenach who never even kissed ye."

She was getting used to his ways. "You don't know that," she returned easily, although he had once again been entirely accurate in his assessment. "How can you be so sure?"

"Here's my method," he said as he stepped forward and drew her into his arms again.

He put his lips to hers and kissed her, this time slowly, gently, inquisitively. With his hands on her back, he pressed her to him. Then he brought his hands up to her shoulders and down to her breasts. He slightly parted the plaid, whose edges he caught so that it would not fall and expose her near-nakedness. His fingers, full of light wool, lodged themselves a moment between her breasts. Then he drew his hands back up to her shoulders, and suddenly she could feel her breasts flattened directly against his shirt. She could feel the heat of his skin beneath, and even the rhythms of his heart.

She was shocked by the stimulating sensations she experienced at this contact with his hands and body. When she tried to pull away, he held her tighter, and his kiss deepened. He nudged her mouth open with his tongue and swirled its tip against hers, then ran his tongue along the inside of her lips. She felt the strangest, most unexpected, most secretive spurt inside her as he kissed and caressed her, less gently now, more insistently, more passionately. She did not know what it was, but it felt like drops of water come to freshen parched plants. Or maybe a summer morning's dew on rose petals. She moved against him, hoping to keep the sensation alive, hoping that the tiny drops would not evaporate. Or extinguish like a flame, for the longer the secretive sensation wavered inside her, the more it felt like liquid flame.

Suddenly he broke the kiss and pushed her away from him. Not all the way away, for the tips of her breasts still touched his chest. He looked down at her and seemed to try to reorient himself. He frowned absentmindedly. "I was tryin' t' make a point. Now what was it?" he asked. His breath of whiskey and heather honey came heavier. He cleared his throat. "Ah, sure now, 'twas t' prove that I knew yer borin' Sassenach had never kissed ye. If he had, and ye had responded like this, he would have never let ye escape him so easily."

Anne was lost for a moment, breathless, in the depths of his blue, blue eyes, which had gone black with desire. "You caught me by surprise," she said, flushing at his words, and at her own unmaidenly response to him.

He shook his head slowly. "We're bound in handfast now," he said low, "and what's good and healthy calls for no shame." He was about to apply his lips to the crook of her neck, but as he closed his eyes to kiss her again, he must have caught sight of his surroundings, for he looked up again. He said aloud, in a very different voice. "We've an audience, Anne o' Siosal." Then he bent toward her again and whispered into her ear, tickling her with his tongue, "Now, that's what I call a shame."

Anne, too, recalled her surroundings. She turned to look at Duncan, who was watching them, nodding benevolently, and at Dugald, who had his hands crossed over his stomach and was wearing an expression of beatific approval. "No more talk now about not meanin' yer pledge, lassie," he said in an affectionate reprimand. Of Gavin there was no evidence. He had apparently gone out again to engage in another serious discussion with the bushes.

Alexander took a deep breath and seemed to have pulled himself together. "That's us away now, lads, t' Dunrobin," he said.

Duncan and Dugald readily approved. Anne tried one last appeal. "You're not taking me back to Tomain nam Mòd?" she asked. Her tone was that of a supplicant who already knew the answer.

"Nay, lass," he said, "not today, at any rate. Eventually, though, ye'll be seein' yer kinfolk again. After we've had the approval of the Sutherland."

Anne accepted this verdict reluctantly. Under the circumstances, she had few arguments or strategies or defenses to mount that would get her back to the Rosses. As they were leaving the bothy, it occurred to her that she would be riding again with Alexander. The thought troubled her.

However, once outside, it was difficult for her to remain troubled, for the day had dawned with glorious promise. Duncan and Dugald had already mounted. Gavin contemplated his horse, then seemingly decided to brave his stomach atop it, for he swung into the saddle with practiced ease. Once there, he looked around with a rather pleased smile on his face at finding himself astride his stallion and steady. Alexander tossed Anne up, then followed her swiftly, and the party took off over the hills.

At first Anne was highly aware of Alexander's body behind hers, and it seemed that he was making every effort to keep her aware of him. He shifted often, so that her curves fitted differently in his angles with every movement; and he seemed to need to move his arms quite a lot, handling the reins, so that they continually rubbed against her waist, the side of her breasts, the tender undersides of her arms. She was surrounded by his touch, his breath on her neck, the feel of his heart against her back. And with the horse working beneath her, it was impossible not to think of him, his eyes upon her, his pledge to her, hers to him, his kisses, his smile, his passion.

The beauty of the natural world beyond his body was dramatic enough that, with the rising sun, her awareness of him blended into her perception of the scenery through which they were traveling. They climbed mountains where sheep and goats skipped, crossed meadows both wild and cultivated, passed through forests thick with trees and foxes and roe deer, and came upon more than one crofter's hut nestled in the valleys called straths.

Alexander explained that the Highlanders were industrious folk, and that the cultivated fields were fuzzy with hemp and flax that the women used for heckling, spinning, twisting, bleaching and dyeing. They stopped to pass the time of day with an old man at his gate. His garden was rank with cabbage and turnips. The old man spoke a strange tongue, to which all four men easily responded. They rode on, the party of four horses fanning out across the wide open space. In reply to Anne's question, Alexander explained that in this corner of the world, "Gaelic is spoken promiscuously."

The landscape was now pleasant and sloping, now rough and precipitous. Anne had the impression that they were climbing, an impression that Alexander confirmed. They were mounting, single file, a rough incline when they came upon the Saunach whose banks were fringed with trees stupendously high, the branches of which met over the stream and intermingled. It was a lean and active river that tumbled down its rocky channel, creating miniature cascades on its way. She was amused by the occasional huge fragment of rock left over from some ancient cataclysm that had been worn into a grotesque shape by the fury of the rushing waters.

The charms of the Saunach were but a foretaste of what they were soon to come upon. They had just crossed a meadow stitched by two winding streams that seemed to play among the flowers, here watering a garden, there turning a mill. The water ran, murmuring and gurgling as it gathered strength. First she heard the stunning roar of some terrible force, and then she looked ahead and to her right and saw an entire glen come into view below her. It was graced by a most extraordinary sight.

The two streams from the meadow had twisted so that they met at the mouth of a craggy steep, at which point they joined to form a muscular cascade, wild and impetuous. Impatient of restraint, this roaring cataract was shooting headlong and desperate down the rock, precipitating itself over the edge, churning at every turn with whitened foam and breaking into a thousand different streams at the abrupt points of the rocks opposing its passage. The spray that rose from it gave a misty obscurity to the surrounding woods, and an air of magic to the whole. At the end of its violent fall, the water pooled calmly, satisfied and sleepy, at the bottom of the glen.

She was momentarily awestruck. Then she realized that Alexander had stopped the horse so that she could see her fill.

"What is it called?" she asked, having to raise her voice to be heard above the roar.

He bent his lips to her ear. "'Tis the Falls of the Kilt-Laurel," he answered. "A bonny sight, when all is said."

She thought back to the two streams moving happily through the meadow. "Where does it begin?"

"In heaven."

She turned and glanced up at him.

His eyes ran deep and blue. They were smiling as mistily and magically as the cataract. "Its earthly origins are at a wee spring to the west of the meadow we just crossed."

"So much force from such unpromising beginnings."

"'Tis the way of it in the Highlands," he said. After a pause, he added, "I wouldn't have wanted t' miss this, lass."

She noticed the reverential tone in his voice. They rode on, exchanging no further words, their ears filled with the great watery shout. Before too much longer, Anne perceived that they were headed straight for the dainty arch of an old stone bridge, which was thrown over the point where the Kilt and the Laurel met.

Anne eyed the structure warily. "Will it hold?" she asked as they approached.

"Let's hope," he answered.

She glanced back at him. "You like to think positive."

He nodded. "That I do."

A few moments later, they were on the bridge. Beneath them, the Kilt and the Laurel rushed to fall in turbulent glory to the bottom of the glen.

"'Tis Sutherland country proper from here on," he informed her.

"And in what country were we before?"

"Sutherland country *im*proper."

When the small riding party left the woods surrounding the magnificent glen, they gave their horses their head across a rough and scrubby country. Judging by the salt in the air, Anne thought they were moving ever nearer to the sea, perhaps to Dornoch Firth.

She was going to ask about their present location, but the words that left her lips were, "What did you mean when you said that you would not have wanted to miss seeing the Falls of the Kilt-Laurel?"

"I've had to spend more time in France of late, and missed summer in the Highlands last year."

"Had to?"

"Me being accounted a political undesirable and all, by yer friends, ye see," he answered carelessly. "My clan sent me away. Oh, aye, I thought them cruel, and I've never been persuaded by any argument that begins, "'Tis for yer own good, lad.' But I went. Then the yearnin' for the hills and valleys grew too great, and I returned a fortnight ago."

She assimilated this, then said slowly, "So you really do have a price on your head."

"And a very low one 'tis, too, which, as I've mentioned, fair blisters me. On the other hand, there's not a body in the Highlands thinks it worth trackin' me down for a few pieces of silver, so my neck is safe enough for the moment."

"But why risk it?" she asked. "I mean, really, you should have let it all blow over—oh, say for a year or two. Let the English and the Scots come to a settlement over the status of the two Parliaments. Then you could return."

"A hundred years from now, ye mean," he answered. He shook his head. "Nay, then, somethin' was pullin' me back. Somethin' strong. Irresistible, ye might say."

It seemed, just then, that his horse's reins needed great attention, such that his arms touched her everywhere. The note in his voice was seductive, provocative.

She knew that she should let this pass, but she prodded anyway. "Something irresistible?"

"Which was, I soon discovered upon my return, that Evan was in sore need of my help. So imagine my surprise t' have bungled the abduction of Claire and t' find myself bound now in handfast." He mused, "How one's plans can go awry."

"Imagine, indeed!" she agreed, a little testily. "Your surprise can be only slightly less than mine!"

He left it at that, but somehow the contact of his arms with her body continued, so that by the time the great weathered pile of stones that was Dunrobin could be seen rising up from the sea, she was feeling rather hot and very bothered by it all.

Dunrobin was an impressive structure, with turrets at all four corners, three great cold walls on land and a fourth stolidly resisting the sea. The castle guard must have been on the alert for them, for, although they were still a ways from the gates, they could see raised arms waving, hailing their return. Not too much later, their horses' hooves were clopping on the cobbles of the courtyard, and they were surrounded by an excited group of several dozen Sutherland men and women.

Not the least of their excitement was due to the bundle that Alexander had in his arms. Anne gathered soon enough that before leaving the castle the night before Duncan and Dugald had announced to at least one of Dunrobin's inhabitants their plan of going to Tomain nam Mòd to fetch back Evan's love. Thus, the exclamations that greeted Anne in the courtyard had the familiar form of "That's not Claire Ross!" and "Where's the Ross lass?" and "Ye've brought a different beauty back for our Evan, lucky lad!"

In one fluid movement, Alexander slid down from his horse and caught Anne, who grasped the plaid around her tightly. One man had stepped forward from the group, and Anne saw at a glance that he was a younger and prettier version of Alexander. She suspected that he was the love-lorn Evan. Despite being lost in a swamp of lovesickness, Evan cast Anne a speculative glance that caused her a lurch of fear. Alexander quelled it with a quick challenge, "Ye can look but not touch, Evan my boy."

"So, then, my clever brother, where's Claire?"

"In Inverness," he answered, "but that's another story. This one is mine in handfast."

Evan's speculative expression took on a different cast. "So, then!" was all he said.

The word *handfast* buzzed through the crowd, and the excitement bubbled up to a boil. Alexander took quick charge of the situation by announcing that he would be happy to explain it all in the hall in a few minutes, then summarily dismissed everyone. His commands were seconded by two more men in the crowd, who bore a striking resemblance to Evan and Alexander, and the crowd broke up.

Anne was just catching her breath from this extraordinary welcome when Alexander turned toward her with his charming smile and a sweeping bow. "Welcome to your new home, Anne o' Siosal."

Chapter Four

Anne looked around her and discovered that Dunrobin's courtyard was much like Tomain nam Mòd's, only slightly larger. It also had a more rugged atmosphere, owing mostly, she suspected, to its proximity to the churning North Sea. As she looked about, she noticed that the crowd was headed off to the left, presumably to the hall and the main living quarters of the manor. Off to the right, she saw Duncan and Dugald and Gavin, along with Evan, taking all the horses in the direction of what must be the stables.

She turned back to Alexander. "But only temporarily, no?"

Not a muscle in his face moved; nor did his smile lose any of its charm. "For a year and a day at least," he said, then added neutrally, "or at most. I can't say, but it'll be as ye wish."

Anne had to be satisfied with that.

"I've told the clan that we'll assemble in the hall, where they can hear me explain everything t' the Sutherland."

"And what, do you think, he'll say about all of this?"

"My father's never had a good opinion of my judgment, I'll confess, and I note that he didn't deign to appear just now in the courtyard." He shrugged off the negative implications of the Sutherland's absence, and he smiled his lopsided smile. "So I'm thinkin' he'll have his reservations."

Anne's eyes had widened, and she wondered whether she would ever accustom herself to the surprise she continually felt in the company of Alexander Sutherland—the son of the clan chief. "I might have known!"

"Ye might have," he said, grinning broadly.

He looked thoroughly disreputable, with his black hair flying around his shoulders and a night's stubble darkening his jaw, but he had the look of the son of the clan chief, nevertheless. She looked down at her equally ragged appearance, wiggled her toes, and unhappily considered presenting herself in such a state before the entire clan, not to mention the father of the man to whom she was—or was not—betrothed.

"Should I not, at least, find something to wear before I make an appearance in the hall?" she asked.

He surveyed her critically, then shook his head. "I wouldn't change a thing if I were ye, lass," he said. His tone was as close as he had ever come to sounding truly serious. "The Sutherland plaid is the best protection ye can mount in going afore this particular chief."

Her image of a terrible patriarch was amply realized not too many minutes later, in the great and gloomy hall, where the cold flagstones bit into the soles of her bare feet and sank her spirits. While Alexander gave a lively, unselfconscious account of the night's misadventure, her heart quailed at the expression on the Sutherland's face, which was as wooden as the grand carved chair in which he sat. He was flanked on either side by his two oldest sons, Jamie and Simon, whose identities Alexander had whispered to her as they walked among the utterly silent clansmen and clanswomen to stand before the raised dais and learn their fate.

The Sutherland was clearly the mold from which his four sons had been stamped. Anne imagined that he would be handsome still, if he were to smile, but she had no way of knowing what transformations a smile could make, for, as he sat listening, his face became harder, his expression darker. She took heart at the thought that he would likely declare this absurd handfasting null and void. She lost heart at the thought of what might then become of her, with or without the Sutherland plaid around her shoulders for protection.

Alexander's easy rumble came to a halt. He had finished his account. No excuses. No apologies. No ingratiating flourishes.

The Sutherland rose. He was of a height with his sons, who dropped back from his sides. He looked down on Alexander broodingly, then shifted his eyes to Anne. She tried to hold his deep blue gaze steadily, but could not. She lowered her lashes and contemplated the flagstones.

"Good work, Alexander," the Sutherland said at last, and quite congenially, too.

Anne's head jerked up. "Good work?" she echoed, too surprised to be demure.

"Very good work," the Sutherland told her, not the least bit put out by her interpolation. "Alexander did right for once, the wayward lad. Naught else he could do under the circumstances." He continued, "To put yer mind at rest, Anne o' Siosal, I'll give my consent in writing and send the document straightaway to the Ross, so that he can affix his name to it, as well. Just to make doubly sure no one can question it, ye know." Then, without missing a beat, he said, "Ye're the very image of Margaret MacKenzie. Do ye have kin in the Clann Choinnich?"

Anne was too taken aback to utter more than, "In fact, my mother was a MacKenzie. Elizabeth was her name. I'm told I resemble her. I know of no Margaret MacKenzie."

To this the Sutherland merely nodded, and thereafter events took on a momentum of their own. The Sutherland called for quill and ink and a sheet of fine paper. He scratched out his lines and subscribed his name. He waved the paper in the air and wanted to know who would transport it to Tomain nam Mòd without delay. Duncan and Dugald came forward to volunteer for the mission, on the impeccable grounds that they had naught better to do and were in need of a wee bit of exercise. The Sutherland put them in charge of the mission and named four other burlylooking Sutherlands to accompany them, in order to prevent "any misunderstandings of our intentions on the part of the Clan Rosich." That done, he put Anne in the hands of three women, close by.

Before she was taken from Alexander's side, she said to him, quite amazed, "That went far differently than I had expected."

"'Twas the plaid," he assured her. "Softened him up."

"It was not," she said with great disgust. "The plaid had absolutely nothing to do with his approval of your actions, and all I can say is that he's apparently as daft as the rest of you!"

"Oh, and did I mention that he's always had a weakness for MacKenzie women?"

Anne tossed her head with what dignity was left her and was escorted out of the hall by the three women. She was grateful that, after having been led through several rather cool and damp corridors and up a corkscrew of a stone staircase, she was brought into a very sunny room, richly paneled and well-appointed. She saw a great copper tub squatting on an otterskin before the low fire in the fireplace, and gathered that she had been brought to this room to be bathed and dressed. For these considerations, too, she was grateful.

The women, whose name were Jenny, Marris and Elspeth, were nice and curious and excited to the point of frequent giggles at the thought of Anne's appearance at Dunrobin and her relationship to Alexander, who was clearly a castle favorite. Jenny and Marris declared themselves to be the chief's daughters-in-law. Jenny was married to the elder son, Jamie, and therefore of higher authority. Elspeth was Jenny's younger sister, and somewhat more curious than nice, Anne thought, and less giggly than the other two. Elspeth looked at Anne from under lowered lashes from time to time, but Anne could not guess her thoughts.

First came Anne's undressing, which was a minimal activity. Marris plucked the plaid from Anne's shoulders, pinching it between two fingers, and held it at arm's length. She eyed it as one would a repulsive insect.

"Duncan's," she guessed, turning up her nose.

"Dugald's, actually," Anne told her. "Duncan was wearing his when he took me from my bed."

The eyes of all three women widened, but not from mention of her abduction.

"'Tis strange t' hear ye speak," Jenny said.

"Have you never heard an English accent before?" Anne asked.

"Aye, often," Jenny replied, "in Inverness and Dundee. I was even once t' Edinburgh, where ye may hear the English accent everywhere in the streets."

"Then why is it so strange to hear me speak?" Anne wanted to know.

"'Tis the way ye look," Jenny said, with a smile and a shrug.

"'Tis an odd effect," Marris agreed, "t' hear yer round and high tones, with no comforting burr, as we call it." She had more immediate problems on her mind, namely the smelly plaid in her hand, at which she was frowning. "Now what am I t' do with this trash?"

Jenny recommended that Marris toss it out the window, whence it would land in the courtyard. Marris was happy to oblige.

Next came Anne's thin night shift. While Marris pulled at the ribbon at the shift's low neck and began untying the ties, Jenny and Elspeth loosened what was left of Anne's braid and finger-combed her knotted curls to prepare them for a washing.

A third and fourth tie were undone, and the shift slipped off Anne's shoulder to fall in a delicate froth at her feet. She stood before Marris a moment, looking for all the world like the red-tressed Venus rising from the sea, and with a goddess's— or a farm girl's—ample curves.

Marris made a low "Mmm" of approval, and Jenny peeped around to survey Anne's charms. She, too, made a sound of approval, then turned to Elspeth and said, "Alex was beyond yer reach, in any case, my El, so there's no need for such a look. Yer curves will come in time!"

Instead of being embarrassed by this unblinking assessment of her body, Anne was pleased. More than merely pleased, actually, for she was unashamed and even proud for once of how she looked. When she stepped into the steam rising from the tub, her sense of well-being increased as she was enfolded by the delicious caress of the warm water. Jenny added some drops of lavender oil, and Anne luxuriated in the sweet scent that gently pushed aside the smell of wool and sweat and frying bacon and horseflesh that had been clinging to her skin over the past hours.

Another dimension to her pleasure emerged when she realized that this was the first time in her life that she had looked right but sounded strange. At Queen Anne's court, she sounded right, but looked strange; her vivid coloring continually set her apart from the other women, as did her body.

Although she had always feigned defiant ignorance of what the gentlemen of the court said about her, she knew that her figure was considered "opulent," and that her red hair prompted the indecorous, shaming nicknames of Cherry Ripe and Fire between the Legs. Her father must have heard the names, for he had allied her to the man least likely to strike a match inside her. His poor choice had prompted such attentions from the least reputable of courtiers that Anne had recently been driven to extremely unbecoming behavior; and that had landed her as far north as her father could send her, namely Tomain nam Mòd.

And now she was here, even farther north, at Dunrobin, naked in a tub, surrounded by Sutherlands, bound in handfast to a man who had carried her off through the woods at night.

Her head was drawn back, water poured through her hair, and mild soap applied. When fingers started scrubbing, a thought inevitably occurred to her. "Is it possible to annul a handfasting?" she asked with her eyes closed, her head moving back and forth under the invigorating pressure.

A small pause was broken by a giggle. "A handfastin' usually makes official what's already occurred in practice," Jenny offered, "so, ye see, 'twould be hypocritical to claim an annulment—after the fact."

"But what if nothing happened in practice? What then?"

Jenny considered this, then said, "I'm not sure I understand yer question. The handfastin' is for two people willin' t' try t' live together. If they choose not t' try, they don't make the pledge. After the pledge, well, then, 'tis official."

"What if a person is tricked into saying the pledge?" Anne asked next.

A long pause fell. Anne opened her eyes to see three women looking at her politely, but evidently puzzled. "Tricked?" Jenny echoed.

"Into pledgin' one's word?" Marris said.

"'Tis not possible," Elspeth opined, her thoughts evidently drifting off into the same philosophical territory that Dugald had charted. "We've a sayin' in the Highlands about one's word—"

"And one's bond," Anne finished for her. "I know it." She abandoned the argument, realizing that her position would have no greater effect on this audience of three women than it had on her earlier audience of three men. She reconsidered the whole, but could not decide whether the Highlanders took the business of handfasting too seriously, or not seriously enough.

Thereafter the talk turned to the problem of Anne's clothing. While Anne was drying her hair and her skin in a large linen, Jenny was very pleased to find, deep in an old trunk, a pretty but old-fashioned dress that had fit the Sutherland's mother, who Jenny had guessed from clan lore had been of a build similar to Anne's. The habit had a bodice and sleeves of scarlet cloth, laced with gold and adorned with buttons of plate, while the skirt was blue. It came with a cloak called an arisaid, which was white striped with yellow, and made of sufficient length to reach from the neck to the ankles. It was nicely plaited all around, fastened about the waist with a belt, and secured on the breast by a large brooch. The belt was of leather and several pieces of silver intermixed, and at the lower end was a piece of plate about eight inches long and three wide, engraved, and ingeniously adorned with pieces of red coral. Next were found hose and black buckled shoes that were a mite too large for Anne, but wearable. Her hair was brushed and plaited on each side, and the ends fastened with blue ribbons.

When Anne was dressed and coiffed, Jenny, Marris and even Elspeth looked happy with their work, although Jenny was aware of one flaw. She sighed and said, "Now, if we could but change her speech."

The Sutherland was to pursue a version of this theme later, in the hall. Anne had spent the rest of the morning and early afternoon with the women. When they had finished with Anne's bathing and dressing, they had taken out their sewing and given her a needle to ply industriously. Just as she was beginning to feel the first pangs of hunger, the dinner was called in the hall. She reentered that great and gloomy space to find it brighter with activity and tables and the smell of food. The Sutherland took one appreciative look at her and crossed the hall to her side. He escorted her to the head table, saying, "If ye're not kin to Margaret MacKenzie, I'm not the Sutherland."

Since Anne had no desire to question his authority, she answered truthfully, "I don't know if I am or not, sir."

"How can ye not know such a thing, lass?" the Sutherland asked, rather shocked by her admission.

"I know little of my mother's family," she said.

The Sutherland shook his head and stated the full sum of the tragedy. "As if speakin' the way ye do is not bad enough, ye've no knowledge of yer clan. 'Tis a shockin' upbringin' ye've had."

Anne was surprised by this observation, for she was used to thinking of her upbringing as unrelentingly strict and proper. She was also offended by it, for she had not been raised Scots. "I'm English, as you know, and know all about that branch of the family."

"But yer name is Chisholm, lass, and yer mother was a MacKenzie!" the Sutherland protested. "Where's the Sassenach in that?"

"My father's mother was English, a Lindsay, and a great favorite at court," she returned, wishing she felt more pride in the fact.

The Sutherland snorted his opinion of the Lindsays.

"And my father's father came to England after Cromwell's victory over the Scots at Dunbar," she continued, "so my father was born and bred in England."

"But he married a MacKenzie woman," the Sutherland pointed out, adding severely, for no Scot liked to be reminded of Cromwell, "and 'tis not entirely t' yer grandfather's credit that he fled Scotland after Dunbar, although the Chisholms suffered during that dark period, and fared no better a generation later, at the battle of Killicrankie, when they lost their ancestral castle." He seated her on the bench next to him on his right and asked, "But did yer father not tell ye about the clan?"

"I'm afraid not," she said. Thinking to please him with a detail, she added, "However, he's always been in charge of Scottish affairs at the court, and has a high rank in the military, as well."

The Sutherland evidently thought poorly of this position and expressed the hope that this one Chisholm, at least, would keep his nose out of the Highlands.

Anne was about to say something to this, but thought better of it and held her tongue. An unpleasant ripple had coursed through her, something akin to guilt. She could not quite identify the uneasy feeling, so she dismissed it.

"And did yer mother never tell ye aught about the MacKenzies?" the Sutherland wanted to know.

"I never knew her, for she died in childbirth with me."

At that moment, Alexander approached the table. Anne looked up at him and saw that he, too, had bathed and changed clothes. With his hair tamed and his face clean-shaven, she had to admit, he was a mightily attractive man.

"Have ye done yer chores, Alex?" the Sutherland asked him.

"Aye, sir," Alexander responded, then addressed Anne. "Ye were told that ye resemble yer mother in looks, and I'm wantin' t' know if ye've been told whether ye resemble her in temper."

Anne was proud of the stories told about her mother, of what a great lady she had been at court, and how thoroughly she had been mourned. "I'm not at all like her in temper, I'm afraid, for she was all fire, but controlled."

Alexander nodded, satisfied. "Ye'll mellow, then, as well. This mornin' I was a wee bit worried about yer tongue, but a man can always tell what the daughter will become by judgin' the mother."

Anne smiled sweetly and reversed herself. "My mother was a shrew until the day of her death."

The Sutherland seemed to think this a great joke, for he threw back his head and laughed. "Too late, lass! The first answer is always the truthful one. Now, Alex, ye'll sit at the end of the bench between yer sisters-in-law and amuse them with yer stories of Paris."

Alexander did as he was bidden, and the assembled clan sat themselves at the table shaped in an L around the hall. The supper set before them consisted of fresh salmon in sorrel sauce and rabbit stewed with sweet roots. The Sutherland threw his plaid over his shoulder to free his arms for eating, which was the sign to begin. He had lost interest in chastising Chisholms past and present, and concerned himself rather with tracing the bloodlines that ran from the Chisholms to the Rosses. Once launched into clan history, he recounted the stories of the MacKenzies, of the great Clan Chattan, and then, inevitably, of the Clan Shutherlanich.

Anne listened, enthralled, and before she knew it the supper was done and she had eaten more than her fill. The whiskey was passed. Encouraged to take a "wee dram," she sipped and, despite her caution, underestimated the alcohol's strength. When she could speak again, she was able to sputter that it was a tasty concoction, but perhaps not for her.

"The smoothest whiskey in all the Highlands," the Sutherland was proud to tell her. "We can improve yer taste for good whiskey in a week or less, but I'm flummoxed t' know what we can do t' improve yer speech."

After that, Jamie, on her right, wished to claim her attention, then Simon. The talk drifted lazily, and she began to expect some festive activity, like dancing to the bagpipes, or at least a toast. However, when nothing special materialized, she came to realize that the plain acceptance of the handfast made it suddenly more real to her than if the occasion had been explicitly marked. The atmosphere in the bothy this morning had been more celebratory than anything she had experienced since.

At the end of the meal, she caught the drift of the conversation between Alexander and Jenny and Marris. Jenny seemed concerned over Alexander's presence in Scotland just now, with English troops in Inverness, and Alexander was making light of it.

Anne caught the drift of Jenny's words, and she imagined that the Sutherland heard them, as well, for he frowned and seemed to wish to cut short that particular conversation. "We'll not worry about all of that just now. We'll hope that Alexander has been clever enough not t' have betrayed his return t' his home."

"I learn from my mistakes, sir," Alexander replied.

"And not t' cause the poor Sassenach garrisons any more trouble," the Sutherland added, "for they're already itchin' t' put a noose around yer neck, lad."

"My only crime last year was gettin' caught," Alexander retorted, "but I'll agree with ye, sir, that the Sassenachs will be less likely t' fall victim a second time t' my method of escape."

Anne leaned her head toward Alexander and asked, "And what was that method?"

Alexander assumed an expression of shocked affront. "My charm of personality, lass!"

A ripple of laughter went through the hall, and Anne decided to rise to the challenge. She said with an innocent smile, "How could I have known? I've seen so little evidence of it thus far!"

Alexander, on his mettle, leaned forward to reply with undisguised meaning, "Because I've not had a chance to show ye. Ye'll learn soon enough, though. This night, in fact!"

The look he gave her caused her to squirm on the bench. She arched a challenging brow and was amazed that her daring could be so well received, rather than condemned, as it would have been by her father. She was also amazed when the meal was over, just like that, and everyone went back to their chores.

So the afternoon went. Anne spent it with the ladies, and did not see Alexander again until the northern sun of high summer was sinking in the sky and supper was announced. In the hall they were served light mutton broth and spinach pie, and in the middle of it all, Duncan and Dugald returned from their mission to Tomain nam Mòd, strolling into the hall as if they had just taken a walk around the castle yard, instead of having finished their second ten-hour ride within the space of twenty-four hours.

Duncan carried the document, signed by the Ross, and handed it to the Sutherland without ceremony. Dugald had his mind on other matters. He was wearing a plaid around his shoulders and holding another one up, saying, " 'Tis wonderful that I just found my own plaid in the corner of the courtyard." He walked over to a far table, withdrew the plaid from his shoulders and handed it to a man. "I thank ye for the use of yer plaid, Douglas," Dugald said, "and I'll return it t' ye now. It served me well, but 'tis not the same as my own."

Douglas accepted the return of his plaid, exclaiming, "Not at all, thank God!" which was met with raucous laughter.

Anne shook her head in amused admiration at the way Dugald shrugged the laughter off his broad shoulders and went with Duncan to the end of the table, where Evan was seated in a swamp of lovesick gloom. Duncan and Dugald nudged him and suggested "a wee ride to Inverness t' see what there is t' see." The Sutherland, overhearing, put a quick stop to that excursion by assigning Evan some chores, saying that hard work would give his thoughts a better tone. So Duncan and Dugald, reduced to staying at Dunrobin for the evening, went in search of a lad or two with whom they could bend the elbow.

Alexander rose from his seat and came to stand before Anne. He extended his hands to her, palms up. With a smile in his blue eyes, he said, "Come walk with me by the sea, if ye please, Anne o' Siosal."

Chapter Five

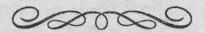

Anne placed her hands in his and rose from the bench. "I get to keep my name, then?" she asked.

"I'm not ready t' take that from ye," he said. "Other things, though."

She couldn't resist. "Such as?"

He bent his lips to hers and touched them lightly. "A kiss," he said, pleasing her greatly. He led her away from the table and asked, as if it were an afterthought, "Are ye a virgin?"

She gasped and looked at him quickly, then away. She could not help it; she blushed. Furiously and modestly.

"I'm glad," he said, correctly interpreting her reaction. "I'll take that, too, then."

She found her voice. "But to speak of it so bluntly..." she said reproachfully.

"Ye'd have me sigh and swoon at yer feet, lass, like yer fine Sassenach lads? I'm tellin' ye no secret when I say that, Sassenach or Scot, a man's got but one idea on his mind when he's with a bonny lass. Especially one t' whom he's pledged. We may as well speak of it bluntly, ye and me, for 'tis what there is between us and afore us."

As Anne assimilated this frank statement, her emotions shifted from wonderment to embarrassment to wonderment again, now shaded with a hint of excitement. They had crossed the hall and were heading toward the dying daylight outside.

"Does this count as courting in Scotland?" she asked.

"Nay, then, that came this mornin', ye'll recall, while ye sat on the boulder by the bothy, half-naked under Dugald's plaid, and afore ye pledged me your troth." He smiled down at her. "This counts as the stroll before I bed ye."

She gasped again but this time could not look away. She blushed again but this time neither modestly nor furiously. "You are very blunt about it!" she managed.

"That's the way I like it," he said. "Blunt. Ye'll see, lass, and I'm sure ye'll appreciate it."

Her head was in something of a whirl. She said the first thing that came to mind. "It's all happening so fast."

"We have but a year and a day, and I have no wish t' waste a one," he replied. He added reflectively, "Considerin' the day we've just spent, from the moment Duncan handed ye up to me, I'd say we're already far along."

She did not know how to respond to that, and he did not pursue the subject. Instead, he seemed more concerned about leading her around the courtyard and behind the stables, to the secret passage in the stout eastern wall facing the sea.

After some tricky maneuvering through odd and ancient passages, they penetrated the castle wall. Suddenly a wide sweep of rocky coastline was spread out before them. The sea was still alive in the light of the lengthening shadows of a very long summer's day. The tang of brackish seawater filled her nostrils, and she accepted Alexander's hand as he helped her down the jumbled rocks so that they could walk along the water's edge. It was a laborious process, and long enough that, by the time they had reached a more level portion of the coast, the great expanse of molten pewter that was the North Sea had darkened by imperceptible degrees to become a vat of sleepy tar. An occasional wind blew up and harped across the water, scarcely rippling its sluggish surface.

Alexander used the occasion of the winds to put an arm around Anne's shoulder, sheltering her at the same time in a portion of his plaid.

She appreciated the gallantry of the gesture. "I'm not cold," she reassured, smiling up at him.

"Ye're very warm, in fact, for which I'm grateful." He had an irresistible light in his eyes.

"Ah, so *you* were cold," she said, teasingly in return.

He shook his head. "I'm as warm as ye, then. Warmer."

She blinked. "Do you never give up?"

"I'm pursuin' a theme, ye might say," he acknowledged, mock serious. Then he said, "T' demonstrate." With the arm he had put about her shoulder, he pulled her closer, into a full embrace. He kissed her at length. Then he lifted his head and smiled dreamily. With his plaid encircling her, he drew back slightly so that he could look at her. "'Tis difficult t' believe that I like the way ye look with yer clothes on. The arisaid becomes ye."

One of his hands moved to the large brooch holding the voluminous cloak at her throat, then lowered, grazing her breasts, and dropped to grasp the end of her belt, which hung at a precise and interesting point below her waist. He fingered the red coral pieces that adorned it. "On second thought, I'm sure t' like ye better with it off."

He turned her, so that his one arm was around her shoulders again, and they walked on in silence. After a companionable while, he asked, "Do ye like my family?"

"I do," she said, without having to give the matter much thought. "It's strange to find myself in the midst of such a large family, since there's only my father and me."

"There are the Lindsays, too, if I heard ye correctly."

But I don't like them, she thought, and they don't like me. Aloud, she said, "I don't fit in there very well." She reflected further, then added, "I could never have spoken to you the way I did at dinner this afternoon without being punished for being forward. I've always been told not to be the center of attention, but no matter what I do, I always seem to find myself there." The corners of her mouth turned down. "It's my hair. It never seems to escape attention."

After a moment, Alexander asked, "What did ye do, then, t' make yer father send ye away?"

Anne shook her head. She did not wish to answer that question.

He said, "Well, now, ye mislike the man yer father chose for ye—which is of no consequence any longer, ye should be glad t' note—and so I imagine that ye were led into indiscretion."

They were climbing slightly, and had come to a particularly treacherous pile of rocks. Alexander stepped forward and pulled Anne up. Grunting with the effort, she confessed, "With a court footman, no less."

"Och, now, lass," he said, with more sympathy than reproach.

"But my father's choice was such an insult," she said, defending herself unnecessarily, "that so many of the 'fine English lads,' as you called them—"

"Sassenach lads, I called them."

"Figured they would have an easy time of it."

"Your father's choice?" he asked.

"Ralph Weathercombe."

Alexander pulled a face. "Is he as lamentable as his name?"

She nodded. "Worse, but from a family very well positioned at court."

"So ye kissed the footman out of spite."

"Something like that."

"And out of a wee bit of frustration."

"Perhaps that, too."

Alexander considered this. "Poor fellow. The footman, I mean, knowing as I do how ye kiss." He asked abruptly, "How old are ye?"

"Twenty," she answered. "And you?"

"Six and twenty," he said. "But why did yer father take so long t' make ye a match?"

"As his position has risen in the past several years, he has been holding out for the best possible offer."

Alexander made a low noise in his throat. "An ambitious Scot. A dangerous sort, I'm thinkin'."

They had arrived at a spot where they could look down into a little cove. Anne was surprised to see a ship bobbing at anchor.

Alexander answered her unasked question. "Aye, she's mine, and carried me safely back from France."

"You sailed such a big ship alone?"

"Nay, I had some fine seafarin' lads with me." He smiled at her. "And t' think that I nearly named her *Anne.*"

"What *did* you name her?"

"The *Marie,* after my dear, departed mother," he said. Then he moved on smoothly. "Ye haven't yet told me why, for yer misbehavior, yer father sent ye t' Scotland and not t' the sober-minded Lindsays. The Rosses have no great reputation for manners, and yer father must have known that in the Highlands ye'd be exposed t' all sorts of rude manners!''

She had to laugh. ''Such as abductions and handfastings,'' she observed. Then she frowned and said seriously, ''I don't know why he sent me here. It was most unexpected, I can assure you, for I had never heard a word about the Rosses until the fortnight before my departure. Maybe he needed an excuse to come to Scotland himself.''

''Yer father's in Scotland?'' Alexander asked conversationally.

''Yes, Edinburgh. We traveled that far together. Then I was taken to Tomain nam Mòd in another party.'' An uneasy feeling swept her, similar to the one she had experienced earlier, at dinner. She looked at him, the frown still between her eyes. ''It's odd that I haven't questioned his motives until now.''

He put a finger to her brow and smoothed it. ''Never mind,'' he said, kissing the place his finger had touched. He moved his lips to her eyes, her nose, the corners of her mouth. He put his lips on hers and tasted her with his tongue. He broke the kiss and bent his forehead to hers, sighing.

''The time has come,'' he said.

She did not ask him what he meant. Standing in the circle of his arms, her head next to his, she could see the steady pulse in his throat in the last light of the day. She nodded.

He took her hand in his and led her back the way they had come, holding her steady over the rocks, catching her when she stumbled, and moving quickly ahead of the night that was rolling in from the sea. By the time they reached the secret passage in the castle wall, the moon was rising. They made unseemly haste across the courtyard, meeting few people along the way. Anne's feet were propelled by the stimulating prospect that what she was about to do was both legal and illicit, that she had been wanting to do it for months and months now, it seemed, and that the man she was to do it with was far, far better than the handsome, well-built footman who had caught her kissing fancy.

And that she would not be doing it out of spite.

But maybe some frustration.

And a good deal of healthy desire.

They were panting when they reached the door to his bedchamber, far off down a long and dark corridor. He shut the door behind them with the whole of his weight, shutting out the world, shutting them in. It was dark in the room, and they agreed to light no candle. The curtains on the windows to the courtyard were not drawn and allowed the silver moonlight to make magical the shadows on his skin as he began to strip down to his trews.

She shed her arisaid, and with it the brooch and belt, but suddenly she stopped. She looked to the large bed, which dominated one wall, the covers already turned neatly back in invitation. She looked back at him and suddenly felt very unsure of herself, despite her desire to get on with it.

He noticed her hesitation. "There's no hurry," he said. He came toward her, took one of her hands and lifted the back of it to his lips. "Allow me t' explain the matter t' ye." He raised his head slightly so that he could look into her eyes. "The Highlands is a cold country in the winter," he said.

"What?" she said, surprised by this turn in conversation.

He smiled and nodded. "And we're a people given to prudery."

"Believe it or not," she said, with a shaky attempt at humor.

"Believe it or not," he repeated, smiling and calm. "Although ye might not think it, the vows of handfastin' are not trivially spoken. But, as I was sayin', 'tis a cold country, and we're a prudish people. So an ardent young man learns how t' keep himself and his lass warm, and a willin' lass learns how t' pleasure herself and him, without causin' him t' violate his honor or her virtue." He kissed the back of her hand again. "If ye see what I mean."

She did, a little. She nodded slowly, holding his gaze, which was gone midnight blue in the dark. She was less afraid than shy, and really very curious.

"The trick for the lovin' young couple is t' find the way without completely undressin'," he explained, "although that restriction should not hamper us in the long run."

He placed her hands on his bare shoulders, and then he put his hands directly on her breasts. He began to stroke them through the material of her bodice, and his fingers found the tips of her breasts. She felt them peak instantly. She gasped and moved against him. He nestled his hips against hers, finding an imperfect, inadequate fit. Then his lips took hers. His tongue seemed to bring to life that little spurt of a spring inside her, the one she had first felt at his kiss in the bothy. This more purposeful kiss made her realize that the spring had been seeping up inside her all day, moistening an already damp ground, with nowhere to flow.

Her hands ran down the muscles of his back. His skin was warm and stimulating to the tips of her fingers, her breasts, her lips. She swirled the tip of her tongue around his, tasting whiskey and broth and the salty sea. He groaned. His hands left her breasts to pull her tighter to him at the hips. They traveled down to her thighs and began to bunch up her skirts, lifting them by handfuls.

"It's not as good," she said.

"What's not?" he managed, a little thickly.

"As this morning," she replied, "in the bothy. When you kissed me, and I was against you. I could feel your skin, and the beating of your heart."

He had raised her skirts to her knees and wedged his legs between hers. His hands ran over the backs of her thighs, which were still covered by whiteclothes. He brought his hands out from under her skirts and held her firmly with one arm around her waist. His free hand went to her back and began to fumble with buttons.

"That's right," he said, nuzzling the hollow of her throat. "Ye were wearin' naught but yer night shift, and I remember that I could feel yer heat through my shirt. 'Tis the thickness of yer bodice that's in the way."

"I thought the trick of this part was to keep the clothes on," she said.

"The trick is not t' undress completely," he said, "which turns on some fine technical points." He pulled the bodice away from her shoulders and down, exposing her chemise. He plucked the ribbon of the neckline, and it sagged prettily. He moved against her so that his bare chest was against her breasts. His hand moved around to touch her pebbled nipples, setting her on fire.

"Is it better now? Is that what ye meant, Anne?"

Skin to skin, hand to skin, was far more than she had meant, and far better than what she had felt before. She kissed him with abandon and explored the ridges and swells of his back and waist and ribs and neck and shoulders with her palms and fingertips. The bunches of her skirts were an increasing nuisance, and she tried to move to escape their weight, but there was no getting around them.

She said, "Yes, but what about the rest of our clothes?"

"In our case, 'twill all end up on the floor," he said, "but I wanted ye t' have the experience of the warmin'-up." By some miracle of agility, he managed to shove his hands under her skirts again and push her drawers off—not smoothly, certainly, but at least without making her fall down in a heap with him on top of her. "Ye see now," he breathed into her ear, as his hands smoothed along the backs of her bare thighs, the sides, down to her knees, up the insides.

She did see, and her knees wobbled slightly.

Holding her again with an arm around her waist, he moved one of his legs behind her for support, then wedged the other leg again between hers. He moved his lips back to her mouth, and she felt them curve up in a smile. He whispered, "Now this is what a clever Highland lad likes t' do for his lass t' keep her warm." His hand crept up the inside of her thigh. His fingers spread moist little lips and found a fruity pearl to touch and stroke, to slide around, to make slick.

Her spring bubbled up, fired up. She was surprised and happy and feeling disobediently forward. "This is what a prudish people do outside of handfasting?"

He took some time before answering. "I can't remember the boundaries at the moment," he said, "but I'm thinkin' that many a Highland lad would be hastily pledgin' his hand t' his lass just now, if he had overlooked the formality—" here he paused to glide the tips of his fingers around the liquid lace he had created "—so that he could proceed t' pledgin' other parts of his body t' her."

"We've already pledged our hands," she pointed out, marveling at the effects of his secret touch.

"'Tis a fact."

Not too many seconds later, the rest of their clothing was in its predicted place, and they had tumbled naked onto the

fresh linens in a lustful tangle. His bed was large and sinfully soft, and with half phrases and inarticulate grunts
between sloppy kisses, they decided not to pull the bed-
curtains, either, so that they could see one another. Then
he took control. He laid her out next to him and covered
her eagerly. He moved her ungently this way and that, at
will, and touched her where he wanted. He spread her
knees, he touched her liquid fire, reveled in it, with it, with
her. He positioned himself for the final pledging.

She felt like golden fire in his arms, from her lips to her
breasts to the apex of her thighs, which she spread like
opening flower petals. She felt as if the goal of her journey north had been predetermined to end at this point. She
felt very wet and desirous and desirable. She felt weak and
hungry. When he grasped her buttocks and made her vulnerable with his legs between hers, about to fill and end her
accessibility, she suddenly felt her loss of control. She remembered being tossed by Duncan into Alexander's arms
as he sat upon his horse. She remembered being torn from
her bed and slung, rump up, over Duncan's shoulders. She
remembered being ripped from the arms of her handsome, tepid but kissable footman, and subjected to an ig-
nominious verbal and physical spanking by her father.

She moved her legs. She struggled against him. "No,"
she pleaded against his lips, as she attempted to push him
away from her. "No, no, no."

The "no" took some time to penetrate, as did her physical resistance. He rolled away from her, onto his back.
"Anne, love, 'tis not fair t' bring a man t' the brink and
then draw back." He stretched out and flung an arm up
and behind his head. He exhaled gustily. He slid his eyes
over to her; they were glittering slits in the night. "I
thought ye wanted the long-overdue end t' yer virginity.
And if ye haven't understood ye want the end of it, I do."

She sat up, folding her legs beneath her bottom, sitting back on her heels, with her thighs together, but not tightly. Her hair tumbled around her shoulders and down her back. Her forearms framed her peaked breasts and pushed them slightly forward. She placed her hands on her thighs, not covering her red delta of hair from his sight, for she was proud of her body and her arousal.

"I do want the end of it," she admitted, meeting his hot gaze with the green fire in her own. "But, you see, from the beginning, I've not been acting, only reacting."

He exhaled again, at length. His eyes rested on her and her beauty. "I like the way ye've been reactin', lass. A lot."

"My whole life, I mean," she continued. "I've never acted, only reacted. I've never *chosen,* only *been* chosen." She considered that. "And not even chosen. Taken, more like. Taken from court, taken from London, taken from my bed last night. Even the words of the handfasting were taken from my mouth."

He was visibly struggling with his desire, and with her sudden and inconvenient sense of injustice. "I'll admit t' bein' desperate, Anne." He gave his head a shake against the pillows and closed his eyes. "Ye know what I want." He nearly sighed. "Ye'll have t' decide what ye want."

He might not have known it, but his unexpected capitulation gave her the choice she needed just then. With his eyes closed, she felt free to look at his body. Really look at it. In all its alarming, exciting detail. From the line of his jaw to his muscled chest, to his narrow hips, to his shapely thighs and calves and feet. After a long minute of inspection, she realized that he had opened his eyes again and was looking at her speculatively in return.

"Like what ye see?" he asked quietly, provocatively. When she did not answer, he prompted, "Touch what ye like. Go ahead, lass. Yer choice." To increase his defenselessness, he put his other arm up and clasped the wrist that was already behind his head. He was hers.

Bravely, even boldly, she leaned forward, put her hands on his shoulders and caressed them experimentally. She put her lips to them and tasted his warm and salty skin. She leaned back and swept her eyes down his body again. She touched his feet. She felt a slight tremor go through him at her touch.

"Naught in between interests you?" he asked.

She accepted the dare and reached out a hand to grasp his manhood, rising straight and eager from its dark nest of hair. He groaned, and his member wiggled involuntarily in her hand.

"Am I hurting you?" she asked as she relaxed her grip.

"Nay," he assured her in a somewhat strangled voice.

She increased the pressure of her hand on him. "Is this too much?"

His eyes rolled back, and his lids closed languorously. "Both too much and too little. But I can't tell ye what to do. 'Tis yer choice. Touch me how ye want."

She was aroused by the look on his face, the sound of his voice, and the feel of her palm and fingers around him, hot and hard and completely hers. She was aware of the fiery wetness between her thighs. She bent over him, her breasts grazing his chest, and whispered into his ear,

"Do I have to touch you with my hands?"

Chapter Six

He cracked his eyes open and rolled his head slightly to meet her face, so warm next to his. Moving his lips against her cheek, he said, "I wouldn't be so restrictive as t' limit ye t' touchin' me with yer hands."

She nodded. "Good." Then she positioned herself over him. She propped her forearms lightly on his chest and arched her back, pressing her breasts against him and raising her rump slightly. She caught his member between her thighs. "This is what I had in mind," she said into his neck, then moved her lips over his chin to his mouth. When she kissed him, she began to move her hips up and down, so that the insides of her thighs slid against him and created the pressure that her hands could not properly gauge. She felt the flow of the fiery spring inside her, no longer aimless, but directed now in its course. The origin of the spring was far below heaven, far below her heart, just above the opening between her thighs. The spring flowed from her center, pulsing now with ever-widening circles of desire that traveled up her belly and down her thighs to her knees.

She took it very slowly, playfully, knowing that she was pushing and pulling him to his limit. She luxuriated in the feel of his length sliding against her, up to the liquid edge

of her, then sliding back and away. She teased herself with
the flaring tip of his shaft, moving around him as his fingers had worked before. She was teasing him, too, meeting him, then winding away, knowing that the spring of his
desire would soon flow with hers, but wanting to hold him
off, to dally next to him and around him, just a little
longer.

She moved up the length of him once, allowing his head
to peek into her surging center. She did it again, permit-
ting him deeper inside her, circling him with her lips, kissing him wetly. And then a third time, inching slowly, so
that his manhood pressed fully against the tiny, swollen
pearl between her legs, from which flowed her desire.

She felt plump and plummy and sinfully ripe. She leaned
her mouth to his ear and circled the shell with her tongue.
"Is this what you want, then?" she breathed.

His reply was low and short and inarticulate.

She increased the rhythm of her hips, shortening the
strokes of her swaying and sliding. With hungry desire, she
sat back down on him, almost sheathing him, hindered
only by the gentle resistance of her maidenhead. She
wanted to force the issue herself, but then she realized that
his hands had spread across her buttocks, helping her,
guiding her movements. She moved forward along him to
reposition herself, her breasts flattened against his chest.
She stretched her neck against his, thrust spread fingers
through his hair, and breathed out and in with a bodily
yawn. She had taken his measure and prepared herself for
a rough and ragged passage. She pushed back upon him,
finally, rude and ruddy and ready to fill herself with him.
Or kill herself with him. Or satisfy herself with him.

She licked his lips. She loved the way he felt beneath her,
strong, hard, hot, and helpless at the brink. She whispered, teasing, taunting, playful still. Into his ear she

dripped the drops of words that made his glass overflow. "Is it fair, now, I wonder, to have brought you this far?"

He replied she knew not what, for there was a muted roaring of blood and desire pounding in her ears. His muscles rippled. She gasped in surprise when he fully entered her. She was flat on her back now, beneath him, filled by him, controlled by him, at the mercy of his strength and his desire. Her frivolous dalliance and feminine teasing vanished, as if diluted in the great sea of a terrible force. His muscle had met her wetness at the mouth of a secret velvet steep, and he joined her to him to form a wild and impetuous cascade, like the merging of the Kilt and the Laurel. One moment she teetered on the edge, the next she was shooting headlong down the precipice with him, feeling foamy and white, churning over rocky desire. Then her ripe fruit burst into a thousand different streams of liquid fire coursing through her body, webbing and flashing over the curves of ancient stone sculpted by eons of rushing life.

She plunged down the gorge with him, breathless, until their falling waters splashed violently against the surface of a deep pool, sending the spray through them, through her, around them. She felt bathed in salty sweat, drowned in the deep pool, then felt herself rise to a misty obscurity. She open her eyes to a midnight world, fractured and dazzled.

A moment passed before she realized that she had surfaced. A magnificent satisfaction pooled between her legs, making her bloated and sleepy. He stirred, still full within her, and grasped harsh handfuls of her flesh. He moaned against her neck, causing her to stretch against him and wrap her legs up around his tight butt. He was breathing heavily on top of her. She moved her head to breathe in the tantalizing tang of his skin, with its first layer of night sex glazing over the clean of the afternoon.

Her first thought was "No fair! It was supposed to be my choice!" She did not seem to have the energy to bring the half serious, half teasing sounds up her throat.

He began to withdraw from her, with a graceful fumbling of legs and arms. A grunt here, a moan there, and he was able to convey the rearrangement he wanted, which was to have her nestled way down into the crook of his arm, her shoulder snuggled into his armpit, with his other hand heavily upon her breast, their legs tangled haphazardly.

They lay cradled a while, until he moved his head to look down at her. His eyes were narrowed to black, glittery slits, but she could see unmistakably that he was a very happy and satisfied man, still dazed by passion and sticky with her dew. He did not say a word. She would not learn until later that he was incapable, just then, of speaking.

She caressed him where her hand happened to have fallen, which was on a muscle of his forearm. She tested it with her fingertips, smoothing over the hardness that flexed convulsively at her touch. She cleared her throat and smiled up at him. Eager and naive and very provocative, she asked, "When do we get to do this again?"

He let her know, of course, at various intervals throughout the night. If his goal was to render her incapable of walking the next day, he certainly tried, and he nearly succeeded.

She had asked her question with no thought that it would be immediately answered. She closed her eyes and drifted aimlessly in a shadowed, luxurious world of desire satisfied. It was pleasure at that moment simply to breathe ever deeper, ever more slowly, and then she entered the dreamworld of disparate impressions and deep-seated knowledge. Patched together came an incoherent picture of red hair unfurled against the Sutherland plaid, and deep male voices with whiskeyed burrs, crosscut by angry English voices decrying Highland barbarism and disobedience. She recognized one of those voices, but could not place it. She waved it away, annoyed, but as she swatted, her hand seemed to come in contact with another hand, and she was back in the arms of the court footman who had caught her fancy. He was pretty enough, and kissed well enough, but something was lacking.

No bubbling spring, she realized. No flow. No desire. No flames. No liquid pool in which to bathe and drown and dirty oneself and cleanse oneself.

But then again, yes. Yes to the bubbling spring. Yes to the flow. Yes to the desire. Yes to the flames. Yes to the liquid pool that seeped around her, that trickled from her, her pores, her fingertips, her tongue.

She opened her eyes and said yes with her eyes to him as he moved over her and spread her legs with authority, giving her no choices this time, parting her moist flower. He cut off resistance top and bottom with his tongue at her lips, her teeth, her tongue, and his manhood at her liquid pool, plunging in like a diver unafraid of the depths. He worked around the tops of her thighs with his hands and his fingers, stroking the slick parts as they came momentarily exposed, until he had drawn her over the edge with him and she was plunging down that precipitous slope again, propelled by churning waters.

The experience was darker this time, with strong undercurrents of mastery, and viscous bonds that had not been there before. It was frightening, too, the force and his strength, and what he was demanding of her, and taking from her. She was nearly overwhelmed by it, submerged in oblivion, until he grasped her buttocks and began to rock against her. She found the leverage she wanted, and they managed to roll over so that she was on top of him, joined to him still. She shook with ecstasy at the movement and the effect of his hands on her backside, and her legs spread over him as she sat upon him. She reared up and arched her head back, groaning her acceptance of his unity with her. His hand came around to the little plum between her legs, now exposed to his touch, and she lowered her head, slowly, to look down at him looking up at her.

She looked. And could not look away. His eyes held hers as he stroked her to distraction, then drew back. He grasped her breasts and moved her with his hips and let her ride him until she folded down across his chest, conceding defeat, and he exhausted himself in her.

As she lay limp across him, he whispered into her ear with a note between triumph and death, "We're not through yet."

She awoke to a half-light in the room and his hand between her legs. She countered with a bold move of her own, and was not disappointed by what she held. He let her have her way a while, before he rolled her over and told her exactly what he wanted to do. Then he did exactly what he wanted to do. The experience, though novel, had a strain of familiarity, and it was less humbling than she would ever have guessed, and, in the end, very exciting.

Through the pulse of desire and the haze of satisfaction, it seemed to her that he had moved through the night around her, with her, in her, with a purpose that lay beyond his own momentary appetites. However, she had neither the words nor the experience to frame what she felt in his arms now, in her head, in her heart, at the juncture of her thighs, after a night of passion and a full morning of love.

Later in the day—after she had lumbered out of bed and rubbed her aching limbs and let him sponge her off and kiss her with lingering lips and they had walked together to the hall and parted for the day after breaking fast—she began to understand. While she was going about the light chores that had been assigned to her, she mulled over her experiences of the past twenty-four hours and more, and tried to mesh her night life with her day life. After the transformation in Alexander's arms during the night, she was a little taken aback, and even strangely pleased that no one at Dunrobin treated her any differently from the way they had the day before. No one commented. No one nudged anyone else meaningfully. No one winked or snickered. No one looked at her askance.

The reason was simple: She had come to Dunrobin already pledged in handfast, and, thus, by Scottish standards, respectable; and she had already spent the night with Alexander on his horse—chastely, although not completely innocently. What they had done together last night was of no different order to the public from what they had done the night before, and no one's business, either.

So she was not the center of attention. She did not feel her face burn at the thought of being the object of scandalized talk. She did not have to hold her head defiantly high. She did not have to fend off the unwanted attentions of men who wanted to conquer her, then strut and crow. She did not have to face her father, and Edinburgh seemed as far away from her just then as London. She gladly embraced the normalized role she was allowed to play as a woman at Dunrobin.

Before the midday dinner, she met up again with Alexander. He caught her in his arms, pecked her lips, and drew back to look at her. She felt her face flush at his regard, not

from embarrassment at remembered passion and expo-
sure, but from desire and happiness. She understood then
that during the night their relationship had been peeled
down to its basic level, leaving no room for coy feints and
modest disclaimers in the morning. He put his lips to hers
again and caressed her rump lightly. Her breasts and thighs
were pressed briefly against his length, sending a quick
course of passion through her. He broke the kiss with a
smile, and she could hardly wait for the night, when she
would be with him again, stripped down to that basic level
of openings and joinings.

After dinner, the Sutherland pronounced the day to be
fine and the wind perfect. He further noted that the links
were in excellent condition and declared an afternoon of
golf. Soon, dozens of sporting Sutherlands had swarmed
out of the castle to warm themselves under a bright blue
summer's sky. They were walking north, toward the
greens, over the sandy knolls, clubs in hand, swatting at
thistles and rough herbage and heather, idly warming up
their strokes.

The men preceded the women, the former group being
rather keener for this manly exercise. Duncan and Dugald
led the entire party, which surprised no one. The Sutherland, along with Jamie and Simon, stayed behind a while
at Dunrobin, planning to make the last party of golfers.
That way they could take their time and play until sunset.

Anne, looking very much a part of the scenery in her
arisaid, walked out with Jenny and Marris and Elspeth.
She was met by Alexander, who was shouldering two
clubs. He put his free arm around her and drew her away
from the ladies, demanding that they play together alone,
behind the first foursome. Anne admitted that her game
was weak, since the English had not played golf much since
the Stuarts had been in power. Alexander was not at all

troubled by this admission, and said that it gave him a chance to impress her all the more with his skill, which, he assured her, was considerable.

Anne and Alexander approached the first of the five long greens, where Duncan and Dugald had assembled, along with Gavin and Evan. The four men were standing around, leaning against their clubs, their plaids lifting lightly around their trews in the mild sea breeze. They were surveying the course, discussing the traps and the treacherous bunkers ahead, and looking as happy and contented as men on this earth could be.

The talk turned to Gavin's interest in a certain castle maiden, who was coming into view, but still at some distance from the greens, and then, inevitably, to Evan's sad state of heart. It drifted from women back to golf and a decision to take three turns of the five holes that made the recognized round. Eventually conversation meandered back again to women, moved on to the order of play and the decision for Duncan to tee up.

Duncan placed his ball, flourished his club, stamped his feet to firm his stance, adjusted his plaid over his shoulder, and paused to scratch himself. He lifted his head to sight the hole, invisible hundreds of yards off, and bent again to fiddle with the pinch of sand on which his ball was poised. He stamped out his stance again, then lifted his head and saw Gavin's lass come into sight. With a grin, he squared his club up to his ball and cried, "Ware a'fore!" although there was not a soul ahead of him. He sent the ball flying with an impressive whack.

"Good shot," Dugald observed.

"Aye, very good," Duncan agreed.

"Good lie, too."

"'Tis a wee bit cuppy," Duncan admitted.

"Aye, 'tis a cuppy lie, but still good."

Gavin stepped up next and hit a most respectable ball that was not as long as Duncan's but had a better lie. He made every effort not to look pleased with himself that the castle lass had seen his excellent shot.

"Now, then, lad," Duncan said with an obvious glance over his shoulder at the bonny lass, "'tis well done, yer stroke, but length will always prevail."

"'Tis not the length," Gavin replied. "'Tis how ye go about it."

"And what about strength?" Duncan wanted to know.

"Strength is a fine thing t' cultivate," Gavin acknowledged, swinging his club easily with a flexible wrist, "but ye must set it up, make it straight, and send it through the fine turf to the hole. That's the way t' go about it, man, for a truly satisfyin' round."

Duncan made a dismissive noise. "Straight?" he said with a wave of his hand. "Do ye think it so important to play it straight?"

"'Tis better for the approach to the hole, ye know," Gavin said. "Come up on it straight. Get it in."

Alexander was leaning against his club, half listening to this earnest discussion. He had an arm draped over Anne's shoulder and had pulled her toward him so that he could nuzzle her neck at will. He chose to enter the discussion at this point. "Length and strength are important, I can't deny," he said, "but I must agree with Gavin that 'tis surely a question of technique—for the satisfyin' round, as he puts it—and of how ye go about it."

"Ye have t' work on yer form, Duncan," Gavin said, nodding in agreement with Alexander's remark, "and add straightness to yer strength. If ye come upon it straight, ye can't miss."

Duncan was unconvinced. "I've missed plenty of times comin' up on the hole straight."

"How is that possible?" Alexander asked, surprised.

"The reason," Gavin said with a superior smile, "is precisely that strength does a man no good at the hole. Finesse is what's needed at the end t' achieve the goal."

Dugald had been listening thoughtfully to this sound advice. "Ye'd best listen t' the young man, Duncan," he recommended. "Although he can't hold his whiskey—'tis a pity—he's got strength and length enough t' approach the hole, and the finesse that ye lack, my fine lad, to get it in."

"My point precisely," Alexander said dryly. "He's got no stayin' power with the strokes, and, as a consequence, scores less with the lass—" Here he broke off and looked blankly around the group. Then, with an expression of spurious enlightenment, he exclaimed, "Ah, I see now that ye were discussin' the game of *golf!* Well, I feel a grand sight better about Duncan's difficulties in the long grasses, I can tell ye!"

This willful misunderstanding, not unnaturally, called for a great many jests of various rude sorts, which did not in the least offend Anne. Duncan wrapped it up by crying shame down on Alexander's head and saying to Anne that she would have to figure a way to curb her man's tongue.

Alexander said, "She's already figured a way."

Three men looked at him in inquiry.

Alexander said succinctly, "Rendered me speechless, she did."

Further explanation was not necessary. Three pairs of male eyes slid to Anne in wonderment and admiration, then returned to Alexander with expressions of great interest and envy. "Well, now, t' imagine Alexander speechless," said Duncan. Then came the immediate inference, "Will ye make through the complete round today, I'm wondering? Fifteen holes is quite a lot."

To which Dugald added, in a practical spirit, "There's a cozy bunker on the fourth hole that might serve yer purposes."

Alexander looked speculatively down at Anne, smiling. "Aye, the sand pit there is dry and snug and surrounded by a screen of whins in full bloom." He looked up again. "We'll just have t' see, then, lads. I thank ye for the tip."

The play resumed. The foursome was divided between two sides of two players each, each side playing only one ball. Since Duncan and Gavin had already teed off, the four men proceeded down the lengthy green to continue the match, with Dugald and Evan taking the second stroke on Duncan's and Gavin's balls, respectively.

When the men were at a reasonable distance, Alexander stepped up, for he and Anne had chosen to play one ball between them, as well. For his shot, he produced a ball made of leather stuffed with highly compressed feathers. He said that he preferred this feathery ball to the boxwood balls that Duncan and Gavin liked so well. Indeed, his tee shot was nearly perfect in form, distance and lie. He explained further that the Sutherland course was long and had originally been designed primarily as a test of hard hitting. However, several years before, he had taken it upon himself to break up the long yardage with sand bunkers and water traps and gravel pits in order to make the game a "less stern and monotonous business." The new hazards, he noted, favored Gavin's game over Duncan's. For himself, he made it clear that he did not mind if all his balls ended up in the warm, soft sand, as long as Anne was there with him.

Anne and Alexander were not, alas, to indulge any of the major side pleasures of the golf course this day, although opportunities certainly existed for minor liberties. Alexander took it upon himself to stand behind Anne, with his arms around her to guide her shots. Anne found the position of his front pressed intimately to her backside not only stimulating, but also very helpful to her as a novice golfer, in terms of correct grip on the club, swing, and follow-through. If her instructor felt it necessary to feel her breast and buttocks as part of the educational process, then she could only determine that there was more interest to the game of golf than she ever would have thought.

They holed out in eight on the first. The second hole went well enough, as well. They were in the midst of the third hole, warming up slowly for the pleasures of the fourth, making all the gestures that would make a stop in the next sand pit necessary, satisfying, and extremely short. They looked up to see a riding party cantering over the greens. At first, Alexander was outraged by this breach of golf etiquette and had something to say about the disastrous effect of horses' hooves on fine turf. At second glance, he perceived his father at the head of the party, with Jamie and Simon and another man behind.

He dropped his outrage and his arm from Anne's shoulder. He took a step away from her, straightened up, and said in the flat voice of prophecy, " 'Tis trouble coming toward us."

Chapter Seven

Anne sensed the doom before she saw it. She heard the note in Alexander's voice, and her heart sank. The instant raising of his guard caused her to sharpen as well, from lazy longings of fleshly love to thoughts of immediate fleshly preservation.

"I was entitled t' a year and a day with ye," he said softly, looking straight ahead at the oncoming riding party. "I had my day but I've the feelin' that my year is t' be cut brutally short."

Anne strained to see who rode behind the Sutherland and his eldest sons. "Are you sure the situation is so dire?"

"'Tis a Sassenach who rides behind my father, judging from the cut and color of his coat."

The party had come close enough for her to discern the set of the Sutherland's features. He was at all times a grim-looking man, but a further stony dimension in his countenance brought her true alarm. Then came into her view the man who rode behind him, and her eyes widened considerably.

"Ye should be happy, lass," Alexander said, summoning a more jaunty smile. "I told ye at the outset that ye'd be rid of me soon enough, makin' ye free t' marry yer borin' Ralph."

Anne was able to squeeze a pip of humor out of the situation, although her heart had sunk to her stomach. "You may soon be hanging at the end of an English rope," she said slyly, "but not, I can assure you, because you are a political undesirable."

Alexander slanted her an inquisitive glance.

"The man with your father," she said, "is *my* father."

Alexander's eyes lit up, and his jaunty smile turned charmingly genuine. "'Tis trouble all the same," he said, "but of a different order entirely." His flat tones had leavened, suggesting that he, too, perceived some humorous dimension to this twist. "And I'll permit myself a gesture. Let us call it 'husbandly.'" He put his arm around Anne again, this time protectively.

The riding party drew rein a few feet from the pair. The Sutherland, his face impassive as ever, remained mounted, as did Jamie and Simon. Walter Chisholm dismounted slowly and deliberately and walked toward them. He did not spare the slightest glance for his daughter. His eyes did not leave Alexander Sutherland's face.

Anne knew that she was being spared her father's fury only momentarily, and her heart pounded painfully in anticipation of when it would fall upon her. As he approached, she suddenly realized how Scottish her father looked, with his ruddy complexion and his light brown hair hesitating between sandy and auburn. She saw, as well, that his coloring matched vividly the scarlet of his military jacket, the smart and arrogant English red that marked such a stark contrast to the rich, earthy reds of the clan tartans.

Walter Chisholm was a tall man, almost the same height as Alexander, and far leaner than the broad-shouldered Sutherlands. He continued to regard Alexander. His voice was chill and superior. "What do you think you are doing," he said, measuring his words. It was not a question.

"At the risk of impertinence, sir," Alexander said, as cool as the North Sea, "we are playing a round of golf. I'm teaching your daughter the strokes."

"My daughter," Chisholm said without change of expression, "has been disgraced."

"She was the victim, ye might say, of a mistake," Alexander replied. "As a result, I've taken the steps t' save her honor." With a hint of challenge, he added, "And that of the Sutherlands."

Every line in Chisholm's face and body was rigid with anger. "A mistake," he repeated hollowly. "And you've managed to save her honor. And yours." He tapped his riding crop against his boots. His sarcasm was thin. "By teaching her golf, perhaps?"

"Nay, then, sir," Alexander said, keeping his voice on the ragged edge of respectful, "by pledgin' my hand t' her in the Scottish manner."

"Pledging your hand?" Chisholm echoed, with a flicker in the depths of his pale green eyes.

"Handfastin', t' be more precise. Betrothal for a year and a day."

"I know what handfasting is, you scoundrel!" Chisholm snapped. From the narrowing of his eyes as he scrutinized Alexander, Anne determined that the Ross must not have relayed the information of how the two clan chiefs had resolved the problem of her abduction day before yesterday. His eyes cut to Anne. "And have you been party to this handfasting, my dear?" he asked, with no hint of fatherly love in his voice.

The way her father's eyes flashed over her then caused fear to ripple through her. She opened her mouth, but no words came out.

"Of your own free will, my dear?" her father said, prodding her.

Alexander's arm rested lightly and reassuringly on her shoulder. She cleared her throat. "Well, Father..." she began. "That is to say... I don't know what you... I was at Tomain nam Mòd and then I wasn't... I'm here now...."

"Have you been party to it?" her father demanded again.

She knew what he was asking. She drew a very deep breath and exhaled the words, "In a manner of speaking, yes."

Walter Chisholm's face was a bloodless white. "The precise manner of speaking we shall discuss, you and I," he said, biting off his words, "back in the keep." With that, he turned on his heels and remounted his horse. He wheeled the steed around without giving either of them another glance, and spoke to the Sutherland as he would to his lowest page. "You shall accompany me back to the castle and provide me with a room where I may speak in private with my daughter."

The Sutherland's face remained set. The manner of his acquiescent nod suggested that, as host, he would not be reduced to the rudeness of his guest. When Chisholm's horse started off again over the greens, with Jamie and Simon following close behind, the Sutherland stepped his horse close enough to Alexander to warn him quietly, "Walter Chisholm has brought several dozen of his redcoated friends with him up from Inverness." Then he galloped off to ride abreast of the English queen's chamberlain and highest-ranking military officer.

The walk back to Dunrobin was not nearly so pleasant as the walk out to the greens. The sun was still shining brightly, but it no longer seemed so warm. Alexander had pocketed the ball and shouldered his clubs, but did not put his arm around Anne's shoulders. They exchanged little conversation. There was nothing useful to say.

At one point, Alexander looked down at her and asked, "What can I do for ye?"

Anne looked back at him and shook her head. She shrugged.

He said, "Ye're understandably worried about havin' t' face the consequences of the changes in yer life. 'Tis a case of sooner rather than later."

Anne nodded, eyes lowered.

They walked on. After a few moments, Alexander said simply, "I'm not a bit sorry for what's happened, lass, and wouldn't change it, even if I could."

She looked up at him and saw a new expression on his face and a new light in his blue eyes. Or perhaps it was that she understood it better now. A lifetime ago, before the extraordinary night and day and night she had just spent, she would have called his look serious. She did not call it serious now, but rather stripped: stripped of the teasing and the easy acceptance of the happenstance of their handfasting; stripped like the basic joining of their naked bodies of the previous night; stripped to the moment before the joining, when he had told her that the vows of handfasting were not trivially spoken; stripped to the morning before, in the bothy, when he had said, "I pledge ye my troth."

She had reveled in her careless freedom of being with him. She had reveled in her fantasy. She had reveled in the smoky desire she felt for him, had indulged it and satisfied it and found it all the more appealing because it seemed forbidden to her, yet curiously and conveniently sanctioned within the walls of Dunrobin. She had not really, truly, *seriously*, pledged him her troth, had she? She did not really, truly, *seriously,* accept the custom of hand-fasting, did she? Was she sorry for what had happened, and would she change anything about the past few days, if she could?

She had no answers to these questions stripped now to their basic parts. She knew only that the origin of what she felt for him began far below heaven and far below her heart. She would not insult him by imagining him reduced to what was between his legs or to a pair of broad shoulders. Neither would she insult him with a response that evaded the stripped simplicity of his comment and his look.

"There is something between us," she said slowly, "but I don't know what."

His expression softened into a hint of a smile. "What we have between us has been good enough t' come together, lass," he replied quietly. " 'Tis not enough t' stay together. There must be more."

Her gaze held his a moment longer. More? she wondered. She lowered her lashes, struggling to understand, and they walked on. They arrived at the courtyard, where, under the ominous eyes of redcoated soldiers, they parted in silence.

Silence did not characterize her meeting with her father—unexpectedly, for Walter Chisholm had always been a reserved and distant parent. Seated upon a hard chair, Anne listened, aghast, to the verbal scourging that hailed down on her from his lips as he stood above her. He had been angry with her for her indiscretion with the foot-man, but the lash of his tongue then had been nothing compared to this. She assumed her customary attitude of hanging head and heavy heart and felt appallingly girlish and confused and convinced that she would never, ever learn to behave correctly.

Then her father turned his attack from her person, her morals and her manners to the specifics of her present situation. She was amazed to hear that he counted her—*her!*—at fault for having been taken, sleeping, from her bed in the middle of the night two days before at Tomain nam Mòd.

At that she sprang to her feet, head erect, eyes wide, heart pounding. "What?" she demanded in the least dutiful voice she had ever dared with him. "You *dare* accuse me of *that?* How, pray, Father, am I to be blamed for anything, when I was asleep in my bed?"

"You attract trouble wherever you go," was her father's immediate response. "Like a magnet to your hair and to your, your—" here he waved an insulting hand "—your person."

She had heard this argument before, and had felt the shame of it. She had even believed it. Now, however, she was finally able to perceive it in its proper, ridiculous light. "Then why," she asked, remembering one of Alexander's comments, "did you send me to Scotland, of all places? Why did you not send me to the well-mannered Lindsays, where I would have been safe and unmolested?"

Walter Chisholm looked momentarily taken aback. He said, "Because I had business in the Highlands, as you'll remember, and I was able to escort you as far as Inverness. You were certainly safe with me for the time of the travel!"

She suddenly recalled overhearing conversations during the trip north between her father and official members of their traveling party. She remembered that her father was on the trail of a particular Highland barbarian, one who had escaped them the year before and dropped from view, but who had, according to reports, once again been sighted. Her unformed impression of a

Highland barbarian jangled against an image of a smooth, broad-shouldered man, but she did not pause to allow the disparate images to settle into a recognizable picture.

Instead, she stayed her course. "And why follow me from Inverness to the Rosses?" she asked. "Was it business? Or were you simply coming to pay me a kindly paternal visit?"

"I was coming west and north on the strength of a report or two," her father replied, "and thought it proper to visit my daughter." His mouth twisted into a joyless smile. "And what should I find but that she was no longer in the castle and was traveling over the countryside, wanton in her night shift!"

"I was taken from my bed in the dead of night," she reminded him. "It was only natural that I should have been in my night shift!"

"Which hardly makes your behavior less wanton," he spat.

"I have done nothing wanton. I'm respectably bound in handfast," she returned, with what dignity she could.

"Respectably bound?" he echoed sardonically. "How far did it go, my daughter, in one day? How far?"

She raised her chin and refused to answer.

"How far?" he repeated, almost taunting. "Far enough that you are no longer sufficiently virtuous to offer yourself to the man I have chosen for you?"

"Far enough," she admitted. Liking the taste of her defiance, she added, "Further."

Chisholm's pale green eyes lit with anger. "Then marriage is the only course left to you now."

Anne blinked. "To Mr. Weathercombe?" she asked, surprised.

"To the man who's defiled you," he answered, eyes hard. He snorted derisively. "You're not fit any longer for your true betrothed. Only the clean cloth of a proper marriage will blot the stain of your lust."

She was stung into retort. "The handfasting continues for a year and a day. After that I will choose whom I wish to marry."

"You will choose nothing!" her father shouted. "I'll not bring another woman from Scotland who's lived under the sinful guise of handfast, to be whispered about and leered at by every man in London! No, by God, I'll not bring another damaged woman down from the wilds and attempt to present her as a respectable woman, creditably and virtuously circumstanced!"

"Another woman?" Anne repeated.

"You'll marry your man with the blessings of a priest and the proper piece of legal paper," he continued without pause. The spittle at the corners of his mouth had dried white with the heat of his anger. "Then, when your man has fallen drunk off his horse over the side of a cliff or impaled himself on the tip of a clansman's sword—perhaps I'll help hasten that day!—I'll take you back to London and exert every ounce of my political skill to see you become Mrs. Weathercombe. And no woman will ever shame me again!"

"Another woman?" Anne was still wondering. "What other woman?"

"Your mother," he spat contemptuously, "as if you didn't know. You're no better than she. Or her sluttish sister, Margaret." He ran narrowed eyes over her, as if perceiving her arisaid for the first time. He shook his head warningly. "You'll be married in a respectable dress. Not in this impertinence."

"I'll not be married at all," she said, stamping a foot. She felt a childish tantrum reverberate through her, one she had never had, one she should have had years before.

"You'll be married to your Sutherland stud before the sun sets today," he said. He turned and strode from the room, slamming the door behind him.

"My Sutherland st—?" At last her tantrum erupted. "I'll make my own choice!" she cried stormily at the closed door. "My own!" she repeated. She shook her fists and stomped around the room, declaring to the four walls that she would marry whom she wanted, when she wanted, why she wanted, and where she wanted.

She was still pacing and muttering angrily, "I say when, and I say who!" and "My choice!" when Jenny and Marris and Elspeth tiptoed gingerly into the chamber.

Jenny was bearing a frothy peach dress in her arms. She held it up and said apologetically, " 'Twas the only dress we could find that was somewhat suitable t' the occasion and that might fit ye. 'Tis not entirely the style for a bride, but 'twas made clear t' us that the arisaid won't do for ye, and so we thought—"

"A bride? I've not chosen to be a bride," Anne had stopped her pacing and was eyeing the proffered dress with displeasure. "And if I *were* thinking to become a bride, I'd wear just what I have on."

Jenny nodded to Marris and Elspeth. The three of them crept forward, calmly apprehensive, as if approaching a skittish colt.

"I've my orders," Jenny said. " 'Tis for the best, ye know, under the circumstances."

"Ye have no choice, Anne," Marris said.

"I'd marry Alexander, if I were ye," Elspeth added.

While Marris unclasped the brooch and unfastened the belt that held the arisaid in place, Jenny continued, "The Sutherland said that we were t' find a dress for ye that would please yer father. He said that we were t' make sure that ye would look the bonny bride and do yer part compliantly."

Marris unwound the striped cloth from Anne's shoulders and waist. Jenny pressed, "The Sutherland said that it would go better for Alex if yer father and his friends had no cause t' be angry with him." Jenny kept up her gentle arguments as Anne's dress was removed. At the moment when the peach confection was floated over Anne's head and adjusted over her curves, Jenny concluded, "The Sutherland is hopin' t' put forward an occasion befittin' the marriage of his third son." Marris stepped back to survey Anne in her wedding dress. "If the Sutherland is hopin' for the occasion to be befittin'," she said, "he'll have t' discover a different dress for the bride."

Jenny and Elspeth looked at Anne, and their eyes widened in unison. Jenny covered her mouth. Elspeth bit her lip. "Perhaps we could adjust the lace at her bosom?" Marris suggested.

"Or perhaps the veil will make her look more modest," Elspeth said as she arranged it over Anne's head and shoulders.

The veil, though very pretty, did not increase the modesty of Anne's appearance. She looked down at herself and had a fair impression of the effect of the beautiful color pearling the immodest expanse of her breasts. "That bad?" she asked.

"Ye look delicious," Jenny said with a hapless shrug.

For a response, Anne said with great satisfaction but rather obscurely, "I'm Margaret MacKenzie's niece." Then, while Jenny and Marris and Elspeth applied themselves to coiffing and binding her hair, Anne said aloud, "I wonder who my mother's man was?" This was followed by rather disjointed musings on handfastings in general and her mother's unknown relationship in particular, all of which she summed up with one unequivocal pronouncement, "But I do not wish to be married, you know."

Elspeth said, "I'd marry Alexander, if I were ye."

Finally, Elspeth's words penetrated. Anne had been so wrapped in a swirling storm of defiance against her father that she had forgotten about the other man in her life. She looked at Marris, who was nodding gentle encouragement, then at Jenny, who repeated beseechingly, as she took Anne's arm and led her out of the chamber, "The Sutherland said it would go better for Alexander if ye were t' marry him right and proper, with yer father lookin' on."

Anne's angry defiance was transformed upon her arrival in the hall, and her heart stopped for a moment. All she could see was Alexander, awaiting her at the far end, flanked by his father and his brothers, standing proud and noble in the full dress of a Highland gentleman. He wore the belted Sutherland plaid, kilted and arranged so that its length also encircled his shoulders, where it was caught on the left with a brooch. Her first impression was of the splendid contrast between the deep green of the plaid and the dull gold of his velvet jacket.

Her second impression registered the details of his magnificence. His breast was left free, and neither ornaments nor arms were hidden; the sword and jeweled dirk at his waist were exposed and hanging visibly on either side of his sporran. His hose were gartered high at the knee, and the brogues on his feet were tied in a traditional pattern. His right hand lay lightly on the hilt of his sword. His left hand held his bonnet, bearing the clan badge, along with two feathers, showing his affinity to the chief. The expression on his face was as proud and noble as his dress, and Anne wondered whether she would ever again lay eyes on another man as appealingly masculine as Alexander Sutherland.

She felt the spurt of something inside her, and its source was in the region of her heart.

Then she noticed that the hall was filled with soldiers, familiar English soldiers, and she felt the tension, masked under the pretense of wedding celebration, but there all the same. The mood struck her as oddly gay and grim.

Walter Chisholm came forward. He seemed perversely satisfied to see his daughter looking peach-ripe and ready for a pretty peeling. He escorted Anne before the groom's party, accompanied by the English soldiers. Behind them, the castle inhabitants filed out of the hall, out of the courtyard, through the open gates, and down the winding path to the little church in the middle of the village carved into the rock at the southern foot of Dunrobin.

There, in the cool dark of the church, standing before the pastor and before the altar, next to Alexander, Anne began to feel the weight of the occasion pressing down on her in a way that she had not felt for the simple handfasting the day before. Here in the church, ceremonial words drifted around her, wrapped her, suffocated her. Then she heard, as if from a muffled distance, Alexander's deep and confident voice, "I take thee..."

Her turn came next, and she could only repeat the ritual formula quietly and without conviction. The irrevocable moment came. The question was asked that began "Do ye, Anne Chisholm, take..." and a small silence fell. She felt herself teetering on the edge of an abyss. She felt her father's eyes boring into her back. She felt a shifting among the English soldiers, who wore their swords and pistols exposed in their belts. She felt the Sutherland clan's collective heart stop. She felt Alexander's presence next to her. She was aware of the very bones in his body, and of the very breath that he drew.

She said, "I do" with her lips and "I don't" with her heart.

She felt Alexander exhale slowly. She felt her father's gaze retract. She felt the soldiers relax. She felt the Sutherland clan's collective heart take its next beat.

They exchanged rings. Alexander lifted her veil and kissed her, officially. When he raised thick, dark lashes and she saw the solemn, self-possessed look in his sapphire blue eyes, the spurt near her heart began to flow. Her eyes returned his regard with a question, but he merely lowered his lashes again, offered her his arm, and led her out of the church as his wedded wife. In the churchyard, they affixed their names to the legal documents. Back at Dunrobin, he carried her over the threshold to the courtyard, and the assembled inhabitants had their sieves ready with bread and cheese to crumble over them and scatter around. An oatcake was broken over her now unveiled head.

The feast in the hall was more than could have been expected for a wedding undertaken on such short notice. Walter Chisholm was an appeased father, but far from a satisfied one. He disdained the bagpipes, which began to wheeze and whine melodiously when a greater part of the food had been consumed. He would not dance with his daughter, but he did sip the fine whiskey, which was poured in abundance.

In fact, the whiskey was so plentiful that many of the men and women could be said to have drunk too much. Midway through the celebration, Elspeth, light-headed and silly with her unrequited love for Alexander, came up to him and put her arms around him. In one disastrous moment of relative quiet in the hall, she said, just loud enough for everyone to hear, ''Tell us more of yer fresh stories from Paris, Alexander.''

Chapter Eight

Anne felt a horrible clattering down her spine. She heard Elspeth's most unwise words, and she was standing near enough to her father to imagine that he heard them, too. She looked quickly at Alexander. His eyes, as blue as the Highland hills in raw dawn, met hers above Elspeth's head. His face had gone grave and stony. Anne glanced back at her father, who was standing in conversation with the Sutherland. She saw his eyes cross the hall to regard Alexander in a newly speculative light, dawning with realization. She easily read the twist of sudden satisfaction on her father's face.

Walter Chisholm quickly had the sum of it. He knew. And she knew that he knew. He had come to Scotland to hunt down the elusive Highland barbarian. He had come to capture the political undesirable who had been working so effectively against the Act of Union. He had come to Dunrobin on the strength of an odd report or two, and, incidentally, to bring his wayward daughter into line. By great good fortune, he had the Highland barbarian's neck within his grasp. Or close enough to taste Alexander Sutherland's death. Close enough to ensure his wayward daughter's widowhood.

It seemed to Anne that all movement in the hall froze for an uncounted second. She looked back at Alexander, who had put Elspeth away from him. He was regarding her steadily, his expression still grave, but with some new dimension now—an appeal, perhaps, or merely a question. She half wanted, half resisted the interpretation that he was giving her a choice—to go with him in peril or stay with her father in safety.

She thought of her father this afternoon, blazing angrily, *You will choose nothing!* She thought of Alexander the night before, stretched out, naked and desiring, surrendering himself to her with the words *'Tis yer choice*. He looked similarly naked and desiring now. Not of the body, this time, but of the spirit. Naked in nobility and desiring in dignity. She remembered clearly what he had said to her that afternoon, upon their return from golfing. He had acknowledged that their physical passion had been enough to bring them together, but that it was not enough for them to stay together. There had to be more.

Did the "more" have anything to do with the spring of emotion that she felt flowing through her heart? Perceiving Alexander noble in dress and body and spirit, she suddenly realized that the spring flowing through her heart was not flowing up from below, from between her legs, where he touched her and joined with her. It was flowing down from above. Its source was in heaven.

Was this the "more," then? Was it truly heavenly? She wanted time, needed time, to know what the more might be, to know her own heart and to commit herself to him with that knowledge. She was not greedy, and would have been content with an extra week, an extra day, an extra minute, to trace the source.

He did not have even an extra second to give her.

The frozen tableau in the hall sprang to life. Alexander was too quick-thinking to draw his sword immediately and raise the interest and attention of the several dozen English soldiers present. Instead, his eyes swept Anne. Then he was a blur of green as he blended quickly into the surrounding Sutherlands, intending to protect himself or defend himself or flee.

Anne cast a glance back over her shoulder and saw her father start forward. The Sutherland, perceiving the dangerous dimensions of the moment, stepped in front of Chisholm to bar his passage. The English queen's chamberlain and highest-ranking military officer called out angrily to his soldiers and shoved the Sutherland aside. The musicians with their bagpipes—misperceiving, or perhaps too well perceiving, Chisholm's words—recommenced on the skirling opening notes of "To the Sutherlands, sans Peur." Suddenly the hall was a confusion of Sutherland men in green and of queen's men in red, not quite fighting, not quite sure what was happening, not quite sure when or where to engage—or with whom—not quite sure where the Sutherland son Alexander had gone.

Nor did Anne know, for she had lost sight of him. When her father thrust her angrily out of his way as he searched for the barbarian, she decided to bend all her energies to saving Alexander's life. Even if she did not have enough of the heavenly "more" flowing through her heart for him, she had more than enough of the earthly flow for him. Even if she did not fully understand the silent, dignified message he had sent her just now, she felt her own crushed dignity rise up to meet his. Even if she never saw him again, she would be happy knowing he lived.

She had a plan.

Despite, or because of, the utter confusion in the hall, rendered all the more incoherent by the piercing pitch of the bagpipes, drowning out specific orders, she made an easy passage around the bodies of the women and the men and the half-drawn, hesitating swords. She scanned the moving crowd intently, until her eyes caught at least one of the objects of her search.

"Duncan!" she called, surging forward and grasping the thick, muscled arm of her initial captor. "Do you know where he's gone?"

Duncan looked down at her darkly, thick brows raised. "He?"

"Alexander, of course!"

"Well, now, lassie, why d'ye want t' know?"

"Because I want to help him!"

"And why should I believe ye?"

"Because...because..." She floundered, then found the perfect argument. "Because we're married, and I naturally wish to help my husband!"

Duncan was unconvinced. "'Tis not yet a real marriage. 'Tis not been consummated," he pointed out primly.

Her mouth fell open. It seemed a mighty prudish, technical point, given everything.

He added suspiciously, "And if ye think I'm t' tell ye so that ye can whisper more of our secrets t' yer father, ye must take me for a fool."

"I told my father nothing," she said, feeling anger and a sense of injustice swirling around inside her. "It was Dunrobin's own Elspeth who exposed Alexander just now."

Duncan had never been the swiftest member of the Sutherland clan. "But all she asked was for Alexander t' tell her more of his stories from Paris," he protested.

"And that was enough to tip my father off," she said impatiently. "Now, we don't have much time to lose! Let me tell you about my plan to help Alexander."

Duncan sniffed. "I'm still tryin' t' discover why I should listen t' a plan devised by a woman raised among the Sassenachs, who has trouble stickin' by her words and whose father is a menace to the Highlands."

"Because I'm not a Sassenach. Not anymore. I'm not my father's daughter. Not anymore. And I mean what I say." She realized, with a fine loosening of internal bonds, that she had been wanting the whole of her long-fettered life to make such a statement. It felt wonderful. "That's right. I'm not my father's daughter," she repeated. "Oh, I'm not saying that my mother played him false. I'm only saying that I owe him nothing. Nothing. Now, whether or not I'm Alexander's wife yet is another point entirely," she said, her Scots temper rising up from her loving heart, healthy and unconstrained, "and I can safely predict that my marriage to him never *will* be consummated, if you and I stand about discussing what's not important and what's none of your business to boot!"

"What's the plan?" Duncan asked, apparently convinced by this display of temper.

She took his hand and led him around the hall. "Get Dugald and Gavin and—and, oh, I don't know, anyone else you can think of that might make a crew."

"A crew?"

"Yes, and if you can find Alexander and get him out of the castle, I'm hoping that enough men can be rounded up to help him sail away, for I don't think he can sail such a ship alone."

Duncan's face assumed a suspicious cast once again.

She misunderstood his look. "No, there really *is* a ship anchored in a little cove off Dornoch Firth. I'm not making this up," she explained, verging on desperation now. "It's a cove that's just above the first ridge on the strand, south of the castle. Do you know it?"

"Aye," he said, "but how do you?"

"Alexander took me there last night after dinner, and before we . . . before . . . well, never mind that! He took me there and showed me his ship and said that he'd sailed it here just recently from France." She looked up at Duncan beseechingly. "The only hope is to get him back to the ship before my father or his men get to him!"

Duncan was nodding thoughtfully. "'Tis a good plan," he acknowledged.

"A very good plan," she replied, for the sake of form. "Now let's get on with it!

Together they wound their way through the dangerous maze of raised arms in the hall and, miraculously, collected Dugald and Gavin. They made their further way around the passageways to emerge out in the courtyard, where Jamie and Simon and the Sutherland were standing, steel blades drawn and glinting in the rising moonlight, ready to engage with a group of soldiers who had exited the hall in search of Alexander.

It was three against six. For now, the opponents were merely eyeing one other tautly, each side waiting for the other to make the first move, if it was going to come to that.

Out of the corner of her eye, off to the left, in the shadows of the courtyard, Anne caught a movement. She could feel his presence in the increased flow from her heart. She dared not look directly, but she knew she had to act before her almost-husband did something exceedingly stupid.

She moved forward into the courtyard and called out with every theatrical fiber of her being, "The man who has cruelly abused me is back in the hall, rousing his men to action!" For increased effect, she positioned herself in the full of the moonlight and bent over a bit, in supplication, her arms clasped in front of her. Hoping that her breasts would not fall out of her dress completely, she pleaded, "Help me avenge my honor!"

To the English soldiers' ears, this was no Highland lass in distress. This was the voice, round and clear, of an Englishwoman. When they turned to look at her, they saw the very pretty sight of Walter Chisholm's daughter in that dress in the moonlight. They abandoned the lesser prey of the Sutherland and his two eldest sons and moved to run back into the castle in search of Alexander.

Anne held her arms out to keep Duncan and Dugald and Gavin from engaging with the soldiers. When the redcoats had hurried past them, Anne dropped her arms and turned. She was surprised to read a disapproving look on Duncan's face. She said, on a triumphant note, "You see, then, Duncan, that my perfect English accent has served some useful purpose!"

Duncan simply shook his head, sadly disappointed.

"What, then?" Anne asked. "Did you think I was betraying Alexander? He's not in the hall, you know."

"Nay, then, he's in the shadows, as we both can see," Duncan said, with a nod in Alexander's direction. "'Tis rather that I'm powerful sorry that ye've turned t' *lyin'*, lass. 'Twas a good trick what you said t' the soldiers just now, but 'twas a lie all the same. Ye've lived too long among the—"

Anne interrupted him on an inspired note. "But, no, Duncan, I was referring to my *father!*" She smiled innocently, "I was not lying at all when I said that a man in the hall had cruelly abused me!"

Duncan's face cleared, and he congratulated her on a "very good trick, indeed!"

Anne did not bask in self-congratulations, but quickly sorted out the rest of the plan. "Now, go, you men, and round up what you can of a crew!" She shooed them off. Alexander was about to step out of the shadows, but she motioned him back. She had looked over her shoulder and seen several soldiers guarding the main entrance to the castle. To the Sutherland, Jamie and Simon, she whispered loudly, "Distract those soldiers at the portal!" Then she ran into the shadows to meet Alexander.

She saw that his hand was still on the hilt of his sword. "I suppose you were thinking to engage with the soldiers in the courtyard?" she asked testily.

"Well, now, the sight of my brothers and father up against a few of them," Alexander replied easily, "brought my hand to my sword and the Shutherlanich war cry up my throat. The words got caught, however, when ye arrived on the scene, rather temptin' in the moonlight. Almost strangled me."

Anne could just discern a smirk on his face and an amused glint in his eyes. She was not similarly amused. "The point is," she said with emphasis, "that it will go very much the worse for you and your clan if any of the English get hurt this night."

Before Alexander could reply, she took his hand and led him farther into the shadows. They were in a dark passageway, one she hoped would lead neither in the direction of the hall nor back to the main courtyard.

"Show me how to get to that odd little opening in the castle walls," she said, "the one we took last night, when we went down to the sea. I want you to exit by that opening."

Alexander obliged her by taking the lead, still holding her hand. "This way," he said. "Why?"

"I want to get you to your ship," she explained. "Duncan and Dugald and Gavin are rounding up a crew to help you sail it."

"A crew, then? Anyone in particular?"

"I told them to get anyone they could find."

"In truth, lass?" Alexander sounded amazed.

"Well, I'm sure qualifications are necessary to sail a ship, but I don't see how you, or anyone else, can be too particular about the crew, under the circumstances."

"Certainly not," Alexander agreed. "And this was your idea?"

"Yes, and I think it's an excellent one," she said, catching what she thought was skepticism in his voice. "So did Duncan, by the way."

"'Tis reassurin'."

They were moving through cool, dank passageways, where skittering shadows spooked them and sparred with them. When Alexander stubbed his toe against some protrusion on the paving stones, he swore under his breath and wanted to know why he could not simply leave the castle by the main portal.

"That would be foolish," she said. "My father has been tracking you for weeks now, and he's probably given orders to have you killed at the least resistance."

"And on my weddin' night, too," Alexander complained, "which, come t' think of it, is not the least of the reasons why yer father would prefer t' see me dead."

"The necessity of my marriage to you certainly adds to his dislike of you," Anne agreed. "Even before he knew who you were, he was hoping that you'd fall drunk off your horse and over the side of a cliff before too long."

Alexander sounded aggrieved. "Such a poor opinion my father-in-law has of me," he said, clucking his tongue with disgust. "I can hold my whiskey and my seat, and both t'gether, very well, as ye have cause t' know firsthand, lass. Why, I can't say the last time I was so insulted t' hear that—"

"For heaven's sake!" she cried, interrupting him. "Instead of being absurd, tell me where we're going!"

Alexander explained that they were heading to the far side of the wing that housed the living quarters where there was a secret passage through the stables. From there they could find the opening in the wall through which he would slip out of the castle.

He pulled her along with him, smoothly negotiating the tricky turns and dark corners. She was getting winded fast, while he was not the least affected by the exercise. He was rather more exercised by the fact that he was having to skulk out of his own castle. He complained that he had envisioned breaking out of Dunrobin after the fun of a stirring set-to with the Sassenach soldiers.

"Yes, I'm sure you are eager for a stirring set-to, as you put it," she panted, "but somehow I'd rather send you out into the world all in one piece."

Alexander paused a moment, bringing her to a halt with him. "Which of my pieces, Anne," he asked gravely, "do ye consider t' be the most important?"

"Which of your pieces—?" she began, then choked. She felt rather than saw the look in his eyes. "How can you be thinking of *that* at a time like this?"

"Easily, lass," he said, "'Tis yer indecent dress. Not that I mind entirely, but I've been findin' it very distractin' the evenin' long, and this *is* our weddin' night, as ye know. So by this point, ye can understand that—"

She interrupted again, this time with some bewildered exasperation. "How can that be? Back in the hall, when Elspeth so foolishly tipped off your identity, you looked at me with such dignity. I thought you were telling me good-bye."

"I was tryin' t' tell ye t' meet me in the passageway."

"I thought you very noble," she insisted.

"Noble?" he echoed. "What do ye mean by 'noble'?"

"You see, I remembered what you said earlier today, that what we had between us was good enough to come together, but not good enough to stay together. You said that there had to be more."

"Have ye had a moment to reflect on what that might be?" he asked.

"Well, something dignified," she said, "and noble."

Alexander considered this. "Noble," he repeated again. "Do ye mean an upliftin' feelin', perhaps?"

"Why, yes, I do," Anne agreed, liking this description.

"At the moment, I'm feelin' noble, as ye wish t' put it, just thinkin' about it." He added thoughtfully, "Very noble."

They heard voices coming down the darkened passage behind them. They paused and caught the cadences of English, not Scots, speech. After a moment, Alexander held up two fingers, and Anne nodded her agreement that there were only two men coming down the hall. Alexander wanted to take them on, but Anne whispered a vehement "No" into his ear. After they glared at one another briefly, Alexander relented and drew her into a nearby alcove, out of the passageway and out of sight.

"Ye'll have t' put up with my feelin' of nobility, then," he said. He drew her to him so that her back was against the wall and he was shielding her from the hallway with his body.

When she was pressed against his length, she breathed, "Good heavens! I can't believe it!"

"'Tis a difficult condition t' be in at the moment, I'll admit," he breathed against her neck. "I could work it off by runnin' my sword through a Sassenach or two. Or we could just stay here in the corner and let me—"

She put her finger to his lips and held on to him tight, but not in a passionate embrace. The two soldiers were coming down the hall. Before they were within ten feet of the alcove, Alexander unclipped the brooch at his shoulder and let the unkilted length of his plaid shift fall over Anne's light-colored skirts, so that no stray light would reflect off the peach silk.

The soldiers came closer. Her heart was pounding against his. The soldiers came even with the alcove. She felt his heart pounding against hers. The soldiers moved on, speaking low as they continued. Then their voices drifted away.

She clung to Alexander still, fear coursing through her veins. When his hand moved to her breasts, her fear turned to indignation, and something else.

"What are you doing?"

"'Tis a daft question, Anne."

"Stop it."

"Why?"

"It's not the time nor place."

He put his lips to hers and began to kiss her passionately. Her breasts were easily accessible to his touch. "'Tis our weddin' night," he argued.

"Which won't last for long," she managed, catching her breath, trying to resist the pleasure of the peaking of her nipples and his hands cupping them, "if you're caught, you know."

He ignored her reasoning. "There's an advantage," he said dreamily against her lips, "when a man belts his plaid in a kilt." His hands left her breasts for her hips. One hand fumbled with various lengths of cloth between them, while the other managed to slip into her whiteclothes. "I've but t' lift my skirts and yours . . ." he explained, at which moment the fingers in her whiteclothes found their goal. He breathed against her with hazy desire and said, "Good God, lass, ye've no cause t' be reprovin' me for the upliftin' state of the wee man pushin' at my sporran. Ye're as active as a Highland stream."

"It's *not* the time nor place for this," she said weakly, though her knees wobbled at his touch. "You've got to get out of Dunrobin and down to your ship."

Thoughts of escape were apparently not uppermost in his mind. "I'm thinkin' that ye must be feelin' as noble as I am," he said into her ear. He caressed her pearled plum with light pressure. He slid his fingers in liquid luxury, spreading her thighs slightly, wedging his legs between them. He was hampered in his search only by the heavy lengths of his kilt, which kept getting caught between them as they shifted against one another.

When he had finally arranged the cloth to his best advantage, and she was next to his nakedness, she breathed in wonderment, "My goodness, you *don't* have anything beneath your kilt."

"I'm not inclined t' dismiss my manly attributes so easily," he said, a low rumble of laughter discernible in his voice and reverberating against her breasts, "and neither should you, lass, if ye've any respect for the man t' whom ye've made yer marriage vows."

"That is, you're not *wearing* anything beneath your kilt," she amended, and provoked him further by saying, "and our vows have not yet been fulfilled." Despite her rising desire, she managed to shove him firmly away from her, although not very far.

He accepted the rebuff, and their skirts fell to their proper positions, but he did not free her from her position in the alcove. Rather, he pinned her there with his arms. His hands were on either side of her shoulders, palms flat against the wall. "Now, here's a crucial point

I'd like t' discuss with ye," he said. "'Tis the vows ye spoke in the church and the document ye signed that made ye my legal wife."

She tried to absorb the meaning of the serious, though smiling, face he presented her, which she could just discern in the dark shadows. "What is the crucial point, then?" she asked cautiously.

"I need t' know the state of yer inward feelin'—I think that's what ye were callin' it yesterday mornin', in the bothy—concernin' the words ye spoke and the name ye signed, namely Anne Sutherland."

"Ah, yes, the inward feeling," she replied. "I think it has something to do with the 'more' between us that you think necessary for us to stay together."

"I think so, too." He paused, looked down, then up again at her. His shadowed face was composed. "I want more, much more, from ye than ye've given me so far," he said, "and I'd like t' know if ye think ye've got it t' give to me. We were properly bound in handfast. Now we're legally bound in marriage." He drew a breath. "I'll admit that none of it counts if ye're lackin' the inward feelin'." He paused again, and then said with endearing solemnity, "What I'm askin' is, do ye wish t' come away with me now, Anne?"

"My choice?" she asked shakily.

"Yer choice," he assured her.

She considered. Having him standing but a breath away from her, the memory of his touch still flowing between her legs, she found it difficult to concentrate on the real question.

"My time is very short, lass," he reminded her.

"I know," she said, "but under these circumstances, it's not easy to recapture the noble feeling, the spiritually high-minded feeling, I had for you earlier in the hall."

He kissed her neck and breasts. "I'm a man who presses his advantages where he sees them." He kissed her lips. "And I'm not about t' tell ye that by wantin' more from ye, my physical desires have disappeared." Then, again, gently, "Do ye wish t' come away with me, lass?"

Although she was fully immersed in the flow of her desire for him, in his touch, in his kiss, in his smile, in his breath, she suspected again the heavenly source of her inner stream. That heavenly suspicion was, however, just a glimmering drop in the larger, more earthly flow inside her. Under the circumstances, she decided, wisely unnoble, that they would have time to explore that exalted, spiritually high-minded plane later—much later—in their love.

"I do," she said finally, and meant it.

Chapter Nine

He was ready to lift their skirts again and make their wedding vows complete.

"No," she protested, holding her skirt down.

"'Twill only take a moment," he said, "and ye want it as much as I. I've touched the evidence."

"No," she repeated, grasping her hands firmly in his and pulling him out of the alcove. "Come on!"

Anne was determined now to get them both out of the castle before it was too late. She began to lead him down the passageway.

"Let me remind ye how it went with me last night, lass," he urged. However, he went with her willingly, and flipped the length of his plaid over his shoulder so that he would not trip over it. He even managed to repin it expertly to his shoulder.

"I remember," Anne said pointedly, "and it's because of my excellent memory that I want to get out of here so we might be able to spend another night together like last night!"

"'Tis an inspirin' thought," he replied.

So inspiring, in fact, that he took the lead, and when her energies flagged, he was able to encourage her with a strong arm around her waist. He led her through the far wing of the living quarters and to the secret passage that led to the stables. There, behind the bundles of straw and bales of hay, they had to hide for a long while, for the soldiers had naturally thought to search for Alexander there, and had rounded up the fine Sutherland horses to prevent his escape on horseback.

When the coast was clear, Alexander showed Anne where to slip out of the back of the stables, toward the castle wall. He was very much disgruntled by the shameful waste of having to hide, chaste, in the straw with Anne. He assured her that a fine roll in the hay was one of life's great pleasures, and he seemed to wish to make up for the lost opportunity in the stables at the tiny passage in the castle wall, where he claimed they would be safe for a moment or two.

Anne was sympathetic, but ultimately unyielding in her desire to get as far away as possible, as fast as possible.

Speed was, in fact, not possible during the rocky descent to the strand that would lead them to the cove. The going was rough on Anne, so much so that she had to kick off her shoes. She decided to leave them behind, since they were too big for her, anyway. She did not pause to strip off her stockings, which, she well realized, would be shredded to uselessness after her flight across the stones. Alexander was unconcerned for the state of her footwear, and extravagantly offered to buy her a dozen new pairs of shoes and stockings as soon as possible.

She wondered if she would ever have a decent dress to wear again, much less shoes and stockings, for they were fleeing with no money, no belongings, and nothing else to serve them in their daily life. None of that seemed terribly important, however, as they stumbled over the shoreline. Anne's eyes were easily tricked by the size of the stones in the shadows cast by the moonlight. When a ghostly fog rolled in on them from the ink black sea that would quickly swallow them in great white billows, she began to panic. Alexander was, by contrast, rather pleased to see the fog, which, he said, would shroud them from view. He knew the coastline well enough, he assured her, to get to the cove without error.

He proved himself not too much later. They scrambled up a ridge that seemed vaguely familiar, but distorted, to her, and then down the other side. They were almost at the water's edge when, through the white web of the fog, she caught the drift of quiet voices. They were the unmistakable strains of men from the Sutherland clan.

As if in a dream, the *Marie* came into view, piecemeal, through the tatters of fog. Anne was able to identify Duncan and Dugald and Gavin and Evan on the makeshift dock, as well as a few other men whose faces looked familiar, but whose names she did not know.

She noticed that the men were already very busy with the boat. Duncan seemed to be in command. When he saw Alexander, he evinced no sign of surprise or relief or gladness. He simply accepted Alexander's presence as a matter of course. Anne's, too. He informed her, "I thought ye'd catch yer cold in such a dress, lass, and so I had Jenny fetch me yer arisaid, along with an extra plaid. I've already stowed the lot in the captain's quarters."

"You knew I was coming?" Anne asked.

"Aye," Duncan affirmed, "although I'll confess not t' have guessed that ye'd need an extra pair of shoes. I've brought none for ye." He shrugged and said confidently, "But we'll find ye stockings. Never ye fear." After that, he consulted Alexander on a few points, then returned to his tasks and to his commands.

Alexander spoke to each man in turn as they came up to greet him and Anne during the course of their chores. Alexander had again unpinned the plaid from his shoulder, and had put the warm, soft length around Anne's shoulders to keep her from the wet chill. It was, as they stood together, as if they were being acknowledged as husband and wife. When Evan approached, Alexander asked what he thought he was doing down here at the dock.

"I'm joinin' ye this time," Evan replied.

Alexander shook his head affectionately. "Nay, then, 'tis better if ye stay at Dunrobin."

"There's naught for me here," Evan said sadly.

Alexander chucked his younger brother on the chin. "I can appreciate the artistic value of lovesick sufferin', lad, and the crew and I would be pleased t' benefit from yer soulful songs. But I'm recommendin' that ye ride straight t' Inverness—this night, if possible—and claim yer Claire. 'Twill be for the best."

Evan sighed deeply at the thought of such bold action.

Alexander smiled an older brother's smile. "I've a bit of wisdom for ye that a man often hears and that I can now happily confirm." He leaned forward and said, low, but well within Anne's hearing, "The feelin' for the lass makes all the difference, if ye see what I mean. 'Tis a powerful experience I'd not want ye t' miss."

Evan's countenance brightened a bit. "Truly?"

Alexander nodded knowingly. "Go fetch yer Claire and test the truth of what I'm tellin' ye."

Evan hesitated.

"I guarantee 'twill be worth the trip," Alexander added, drawing back to bring Anne closer in the circle of his arm. "And I'd stay t' convince ye further, but I'm wantin' t' get on with it myself." He kissed her neck, then raised his head again to smile upon his brother. "Ye'll see, lad, soon enough, I hope, the worth of stayin' here t' be with yer Claire. And be sure t' thank me for it in yer prayers."

Evan accepted the suggestion finally with a nod of conviction. "We'll miss ye, Alex," he said.

Alexander asked, "Jamie and Simon are still fightin' shadows in the keep?"

"All's well," Evan said. "Half the soldiers are searchin' the bedrooms. The other half have taken to the hills on horseback, searchin' for ye."

"And the Sutherland?"

"He's seen the error of his ways and is cooperatin', I suppose ye might call it, with Walter o' Siosal," Evan said with a brief glance at Anne and a rather ill-concealed smirk. "He can't, for the life of him, imagine how ye've disappeared, although he's offered some prime suggestions about where t' look for ye. I'm guessin' that Father and the Siosal are bound t' become fast friends."

Alexander was not going to make much of the goodbyes. He released Anne momentarily, clasped his brother's hand and drew him to his breast. A brief embrace, and Evan disappeared into the fog.

Duncan appeared the next instant to engage Alexander's opinion on a variety of nautical matters, and Anne listened with growing surprise to the rather involved discussion. When Duncan left to carry on with his preparations, Anne asked, "Do I infer correctly that Duncan is a rather experienced sailor?"

Alexander turned her toward him and, with warm hands on her bare shoulders, said, "He and the lads sailed with me to France and back."

"Duncan and Dugald and Gavin?" she asked, amazed.

"And Jonathan and Bruce and Douglas," he added, "not t' mention Hugh over there stockin' the barrels."

"But I thought...that is, it seemed to me that...and here I was thinking— Well!" she exclaimed, both amused and disgusted by this news. "Wouldn't you just know it!"

"They're honest men, all of them, and as reliable on sea as they are on land. The day we arrived, we established our plans to leave again. On a moment's notice, if need be."

Anne felt utterly useless, or at least redundant. "No wonder Duncan thought my plan was a good one," she said, somewhat crestfallen. "And no wonder you seem so remarkably organized. Here I was thinking that I was acting on your behalf in a manner that no one else was capable of!"

"Well, if you put it like that," Alexander said with a determined light in his eyes, "I'm thinkin' that there is a manner in which ye can act on my behalf that no man on this miserable crew is capable of."

"No, I mean it, Alexander, my disappointment is real," Anne said. "I've been learning to act, not react. To take, not be taken. To choose, not be chosen. I thought I was *doing* something by organizing your escape!"

"You were actin', and most efficiently," he replied. "'Tis not a point in yer disfavor that yer excellent plan happened t' coincide with ours. And as for takin' control of yer life, Anne, I can only hope that I live t' see the day when I'm in control of mine."

"What do you mean?"

"That if I had my way, I'd stay in my bonny homeland and tend t' my land."

"Yes, but you chose to act against political events," she argued. "You were taking control of your fate."

Alexander shook his head, his expression a little sad, a little wise. "I was reactin', as ye have complained, t' events beyond my control. I've had my measure of success, but it's come at the price of my neck, and I've my doubts that Scotland can remain independent of English rule in the long run. So ye see..."

Anne did see, suddenly, and she also saw a man who understood some of the constraints that had governed her own life. However, Alexander, for all his subtle understanding, really did have other, less lofty issues on his mind.

"So ye see," he repeated, drawing her to him with purpose, "that we make a good match, you and I, in more ways than one. Speakin' of one way in particular, and at the risk of belaborin' an obvious point, I'd like t' remind ye that this is our weddin' night."

He carried her over the gangplank and set her down on her feet again once they were on the main deck. The seafaring Sutherland men came aboard then, drew in the plank, and raised the anchor, spirits high, eager for adventure. Expressing his confidence that Duncan could guide them safely out of the cove, even in the fog, Alexander took Anne's hand and led her down the few stairs to the captain's quarters.

Once inside the cabin, she was surprised at how well-appointed, although not quite luxurious, were the surroundings. She hardly had a moment to take in the details before Alexander wrapped her in his arms and began to kiss her with the passion that had been building throughout the evening.

He was just placing his hands on her breasts when the ship heaved in departure, and Anne found her back up against one wall, pressed intimately to Alexander.

"That's it!" he breathed, in pleased discovery. "Against the wall, then! Just as we were about t' try it back at Dunrobin." He shifted his hands and easily released her breasts from the meager confines of her bodice. "My jacket," he murmured with a certain urgency, indicating that she was to get it off him as quickly as possible. She was minimally reluctant to do so, since she had found the velvet rubbing against her breasts to be very stimulating.

She found the linen of his shirt beneath equally stimulating, but neither of those sensations compared to the feel of his warm skin against hers, when jacket and shirt had been cast aside. That left only his kilt, which fell unceremoniously with a quick unbuckling of his belt. Its soft green folds caught around their legs and between their bodies.

"Yer skirts, Anne," he breathed.

"Let me get them off."

He shook his head as he kissed her. "No time."

Launched now, the ship was rocking gently, creating an extraordinary sensation as their bodies moved together, lapping against one another at all the right places. His hands were under her skirts, which he had pulled up and away as much as possible. Her whiteclothes were down, and hardly a second passed from the moment he pressed eager fingers, touching and testing her ripe fruit, to the moment he moved her slickly over him, plunging hot into her. She was filled and fulfilled by him, open and unconstrained, moving happily with him, rocking with him and the boat.

After a gloriously brief union, still panting with the effort and heaving with the movements of the boat, he said, "The wall was a good start."

She sighed, happy and satisfied and continually provocative. "I've other ideas for it."

He caught his breath. He held her firm against him, around him. "Takin' control of yer fate, lass? Choosin' yer positions? Actin' on yer desires?"

"Yes, yes, yes," she answered him. "And my first act will be to rid myself of this dress."

He kissed her sweetly, tongue to tongue. "Good lass," he said approvingly, "and show me yer other ideas when I recover."

She did.

They awoke the next morning in a pleasant tangle of limbs on the narrow bunk, having sunk, exhausted at last, into a horizontal position on the mattress.

She had developed a great hunger as a result of the vigorous night's exercise. She was not surprised to learn, when her stomach rumbled ravenously, that she was on board a ship that was well stocked with food. When she heard the morning menu, she was not wildly overjoyed, but he assured her that she would grow used to the taste of porridge, and would even come to like it.

She doubted that, but as for agreeable Scottish customs, she did like having the arisaid to wear. She dressed happily in the knowledge that she would be able to undress again with Alexander naked next to her. They emerged in midmorning from the captain's quarters to behold a magnificent day for sailing. The gulls circled in the wide blue bowl of the sky. The Scottish coast was distant but discernible. The sea air was invigorating. The mood of the crew was happy, despite the fact that, to a man, they were leaving their homeland reluctantly.

Alexander showed her proudly around his ship, explaining this and that to her, giving her certain tasks to do, since she demanded it of him, and doing his own work. A moment of relative inactivity arose in the middle of the afternoon. Anne and Alexander had met at the railing and were gazing idly over the silver sea. Her arisaid was arranged around her shoulders, shielding her from the fresh sea breezes. She wore no shoes, but needed none. She liked the feel of her wedding band around her finger and admired the glint of the sun against the gold.

She asked, "By the way, where are we going?"

"Back to France," he replied.

"To France?" she repeated, surprised. "I did not imagine that you would go to the same place twice."

"Why not? 'Tis where I have my manor."

Anne's surprise increased. "Your manor?" She had imagined that she was sailing off shoeless, homeless, penniless and directionless.

"Aye, in the Loire valley," he said.

She had a vague idea that a manor in the Loire valley was no small accomplishment for an outcast Scot. "How is it possible that you have a manor there?"

"Ah, did I not tell ye, lass, that I'm a great favorite at the court of King *Louie?*"

"King Louis? The Fourteenth? Of France?" she asked skeptically. She decided that he was teasing her.

"Aye." His voice and face were serious.

"And how is it that you're a favorite of the court?" she asked, then held up a hand. "I know! Don't tell me! It's your charm of personality."

He smiled a very charming smile. "Nay, then, 'tis my father's gold that attracts the French lads and lassies. He has a deal of it, ye know, and has been generous enough t' make it available t' me. Now, I'm predicting that ye'll be a grand favorite at court. There's not another redhead among 'em."

Duncan and Dugald had joined them. Anne still believed that Alexander was teasing her, but when Duncan offered a detailed description of the manor that included an enthusiastic discussion of the merits of the five-hole golf course they had laid out during the past year, she began to imagine that perhaps he had been telling her the truth.

After some reflection, she asked, "But, then, Dugald, why was it that, when you were first thinking of binding me in handfast to Alexander, you said he had nothing to lose? Now I discover that Alexander has a manor with a golf course."

"But the manor is in France, lass!" Dugald replied, in a tone that suggested she had not understood the true dimensions of the tragedy.

"It's a nice enough place to live, no?" she ventured.

Duncan confided seriously, "'Tis a grand country, France, but I'll tell ye that no one there speaks decent English, much less a word of the revered tongue."

"You mean Gaelic?" she queried.

Duncan looked at Dugald and Alexander blankly, then back at Anne. "'Tis what I just said, lass!"

She shook her head and had to laugh. "I guess that they speak French rather well, though."

"Do ye speak it, lass?" Duncan asked.

"Badly," Anne admitted.

Alexander was encouraging. "Ye'll improve."

"'Tis a strange tongue," was Duncan's considered opinion.

"A body can hardly understand what they're sayin'!" Dugald added.

"And when a body does come t' understand, why, more often than not, 'tis an insult or an absurdity! Bah!" Duncan said. "Now, Alex here thinks it none so bad, and likes his manor well enough, but when all is said, he's a man with naught to lose! Or was, lass, until he married ye."

Duncan and Dugald wandered off, trading sorrowful observations on what they were to encounter in France.

Anne felt flattered by Duncan's last remark. "Despite his opinion," she said to Alexander, "you were not quite the man who had nothing to lose."

"Before I met ye, I had thought that there was naught left for a man t' lose but his life, once he'd lost his homeland," he replied simply. He leaned forward and took her chin in his hand. "I'm glad t' discover that I was wrong. I've a wife now, and the perfect one for a man who might never see his Scotland again." He drew her against him. "I've a livin' piece of Scotland t' hold in my arms and t' take with me t' my bed."

"Is that how you see me, then, as your Scottish lass?"

"'Tis an excellent beginnin', t' my way of thinkin'," he replied.

She felt very happy in Alexander's arms, breathing in the sea air, with the summer sun on her face. She did wish, however, to raise an objection. "You know how I look, but you really don't know too much about me yet."

"Nay, then, but I know ye enough," he said, "and 'twill be a pleasure gettin' to know ye better."

She could only agree that that particular pleasure would be returned in full measure. After a moment, she said, "We might not suit in the long run."

He shook his head. "I'm not worried about that, lass."

She was at first surprised by his confidence, but then she smiled affectionately. She realized that she might, in fact, know much more about him than she had thought. She even shared his optimism, for she had discovered something about herself, as well, in the past day or two.

"That's right," she said. "You like to think positive."

He returned her smile, and the light in his eyes as they rested upon her seemed to her to be the kind reserved for a good friend, or for the sight of his Highland hills and valleys. He said, "Ye've the right of it, lass, and 'tis a cast of mind that has long served me well." He nodded. "I like t' think positive."

* * * * *

Dear Reader,

Imagine the drama of being carried off into the wild Scottish Highlands by a band of ruffians from a rival clan. Imagine the excitement of discovering that your captor is a smart, handsome man named Alexander and that his sidekicks are as amusing as they are strong. Imagine the surprise to discover that you are bound to Alexander in handfast—almost without your knowing it. Imagine the passion of this "marriage for a year and a day." Imagine the unexpected consequences of this passionate handfast when your father learns of it....

Don't just imagine the drama, excitement, laughter and love. Live the adventure with Anne in "The Handfast"!

I hope your summer is filled with the sweet, satisfying emotions of all your favorite romances.

Enjoy!

Julie Tetel

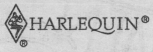

Fifty red-blooded, white-hot, true-blue hunks
from every State in the Union!

Look for MEN MADE IN AMERICA! Written by some of
our most popular authors, these stories feature fifty of
the strongest, sexiest men, each from a different state in
the union!

Two titles available every other month at your favorite
retail outlet.

In May, look for:

KISS YESTERDAY GOODBYE by Leigh Michaels (Iowa)
A TIME TO KEEP by Curtiss Ann Matlock (Kansas)

In June, look for:

ONE PALE, FAWN GLOVE by Linda Shaw (Kentucky)
BAYOU MIDNIGHT by Emilie Richards (Louisiana)

You won't be able to resist MEN MADE IN AMERICA!

This July,
Harlequin and Silhouette
are proud to bring you

WANTED: Husband
POSITION: Temporary
TERMS: Negotiable—but must be willing to live in.

And falling in love is definitely not part of the contract!

Relive the romance....

Three complete novels by your favorite authors—in one special collection!

TO BUY A GROOM by Rita Clay Estrada
MEETING PLACE by Bobby Hutchinson
THE ARRANGEMENT by Sally Bradford

Available wherever
Harlequin and Silhouette books are sold.

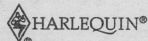 

HREQ6

Where do you find hot Texas nights, smooth Texas charm and dangerously sexy cowboys?

Crystal Creek reverberates with the exciting rhythm of Texas. Each story features the rugged individuals who live and love in the Lone Star state.

"...Crystal Creek wonderfully evokes the hot days and steamy nights of a small Texas community...impossible to put down until the last page is turned."
—*Romantic Times*

"...a series that should hook any romance reader. Outstanding."
—*Rendezvous*

"Altogether, it couldn't be better."   —*Rendezvous*

Don't miss the next book in this exciting series.
SHAMELESS by SANDY STEEN

Available in July wherever Harlequin books are sold.

Harlequin® Historical

LOOK TO THE PAST FOR FUTURE FUN AND EXCITEMENT!

The past the Harlequin Historical way, that is. 1994 is going to be a banner year for us, so here's a preview of what to expect:

* The continuation of our bigger book program, with titles such as *Across Time* by Nina Beaumont, *Defy the Eagle* by Lynn Bartlett and *Unicorn Bride* by Claire Delacroix.

* A 1994 March Madness promotion featuring four titles by promising new authors Gayle Wilson, Cheryl St. John, Madris Dupree and Emily French.

* Brand-new in-line series: DESTINY'S WOMEN by Merline Lovelace and HIGHLANDER by Ruth Langan; and new chapters in old favorites, such as the SPARHAWK saga by Miranda Jarrett and the WARRIOR series by Margaret Moore.

* *Promised Brides,* an exciting brand-new anthology with stories by Mary Jo Putney, Kristin James and Julie Tetel.

* Our perennial favorite, the Christmas anthology, this year featuring Patricia Gardner Evans, Kathleen Eagle, Elaine Barbieri and Margaret Moore.

Watch for these programs and titles wherever Harlequin Historicals are sold.

**HARLEQUIN HISTORICALS...
A TOUCH OF MAGIC!**

HHPROMO94

Harlequin® Historical

Looking for more of a good thing?

Why not try a bigger book from Harlequin Historicals?

SUSPICION by Judith McWilliams, April 1994—A story of intrigue and deceit set during the Regency era.

ROYAL HARLOT by Lucy Gordon, May 1994—The adventuresome romance of a prince and the woman spy assigned to protect him.

UNICORN BRIDE by Claire Delacroix, June 1994—The first of a trilogy set in thirteenth-century France.

MARIAH'S PRIZE by Miranda Jarrett, July 1994—Another tale of the seafaring Sparhawks of Rhode Island.

Longer stories by some of your favorite authors.
Watch for them this spring, wherever
Harlequin Historicals are sold.

EXPECTATIONS
Shannon Waverly

Eternity, Massachusetts, is a town with something special going for it. According to legend, those who marry in Eternity's chapel are destined for a lifetime of happiness. As long as the legend holds true, couples will continue to flock here to marry and local businesses will thrive.

Unfortunately for the town, Marion and Geoffrey Kent are about to prove the legend wrong!

EXPECTATIONS, available in July from Harlequin Romance®, is the second book in Harlequin's new cross-line series, **WEDDINGS, INC.** Be sure to look for the third book, **WEDDING SONG,** by Vicki Lewis Thompson (Harlequin Temptation® #502), coming in August.

HARLEQUIN®

Diamonds of the first water, these exceptional heroines reflect the rare beauty and exquisite nature of priceless gems.

Fall in love with the past as Harlequin presents its latest Regency Romance collection, *Regency Diamonds.*

The collection features two stories by your favorite Regency authors. Brenda Hiatt brings us the passionate story of a heroine who must rekindle both the memory and the love of her husband in "Azalea," and Paula Marshall brings us a case of mistaken identity in "The Cyprian's Sister."

Capture the spirit and the passion of the Regency era with our latest collection, *Regency Diamonds.*